CU00983727

THE OMEGA SANCTION

Tomas Black

First Published in Great Britain in 2019 by

TEARDROP MEDIA LTD

Copyright © 2019 Teardrop Media Ltd

The moral right of Tomas Black to be identified as the author of this work has been asserted in accordance with the Copyright, Design and Patents Act 1988.

All rights reserved. No part of this publication may be reproduced, stored in a retrieval system or transmitted in any form or by any means, without the prior consent of the publisher, nor to be otherwise circulated in any form of binding or cover other than that in which it is published without a similar condition, including this condition, being imposed on the subsequent purchaser

This book is a work of fiction. All names, characters, businesses, organisations, places and events are either the product of the author's imagination or are used fictitiously. Any resemblance to actual persons, living or dead, events or locations are entirely coincidental.

To friends and family who supported my efforts.

Foreword

The financial heart of Great Britain is a square mile in the centre of London simply called the City. It's one of the biggest financial centres in the world and responsible for transacting trillions of dollars of financial products. It is also where most of the world's gold is bought and sold.

With so much money pumping around its financial heart, the City is under constant threat from organised crime, unscrupulous institutions, cyber attacks and foreign governments to name but a few. A number of agencies work to combat these threats. The most prominent is the National Crime Agency (similar to the FBI) or NCA. There are also private companies that assist the NCA. These companies are not so well known. They provide financial expertise, computer forensics, information security and even special investigators who secrete themselves into companies that are suspected of bad deeds. In The Omega Sanction, I've created one such company called Roderick, Olivier and Delaney and this is their story.

Prologue

Harry was unaccustomed to waiting patiently, but the young Hans Mueller had left her no choice. She looked down from her small apartment's window onto the darkened street below, just off from the main Bahnhofstrasse. All was still and quiet. It was gone midnight, and the good people in this part of Zurich had retired to their beds long ago.

The apartment was a one-room affair, situated above a small shoe shop not far from the central railway station. It wasn't luxurious, but it was all Harry could afford. Zurich wasn't a cheap city to live in unless you worked for one of the many financial institutions that were based there. Then they trapped you in the town with rent-free accommodation and an expense account.

God, she hated Zurich.

Hans Mueller had stopped typing, the only sound coming from the three computers, whirring away under her small table in the centre of the room.

Harry tore herself from the window and peered anxiously over Hans' shoulder, willing him to hurry up and complete the hack.

"What's taking so long?"

"Please, don't rush me. This system is littered with TripWires. If I attempt to move the wrong file it will trigger the IDS."

"IDS?"

"Intrusion Detection System. Then we're fucked." Hans' fingers gracefully stroked the keyboard and a list of files scrolled up the screen. "Wait a minute…"

Harry leaned closer. "What … what is it?"

"Sohn vonere huere!"

"English, Hans. What just happened?"

"This is not the production machine." He rapidly tapped out a short command, and a long list of numbers appeared on the screen. "No, no …"

"What, Hans, tell me!"

"I must have activated a TripWire program, which in turn alerted the IDS. I've never seen a security system like this. It didn't just shut me out, but shunted me off the production server to a another machine."

Harry was still in the dark. "Ok, so we just shut down and try again –"

"No Harry, you don't understand. This server is a Honey Trap – a machine with just enough valid information on it to keep me interested, all the while it's logging every keystroke I make and relaying my IP address to the IDS. I've been hacking the wrong machine."

"For how long?"

"Possibly hours. Fuck, they must have traced my IP address by now."

Harry knew they couldn't go back and resume their attack on the server – at least not tonight. "Did you get the information we were looking for?"

"Some – before I was shunted off. But Harry, there are some major players involved in this – foreign agencies. It's bigger than we thought …"

"Later. Did you trace the last shipment of gold?"

Hans nodded. "A bank in London. Reinhart Benson International."

There was a squeal of tyres from the street below.

"C'mon," said Harry. "Time to go…"

The Digital Imperative

1

Victor Renkov glanced down at the diminutive figure of Anna Koblihova, strapped tightly in the seat harness of his brand new Ferrari Enzo. The scant black number she called a dress rode high on her thighs, exposing her strong pale legs. She was playing a dangerous game.

He brushed the accelerator, and they roared down Lower Thames Street in the City of London, the big V12 engine echoing down the canyons of glass and steel. The low sun of a bright Autumn morning glinted off the sloping windscreen. He reached for his sunglasses and smiled. No, it wasn't a good idea to distract a man driving a machine capable of two hundred and six miles per hour. Dress for business he had told her, although he hadn't been very specific. Perhaps the way she dressed was the business?

He flicked a paddle on the rim of the steering wheel and moved up a gear. The car screamed past Old Billingsgate Market. "What do you think, Anna? Fantastic, yes?"

Anna gripped the plush, leather-clad dashboard with one hand and the door panel with the other, her wide hazel eyes fixated on the road ahead. "Victor! Why did you buy such a ridiculous car?"

He pulled down his sunglasses and peered at her over the rims, incredulous. "It's a Ferrari!"

Victor followed a route that hugged the river, slowing briefly for traffic at the London Bridge underpass before accelerating, once more, onto Upper Thames Street and towards Blackfriars Bridge.

"Where are we going, Victor?"

"We're visiting a bank," he told her in a tone that was a little too petulant.

He had known her less than a week but was already regretting the encounter. She had caught his eye at his Mayfair club, draped over the arm of her patron, Vladimir Abramov. She sashayed over, smiling sweetly. Her short, black hair framed an oval face, softening her strong, pale features while lending her a youthful, angelic appearance. He'd flirted with her, but only to make Vlad jealous. But Vlad's jealousy came with a price.

He moved up a gear, accelerating as they entered the shade of the Blackfriars Underpass before re-emerging a few seconds later into the bright sunlight of the Thames embankment.

Victor grinned. "Fantastic!"

Anna pleaded in Russian, *"Please God, Victor!"*

"English, my dear. We must improve our English."

She rolled her eyes at him. When introduced, they naturally spoke in Russian. He had grown up in a small town on the outskirts of Moscow, so his accent was that of a Muscovite; he couldn't place hers. He remembered they switched to English so as not to bore the rest of their party. While she spoke the language very well, there were echoes of heavy Russian tones. It made her sound dull. When arriving in London, he had worked hard on his English and to lose his accent. That was a little over ten years ago.

"What is so special about this bank anyway?" asked Anna.

"It belongs to Reinhart Benson International. They specialise, among other things, in gold bullion. We're heading for their vault."

"A bank vault? And this is where you work?"

Victor laughed. "No, not quite. I have an account with them."

He never tried to explain what he did for a living. Most people were clueless about the workings of the financial institutions of the City, and he supposed she was no exception. And what did he do? He gambled with other peoples money.

"You have money in this bank?" she asked.

"Yes – well, sort of. Clients give me their money, and I invest it in gold. This bank vault stores the gold – gold bullion to be precise, big bricks of it. Tell me, Anna, have you ever walked into a room filled to the ceiling with solid gold bricks?" He watched her face light up. "And the colour, Anna, a warm, radiant yellow like nothing you have ever seen. You never forget the colour of pure gold." Yes, if you wanted to impress a woman you showed her a room full of gold.

"Oh, Victor, it sounds exciting." She half turned to face him and smiled. "And is this where you keep Vladimir's gold?"

Perhaps she wasn't as clueless as he first thought. He glanced at the buildings on the opposite side of the road. "Shit, we've passed it."

He pulled smartly into the right-hand lane and slowed to execute a sharp U-turn through a gap in the central reservation, ignoring a sign that told him 'No U-Turn'. Drivers coming from the opposite direction sounded their horns. Victor simply waved, accelerating swiftly back along the Victoria Embankment for a short way before turning sharply left into a narrow side street and stopping beside a large Victorian building.

"We're here," he announced.

Anna breathed a sigh of relief. "Thank God." She peered out at the ornate building. "And this is a bank? Looks more like a French chateau."

"Yes, well, they don't advertise the place as a bank for security reasons," said Victor. Now that he was here, he had a bad feeling in the pit of his stomach.

"Are you ok?" she asked.

"Yes. Just thinking …"

He had received the call at around 10.00 pm the night before. A woman from the bank. Harriet Seymour-Jones, an Auditor with Reinhart Benson. A funny time to call, he thought. It was about his gold account. There appears to be a problem. Can't say over the phone. Best we meet at the vault. The appointment was made for 10.30 am.

He checked his watch. They had time to spare. He flicked a switch and his door clicked open, pirouetting out and up. He ducked and climbed out onto the pavement. Anna was right, even from here the building looked very out of place, wedged between its more modern counterparts of glass and steel. Definitely Victorian or possibly Edwardian, he could never remember which.

He walked around to the passenger side door and flipped a recessed catch. There was a knack to opening a door on a Ferrari. Anna freed herself from her seat harness and nimbly stepped out. She smoothed down her dress then remembered she had a bag and bent down to retrieve it from the seat well. Several passing motorists tooted their horns in appreciation of the manoeuvre.

They walked a short way to the front of the building which faced the Thames. Tourist boats motored by, along with the occasional police launch. Several commercial lighter barges were moored to a temporary pier close by, not a stone's throw from the building's entrance, providing, of course, you could throw a stone across a four-lane highway. They entered through a set of large oak doors and into a spacious reception area, Anna's bright red heels clicking on the polished marble floor. They were met by a thick-set man in a grey suit that stretched across a large barrel chest. Victor assumed he was security.

"Can I help you, Sir?" His gaze fell on the petite but beautiful form of Anna who gave him an impish smile. "And Madame," he added as an afterthought.

"Victor Renkov to see Harriet Seymour-Jones. She's expecting us."

"This way, sir. You'll both need to sign-in," he said and led them through a set of glass doors where a young woman in a dark-grey suit sat behind a large, ornate writing desk. More Regency furniture lined the walls of the room. "I'll make Ms Seymour-Jones aware of your arrival," he said and left the room.

The young woman beckoned them to take a seat. "Rosalind Baxter", she said, offering Victor a limp handshake. She was a thin woman with short mousy hair. She presented Victor with a leather-bound ledger. "Please sign-in Mr …"

"Renkov, my dear. Victor Renkov." Victor pulled the ledger towards him and drew his favourite Mont Blanc pen from his jacket.

"And this is …" hesitated Rosalind Baxter, her hand waving vaguely in the direction of Anna.

Victor gave Anna a sideways glance, as he scribbled their names in the book. "Who are you, my dear?"

Anna gave him a caustic smile. "Your personal assistant, I think, Victor."

Baxter showed no sign of surprise at Anna's title or her choice of business dress, but merely took back the ledger from Victor and examined the entries. "Victor Renkov and Anna Koblihova, PA. She entered their details into a computer on her desk.

"PA, I like that," said Victor.

"Are we really going to enter the vault?" said Anna, gazing around at the room.

"Bloody well hope so," said Victor, "otherwise this has been a complete waste of time."

"But why do you need to see the vault?"

Another good question, thought Victor. *It was about his gold account. There appears to be a problem.*

Baxter stared at her screen. "Ah, yes, here we are. Victor Renkov. You have an allocated gold account, number 02540123, and you have executed your right to Audit." She smiled with satisfaction at having reconciled their appearance at the bank with her computer records.

"My right to Audit …" said Victor, trying not to sound surprised by this latest revelation.

"That's right," said Baxter. "As stated in your contract, you can request a total of two audits of your account a year. Ms Seymour-Jones will conduct the audit, along with Ms Sally Choong from our Custody department and Mr Walter Baker, the assistant Vault Manager." She gave them her best customer service practised smile. "I'll walk you down."

Victor hesitated. "Wait. You said assistant Vault Manager. Where's Harvey Pinkman?"

"Who is this Pinkman?" asked Anna.

"Mr Pinkman hasn't come in today," said Baxter, smiling sweetly and ignoring Anna.

"But I always deal with Pinkman," said Victor. He felt his stomach knotting. "Where is Harvey Pinkman?"

Baxter's smile quickly faded. "I can't really say, Mr Renkov," her voice rising slightly. "He didn't turn up for work today. I'm sure there's a reasonable explanation. Probably just a tummy bug or suchlike. There's a lot going around."

"Come, Anna," said Victor, standing. He turned to Baxter. "Take me to the vault."

"Right. Jolly good. This way," said Baxter and headed for the door. Victor followed close on her heels.

The reception area receded into the building with two more offices located to the left and the right. Two large stone urns stood guard at the entrance to each room. At the rear of the area, a large oak stairway led up to another floor. Baxter led them around the side of the staircase to a set of ornate steel doors on the opposite wall. It took Victor a moment to realise that they were the doors of an elevator.

"How do we call the elevator? There are no buttons," said Anna.

"No, that's right," said Baxter. "You need a special card key." She indicated a plastic card, fixed to a lanyard around her neck with her photo-id displayed on one side. She leaned forward and placed the card against a small black square beside the doors, which immediately parted, revealing a spacious, wood-panelled interior. "After you, please," she said.

Once inside, Baxter pressed a yellow button, and the steel doors slid shut. The elevator gave a soft whine and descended. "What is that for?" asked Anna, pointing to a red button."

Baxter looked at Victor and then to Anna. "You know, I'm not sure. My card only allows me access to the vault. I believe there may be a storage level below that, but I could be wrong. Only Mr Pinkman has access to that level. This building was used during the war to store works of art, I believe. It's had many uses since then. Rhodes Metals converted it into a vault when they took it over a few years ago."

"I thought this belonged to Reinhart Benson International," said Anna.

"That's right," said Baxter. "RBI is the parent company, and Rhodes Metals is one of its many subsidiaries."

"Would that be Damian Rhodes?" asked Anna, with just a hint of excitement in her voice, "I hear he's very handsome –"

"You ask too many questions," said Victor.

The elevator completed its short descent, letting out a small sigh that decreased in pitch as its motor spun down. There was a soft bump and the doors opened smartly. They walked out into a short, wide corridor. Anna looked around in wide-eyed amazement.

"It's beautiful," she said.

Blue-grey marble dressed the floor, walls and ceiling. Elegant up-lights, in an Art Deco style, lined each wall, throwing up a warm, soft glow that receded along the corridor where harsher spotlights illuminated the round, monstrous door of the vault that made up the entirety of the far wall.

"It is impressive," said Baxter. "Mr Rhodes wanted only the best Italian Carrara marble for the vault entrance." They walked towards the vault door. "The walls of the vault are half a metre thick and made from reinforced concrete; special steel lines the outer wall making it resistant to explosives and thermal torches. And the door –"

"And the door is is over a metre thick and weighs 45 tons," said Victor, now plainly irritated by Baxter. "Yes, yes – I've been given the tour. Can we get on?"

"Yes, of course, Mr Renkov," said Baxter, looking a little harried. "This way."

As they approached the end of the corridor, a small side room came into view a few metres from the vault door. A security guard stepped out to meet them, signalling with his arm that they should enter.

"I'll leave you here," said Baxter. "Please sign out when you're finished." She gave them her best VIP smile, then promptly headed back to the elevator.

They entered what appeared to be a small utility room, its thick oak door wedged ajar. The walls were of smooth, unadorned concrete and a simple overhead fluorescent strip cast a harsh light on the bare, concrete floor. Obviously, not a room that VIPs generally entered, Victor noted. Around the sides of the two far walls were a set of wooden cabinets which supported sets of brass scales of various sizes.

A tall, slim woman in a black pencil skirt and plain white blouse was resting on the edge of a large oak desk which took up most of the remaining space, making notes on a tablet, her long slender legs outstretched before her. Victor noticed that she had the most beautiful head of copper coloured hair, drawn back and neatly braided into a thick copper plait that extended down to the small of her back. Sat behind the desk was a short, young Asian woman in a dark suit.

"Mr Renkov," said the woman on the desk. She stood and extended her hand in one fluid movement. "I'm Harriet Seymour-Jones. Please call me Harry. I'll be your Auditor for this assignment."

Victor automatically proffered his hand which she clasped firmly and held longer than etiquette required. Harry looked him straight in the eye and gave him a slight smile. He got the impression that she was telling him to play along – don't make a fuss. She noticed Anna staring back up at her. "Nice Shoes."

Anna smiled her most caustic of smiles. "Valentino Garavani," she said, then raised her bag. "Prada."

"Nice combo," said Harry. "And you are?"

"Anna Koblihova. I am Victor's PA."

"Personal Adornment?" said the Auditor, smiling broadly.

Before Anna could riposte, there was a slight cough from behind the desk. "Oh, and this is Sally Choong, from Custody. She's here to keep us honest."

The young Sally Choong hesitated, looking between the improbably dressed Anna and Harry. "Oh, yes - well, not really. Actually, I'm here to ensure we can account for all gold movements, to and from the vault. The Vault Manager and I will remove your gold from the vault and bring it here to the balance room where your Auditor will weigh each bar, and record the serial number." She studied a file on her tablet. "Mr Renkov. You have an allocated account containing just over one metric ton of gold, 32,150 troy ounces to be precise." She looked up at Victor and smiled her best VIP smile.

Victor paid no attention to the Custody Officer. The Auditor was clearly the one in charge. She had a confidence and directness that

Victor admired. He also found her to be a strikingly beautiful woman - even in this light.

"Let's get on with it, shall we," said Victor, dragging his thoughts back to the task at hand. He had a bad feeling about the whole setup. Until yesterday, he'd never spoken to this Auditor – let alone requested an audit. What exactly does she know?

"Ok, let's open the vault, shall we," said Harry, striding out of the balance room and into the corridor. The remaining trio followed her out and waited in front of the cavernous vault door. Victor noticed that the security guard was standing beside a small panel on the opposite wall, whispering something to the Auditor. He then reached for a wall mounted phone and started making a call.

Harry walked over to Victor. "Slight problem. Can't find the Vault Manager and we need him to enter his biometrics."

"Biometrics?", queried Anna.

"His hand," said Victor, his agitation rising, "he needs to place his hand on the panel." He turned to the Auditor. "Where is Pinkman?" He pulled out his phone. "I need to make a call."

"Your guess is as good as mine," said Harry. "And you won't get a signal down here. Too deep."

Just then the elevator door opened at the far end of the corridor, and a young man stepped out. Victor thought he looked about twelve. He walked briskly towards them. "Who's this?", asked Victor.

"This is Walter," said Harry, "He's the Assistant Vault Manager."

"Good grief," retorted Victor.

"Sorry, Harry," said Walter, a little breathless, "I need …" He stopped as his gaze fell on Anna. She gave him a warm smile.

"Eyes up here, Walter," said Harry, all business. "We need you to open the vault. Smartly now."

Walter dragged his eyes back to face Harry. "Yes, of course – slight problem. Word from the boss. Pinkman needs to be the one to open the vault."

"But Walter," explained Harry, patiently, "Harvey is not here. And this audit was arranged over a week ago. Mr Renkov is waiting." She nodded to the security guard who entered a code into a keypad on the wall. The small, hand-sized panel lit up with a pale green colour. "Place your right hand on the scanner, Walter," said Harry, more firmly. "I'll take responsibility."

Walter's face took on a pained expression. "Harry, I'd love to help, but I was told that only the Vault Manager could open the vault for an audit."

"Who told you that, Walter?" asked Harry.

"Damian Rhodes," said Walter, with more than a hint of awe in his voice.

"Fuck Rhodes," exploded Victor, "open this bloody door now!"

"Victor, Victor, calm yourself," implored Anna, soothingly. She moved closer to Walter.

"Walter, you look like a smart man – important man, yes?" She took his right hand in hers and squeezed gently. His eyes drifted down to her angelic face, then to her cleavage. His mouth parted as if to say something, but no words came out. "Come Walter."

Anna led him slowly over to the green, glowing panel. Walter followed as if in a daze. The security guard stepped to one side, a bemused look on his face. Something seemed to snap inside of Walter. "Sorry, Ms … I don't think Mr Rhodes –"

"Don't worry," purred Anna, then quickly grabbed his wrist in a vice-like grip and slammed his palm onto the panel. There was a small increase in the panel's brilliance, then a loud ding. Walter looked on in horror.

A klaxon started. Victor felt a slight vibration through the floor. He heard the sound of electric motors spinning up, their whine growing louder. "Please stand back," said the security suit, his arms outstretched. Anna released the hapless Walter and everyone took several steps back as the enormous vault door cracked open a few centimetres, then started to swing out slowly.

Anna clasped her hands together, playfully. "Victor this is so exciting!" she squealed.

Victor's heart was pounding as fluorescent lights flickered on, one by one, inside the vault, first illuminating the entrance, and then the interior. He could make out racks of safety deposit boxes at the back of the vault.

The sound of the door's electric motors dropped in pitch as they slowly spun down, the vault door silently swinging to a halt on its two gigantic hinges, revealing a spacious stainless steel room.

Victor was the first inside, followed swiftly by Harry, then Anna. The three stood in the middle of the room looking around. Sally Choong finally entered the vault, tablet in hand. She let out a short gasp. "I don't understand," she said. "It's empty."

"Sally, how much gold do your records show is stored in the vault?" asked Harry.

Sally Choong examined her tablet, scrolling through several pages. "Approximately, six metric tons, of which one metric ton belongs to Mr Renkov."

"Vladimir's gold," said Anna to no one in particular.

Victor felt physically sick. Where was Harvey Pinkman?

2

To the denizens of London's Square Mile, it is known prosaically as The Leadenhall Building, a manifestation of glass and steel erected on a small plot of land between the Lloyds building and a nondescript black monolith, the name of which no one cares to remember. To the rest of the capital, it is known as the Cheese Grater.

To Fabio DeLuca, it was a beautiful building, no matter what people called it. In his native Rome it would have been given a grand name; to his colleagues in Reinhart Benson International, it was just another place to make money.

He arrived outside the office on Leadenhall Street earlier than was his custom. For a City trader, 7.30 am was not an uncommon time to start work, but he was nursing a hangover and feeling fragile. The young Italian chided himself for being so reckless the night before. Today was not the day to screw up. He'd only had time to grab a coffee and a bagel on the way in.

He walked to the cavernous atrium that was the entrance to the building and through the public space of lawns and trees until he reached the escalators that rose thirty metres to the mezzanine level above. He walked across the reception hall until he came to a row of glass turnstiles where he was greeted by a short, stocky man in a light-grey suit.

"Good morning, Mr DeLuca."

"Hey, morning, George. How are you?"

"Very well, thank you. Word to the wise: Mr Rhodes has already arrived."

Fabio's heart sank. He looked at his watch. He was only a few minutes late. If he caught a high-speed elevator, it would take him to his floor in no time.

"Thanks, George, I owe you one. Ciao!"

He juggled his bagel and coffee in one hand while he retrieved his pass from his jacket pocket, careful not to spill anything down his expensive Italian suit. He slid the pass over the top of the turnstile, causing the glass barrier to slide open with a satisfying hiss. He hurried to the elevator banks located at the back of the building.

To describe the building as a Cheese Grater was a bit of a misnomer. To Fabio, it was more of a wedge with its base at street level and the office space above diminishing in size, floor after floor, to accommodate the sloping frontage of the building. The RBI offices were located on the fortieth floor and thus considerably smaller than offices situated in the lower levels.

His colleagues in Rome had joked when they'd heard he was moving to the new London office: "Hey, Luca. Better pack your Parmigiano. They're sending you to the Cheese Grater." He'd ignored their comments but was surprised by the assignment. Firstly, because he was relatively new to the bank, and secondly, he traded in gold bullion. RBI in London dealt mainly in Foreign Exchange and Investment Banking. The head dealer in Rome had summoned him to his office. RBI had bought a small Precious Metals dealer in South Africa, he confided, and they're putting together a new team of dealers in London. Fabio knew of the outfit – anyone who traded precious metals had heard of Rhodes Metals and the maverick owner and CEO, Damian Rhodes.

He arrived at the back of the building and punched in the floor on the panel in front of him. They say the elevators in The Leadenhall Building are the fastest in Europe; Fabio's stomach never doubted it. He barely had time to admire the view before it sharply decelerated and opened onto his floor. He stepped out into a small reception area and was greeted by Samantha Jenkins, the latest addition to the Rhodes stable of PAs.

"Morning, Luca. He's waiting for you in the conference room."

While most execs he had worked for usually had one Personal Assistant, Rhodes had three and sometimes four. And they were all of a certain type: tall, blond and stunningly attractive. Sam brought this months total to four. Why Rhodes needed so many PAs, Fabio could only guess.

"Morning, Sam. Thanks."

She smiled and picked up the phone. "Mr Rhodes? He's on his

way."

The conference rooms were all-glass affairs that took full advantage of the sloping frontage of the building, providing panoramic views of the City. Damian Rhodes was standing with his back to the door when Fabio entered. He appeared to be in a contemplative mood as he stared down upon the stainless steel of the Lloyds building across the street. In the distance, the sun glinted off the gilded stone flame atop the London Monument.

"You're late."

Rhodes was not a tall man. In magazine photographs he appeared of average height; in person, he gained a few centimetres by making those around him feel small. His blackish hair was kept short and well-groomed, flecks of silvery-grey around his temples marked his advancing years. Fabio thought he had the look of an Italian, with a strong nose and the thin, small mouth of a Mafioso. He favoured the English style of suit from Saville Row and always in dark wool. He looked lean and fit for his age, which Fabio estimated to be the early forties.

"Sorry, sir. Metro delay."

Rhodes turned to face the young Italian. "It's called the Tube, Luca. No one over here calls it the Metro." He paused. "And you look like shit."

"Sorry, sir …"

"It's important you don't screw this up, Luca." He paused to study Fabio carefully. "We have a major client who needs to offload their gold holdings, and it needs to be done today. Understand?"

"Yes, sir."

Rhodes moved over to a green file that lay open on the conference room table and retrieved a single sheet.

"Here are your instructions." He handed the sheet to Fabio and glanced at his watch. "One last thing. It's important you sell before 8.00 am."

Fabio scanned the dealing sheet. He hesitated then read the instructions more carefully. The sell order amounted to five metric tons of gold. It was a considerable amount to offload onto the market in one go.

"But sir, the London market will still be closed …"

"Hong Kong is open. You'll be selling using our counter party."

"Sir …" again he hesitated. He wanted to be sure. "If I place this amount of gold in Asia before London opens …"

"Our client was very specific," repeated Rhodes, a little testily. He looked at his watch again. "Carry out your instructions and report back to me when it's done."

Fabio looked once more at the deal sheet and felt a little sick.

"Yes, sir."

He exited the conference room and made his way back to his desk. He turned on his computer and brought up his dealing system. Other dealers were beginning to file into the office. "Hey Luca, you look like shit … "

Fabio ignored them. He was still confused. The London gold bullion market was the biggest and most liquid in the world. It could absorb a massive amount of buying and selling of the precious metal without so much of a hiccup in price; the Hong Kong market was much smaller, which meant that placing a sell order of such magnitude would cause the spot price of gold to crash – at least until the next gold fix which was 10.00 am London time.

He glanced at the world clocks displayed on the far wall of the office. It was 7.50 am. He rapidly typed in the sell order, noting that the client was Borite Metals Holding. He'd never heard of them. His finger hovered over the Enter button. He hesitated. On a hunch, he flicked on a second screen which showed the price of gold futures. The current or spot price of gold was $1,500 an ounce. The short-term futures contract for gold was slightly higher. This meant that most traders thought the price of gold would rise over the next few days. Then he saw it. A large contract shorting the price of gold. Someone had just bet on the price of gold falling.

The clock's minute hand ticked forward. It was now 7.55 am. Fabio looked over at the conference room. Rhodes was still there, glaring at him. He moved back to his dealing screen. The order was waiting to be executed. Tick, tick, the minute hand advanced: 7.58 am.

A tall woman was walking towards him. She had beautiful, long red hair, pulled back and plaited into a rope. She was smiling at him. He turned to look at his screen: 7.59 am. He pressed the Enter button, and the trade was executed. Five tons of gold bullion had just been dumped onto the Asian market.

The London market opened just as the spot price of gold plunged nearly five per cent. Someone had just made a lot of money. There were cries of dismay from the other dealers in the room, the price of gold had fallen off a cliff.

"Fabio DeLuca? Hi, my name is Harriet Seymour-Jones, and I'm here to audit your trades."

3

Ben Drummond breathed in the cold night air as he ran up the steps leading to the south-side footpath of Tower Bridge from the wharf below. It was 2:00 am, and traffic heading into the City was light. He stepped up the pace and quickly made it to the first stone-clad tower. A young couple were sharing a lovers embrace, oblivious to the rushing, inky-black river of the Thames below. He ran passed them and headed over the central span and towards the lights of the City beyond.

He had received the call in the early hours of the morning: "Captain Benjamin Drummond? NCA Operations Centre. You're needed urgently at the Leadenhall Building. Yes, tonight. Please report to Commander Alex Fern. She'll brief you on the assignment."

The operator had been curt and to the point. He thought it strange. The fact that the National Crime Agency had called him was not the problem. He was registered with them as a Computer Forensic Investigator and had carried out several assignments on a contract basis, but NCA operations were generally planned at a more leisurely pace, and never in the middle of the night. So he had thrown on a navy tracksuit and a pair of trainers, gathered up his gear in a small rucksack, and headed out of his apartment on Butler's Wharf, just below Tower Bridge. He reckoned it was quicker to jog than wait for a cab.

He crossed the bridge and carried on jogging past the Tower of London, it's limestone battlements lit-up in all their splendour. He picked up the pace again and was reminded of his old drill sergeant: "Soldiers don't jog, Drummond. They fucking run." He had fucking run for Queen and Country, that was for sure.

He rounded the corner of the Tower and carried on at a steady pace along Tower Hill Road, coming at last to Old Billingsgate Market. The Monument rose up from between the City buildings on his left, a brightly lit beacon against the dark London skyline. He stopped and looked at his watch. It was 2.30 am. *Run you fuckers, run!*

He sprinted across the four-lane highway of Lower Thames Street and along the narrow passageway of St. Mary at Hill until he reached EastCheap and the improbably constructed Walkie Talkie building. A few late night revellers cheered him on: "go on, ma' son."

He ran hard between darkened buildings, turning right into Lime St and past Leadenhall Market where the street narrowed before opening out beside the illuminated, steel-clad Lloyds building. He remembered his father, William, bringing him here when it had first been built. They both thought it looked like a brewery. He slowed and walked to the end of the street where he was greeted by the sight of the Leadenhall Building. William always called it The Cheese Grater.

He crossed the road and walked towards the building entrance. The street was empty and quiet. He headed for the escalators. As he drew near, two armed police officers in full, tactical gear approached him from his left and right. He stopped and kept his hands in plain sight. Experience had taught him to be cautious around men carrying automatic weapons in the middle of the night.

The officer on his right did the talking. "Sorry sir, this area is closed. Move along."

He thought them well trained. The man kept his distance, his hands never leaving his weapon. His partner stood off at the ready, alert for potential threats. Drummond cast an experienced eye over their guns: Heckler & Koch MP5s; Glock 9mm for sidearms. Their black, tactical dress was branded with the letters NCA: National Crime Agency.

"Ben Drummond, Computer Forensics, reporting to Commander Alex Fern."

The officer nodded to his partner. She keyed her radio and started up a conversation.

"Show me some ID," said the officer.

He slowly reached inside his top pocket and retrieved an ID card bearing his photo. He handed it to the officer who studied it for a minute and waited for his partner who finally nodded.

"Commander Fern is waiting for you on the mezzanine level," said the officer. He leaned in closer. "And she's pissed off."

Drummond took back his photo ID. There wasn't much he could say. He had been dragged from his bed in the early hours of the morning, and *she* was pissed off. He walked to the bottom of the escalators, which had been switched off, and started the long climb up.

Commander Alex Fern was waiting for him at the top of the escalators. He had served with some tall women in the army, but Alex Fern was the biggest woman he had ever seen. She stood a good head taller than him with strong, broad shoulders. The Commander wore the same black, tactical gear of her officers, complete with a Glock 9mm sidearm. Her jacket was unbuttoned at the neck revealing a white t-shirt instead of the regulation stab vest. Tufts of blond hair were trying to escape from beneath her cap which she wore in place of the standard ballistic helmet of the junior ranks and which was branded with the bold white letters of the NCA.

"You the tech guy?" she enquired.

"Ben Drummond, Ma'am. Computer Forensics."

She studied him for a while. Drummond felt as if he was back on parade – except the only thing he was packing was a laptop.

"Someone must think very highly of you, Drummond. They cancelled my regular tech and said it had to be you. We've been hanging around for the past hour."

"Sorry, Ma'am." He didn't know why he was here either. But he kept that thought to himself.

"You run here?" she asked

"Thought it would be quicker than calling a cab. I live just across the river … a little over three kilometres," he replied

"Ex-Army," she said. It was more a statement than a question.

"Yes, Ma'am."

"I can always tell."

Drummond never liked being labelled 'Army'. He'd resigned his commission over ten years ago and had worked hard to lose some of the rough edges that armed service had ground into him. Still, the Military had a way of leaving an indelible mark.

Drummond surveyed the mezzanine level which served as the central meeting point and reception area of the building. He'd been here before on other contracts. During the day it would be full of bustling office workers, chatting and waiting for meetings. The large hall was now empty, except for two armed NCA officers waiting over at the turnstiles that led back to the rear elevator banks.

"Expecting trouble?" he asked.

"Got a tip-off that someone is in the building. Probably nothing," said Fern.

She turned quickly and started walking towards the turnstiles. Drummond marched in double-time to keep up with her broad back.

"You have your gear?" she asked.

"Yes, Ma'am."

She stopped and spun around to face him. "Look, I appreciate the chain of command and all that, but just call me Fern. Ok?"

Drummond smiled. "Sure, no problem. Most people just call me Drum."

They carried on towards the two officers.

"I don't have to explain Chain of Custody and all that crap, do I Drum?"

"No, not my first day on the job."

"Good. We've been planning this raid for some time, and I don't want any balls-ups with the evidence."

The two officers at the turnstile straightened their stance as they approach. If nothing else, Commander Fern had their full attention, and he guessed their respect.

"We're going up. No one goes in or out," said Fern.

The two officers acknowledged their orders with slight nods. They were a tight team. No superfluous chatter; no, yes sir, three bags full, sir, no questioning their orders. He knew what it was like to be part of such a team.

Fern opened the turnstile with her ID card, and they passed on through towards the elevator banks.

"What am I looking for?" asked Drum.

"We've been following the activities of a bank called Reinhart Benson International for some time now, as part of a joint money laundering effort with the Department of Justice in the States. We got a tip-off from a whistleblower – something big going down with their bullion trading. DOJ wants us to go in and find out what's going on."

Drum thought about this. He was familiar with the way these systems worked. "You understand that their trading system is likely to be centralised, offsite somewhere – probably not in this building?"

They had reached the rear of the building. Fern scanned her pass over a central console, activating the elevators.

"Yep, we understand that. But our insider told us to grab the computers and any related material belonging to Harvey Pinkman and Fabio DeLuca. They're located on the fortieth floor," replied Fern.

"What's special about these guys?" asked Drum.

"Don't know yet. Our insider tells us that DeLuca has been carrying out some illegal trades and the evidence is probably on this Pinkman's laptop."

"What's Pinkman been up to?" asked Drum.

"All we know about Harvey Pinkman is that he's the bank's Vault Manager – handles all the gold transfers. Other than that …"

The elevator car appeared from out of the glass and steel of the building's elaborate external shaft. Fern stepped inside as soon as the doors opened.

"Jesus, they're fast," said Fern, momentarily caught off guard as the elevator started its rapid ascent.

A thought occurred to him. "Where's the building security guard?" asked Drum.

"Fuck!" Fern keyed her radio. "Harris. You laid eyes on building security tonight?" She waited. "No … shit! Go and look for him. Why didn't you tell me no one was manning the desk? Yes, it is a problem. We're on the fortieth floor. Call me when you have something."

Drum made no further comment. They both knew someone had screwed up. The elevator performed a rapid deceleration before stopping. They stepped out into a small reception area. A large sign on the wall told them this was Reinhart Benson International.

Fern pointed towards two glass doors. "That leads to the main office space. We understand DeLuca has a desk towards the front of the building and Pinkman has an office on this floor. Find DeLuca's desk, and I'll search for Pinkman's office. Shout if you need me."

He nodded and made his way towards the doors. The lights in the office space beyond were dimmed. He pushed aside one of the doors and walked through. Overhead lights began to flicker on as the building management system detected his movement. Orderly rows of desks lined each wall, extending part way to the sloping front of the building where a large, glass meeting room was located. In the centre of the main floor was a partially enclosed room which Drum guessed to be another ad hoc meeting space.

He stood still and listened – something he had been trained to do. There was a faint hum of the air conditioning, but otherwise, the area was empty and quiet. He moved slowly along the row of desks, looking to see if any bore the name DeLuca. Fern was nowhere to be seen. She seemed quite happy to leave him to his own devices.

He came to the last desk on the left-hand side of the space, in sight of the glass-enclosed conference room. An embossed plate proudly displayed the name of Fabio DeLuca. Drum surveyed the area noting that the desk had been cleared of all paperwork. This was standard policy for financial companies operating in the City. He took off his rucksack and rummaged around inside until he found a toolkit of assorted screwdrivers. He laid them out neatly in a line on the desk.

There was nothing remarkable about the desk. It was similar to others in the room with two sets of drawers. Now, Fabio, he mused, are you a bad boy? He tugged at the top drawer which glided open. Fabio, you bad boy. You didn't secure your desk. Sitting on top of a pile of papers were two memory sticks. Bingo! Evidence – or maybe just Italian porn. Either way, he tagged and bagged them. He opened the main drawer and was surprised by the sight of a laptop. Fabio, what have you been doing? He pulled out the laptop and placed it on the desk.

He thought he heard a noise in another office. "Fern?" He listened. He heard nothing but the hum of the air conditioning.

He started to examine the laptop. It was powered down. He would bag and tag it for later.

Drum saw him first, a large man in a dark suit with close-cropped hair coming out of a corner office near the reception area. He carried a laptop under his arm. He spotted Drum and stopped. They both stared at each other. He muttered something that Drum couldn't make out then cursed in a language that Drum was familiar with – he had been cursed in Russian many times in Afghanistan.

"Hi," said Drum. "Are you security?"

The Russian pulled a wicked looking knife from a sheath on his belt and manoeuvred himself between the desks.

Drum guessed he wasn't the security guard. *No heroics, Drum.*

The Russian moved slowly towards him, beckoning him out from behind the desk with his knife and pointing to DeLuca's laptop. It looked like they were after the same thing – whatever that was.

Drum stood his ground. He slowly moved the desk chair between himself and the advancing Russian. The big man slowed, recognising, perhaps, that his opponent was not about to cut and run. He started speaking softly. Drum reached down and let his hand explore the surface of the desk, his eyes never leaving the Russian. He felt for his toolkit. It was the best he could do.

The big Russian was less than a metre from him when he lurched forward with a straight-arm thrust of his knife. Drum's left-hand and wrist snaked around his opponent's outstretched forearm and gripped it firmly, deflecting the blow, while at the same time kicking the chair hard into his legs. The Russian cursed loudly and fell forward, bringing him within range of Drum's other hand which now gripped a long, thin screwdriver. Drum slammed it down hard into the man's extended shoulder, its blade penetrating deep to the bone.

The Russian screamed, letting go of both his knife and the laptop, which bounced and then clattered off the desk before hitting the floor and shattering. He staggered back, clutching his shoulder and cursing loudly.

Fern strode into the office space and advanced towards the Russian. She didn't seem to be in any hurry. Better late than never, thought Drum. The Russian saw her and abandoned his attack. He bent down and retrieved his knife and staggered towards the conference room, still clutching his wounded shoulder which was now bleeding profusely. Blood dripped down his hand and the tip of the blade, leaving a crimson trail across the floor.

Fern stopped beside the meeting room and waited for the Russian to come to her. Now would be a good time to draw your weapon, thought Drum. The Russian advanced slowly on Fern, mumbling to himself. He took the knife in his other hand and expertly flipped it around so that the blade was pointing down with it's cutting edge facing out. Drum recognised the move. He meant to stab down or sweep across the throat in one cutting motion. Fern crouched into a fighting pose. *Just shoot the fucker.*

The Russian made a poor attempt at a feint before telegraphing a wide sweeping slash of his blade that was intended to cut across Fern's throat. She saw it coming and nimbly stepped to one side, grabbing his wrist in a vice-like grip with her left hand and the upper arm with her right. Using the Russians forward momentum and her considerable strength, she pivoted her whole body, accelerating her opponent in a wide arc, sending him careering into the glass wall of the conference room with incredible force.

The glass shattered with a deafening crash, turning the wall into a cascade of sparkling diamonds. The Russian fell backwards through the broken glass before coming to rest, face-up, on the conference room table. He lay there, spreadeagled, not moving.

Fern stood staring at the prone figure. Drum said nothing. He moved from behind the desk and carefully made his way into the shattered conference room, the broken glass crunching beneath his feet. The guy looked dead, his screwdriver still embedded deep in his shoulder. Drum leaned over and felt for a pulse in the Russian's neck.

"He's still alive."

Fern made her way through the shattered wall, her combat boots scattering shards of glass in her wake. She pointed to the screwdriver.

"Good improv' …"

4

It was 5.30 am by the time Drum had completed bagging and tagging all the evidence. The first rays of dawn were beginning to brighten the City skyline. The office space had filled with armed NCA officers, regular City police and ambulance crews. The place was now a crime scene.

Fern had found the building security guard with his throat cut in Pinkman's office. The guy had never stood a chance against a trained killer. It would have been better if Fern had shot the guy. They took him out, handcuffed to a stretcher with an armed NCA officer for company. Drum explained to one of the medics that he wanted his screwdriver back: it was part of a set.

Fern was slumped in one of the office chairs, legs outstretched with her hands behind her head and her eyes closed. He walked over to her carrying his rucksack. She looked beat.

"I'm all done here," said Drum.

She opened her eyes and looked at him and wearily pushed herself out of the chair.

"I'll walk you down." She turned to one of her NCA officers. "Harris, I'm going down. I'll be on my mobile if you need me." The guy nodded.

They rode the elevator down in silence, each contemplating the events of the night. They picked their way through the yellow police tape that now cordoned off most of the mezzanine and climbed onto the escalator that led down to the atrium.

Drum was not a small man, but Alex Fern was a good head taller and broader in the shoulder than him. It took great strength to throw a man of the Russian's size through a plate-glass window.

"I know what you're thinking," she said.

"What am I thinking?"

"I shouldn't have thrown him through the window."

"Ballsy move."

"Yeah, well … I was angry – after I saw what he did to the security guard. And I shouldn't have left you alone. God knows what would have happened if it had been one of my regular tech guys …"

Drum changed the subject. It was never a good idea to play 'what if' after a fight; that you survived was all that mattered. "Did you notice the tattoos on his neck? Not your regular thug. And he spoke to me in Russian," said Drum.

She was silent for a while. "Yeah, you noticed that too …"

They were both quiet as they walked out onto Leadenhall Street. There were few pedestrians at this time in the morning and traffic was light. Fern raised her arms to the sky and stretched.

"God, I'm tired." She studied him for a while. "You don't look too good yourself."

He ran a hand back through his light-brown hair. He needed to get it cut. He wore it longer since leaving the Army. He was approaching forty and flecks of grey peppered his temples. *Git your fucking haircut, Drummond.*

He was hungry. "Hey, why don't I buy you breakfast?"

She thought for a moment then seemed to come to a decision. "Why not. I'm starving." She hesitated. "What's open at this time in the morning?"

"I know a place in the market. Trust me, you'll like it," said Drum.

"Ok, but first I need to shed this gear." She pointed to a large, black van parked outside the Lloyds Building with the letters NCA painted boldly in white on its side. "I have my civilian kit in the back. This won't take a minute. Let's go."

Drum followed her across the road to the NCA van. She banged on the doors which were opened by a young female officer.

"Joy, I need to change," said Fern.

The young officer jumped down. "Yes, Ma'am." She landed nimbly beside Drum and smiled. "Hi".

Drum returned the smile.

Fern climbed into the back of the van and carefully removed her sidearm, placing it on top of a black holdall. No one attempted to close the doors. She quickly removed her black tactical gear until she was down to a black bra and briefs. She retrieved a clean t-shirt from the bag and a carefully folded grey trouser suit, then did a quick limbo to get them on within the small confines of the van. She then donned her sidearm beneath her jacket.

"Right, let's go," she said, jumping down.

Joyce pointed to her head. "Lose the hat."

"Oh, right." She tossed her hat in the back of the van then mussed up her short blonde hair. "That will have to do."

Drum was beginning to warm to Alex Fern. There was no pretence of coyness about the woman – no false modesty. What you saw is what you got. And there was a lot of Fern to like.

Joy smiled once more at Drum. "Be seeing you."

"*Bye*, Joy," said Fern, striding off.

Drum marched in double-time to keep up. "What marked me as Army," said Drum, curious.

She grinned. "The first time I'm introduced to a tech, they stare first at my tits, then my sidearm. It's probably the first time they've seen either outside of a computer screen. You clocked my sidearm, then my tits."

Drum laughed. "Your sidearm is a Glock 17, 9mm – standard issue for security forces." He paused. "And I noticed you weren't wearing a stab vest."

It was her turn to laugh. Her whole demeanour was transformed when she smiled. "Yeah, well, they don't make a woman's vest in my size, and a man's vest just wouldn't cut it."

They were passing the entrance to the Lloyds Building when Drum noticed a tall man in a light-grey suit with straw-coloured hair leaning nonchalantly against the side of a sporty silver Mercedes. He was smoking a long black cigarette. He could have been a chauffeur, but as they drew closer Drum could tell he was powerfully built. The guy wore a white shirt, unbuttoned at the neck which partially exposed a set of distinctive tattoos. His previous encounter with the Russian had put him on edge.

"On your right ... big guy – eyeballing us."

Fern turned slightly. "Yeah, spotted him back at the van."

She unbuttoned her jacket so her sidearm was in full view then stopped and faced their observer. The tall man threw down his cigarette and leisurely got back into his car. The engine started, and the car lurched forward and headed back down Lime Street.

Drum walked over and retrieved the cigarette. It was a Sobranie – a Russian brand.

* * *

There has been a market at Leadenhall as far back as 1445. It was one of Drum's favourite locations with its ornate Victorian roof and red painted colonnade. There was something of the Dickensian about the place, except it was now frequented by well-heeled Lloyds Underwriters and City traders. The Ives restaurant was situated just inside the market, off Lime Street, and above a fishmongers that was famous for its smoked salmon and oysters. The restaurant was the fruition of the long-held ambition of Sergeant Ian (Brock) Ives, NCO of her Majesty's SAS, retired.

The seed of the idea to open a restaurant in the heart of the City of London had been sown one evening on his last tour of Afghanistan in some desert between Helmand and Kandahar. There had been Ives, Dick Davis, Joe Cairns, Tommy McPherson and Ben Drummond. They had been surviving on rations until Dick (Poacher) Davis did some negotiating with one of the local tribes for a goat and some spices.

The Poacher, as the troop called him, had been a gamekeeper in civilian life. He was a tall, lanky man with a soft West Country accent that could charm a bird from a tree. The Poacher could also look up at the sky and give you a fairly accurate assessment of the weather. On that particular tour, he would look up at the beginning of each day and without fail declare that it would be 'bloody hot'.

Ives then preceded to cook them the best goat curry they had ever tasted. Drum said he should open a restaurant. He and Ives had been friends ever since.

The restaurant had been open for a little over a year but had already acquired a reputation among the City elite for serving a great breakfast. Their doors opened at 6:30 am to take advantage of early morning traders, and those power brokers that liked to do deals before the lunchtime rush.

They arrived at the restaurant a little past opening time. Drum led the way up a flight of stairs to a large dining area. City traders were already seated at several tables, and waiters were taking their orders. The place had a rustic feel, with its rough wooden floor and cast iron columns that supported the Victorian roof. Long down-lights with glowing orange filaments gave it a cosy atmosphere.

A short, stocky man in a white apron came barreling out of the kitchen at the back of the restaurant carrying two steaming plates. He had a hard, craggy face and bushy eyebrows that hid soft brown eyes. A silvery-white stripe cut through the centre of his salt and pepper hair. He stopped when he saw Drum.

"Benjamin! Good to see you. Let me get rid of these."

He served the diners with the plates and made some small talk for a minute or two. Ives had become quite the bon vivant. He signalled to Drum and led them to a table marked 'private', tucked away discreetly in a corner at the back of the room.

"My special table for those patrons carrying concealed weapons."

Drum smiled. "Brock, meet Commander Alex Fern. NCA."

Brock took Fern's hand and shook it enthusiastically. "Nice to meet you, Commander."

"Call me Fern. Another military man, I'm guessing?"

"Why yes. How did you know?"

Drum and Fern both laughed.

"Sorry, Brock," said Drum, "long story. We've been up all night on a job, and we're starving."

Brock beamed. "Of course. How about the morning special? Poached Haddock with Poached Egg and Rustic Loaf."

"Sounds amazing," said Fern.

"You sit tight. I'll be right back with some coffee. You both look knackered."

They wearily eased themselves into their chairs. Within minutes, Brock kicked open the kitchen doors carrying a large coffee pot. "Food's on its way." He then disappeared back into the kitchen.

"Brock?" said Fern.

Drum poured them two coffees. He added cream to his cup from a jug on the table. Fern declined.

"He's always had that stripe of white hair. Born that way. So he got the nickname 'Brock' after the badger."

Brock came backwards out of the kitchen doors carrying two steaming plates of food.

"And what did they call you?" asked Fern.

"He was called 'The Package'", said Brock, placing the plates on the table.

Drum rolled his eyes.

Brock winked. "Well, I'd better be getting back to the kitchen. Give me a shout if you need anything."

"You two obviously served together," said Fern, grabbing the Rustic Loaf.

"Afghanistan."

She looked at him and raised her eyebrows, wanting more of the story.

Drum's mind drifted back to a cold night in the desert and a hot goat curry.

"I was the assigned mission specialist to Brock's troop. The SAS call non-troop members 'Packages'. It's their job to get them to a location and to get them out." He rarely spoke of those times, and darker memories came flooding back. "Anyway … enough of my war stories. Tuck in."

They ate in silence, Fern cutting the Rustic Loaf into great slabs and thickly spreading the butter, Drum demolishing his fish and eggs.

"God that was good," said Fern, pushing her clean plate away and leaning back in her chair.

Drum poured them some more coffee. "So tell me, what does the Russian Mafia want with these two laptops?"

She looked at him over the rim of her cup and slowly sipped her coffee. She was obviously debating something with herself.

"Well, it's no secret that the NCA has been keeping tabs on organised crime involving the Russian Mafia. We've seen their operations expand this past year – drugs, people trafficking, money laundering – the usual. There's a growing concern they're targeting City institutions. But why they'd be interested in these particular laptops … I really have no idea."

Drum finished his coffee and regarded her across the table. She wasn't telling him everything.

"Your turn," she said. "Why did NCA Operations call you and not my regular guy?"

That was a good question. Drum didn't know either. Then a thought occurred to him.

"You've heard of Phyllis Delaney?"

"Everyone knows Phyllis Delaney in our business. Why do you ask?"

Of course, he thought. Anyone involved in rooting out financial crime knows Delaney. She has her fingers in every major government body involved in the financial sector. When bad shit hits the corporate fan, the Fed and other financial regulators call in the firm of Roderick, Olivier and Delaney. Those in the financial community simply called it the ROD.

"You mentioned the raid was initiated by the Department of Justice. I think ROD are somehow involved – at least on the DOJ side."

Fern frowned. "Possibly. But why call you?"

"I used to work for ROD – until recently, that is."

"What happened?"

"Delaney and I had a falling out."

Fern pursed her lips. "Not a good person to fall out with, I would have thought."

Drum had to agree. Still, this was just like Delaney. She never liked anyone to quit the firm – unless it was on her terms.

"Anyway," he said, "looks like you're stuck with me."

She smiled. It was a smile he could get used to.

"I'd better be going," she said, looking at her watch. She pushed back her chair and stood up, straightening her jacket, making sure her weapon was concealed. Bad form to frighten the diners. "You'll let me know asap when you've finished with your forensic examination of the laptop data."

Drum stood and said, "I'll get to work on it today."

She nodded. "Thank Brock for a lovely breakfast." She handed him a card. "In case you need me."

Something was still bothering him. "Quick question. Do you know the big guy – the one outside Lloyds?"

She hesitated for a second. "Yes. He's an enforcer for a guy called Vladimir Abramov – the head of the Russian Mafia."

5

Drum was late leaving the restaurant. Brock had plied him with more coffee and insisted on knowing every detail of his encounter with the Russian and his thoughts on Commander Alex Fern. Spetsnaz for sure was Brock's expert opinion. The move with the knife – classic Russian military. Lucky to be alive. "And she threw him through a plate-glass window. Bloody hell. Good job she was there to protect you."

It was after 8:30 am when he finally made it back to his office on Butler's Wharf. Drum's father had bought the lease on the property when London's docks were being re-developed. William had always been a canny trader – even when he was selling fruit and veg. He now owned the leases on several prime properties on the south side of the river. When asked about the money he had made, William would always say he was comfortable.

Drum's office was a corner property, tucked just below Tower Bridge with a view onto the river. The ground floor comprised mostly of office space; it was not big by commercial standards but sufficient for his needs as a specialist contractor to the City. The level above was given over to a small apartment which was accessed by a wrought-iron spiral staircase from the office below. William said it lacked a woman's touch. Drum called it home.

The sign on the large plate-glass window of the office read Security Risk Dynamics. Raj Patel was waiting outside for him, taking a break.

"Ben! Glad you could make it." He nodded to the small reception area just inside the entrance where two women sat. "I was about to send them home."

Raj Patel was Drum's only employee, a young security analyst from Delhi hired over a year ago as a favour to a friend in one of the banks.

Drum had sponsored his visa – a long, drawn-out process that he thought would never end. But Raj had proved himself invaluable and one of the best cybersecurity analysts he'd ever met.

"Oh, Christ, I'd forgotten all about the interviews. How long have they been waiting?"

"Since eight this morning," said Raj. "They're overflowing with my tea."

"Sorry, Raj. Long night. I'll fill you in later." He handed Raj his rucksack. "There are two laptops in there – all bagged and tagged – register them in the evidence log and remove the hard drives. We'll need a forensic examination as soon as possible. The NCA is in a hurry. You know the drill."

"No problem, Ben," said Raj. He hurried into the office, glad to have something to do.

Drum followed him. Of the two people waiting one was a young woman in her early twenties, thumbing her mobile, oblivious to her surroundings; the other woman was much older, waiting patiently with her hands resting in her lap. Drum guessed the older woman to be in her mid-sixties. Seeing her reminded him of something William had said, but he couldn't think what.

"Hi, I'm Ben Drummond. Sorry to keep you waiting." The young woman looked at him, mouth agape. The older woman smiled warmly and with mild amusement. He suddenly realised he must look a mess. There was blood on his trainers, and he hadn't shaved since yesterday. He was hot and sweaty from the run back from the market.

The older woman stood up and held out her hand, unfazed by his appearance. "I'm Alice. Pleased to meet you." She tilted her head to one side and studied him. "Looks like you've had a busy night?"

He knew what was nagging at him.

"I've met someone," his father had said on one of the rare occasions they shared a pint together. "Nice lady. At the bowl's club. We're … you know, seeing each other. Dating, if that's the right word for people of our age. I told her you were looking for someone to help with the office work. I think she can type. Even does shorthand. Her name is Alice."

Alice was still waiting for him when he returned to the office after a shower and shave. He'd donned a charcoal-grey suit and a clean white shirt, open at the neck. He'd not worn a tie since leaving the army.

"Where's our young friend?" said Drum, pointing to the empty chair.

"I think she had a social media crisis," replied Alice, straight-faced. "Said she couldn't wait any longer and left." She cast an eye over his new appearance. "That's better."

Drum escorted her to his office which looked out over the Thames. A tourist boat sounded its horn as it passed under the bridge. Drum wasn't the tidiest person on the planet, but he had to admit his office was a mess.

A pathetic looking Lily on the window sill had succumbed to neglect and given up the ghost. Various papers and folders were scattered over his desk, and more files stood sentry on the floor by the door. He had to clear a chair before Alice could sit down.

"Sorry about the mess. Things have been a little hectic of late," he confided, sheepishly.

Alice didn't seem a bit put out. She dusted the chair with her hand and sat down. She looked around the office. "I think your plant has expired."

Drum regarded the shrivelled specimen. "It's just resting."

She reached down and retrieved her bag, a fine leather satchel, taking out a slim bound document which she handed to him. Drum realised it was her resume.

Drum skimmed the neatly typed pages: Public school, moving up to Cambridge to study Modern Languages as an undergraduate; then to Oxford University for a Masters in Russian; a year off travelling after graduation and then recruited to the Civil Service. A long but undistinguished period in the Foreign Office and, towards the end of her career, a few years in the Treasury. Her life, on paper at least, was a correctly ordered timeline from Public School to retiree - no gaps, no blemishes, no deviations. A career Civil Servant was Alice - or so it seemed.

She sat upright and perfectly still, intently watching his every move. She did not speak, patiently waiting for him to finish reading, her small, white manicured hands folded in her lap. She wore little makeup, yet her skin was fair and glowing, softening the crows-feet of age etched around her pale-blue eyes. It seemed to Drum that she was assessing him; not him assessing her. Her silvery-white hair would have been quite long, had it not been fashioned into a neat bun and held in place by an elaborate enamelled pin, shaped in the form of a butterfly.

All in all, Alice was a handsome, yet unremarkable woman. But it was how she dressed that caught Drum's attention.

They were the clothes you thought a Civil Servant should wear: a plain, dark-blue suit jacket, perfectly tailored to her slim frame and a matching knee-length skirt. Her plain white silk blouse was open at the neck, revealing a string of small, luminescent pearls, and her shoes were what William called, 'sensible shoes': low heeled and soft leather, the colour of her suit. This was all perfectly fine, except that her clothes were obviously very expensive.

"A super resume," said Drum.

"Curriculum Vitae."

"Sorry –"

"We call it a 'Curriculum Vitae' over here," she said. "Latin: the course of one's life."

Drum looked up and smiled. "Guess I've spent too much time over there, Alice."

She blushed. "I'm so sorry. That was very rude of me. Haven't had an interview in years –"

"Chanel?" Drum said.

"Sorry – what?"

"Your suit. Worked with a colleague from Paris once. She wore something similar."

Alice instinctively looked down, as if worried something was out of place. "Why – why yes it is. You're very observant." She absentmindedly flicked at her skirt. "More than you can say about your father …"

Drum could tell she instantly regretted mentioning his father. He laughed. "You're not far wrong there, Alice. Now, on the other hand, if you were to wear a string of jellied eels around your neck, instead of those pearls, he might take more notice."

She looked at him and inclined her head then burst into a cackle of laughter. "Oh, my. You're so like your father."

They both sat there laughing at William's expense. And when she laughed, she became a completely different person - more animated, the crows-feet around her eyes softening her face.

"Oh, look …" She hesitated.

"Call me Ben."

"Yes, thank you, Ben. Look, I told William that this was probably a bad idea –"

"Nonsense. You're the best candidate I've seen all morning."

She looked around at the empty reception area. "I appear to be your only candidate ..." and they both burst out laughing once more.

"Look, Alice, the job's yours if you want it. But frankly, with your – " he chose his next word carefully " credentials, I'm worried you'd find the work boring."

She allowed herself a wry smile. "Oh, I don't think so. Looks like you could use a little help around here." She cast her eye once more around the office. "I can start tomorrow if you like?"

And with that Alice Pritchard became the newest recruit to the business.

6

The offices of RBI were now a crime scene which meant that Rhodes and his cohort of traders had to find temporary accommodation elsewhere if they were to continue trading. Murder, it seemed, was not considered too big an obstacle to the continued creation of wealth. The bank's alternate location was activated.

The secondary dealing room of Rhodes Metals was a squat redbrick relic of the Victorian era, located just behind the Leadenhall building. It sat incongruously between the small, medieval church of St. Helen's and the towering phallic icon Londoners called the Gherkin. If the relic had a name, Damian Rhodes and his traders never used it: since moving into the building they merely referred to it as The Undershaft.

Rhodes arrived early. He liked to prepare for his morning briefing, scheduled for 7:30 am. Anyone turning up late to the meeting was fined one hundred pounds – no matter how senior they were. Since moving to the new location, traders referred to this process as being shafted.

Rhodes handpicked all traders himself. They had a reputation in the market for being uncompromising and tough; those that survived the dealing room were those that made a profit – no questions asked. Rhodes knew that DeLuca was not one of them. He was disappointed with the young Italian – DeLuca had delayed the execution of his dealing instructions, a delay that could have cost him millions. Then the Auditor had turned up.

Rhodes didn't mind his new office. He didn't miss the vertical commute each morning. There was something civilised about just walking into a building through the front door at street level. His new PA was waiting for him.

"Good morning, Mr Rhodes." She handed him an espresso.

"Morning, Sam. No calls until after the briefing."

"I'm sorry, but you have a visitor."

He stopped in his tracks. "What – at this time in the morning?" He looked at his watch. It was 7.05 am.

Samantha Jenkins looked pained, a deep frown cutting across her perfect forehead. "It's Sir Henry. He's waiting in your office."

His office in The Undershaft had an Edwardian feel, an old boys club smelling of brandy and old cigars. A brown leather Chesterfield couch furnished each wall together with a large central bookcase. His desk was an antique behemoth of satinwood-inlaid mahogany with a green leather top. Sir Henry was ensconced on one of the couches enjoying a cup of tea, courtesy of the ever-thoughtful Samantha.

"Sir Henry," said Rhodes, throwing his coat over the back of his desk chair. "To what do I owe the pleasure?"

Sir Henry Minton was a thickset man in his late-sixties with steel-grey hair. He was old money, the family cash having come from shipping and banking for generations. His wealth was inherited not earned, and Rhodes despised him for it. He was also chairman of Reinhart Benson International.

"The board is worried," said Sir Henry.

Rhodes thought this to be an understatement given recent events. He sat down on the adjoining couch and sipped his espresso.

"Sally Choong of Custody reports that bullion is missing from the vault … and now this raid?"

And not a mention of the poor bastard who had his throat cut, thought Rhodes. He placed his espresso cup on a small table beside the couch. "Let me assure you, Sir Henry, that no gold is missing from the vault. Custody doesn't know their arse from their elbow. The gold was moved on Friday to the alternate vault in Eastcheap. Unfortunately, our Vault Manager – Harvey Pinkman – had a family emergency and didn't have time to update the inventory system."

Sir Henry looked sceptical. "So, you're telling me that the six metric tons of gold that should have been in the vault is all accounted for."

"Precisely."

"But why move it in the first place?"

Rhodes knew Sir Henry was clueless about the workings of a bullion vault, despite his position in the company. It was one of the reasons RBI had bought Rhodes Metals. He tried to make it simple for the chairman. "The vault sprung a leak."

Sir Henry looked incredulous. "Sprung a leak! What are you talking about?"

"The vault is located beside the Embankment – beneath the level of the Thames in fact. We noticed there was water seeping in from somewhere – the construction is relatively new. Pinkman was investigating. The vault was cleared so that work could be carried out to correct the problem. Can't have workman helping themselves to bars of gold, now can we."

Sir Henry might be a dinosaur, thought Rhodes, but he was no fool. He waited for the inevitable.

"Well," replied Sir Henry, "that being the case, you'll have no objection to a full audit of the bullion inventory. The Audit and Risk Committee are insisting on it."

"Of course," said Rhodes, helpfully. "I'll give the Audit Manager a call and set one up."

Sir Henry paused sipping his tea. "That won't be necessary." He eased himself out from the comfort of the couch. "We might have a bigger problem." He walked over to the window and stared out as if searching for inspiration. "Our American friends at the Department of Justice are putting pressure on our regulators on this side of the pond to look into irregularities regarding our trading."

Rhodes sat forward. "What irregularities?"

Sir Henry turned to face him. "They won't say, exactly – playing their cards close to their chest, as it were. But it's clear your bullion trading has come under scrutiny. Apparently, there's a whistleblower."

Of course, thought Rhodes, the Auditor with the red hair – it could even be DeLuca. "Look, Sir Henry, let me reassure you that our trading is squeaky clean –"

"Oh, well," interjected Sir Henry, "not for me to say – up to the board." He paused. "That's why it's been decided to bring in outside expertise – in fact, the DOJ is insisting on it."

"Who do they want to bring in?" asked Rhodes.

"Roderick, Olivier and Delaney. They'll be liaising with the NCA."

Rhodes knew of ROD's reputation. Their investigation would be no picnic. They hired the best and dug deep. Things had just gone from bad to worse. "How long have we got?"

"A week – maybe two. I'm flying to New York to be briefed by the DOJ." The chairman looked at his watch. "Well, better go …" He hesitated. "Look, Rhodes. If you're as squeaky clean as you say, you have nothing to worry about."

Rhodes stood up and forced a smile. "Of course – thank you for stopping by."

Sir Henry nodded and walked swiftly out of the office.

Two weeks. That's all he had to put his house in order. The most pressing issue was the whereabouts of Harvey Pinkman and the six tons of gold bullion that should have been in the vault.

Rhodes was still pondering the problem when Samantha Jenkins poked her head around the door. "Sorry to interrupt you, Mr Rhodes, but the team are waiting."

He looked at his watch. It was 7:45 am. He had just been shafted.

7

It was early Friday morning, and Drum was already awake. His mind had been churning with the events of the previous night and sleep had evaded him. He raised the blinds of his bedroom window and stared out across Tower Bridge. The low Autumn sun danced playfully on the waters of the Thames, showering the river with a myriad of dancing lights. He was reminded of the Russian crashing through the plate-glass window. *Good improv'.*

Someone had wanted him there, that was for sure. At first, he thought it had been Delaney's machinations, but the more he thought about it, the more unlikely it seemed. After all, she would have just called him. And why had they used his army rank? *Captain Drummond? You're needed at the Leadenhall Building.*

Drum's apartment was a spartan affair – more like an army barracks than a home, said his father. A large bed was placed against one wall of a relatively spacious lounge which adjoined a modern kitchen-diner. A large, well-equipped shower cum-wet-room made up the rest of the space.

Drum showered and dressed in a grey wool suit and plain white shirt. He would have liked to have dressed less formally, but he never knew when a client would stop by or want an impromptu meeting across the river in the City. He observed his appearance in a full-length mirror. He was approaching forty but still looked lean and fit. He swept a hand through his long damp hair and thought about getting it cut. A dark shadow of stumble completed the look.

By the time he had made it downstairs, Alice had arrived. She was smartly dressed in a matching grey-check jacket and skirt with a dark grey sweater and carried her leather satchel over her shoulder. He was reminded of someone he used to work with. Alice wanted to reorganise his filing system, she told him, and clear his office of all stray papers. So, he headed out and took a walk along the wharf and grabbed himself a coffee.

It was gone eight when he arrived back at the office. Alice was sitting behind the small reception desk sorting through a pile of papers.

"Raj is out back – in the tech room, cloning the drives," she said matter-of-factly. "At least, that is what he said he was doing." She nodded in the direction of his office. "And you have visitors."

He was surprised to see Victor Renkov sitting in his office. His life was inexplicably full of Russians.

"Benjamin!" said Victor, standing and enthusiastically shaking his hand.

"It's been a while, Victor."

Drum hardly recognised his office: the scattered papers had all been removed, and his desk looked neat and tidy; in place of his expired plant now stood a beautiful, purple orchid – at least, that is what Drum thought it could be. On his black couch, which previously had been used as an impromptu filing system, now lounged a young woman in a dark purple dress, split modestly at the knee. A thin, black belt was fastened around her slim waist.

 Drum turned to face the young woman.

Victor paused. "Oh, yes. This is Anna. My ... PA."

"Please to meet you, Anna."

Anna smiled warmly.

Drum returned the smile and sat at his newly-cleared desk. "How long has it been, Victor?"

Before Victor could answer, Alice entered the room. "Can I get you some tea, Mr Renkov?"

"No thank you, my dear." He turned to Anna and spoke to her in Russian. Anna fired back a sharp rebuke. It seemed to Drum that Victor was having a little PA trouble. Victor was about to reply when Alice spoke to her in Russian. The woman looked a little surprised, shrugged her shoulders and eased herself out of the couch in one smooth movement.

"Anna and I will chat outside," said Alice. "We'll leave you gents to catch up." She held the door open until Anna had left the room then followed her out and closed the door.

"I didn't know you'd hired a Russian," said Victor, in amazement.

"She speaks like a native Muscovite."

"A Masters in Russian, apparently", replied Drum, remembering Alice's resume. "What did she say to your PA?"

Victor laughed. "Basically told her not to be a bore and let the men talk."

Victor was always the charmer. A son of a minor government official, he had saved and borrowed money to study business at a little-known educational establishment in central London that specialised in acquiring visas for foreign students. The scheme turned out to be a scam, by which time most of his money was gone. Not wanting to return home to his family in disgrace, he spent his last few pounds in a charity shop on a well-worn suit and a pair of brown leather brogues. He then headed for the City of London and made a fortune in the money markets. Drum never entirely bought into the story, but Victor's rise in the City had been remarkable.

Victor removed his overcoat and threw it over the back of the couch. He was dressed for a City boardroom in a three-piece navy suit with a narrow pinstripe. A red and blue striped regimental tie secured the neck of his off-white shirt, the collar of which was held in place by an ornate gold pin. He moved to the window, hands in his pockets, and stared out.

"Nice view you have here," he said, half to himself.

"What's troubling you, Victor?"

"I have a problem." He moved back to the couch and flopped down. "At least I think I do."

Drum knew that this was going to take a while. It was time he didn't have. "C'mon, Victor. Cut to the chase."

"Right. Well, since we last met, I've branched out – currency trading not as profitable as it used to be. China catches a cold, and the markets take a dive. So I started investing in precious metals – gold especially – as a hedge against the bad times and the volatility of the markets. It's always been a safe haven when times get tough. So far, so good." He paused. "Looks like your Alice is getting on with Anna …"

Drum looked out into the reception area. That was the trouble with modern office designs, they were almost entirely constructed of glass. Like working in a goldfish bowl. Alice and Anna were having an animated conversation about something.

"Anyway," continued Victor, "news gets around, and some of my investors want in on the action – but they want physical bullion, not interested in the paper investments around gold. No, they want to see and touch the stuff. So, I open what's called an 'allocated' account with RBI. Been buying and storing gold in their vault for the past year –"

"RBI?" interrupted Drum. "That would be Reinhart Benson International?"

"Yes, do you know them?"

Certain sounds remind Drum that trouble is coming his way. The sounds of weapons being checked just before combat; the snap of a slider being pulled back on Glock; the sound of the front door slamming when his father returned home from work. There was something in Victor's voice that had a similar effect.

"I've heard of them," said Drum, casually. "Go on."

"So I get this call - late one night," continued Victor. "One of the Auditors from RBI – telling me there's a problem with my account. I need to come to the vault."

"Wait. Why would an Auditor be calling you?" said Drum, a little confused.

"That's what I thought," replied Victor. "So, I arrived at the vault the next day. I take Anna - thought to impress the girl. Trouble is the vault's empty!"

Drum leaned back in his chair and frowned. "The vault was … empty? What were you expecting to see?"

Victor stood up and began to pace. "I'll tell you what I was expecting to see: just over a metric ton of my gold – or strictly speaking, my clients gold!"

"And the Auditor …"

"Right, right. She was as surprised as I was. According to the Custody Officer who was present when the vault was opened, I should have had eighty bars of gold bullion tucked up nice and safe inside."

"And it was empty …"

"Nichevo," said Victor, reverting to his native Russian. "Zilch, nada."

"So let me get this straight," said Drum, rubbing his temple, "you get a call from one of the bank's Auditors who tells you there's a problem with your gold account."

"Right."

"You turn up with … Anna and you're told you have eighty bars of gold bullion sitting in the vault – how much is that worth, by the way?"

"About forty-eight million US."

Drum was used to working with large numbers in the City, but still

... that was a large amount of money to misplace.

"Ok, so the vault is opened and zilch. The vault is empty."

"Precisely."

It made no sense to Drum. "There must be a mistake in the inventory – the gold is at another location, perhaps. And this was Monday, you say?"

"Yes."

"So, today's Friday. Have you gone back to the bank and queried the problem – spoken to the Auditor?"

"Look, Benjamin. Do you think I'd be here if everything were fine? I've tried calling the bank – asked for the Auditor. They tell me she no longer works there. I've asked for the Custody Officer. Guess what? She's moved back to Hong Kong!" Victor paced over to the window. "Ben – you have got to help me sort this out. I thought with your contacts you might have heard something?"

"Heard what exactly?"

Victor glanced at Drum. "Well, I thought that since you work with the NCA, you might know what's going on at RBI – they're all over the news. Something about a murder?"

Drum had yet to look at a newspaper, let alone turn on the TV. He shouldn't have been surprised that the murder had made the front pages. But there was someone in this whole saga that Victor hadn't mentioned, or had left out for some reason.

"Victor, I don't know too much about dealing in gold, but I understand enough about vaults to know you need a representative from three departments to be present before it can be opened: Audit, Custody and Vault Services. Where was the Vault Manager?"

Victor thrust his hands back in his pockets and stared out of the window, chewing things over. A pleasure boat sounded its horn as it approached Tower Bridge. Drum had heard the sound many times before, but on this occasion, it resonated with the warning ringing in his head.

Victor watched the boat disappear under the bridge, and this seemed to break his reverie. He turned to face Drum. "Ah, yes. The Vault Manager. The person I normally deal with didn't turn up. They sent a snot-nosed assistant in his place."

"Who were you expecting?" said Drum, although, by now, he thought he knew.

"Pinkman," replied Victor, "I always deal with Harvey Pinkman."

* * *

Victor was disappointed when Drum declined further work at the bank. It's not that he didn't want to help, it was just he was fully committed to his current assignment. Victor looked crestfallen and left shortly after.

Drum was still digesting the information gleaned from Victor when Alice walked in with a tray.

"Thought you might like some tea after your Russian experience," she said, placing the tray on his desk. She sat herself down on the couch, fussing with her jacket. "Raj is coming."

Drum was beginning to like having Alice around. She'd handled Victor's arm-candy with consummate ease. And his office looked great.

"Thanks, Alice. You didn't have to go to all this trouble –"

"Oh, tsk, tsk," she said, picking at her skirt, "it's nothing – and we could all do with a break. Why don't you be mother?"

Drum poured them both some tea. He didn't know they had a teapot. They both sat in silence for a minute or two, sipping their tea as English people do. Drum broke first.

"Thanks for dealing with Victor's PA. You were very professional."

Alice gave him a wry smile and chuckled to herself. "Oh, my. What did you make of her?"

Drum thought it an odd question. She was looking at him, assessing him. "Well, an attractive woman –"

Alice rolled her eyes. "Apart from the obvious – her demeanour. What did you think?"

Drum thought back to his first impression of the young woman lounging on his couch, her tone with Victor. You didn't have to understand Russian to know she had told Victor to take a hike. "Well, thinking about it … she certainly wasn't Victor's PA, neither was she a piece of arm-candy. You seemed to have a long chat with her. What did you think?"

"Hm, I think she was looking after someone else's interests. Certainly not Victors." She sipped her tea and looked at Drum over the rim of her cup. "And her accent … Ukrainian, I think."

"Victor complimented you on your Russian. Thought you were a Muscovite."

"Oh, the sweet boy. Bit of a charmer is our Victor. Wouldn't trust him as far as I could throw him."

Drum smiled. Alice was very perceptive. "Really, Alice. What makes you say that?"

"Oh, past experience, I guess. Russians – can be devious bastards.

Dealt with too many of them."

"This would be at the ... Foreign Office?"

Alice slowly returned her cup to her saucer, the clink of china signalling the end of the conversation. "Oh, tsk, tsk. Just me being silly. I'm sure he's a very nice man. Are you going to help him out?"

Drum wondered what Alice had learned from her conversation with Anna. "I can't. Told him it would be a conflict of interest. Already fully committed to this job with the NCA. But it didn't stop him pumping me for information concerning RBI."

Drum was debating whether to tell Alice about the raid on the Leadenhall Building when Raj walked in.

"Good news, bad news," he chimed, helping himself to some tea. "I didn't know we had a teapot?"

"Bad news first," said Drum.

"Bad news is the Pinkman laptop is encrypted."

Damn, thought Drum. Fern will be pissed. "What's the good news?"

"The good news is the DeLuca laptop is wide open. I'm running the data analysis now."

"The encryption on Pinkman's laptop. Can we crack it?" asked Drum.

"I don't think so," said Raj, blowing on his tea. Looks like someone has used a strong key sequence." He paused. "You didn't find a post-it note on his desk, perchance?"

Drum laughed. "Sorry, Raj. I was a little busy."

Alice sat up and gave him a hard look, the crows feet around her eyes deepening. "This job of yours ... it wouldn't have been in the Leadenhall Building, would it?"

"Why, yes," said Drum.

"It's all over this morning's news," said Raj. "Poor man was murdered – arrested some Russian."

Great, thought Drum.

"Alright," said Alice, "spill the beans."

So Drum recounted the events of the raid and the discussion he'd had with Victor.

"And this Russian tried to kill you," repeated Raj, incredulous.

"Bastard!" cried Alice. They both looked at her in surprise. "Sorry, chaps ..."

"And this Fern woman shot him," said Raj.

"Threw him into a plate-glass window. He was still breathing when I checked."

"Pity," muttered Alice.

Raj finished his tea. "I'd better get back to it. Shame about the Pinkman laptop. Seems he's now a person of interest."

Alice was looking thoughtful. She turned to Drum, "Did you tell Victor that you had this Pinkman's laptop?"

"No, I thought it best to keep quiet about that," said Drum.

"Good. The less Victor knows about your involvement in the raid the better."

Drum frowned. "You really don't trust him?"

Alice forced a smile. "Well, just me being silly …" She picked at something on her skirt. "It's a bit of a coincidence, don't you think … Victor coming here asking about this Pinkman?"

Drum had to admit she was right. Victor was after information. About what, he didn't know.

Alice rose from the couch and was about to leave when she hesitated. "It's Saturday tomorrow. Why don't you visit William? He'd love to see you."

Drum thought about this. "Why would I want to do that?"

"Well, for one thing, he's your father, and for another, you haven't seen each other for a while."

Drum leaned back in his chair and sighed. "Ok, Alice. I'll give him a call – because it's you."

Alice beamed. "Thanks, Ben. He'll like that."

She was about to leave when Drum had a thought. "Alice, just one thing."

"What's that, Ben."

"Let's keep office work between us. I don't want William hearing about Russians trying to kill me."

Alice gave him a conspiratorial smile. "Of course, Ben. I know how to keep a secret."

8

Drum threw on a pair of faded blue jeans and a t-shirt for his meeting with his father. It had been a while since they had sat down and had a proper talk. He knew it was important to Alice that they meet, so he guessed William had something to tell him. He grabbed his old leather jacket and left his apartment. It was a crisp Autumn morning, so he decided to walk, heading out over the bridge to the City beyond.

William had business near Liverpool Street, so Drum had agreed to meet in Spitalfields Market. William had complained once that the market was becoming too 'trendy'. It's only saving grace, according to William, was you could still get served a decent bowl of jellied eels.

As a boy, William would take him to the fish market at Old Billingsgate and buy three or four live eels. He would carry them home, wrapped in newspaper and held tightly under his arm lest they escape. They did once, and he received a sharp cuff around the ear for his trouble. Once back home, William would decapitate the eels, gut, chop and boil them in a spiced stock and allow the evil brew to cool until set in their own jelly-like fluids. They would then be eaten cold. The dish goes back to the eighteenth century and indeed only found in London's East End.

Drum found William sitting on a bench, in the food hall of the market, a bowl of his favourite eels before him.

"Hello, William," said Drum, sitting down opposite his father. "Don't wait for me. Tuck in."

William was dressed in a smart green, waxed jacket with a matching flat cap. His silvery-grey hair beneath looked recently trimmed, and he was cleanly shaved. Drum thought his father was looking well; Alice was apparently having an effect.

"Hello, son – an' I wish for once you'd call me Dad."

"Hello, *Dad*," said Drum, humouring his father.

William eyed an unusually large piece of eel and stabbed it with his fork. He raised it slowly to his mouth, a portion of the jelly-like mass dripping from its decapitated body.

"How's it going then, son? Met anyone interesting?"

Drum had grown up eating many different types of food in London's East End, he'd even watched Brock eat a whole sheep's head in the deserts of Afghanistan, but he still couldn't bear to watch his father eat eels.

"Met a Russian the other night – on a job," said Drum.

William looked past his piece of eel. "A Russian, eh."

"Yeah, I lent him my screwdriver."

"That was nice of you," replied William.

"Never gave it back," said Drum.

"Bastard."

"That's what I said. Told a lady friend I was with –"

William was about to bite into his lump of eel when he paused. "A lady friend, eh. Bout time you met someone …"

"Tall girl –"

"You like em tall," said William.

"He only goes and swears at her – in Russian."

"No. The swine!" exclaimed William.

"That's what I said."

"What she do then – this girl of yours?" asked William.

"Grabs hold of him and throws him through a plate-glass window."

"No … 'ang on, you're pulling my leg …"

"That's what he said!"

They both burst out laughing.

It's good to see you, son. Are you sure I can't get you some eels?"

"No thanks."

They sat in silence together, father and son, just enjoying each others company. As relationships go, theirs had been a difficult one. William had married young, his Spanish flower, he called her. A romance that blossomed while visiting a flower market in Barcelona. Benjamin had been their only child. But a tragic road accident robbed him of his only true love when Benjamin was just five years old, leaving William to struggle as a single parent.

William raised his son as best he knew how – as his father had raised him. Don't mollycoddle the boy, his fellow traders warned;

spare the rod, spoil the child was their sage advice. But William loved his son; he just kept it a secret from him.

With William off working and coming home late, Benjamin was left to fend for himself. He did well in school but was often in fights; at one point the Social threatened to take him away. Then a friend in the market suggested the Army. Put my lad straight, it did, his friend confided. So Benjamin was conscripted to the cadets and never looked back.

Ben Drum was smiling.

"What's so funny, then?" asked William, sucking on an eel bone.

"I was thinking about the time that eel escaped."

"Oh, yeah." William laughed. "We chased it all around the market. Shouldn't 'ave clipped you around the ear, though ..."

"Yeah, well – don't go all politically correct on me, now. I survived."

William beamed. "Yes, you did, son. You did." He paused between bites of eel. "Talking of survival. How's Alice doing?"

It was Drum's turn to smile. "Well, actually, she's been a real help."

"I thought so," said William, eyeing another piece of eel, "she knows shorthand and stuff."

"Where did you say you two met?"

"I told you. At the bowls club."

"Since when did you play bowls?" asked Drum sceptically.

"Joined a few months ago. Henry suggested it. Ya know, my mate from the Nag's Head. Got to get out more, says Henry. Join the bowls club. Meet people. And he was right. I met Alice. We've been ... you know –"

"Seeing each other," added Drum.

Drum thought it was nice that his father had finally met someone – but Alice? Talk about chalk and cheese.

"Did she tell you what she did – before retiring, that is?" enquired Drum.

"I dunno, really. Something to do with the government. Typing and stuff. She said they screwed up her pension or something. Just needed a little job to tide her over. Why?"

"Oh, you know. Just curious. Anyway, I hope she doesn't find us too boring."

"You just watch your language around 'er – you and your Army mates. Sensitive, is Alice," said William, spearing at another morsel of eel. He paused. "Look, Ben. There's something I've been meaning to tell you – about Alice and me ..."

Drum noticed his father staring past him. "What's up?" said Drum, deliberately not turning around.

"Don't look now but there's this big guy, watching us across the hall for the past ten minutes."

"Does he look like a fighter – blond hair?" said Drum.

"Yeah, do ya know him? Looks like a mean bastard."

Drum thought he knew who it was. He pulled out Alex Fern's business card. "Listen, Dad. Take this card and phone my friend –"

"The big girl? Wouldn't you be better off calling the police?"

"She is the police. Tell her I have a Russian problem."

"A Russian problem? I don't understand ..." William looked concerned. "Listen, son, I'm not leaving." William's face took on a grim expression. "You and me, son. We can take him."

Drum smiled. "It's alright, Dad. He just wants to talk. Probably waiting for you to leave. Alex will know what to do. You shoot off."

William looked unconvinced. "You sure? I don't like to run off and leave you."

"Course not. You'd be helping me out. Got your phone?"

William patted his jacket pocket.

"Off you go then. I'll call you later – promise."

William reluctantly stood up from the table. "You'd better call me."

Drum watched his father start to walk away, his hand reaching for his phone. He waited until he was out of sight and turned to face the Russian walking casually towards him. He was smoking a black cigarette.

9

The Russian sat himself down in a casual manner. No rush, no fuss. For a big man, he moved with elegant ease. He said nothing, just regarded Drum and continued to smoke his cigarette. For the second time this week, Drum thought he was being assessed.

"It's self-service here if you're looking for some tea," said Drum.

The big man looked around, then raised a hand the size of a ham. He took one last drag on his cigarette before extinguishing the end, with a sizzle, in the entrails of William's eels.

"The old man," said the Russian in heavily accented English, "he is your father, no?"

The Russian's voice was deep and sonorous. Drum detected no implied threat in his tone. It was more a statement than a question.

"Just some old guy trying to scrounge some money," said Drum, unconvincingly.

"He looks like you, I think, Ben Drummond."

Someone had done their homework. "And what do I call you?"

The Russian shrugged as if the question was pointless. "People know me as Misha."

One of the stall holders, a bearded man in a white apron that Drum had not seen before, approached their table carrying a large tray. The tray held a small silver urn, some small glasses and a plate of what looked like biscuits. The man placed the tray carefully between the two of them and spoke to Misha under his breath. Drum couldn't make out what was said, but the Russian nodded and sent the man away with a wave of his hand.

"We have time," said Misha. He reached inside his suit and retrieved a slim silver case. As he did so his jacket parted, revealing the grip of a heavy looking handgun. And here's me, thought Drum, without even a screwdriver.

Misha flipped open the case, one-handed, with practised ease, revealing neat rows of black cigarettes. He offered one to Drum.

Drum shook his head.

Misha took no offence but retrieved one of the slim black smokes and placed it between his lips, snapping the case shut and returning it to his pocket. With his other hand, he produced a battered old lighter which he flipped open, striking the thumbwheel in one smooth motion before putting flame to tobacco. He breathed deeply, inhaling the smoke.

Drum thought he recognised the crest on the lighter. "Spetsnaz?"

Misha examined the worn and faded crest as if seeing it for the first time. "Da. You are a military man?"

"I served my country, yes."

"Your country. Da. I'm sure your country is very … grateful." He gave Drum a sardonic smile and put the lighter back in his pocket.

The bearded man returned and poured a black liquid from the urn into the two glasses, before departing to whatever corner of the market he had surfaced from. Misha continued lazily smoking his cigarette and proffered his hand towards the tray. Drink.

"It's been a while since someone has poured me tea from a samovar," said Drum, taking a glass of the steaming hot liquid. The tea had a rich, smoky aroma to it. "And these must be Nuql, sugar covered almonds," pointing to what he first thought were biscuits.

The big Russian regarded Drum through a cloud of cigarette smoke. He picked up his glass and drank some tea. "You served in Afghanistan, I think."

Drum tasted his tea. It was flavoured with cardamom. It reminded him of cold desert nights spent in Helmand with the local militia. "Two tours," said Drum. "And you?"

"Afghanistan, Iraq, Chechnya – too many, I lose count."

"And now you're a gun for hire."

The Russian looked at him. "We are all – how you say – guns for hire, Benjamin Drummond."

He tapped his watch. "We go now, I think. Please stand up."

Drum stood up. He knew the drill. With thumb and forefinger, he parted his jacket. Misha stood and merely nodded. It wasn't the most thorough of searches.

"Where are we going?" asked Drum.

"Mr Abramov would like to speak to you. He is waiting for us. I drive." He stood up, and Drum felt very small. "I park over here." He pointed to one of the side entrances. A silver Mercedes was parked beneath a sign that said 'Emergency Vehicles Only'.

They walked towards the car. Drum knew it was pointless to argue. If he'd refused, Misha would have probably just picked him up and stuffed him in the boot. Sooner or later he would have to talk to Abramov. At least the big Russian hadn't tried to kill him – yet.

Misha stopped. Something was on his mind. "The policewoman …"

"You mean Alex Fern?"

"You sleep with her?"

Drum smiled. "No, at least not on our first date."

Misha nodded approvingly.

They reached the car. Misha paused and leaned on the car's roof. "I know what you are thinking."

"Not to play poker?"

"You are thinking you can take me. I think not. It would be foolish to try."

Drum grinned. "No, Misha. I can't take you." He opened the passenger door. "But I'm sure Alex Fern could."

The big Russian looked surprised, then roared with laughter. People turned to look. He slapped the top of his Mercedes. "I think you are right, Benjamin Drummond! I think you are right."

Misha drove at a leisurely pace, keeping to the speed limit. It wouldn't have been wise for him to have been stopped for speeding when carrying a concealed weapon. He left the market via Commercial Street before turning into Whitechapel. He made no small talk, and Drum was content with his own company. After a few miles of light traffic, he headed South towards Wapping and the river. At least he wasn't smoking.

It was no coincidence that since the raid on the bank his life, once more, was full of Russians. It was a fair assumption that the thug in custody was Abramov's man; he'd wanted Pinkman's laptop, which meant that Abramov wanted Pinkman's laptop. Somehow it was connected to Victor's visit to the vault.

They drove through the backstreets of Wapping and turned into a narrow cobbled street, between a canyon of Victorian warehouses, fashionably refurbished. Where once there had been a bustling dock, filled with the flotsam of global trade, there was now the chink of cappuccino cups and apartments filled with the City's elite. William must be laughing: he had bought property here when they were tearing down the place.

Misha slowed and turned into the narrow entrance to a large warehouse complex. The enormous lintel embedded in the scrubbed Victorian brick proclaimed this to be Regency Wharf. Security cameras were everywhere. The car squeezed through a narrow passageway and emerged into a small, cobbled courtyard surrounded by apartments and offices. He cut the engine and sat back in his seat and turned to Drum. "Abramov is not a patient man. Don't be smart ass." With that succinct piece of advice, he exited the car.

A brick staircase, with wrought-iron balustrades, lead up to another level and a pair of faux warehouse doors. A security camera monitored the entrance. Misha took the steps two at a time and waited for Drum to catch up. A buzzer sounded, and one of the doors snapped open with a loud clack.

The Russian waited for Drum to enter first. It was never a good idea to have a potential adversary at your back. They emerged into a spacious apartment, or it could have been an office; Drum couldn't quite tell. Whoever had designed the place had done well to incorporate the industrial fixtures of the original Victorian warehouse, with its exposed iron roof beams, supported by ornate, iron columns. Drum noticed a rusty pulley wheel, hanging from one of the beams. Industrial loft meets Mafia chic. Handy if you wanted to restrain an uncooperative visitor.

The walls were of the same bare tan brick as the outside of the building. A large oval window looked out onto the small courtyard and flooded the room with natural light, illuminating a large couch against one of the walls where Victor's PA lounged.

"Hello, Anna. Fancy meeting you here."

She acknowledged him with just the slightest of nods then looked away as if bored by his presence. As before, she was impeccably dressed in a pale-grey pencil skirt and matching jacket. A simple low cut blouse completed the ensemble. She looked every bit the corporate moll.

Misha placed a large hand on Drum's shoulder and pointed to a red leather couch in the centre of the room, indicating he should take a seat. In front of the couch was a large oak desk. Various papers lay scattered on its surface. Placed in a prominent position on the edge of the desk was Drum's screwdriver.

He sat back on the couch and waited, doing his best to relax. A door opened at the back of the room. A bearded man in his mid-forties wearing a tailored black suit entered, followed by two henchmen dragging a dishevelled Victor Renkov.

The bearded man took up his position of power behind the oak desk, while the two henchmen manhandled Victor roughly into a chair on the opposite side of the room. He looked like shit. His ordinarily slicked-back hair was messed up and matted; his once immaculate suit was now dirty and torn, and his shirt was tieless and bloodied. Drum looked up at the pulley. Every Mafia home should have one.

"Hello, Victor. Been burning the candle at both ends, I see."

Victor looked up. One eye was half-closed and bruised. He smiled at the joke. One of the henchmen cuffed him hard about the head, almost knocking him off the chair. *Don't be smart ass.*

Drum glanced at Misha who was leaning against one of the columns. He looked bored by the whole opera. Drum said nothing.

"Benjamin Drummond," said the bearded man, in heavily accented English. "My name is Vladimir Abramov. You have heard of me, perhaps?"

Vladimir Abramov looked at him over hooded eyes, as black as coal. A sharp angular face intensified his gaze, while his thin hard mouth was without mirth.

"Only by reputation," said Drum, as pleasantly as he could.

Abramov seemed to notice something and spoke rapidly to Anna in Russian. She shrugged.

"Forgive me. We have no manners. You would like coffee, perhaps?"

Drum bit his tongue and forced himself to be civil. Just another Saturday morning, hanging out with the hood. "Yes, coffee – espresso, a little cream."

Abramov spoke curtly to Anna. She nodded and got up from the couch. She gave Drum a hard look as she left the room.

"Victor tells me you are old friends?"

"I wouldn't go that far," said Drum. Misha laughed under his breath, and Victor groaned.

"No? That is a pity. Victor says you can help us. Vladimir, he says. My old friend Benjamin Drummond will help us. Leave it to me, he says. I think not, perhaps."

"Help with what?" asked Drum, although he thought he knew.

"Here is the problem," replied Abramov getting up from his chair. He moved to the front of the desk. "Victor comes to me. He has a business proposal. Vladimir, he says, the markets are shit give me your money, and I will keep it safe. I say, are you sure Victor? Gold Vladimir, I'll turn your money into gold. It is safe as houses."

Victor groaned. One of the henchmen shook him and spoke roughly to him in Russian.

"So," continued Abramov, "I say to Anna, keep an eye on Victor. I like him but – how you say – he burns his candle at both ends."

That was one way of putting it, thought Drum. "Victor told me about his visit to the bank. As I said, the gold is probably in another vault –"

"This is bullshit," interrupted Abramov. He stood and began to pace in front of the desk. "Total bullshit. Harvey Pinkman is missing."

"The Vault Manager?" said Drum.

"No one has seen or heard from him since Monday. And now my gold is missing," continued Abramov.

Drum had to admit it wasn't looking good. He looked at Victor. His nose had started to bleed. "You need to find Pinkman," said Drum.

Abramov stopped his pacing and sat on the edge of the desk. He picked up the screwdriver and looked at Drum. He smiled. Drum thought it more of a grimace.

"No, Benjamin. You need to find Pinkman." He tapped the screwdriver in his hand.

Anna came back into the room carrying a single espresso cup. She sashayed over and leaned close to give him the cup and whispered in his ear: "say yes."

"Thank you," he said, a little confused about her message. She walked back to the other couch, sat and carried on looking bored.

Drum sipped his coffee. He was between a rock and a hard place. If he told Abramov to go fuck himself, it wouldn't bode well for Victor; he was also sure that Abramov would insist on returning his screwdriver, but not in a nice way. If he said yes, it meant he'd be working for the Russian Mafia, and that wouldn't look good on his resume; Alex Fern wouldn't be too pleased either. Drum drained his coffee.

"Look, Vladimir," he said, placing the cup on the arm of the couch and standing up. One of the henchmen flinched and moved towards him. Misha stood from his slouch at the column. "I'm going to have to decline your invitation."

Victor groaned loudly, and Anna turned swiftly to face Drum.

"That is unfortunate, Benjamin. Not only for Victor –" he tapped the screwdriver against the table "– but also your father –"

Drum advanced quickly towards Abramov who was taken aback by the move. He had taken only a few strides when he was met halfway by the henchman who was already drawing his gun. Drum opened the palm of his hand and, keeping his fingers straight, viciously jabbed the guy in the throat just as the gun cleared his holster. The henchmen's hand reflexively moved to his neck as he wheezed and gasped for breath. His eyes bulged and his head bent down allowing Drum to snatch the gun from his hand. He finished him off, by smashing the butt of the handgun against the side of his head, before bringing the weapon to bear with both hands into the face of a surprised Vladimir Abramov.

Drum heard the distinctive double-click of a gun's hammer being cocked at the back of his head. The soft, calm voice of Misha whispered in his ear: "Benjamin. Big mistake."

There was a banging on the door. Time froze. Nobody moved. Drum held the gaze of Abramov's black, soulless eyes. The banging became more insistent. Then a familiar voice: "Open up. Police!"

Drum heard the click, click of a gun's hammer being carefully replaced behind him. He stepped back and lowered his own gun. Abramov looked shaken but undeterred. He straightened the jacket of his suit and moved behind his desk. Misha returned his gun to its holster and was walking towards the door. Abramov waved at the remaining henchman, who holstered his weapon. Drum stuffed his newly acquired gun down the back of his jeans and covered it with his T-shirt and jacket. Victor groaned quietly.

Misha opened the door just a crack. He spoke softly, almost sweetly to the person on the other side.

"Go fuck ya self, you bloody idiot, shouted Fern, pushing past the big Russian and into the room.

Abramov sat back down. "Ms Fern. How can we help?"

"Noise complaint," she replied, unconvincingly, waving her warrant card. She looked first at Drum and then Victor. "Bloody hell, what happened to him."

"Accident," replied Misha.

"No shit," said Fern.

She pointed to the henchman lying unconscious by Drum's feet. "What about this guy?"

"Accident," replied Drum, straight-faced.

"Good grief, Drum. Let's go."

"Give me a hand with Victor," said Drum.

Fern strode over to Victor, pushing the remaining henchman roughly to one side.

"Mind the windows," said Drum.

"Piss off and give me a hand."

Drum stepped over the prone body at his feet and bent down to help Victor up. They shuffled him over to the door. Misha was waiting, holding the door open.

"Wait a minute," said Drum, letting go of Victor's arm.

He walked back over to the desk. Abramov sat there, looking amused. Drum took the screwdriver from his hand. "This is mine, I think. Part of a set."

"Drummond," said Abramov. "I still want to hire you."

Drum looked at the Russian, wondering what made the guy tick. "I'll think about it." He walked back to Fern and helped carry Victor out of the door.

10

It was late afternoon when Drum and Fern finally made it back to Butler's Wharf. For the second time that week he had a Russian's blood on his hands. Fern had said very little on the drive back. They had taken a detour to Victor's apartment in Canary Wharf and dropped him off. He had refused to go to a hospital and resisted Fern's attempt to persuade him to make a complaint against Abramov, a course of action that would have inevitably resulted in his swift and untimely death. But you couldn't fault her for trying.

Alice was waiting in his office.

"You look like shit – oh, sorry," she said as Fern walked in behind him. "I'm Alice." She held out her hand to Fern.

"Alice meet Commander Fern of the NCA. Fern, Alice."

"Your mother?" asked Fern, taking Alice's small manicured hand in hers.

Alice cocked her head to one side and let out a cackling laugh. "Good Lord, no. Office Manager." She turned sharply to face Drum, with a look on her face that said he was in deep trouble. "And you need to call William. He's worried sick. All I could do to stop him from calling the police."

"I am the police, Alice," said Fern, slumping down onto Drum's couch.

"No, my dear. I mean to say, the NCA is not the regular police. I'm talking about the plod."

Fern let out a hearty laugh. "The plod! Crumbs haven't heard that expression in a while."

Drum was about to sit down when he remembered he was still carrying the Russian's gun. He took off his jacket and slung it over the back of his chair, retrieving the gun from his jeans and placed it on the desk.

Alice looked at the gun and frowned.

Drum sat back in his office chair. He noticed Alice staring at the gun and realised he'd been thoughtless brandishing the weapon in front of her. He'd probably terrified the poor woman.

Alice moved over to the desk and picked up the gun.

"Alice," exclaimed Drum, "be careful. It's loaded."

"Good grief," sighed Fern. "Put it down, Alice. You'll shoot someone."

Alice smiled as she examined the weapon. "I don't think so." She turned the big gun over in her hand, feeling the weight of the black metal casing, examining both sides, then held it in both hands, one hand under the other for support and pointed it at the wall. She sighted down the barrel, both eyes open. "Glad to see you've kept the safety on." She looked up from the sight and turned the gun over, flipping a small lever on the side. She deftly caught the gun's magazine as it slipped smoothly from the recess in the grip; she pulled back the slider on the top of the barrel and checked that the firing chamber was clear. She placed the magazine on the desk.

"A Sig Sauer, P320, recently upgraded. Magazine carries seventeen, nine-millimetre rounds. It's been fitted with a mag-well for fast loading." Before Drum could say anything, her hand moved swiftly back to the magazine and, in an instant, the gun was reloaded.

Fern looked at Alice open-mouthed. Drum was speechless.

"Oh, tsk, tsk. It's nothing, really," she said, ejecting the gun's magazine once more and checking the chamber. "Army brat. Father was a Colonel in the guards. Taught me to fire all sorts of weapons as a teenager." She looked at them in turn and smiled. "Well, I'll make some tea, and you can tell me all about your adventures with the Russians." She turned to walk out of the door taking the gun with her. "I'll lock this in the safe – and call William."

They watched her in silence as she made her way back through the reception area and into the small kitchen. Drum could hear a clinking of crockery.

"Office Manager," said Fern. "Really?"

"Speaks Russian like a native, according to Victor."

Fern looked at him, a wry smile spreading across her face. "Well, that should come in handy."

They both burst out laughing.

Drum called his father and reassured him he was alright in the time it took Alice to return with her beloved teapot. She was a civilising experience, and Drum liked having her around. He felt the same about Fern. He must have been staring at her because she gave him a warm smile.

He loved that smile.

"How did you two meet," asked Alice, pouring the tea.

"We work together," said Fern, a little too hastily. "We don't know each other socially ..."

"That's a shame," said Alice, half to herself. She handed Fern a cup of tea and sat down next to her on the couch. Drum thought the size difference a little comical but kept it to himself.

They drank their tea in silence. Fern obviously thought that Alice was going to leave but, when she didn't, she ploughed straight in with a question.

Fern said, "So, what were you doing at the Abramov's residence?"

"I was invited."

"Kidnapped more like," said Alice "– at least that's what William told me."

"Our friend outside Lloyds," added Drum.

"You mean Molotok?" said Fern.

Alice snorted with derision. "Molotok – utter rubbish. That's not his real name."

Fern looked surprised. "No? That's the name we know him by."

"That's probably just some gangster's name this bunch made up to scare people. It means 'The Hammer'," said Alice.

Drum said, "Told me his name was Misha. Didn't make him any less scary. Picked me up at Spitalfields market when I was talking to William." He thought back to the meeting. "Actually, we had a decent conversation." He neglected to mention Misha's interest in Fern. He looked at her over the rim of his cup. "What did he say to you at the warehouse?"

Fern looked down at the floor. "Stupid shit, really. Tried to wind me up. Told him to fuck off – sorry, Alice."

"Good for you," replied Alice, beaming.

"You didn't tell me you knew Victor Renkov," said Fern, regaining some of her composure. "How's he involved in all of this?"

Drum leaned back in his chair and thought about the time he met Victor.

"He was one of my early clients. Some of his fellow Russians back home had been intent on hacking into his dealing system. I helped install Firewalls and Intrusion Detection systems to keep the bad guys out. Basic stuff, really. We became drinking buddies." Drum thought about some of the parties that Victor had taken him to. There should be a warning sign pinned on the lapels of all young Russian males: we drink until we drop. It wasn't Drum's scene. "We lost touch over the years."

"I told you he was trouble," said Alice, with an air of satisfaction.

"He came to see me," continued Drum. "Asked me for help. Apparently, a ton of gold has gone missing from his account at RBI –"

"Let me guess, " interrupted Fern. "This gold – it belonged to Abramov."

"You got it in one."

"Bloody hell," said Alice, setting her cup down on the tray with a loud clatter. "You realise your friend Victor is a 'Dead Man Walking'?"

They both looked at her.

"Just saying."

Drum pressed on. "It gets better. Looks like the Vault Manager has also done a runner."

"Pinkman?"

"The same. Abramov is desperate to find him."

"I bet he is," said Fern. She frowned. "Does he know we have Pinkman's laptop?"

"I suspect he does – our Russian friend you threw into the window is probably talking."

"About that … he's dead.

"He can't be," said Drum. "His injuries didn't look that life-threatening, and I've seen a few."

"You're right. His injuries weren't that bad."

"Abramov," said Alice.

Drum reached back and found his jacket. He retrieved his screwdriver and handed it to Fern.

"Looks like they got to him."

Fern was silent, a frown creasing her forehead. She ran a hand through her short blond hair. "Any luck with the Pinkman laptop?"

"Encrypted," said Drum. "Raj has been trying various decryption algorithms – no luck. He'll need more time."

Alice said, "Abramov knows you were on the raid, and now your friend Victor has dropped you in the shit, he'll be coming for you." She turned to face Fern. "You need to find Pinkman or else Victor is toast

... it doesn't look good for Ben either."

Fern shifted uneasily on the couch. She stood, replacing her cup back on the tray with a clatter and smoothed down her jacket.

"About Pinkman," she said. "I've been taken off the case."

11

It was Monday morning, and Drum was in his office, staring out at the river, deep in thought. He'd spent most of Sunday brooding over the NCA's decision to remove Fern from the case. He'd called and offered to take her out for Sunday lunch at one of the many restaurants by the river, but she'd made her excuses, and that was that. She'd confided to him, before leaving the office on Saturday night, that it seemed the NCA would likely drop the case at RBI. Without a statement from Victor concerning the missing gold or the bank reporting a crime – unlikely – there was nothing the authorities could do. The whistleblower had also mysteriously disappeared. The agency was blaming the Russian's death on Fern and, without anyone to prosecute for the death of the security guard, it looked like case closed.

The one person who might have some of the answers was Harvey Pinkman, and he was nowhere to be found.

He was wondering what to do with the evidence confiscated from the raid and whether he should be looking for Pinkman when Alice poked her head around the door.

"Sorry to interrupt, but you have a visitor."

Drum looked out into the reception area, but all he could see was the back of a large man in a beige trench coat.

"Who?" mouthed Drum.

Alice stepped quickly inside the office and closed the door. "Seen his type before – Thames House. Arrogant bastard. Wouldn't give me his name."

Thames House was shorthand for MI5. Drum was beginning to wonder what Alice really had done at the Foreign Office.

"Better show him in."

He recognised the man as soon as he walked through the door.

"McKay"

"Drummond."

Major Angus McKay was a great bear of a man. He was thick set with a barrel chest and seemed to fill the room. His beige trench coat draped him like a tent, and an old battered trilby partially hid a head of closely cropped ginger hair. The last time they'd met was in Helmand. Drum and Brock were at a mission debriefing. Brock swore then that if he ever met McKay again, he'd kill him. Drum felt much the same.

"You realise that people working in the intelligence service in the twenty-first century don't dress like that anymore."

McKay ignored his sarcasm. "I'm here as a courtesy."

Drum made a point of not offering McKay a seat. "I'm listening."

"You're to drop any investigation into Reinhart Benson International."

"And why would I want to do that."

"Look, I know we've had our differences –"

"Fuck you, McKay."

"Look, Drummond. I know you blame me for that last mission in Helmand but, in war, shit happens."

Drum clenched his fists. "How did an incompetent bastard like you end up back in the intelligence service? We can't be that desperate in this country."

"I wanted to keep this civil. You've rattled some cages with this case of yours. Take my advice and walk away –"

"Or what?"

McKay thrust both hands into his trench coat pockets. "I have my orders. I need all of the evidence you took from RBI."

Drum took a step towards McKay and the two men squared off, eye-ball to eye-ball.

Alice poked her head around the door. "Can I get you gents some tea?"

Neither man spoke.

"I bought some ginger nuts."

Drum moved back to the window, turning his back on McKay. "Major McKay is leaving, Alice. Please show him the way out."

McKay turned and strode out the door, almost knocking Alice over as he headed for the lobby.

"Charming," said Alice. "You know he'll be back – probably with a warrant."

Drum looked out across the river at the City beyond and wondered who had the kind of influence to bring the security services to bear on the case. The Russians were one thing, but he'd never expected MI5 to give him grief.

"You two obviously know each other," said Alice.

Drum turned to face her, trying to keep a lid on a mix of emotions he hadn't experienced in a while. He wondered if he should tell Brock. He didn't give McKay much of a chance if Brock decided to keep his promise. He let out a sigh.

"Major Angus McKay, army intelligence if that's not a contradiction in terms – or at least he was. God knows who he's working for now."

"Tell me what happened between you two," said Alice. She sat down on the couch and made herself comfortable.

Fuck McKay.

Sergeant Ian (Brock) Ives had said as much ten years earlier in a nameless desert in Afghanistan, sitting cross-legged atop the bonnet of his Land Rover as he lazily smoked a long, thin roll-up. He'd long ago run out of his regular smokes. Flecks of grey sandy desert clung to his three-day growth of beard, making him look prematurely old.

It had been a long night, and the men were knackered. They had spent hours searching the cold barren desert for their man. He had performed a HALO jump, so desperate was London to get him there. Brock shuddered as he remembered his own experience of the manoeuvre. His had been a training exercise, jumping from the back of a Hercules from five thousand metres. He'd felt claustrophobic in the breathing mask; without it, he would have been unconscious in less than thirty seconds. And the cold. Like flying through a meat locker. That was the 'High Altitude' part over. Then the warm air hit you like a brick, and you gritted your teeth waiting for the chute to open at a little under one thousand metres or the 'Low Opening' part – you hoped.

They had eventually found their man a few hours before dawn. At least he'd had the good sense to stay put and not try to wander off. He looked over at the new man tinkering with his gear. He seemed none the worse for wear after his ordeal. Tall, lean and fit. He didn't strike Brock as a signals bloke.

Brock watched the cold Afghan sky begin to pale and swore quietly. If they sat here much longer his arse would become permanently welded to the cold metal of the Land Rover. With so little planning, none of them had thought to pack any warm gear. He shifted the M16 lying across his legs and tried to get more comfortable. Shit, if they stayed exposed on this flat, open desert, the Taliban would have more than his arse.

He regarded what remained of his roll-up with disdain and scrutinised Dick (Poacher) Davis out of the corner of his eye. The tall, lanky man was leaning against the side of the Land Rover, smoking a filtered Embassy.

"Hey, Poacher."

"Yes Brock."

"Got any Embassy?"

"Yes, thanks."

"Fuck you, Davis."

"Charmed! I'm sure."

He glanced at the tall trooper taking long calculated drags on his cigarette, relaxed and apparently without a care in the world. An ex-gamekeeper with a soft West Country accent, Poacher was used to playing the waiting game.

Brock returned his gaze to the sky. "It'll be light soon."

The Poacher nodded. "We'll stick out on this plain like a boil on a whore's arse alright."

Fuck McKay. He'd personally kill the bastard if they were compromised out here in the open, Major or no Major.

Brock flicked away the remnants of his cigarette and slowly unwound his legs from beneath him, easing himself down from the bonnet, stretching, rubbing his arse with both hands. He turned to find Joe Cairns, the driver for this mission, still asleep, head back, mouth open and snoring loudly. What a racket. If the insurgents don't see us, they won't fail to hear us. Brock had not known Cairns long. The rest of the troop had named him 'Charming' owing to his complete lack of social graces. What luck to be stuck with the guy for 6 hours solid!

He looked across to the other Land Rover. Tim Weekes was arguing the toss with Tommy McPherson on what to do next. McPherson - known as 'Hazard' on account of the scary things he did with explosives - was pointing animatedly at the map. Whatever Weekes was selling, Hazard wasn't buying.

He mentally went through the game plan. Get the man in, Weekes had told them. He recalled the Major's gaunt features illuminated in the harsh light of the projector in the cramped mess room of Station

One. "The enemy has something interesting," he'd said, "and we need to know about it - or at least London does." He tapped a fresh cigarette on top of the projector and used it as an impromptu pointer. He ran a hand through lank blond hair. "It was spotted during the last recce and photographed. We don't think its radar - probably communications. London's sending a specialist."

What a blinder of an idea, thought Brock. The insurgents are kicking our arse in Helmand and London wants to send a 'specialist' for a peek at a satellite dish. A few more Tornados would be more like it. Poacher had had the right idea.

"Why not pound it from the hillside?" asked Poacher, stretching out his long legs, trying to get comfortable on the hard mess chairs.

A match was struck from the corner of the mess, its light revealing the thick-set features of McKay hewn from the shadows. The white smoke of a cigarette rolled over the flame and extinguished it. "Its information that wins wars don't let's forget that. We need to know what information this technology is sending - or receiving."

The room remained silent.

Weekes contemplated the end of his cigarette. He rolled it between finger and thumb, then tapped it once more on the projector. "As I was saying, London is sending a specialist – a chap from GCHQ. His name is Captain Benjamin Drummond. He'll be the package."

The whole operation had been McKay's idea.

Getting the man in wasn't going to be the problem; but, getting the man out … not even Weekes believed that.

Fuck McKay.

12

Drum took an early lunch. He didn't know Alice well enough to confide in her the complete story. The memory of that last mission had opened old wounds. It had been a shambles. Hazard had persuaded Weekes to move off the plain and make for the ridge. That's when they saw them. A group of well-armed men heading straight for their last location on the plain. Their position had been compromised.

Drum spent most of his lunch break walking by the Thames trying to clear his head. He wanted to head over to Ives and talk things through with Brock, but he knew the restaurant would be rammed at this time of day and Brock would be up to his apron strings with customers.

Whatever was going on at RBI, someone there had serious influence if they could close down an NCA investigation and then bring the intelligence services to bear on the case. It didn't look too good for Victor either. Abramov didn't buy Victor's plea of innocence and was sure he was somehow involved with the missing gold. He needed to give Abramov what he wanted. He needed to find Harvey Pinkman.

He headed back to the office, along the Embankment past H.M.S Belfast, until he reached the underpass below Tower Bridge which led to Butler's Wharf. He was about to head into his favourite coffee shop when his mobile rang. It was Alice.

"I have a Phyllis Delaney on the line, phoning from New York. Can I transfer the call?"

He walked into the coffee shop, the aromatic smell of fresh ground coffee filled his senses. He pressed his mobile tightly to his ear to shield it from the buzz of a dozen conversations.

"I don't know any Phyllis Delaney," he lied as he caught the eye of the barista. *The usual.*

"That's what she said you would say. I'm patching her through."

Damn, that woman was good. He paid for his coffee and grabbed a seat by the window.

"Hi Ben, Phyllis."

The last time he'd spoken to Phyllis Delaney was over a year ago in her office on 46th and Sixth, Avenue of the Americas. He'd told her to go fuck herself. He regretted losing his temper. It seemed she was prepared to bury the hatchet – more likely, a hatchet was heading his way.

"Phyllis. To what do I owe the honour?"

"Listen, Ben. I need your help."

This was new. Phyllis never asked for help. The shit must have really hit the fan.

"I thought I made my feelings clear about working for Roderick, Olivier and Delaney the last time we spoke," he said.

There was a pause on the line. It sounded like he was put on hold.

"Hi Ben, yes sorry. I have several people talking to me at once. It's about Harry. She's missing. Last seen in London."

Drum conjured up a picture of Harriet Seymour-Jones. An attractive woman with fiery red hair and a wicked smile. He and Brock had helped get her out of Mexico City along with her partner, Jimmy Miller.

"They have got themselves into a bit of a pickle", Phyllis had told him. "Just a quick in and out job. Close protection detail. Nothing you boys can't handle."

It had been a close call and the cause of the rift between him and Delaney.

"You know Harry, Phyllis. Probably taking time off skiing somewhere."

"Not this time, Ben. We think she's gone dark. She called Jimmy Miller a week ago."

Drum recalled the Mexico City debacle. Harry, her first big assignment; Jimmy Miller, the young ROD analyst; and Rachael Mansfield, dead.

"What was she working on in London?" asked Drum.

"That's the thing. We think she was moonlighting on the Mexico City case and ended up in London. We suspect she was tracking a shipment of gold bullion from Zurich, heading for the London market – the gold she uncovered in Mexico City."

The noise in the coffee shop had grown louder, and he had trouble hearing Phyllis. He thought she mentioned gold. He drained his espresso and headed out the door.

"Listen, Phyllis. Reception here is not that good. Let me call you from the office."

The call was ended abruptly. Phyllis was not known for her small talk. In a few short minutes, he was back in the reception area of his office.

"Did you talk to Delaney?" inquired Alice.

"Yes, thanks." He had a hunch about Harry. "I need to call Phyllis back. I'll dial from my office. In the meantime, give Victor a call – his number is in our directory."

"Why would I want to do that?" said Alice, with a look of disdain on her face.

Drum ignored her look of protest. "I need the name of the Auditor at RBI – the one that called him about his gold account."

"Really?"

He moved to his office and closed the door and hit the speed dial for Delaney's direct number. Few people even knew she had a private number. It took one ring for Delaney to pick up.

"Phyllis? It's Drum."

"Hi Ben, I have you on speaker." This was Phyllis code for keep the conversation civil.

"Mr Drummond, it's Tom Hammond here. I represent the DOJ special task force investigating corporate money laundering."

"How can I help you, Tom," replied Drum.

"Ms Delaney informs me you're working with the NCA on the RBI case," said Hammond.

Someone was well informed, but then Phyllis did have her fingers in all sorts of agencies. "I was," Drum answered. "The NCA has decided to close the case."

There were suddenly several conversations taking place simultaneously in Delaney's office. Eventually, Phyllis managed to restore order.

"Ben, Phyllis here. Did the Agency give you a reason for closing the case?"

"Not really. Unclear from my end. A Commander Alex Fern was in charge of the investigation. They appear to have pulled her off the case."

There was a silence on the end of the line. He thought an open conversation no longer a wise option. "Phyllis, please pick up."

There was a click on the line which told him only Phyllis could hear him. "I don't know what's going on at your end, but I've had a visit from Thames House warning me off the case."

"What? I don't understand. Why would the security services be involved?"

"I don't know – but it was a very unsubtle warning." The image of McKay filling his office came to mind, and he felt his anger rising. "They sent me a very blunt instrument to tell me to fuck off."

Phyllis was silent.

Alice came into his office and gave him a neatly folded note. He nodded his thanks before Alice retreated back to her desk.

"Phyllis, you there?"

"Yes, I'm alone for now."

"What has this got to do with Harry?" asked Drum.

"We think Harry tracked the Mexico City gold to an RBI account in London before she disappeared."

Drum pressed the phone to his ear and unfolded the note Alice had given him and read the name printed in Alice's neat hand-written script: *the Auditor's name was Harriet Seymour-Jones.*

"How can I help, Phyllis."

There was a pause on the line. "We were thinking – that is to say, Director Hammond and I would like you to join the ROD team investigating RBI from this side of the pond. Seeing as the British authorities have closed the case at your end, that is. And I'm sure Harry was investigating RBI – off the record."

Drum thought about McKay demanding he walk away, and Fern being pushed off the case. Something didn't smell right that was for sure. Working for ROD at the behest of the DOJ would get him back into RBI and the possibility of helping Victor – providing he was still alive, of course.

And then there was Harry.

Harry wasn't playing by the rules and Phyllis couldn't have a ROD investigator running around London, conducting her own rogue investigation. He liked Harry.

"What do you say, Ben?"

Drum remembered Mexico City, how he and his team had barely made it out alive; how Rachael, a young computer analyst, had died. He understood why Harry couldn't let it go. She had moxie, as Phyllis would often say: true grit. He'd blamed Delaney for putting the young

ROD team in harm's way. What started as a routine investigation of a small Mexican company, unearthed a major operation of a drugs cartel. Delaney, the grand chess master, moving her investigators across the globe like so many pawns. But Rachael had been a sacrifice too far. He'd said goodbye to ROD; Jimmy Miller, traumatised by the loss of his colleague, had retreated to his native Boston; and Harry? Harry had moxie.

And what did he have?

"I'm in."

"Excellent. I'll send your Office Manager the details."

The line went dead. No thanks, goodbye, be seeing you. That was Phyllis Delaney all over.

Alice poked her head in. "All done?"

"I hope you weren't ear-wigging."

Alice gave him a wry smile. "Goodness, no. If I'd wanted to eavesdrop, you'd be the last person to know about it."

"Right."

"And it looks like you're heading for New York."

"What makes you say that?"

"This was couriered over while you were at lunch."

Alice dropped an envelope on his desk. He looked inside: a business-class ticket to JFK, courtesy of Phyllis Delaney.

Damn, that woman was good.

Don't Spare the ROD

13

The problem with JFK International was the long queues at immigration. Drum stood in line for what seemed an age but, in reality, it was probably no more than thirty minutes, shuffling along with other the passengers until he reached the head of the queue. Despite travelling business class, he'd dressed in a pair of old faded blue jeans, a tee shirt and his favourite tan leather jacket. His fellow business travellers seemed content to fly suited and booted, pecking at their laptops for most of the flight. He had taken full advantage of his spacious reclining seat and slept most of the way. When his turn finally came, he grabbed his battered canvas holdall and headed over to the immigration desk.

He handed over his passport. The young man behind the desk eyed him suspiciously. He had to admit he probably looked a mess with his hair longer than it should be and a shadow of a beard.

"Business or pleasure – Mr Drummond."

"Business, I'm attending a meeting."

The young officer swiped his passport through a reader and waited. He looked at the screen and frowned. He looked back at Drum, then back at the screen. He picked up his phone.

"Everything alright?" asked Drum.

"Just stay right there."

Drum waited as the officer spoke animatedly into the phone. He nodded several times and put the phone down. He gathered up all of Drum's documents and put them to one side.

"Someone will be with you shortly." He got up from his seat and walked out of his booth.

Drum waited for a few more minutes then looked up and saw a lean man in a charcoal-grey suit sauntering in his general direction. The man paused and chatted with the young officer then entered the immigration booth and stood in front of the terminal.

"Mr Drummond, I'm Tom Hammond."

Tom Hammond spoke in a precise, slow, southern drawl. Drum put him somewhere in his mid to late forties. He ran a hand through thick black hair which he wore swept back.

"Evening, Tom. Surprised to see you're here in person. Is there a problem?"

Hammond looked up from the terminal, unsmiling, his lean features studying him with a calculating gaze.

"Well, I have to say, we are confused." He looked down at the terminal, a wry smile creasing his mouth. "You have been red-flagged by your security services." He looked up at Drum, his smile fading. Don't suppose you can explain that?"

"Popular, I guess."

"Then we get a call from someone in your Ministry of Defence, telling us the flag is a mistake and you should be allowed to enter." He looked down at the terminal again and pointed at the screen. "But here it is still. A red flag."

Drum guessed that McKay had been up to his old tricks. Someone was desperate for him not to take this case.

"What did Phyllis - Ms Delaney have to say?"

This time Hammond's face split into a wide grin. "Why, she was madder than a wet hen when we told her."

Drum smiled. He'd been on the sharp end of her tongue on more than one occasion. "What now?"

"I reckon we let you in. Ms Delaney thinks we need you." He picked up an immigration stamp, adjusted the date and stamped Drum's passport. "Welcome to the United States." He handed the passport back to Drum.

Drum picked up his bag and pocketed his passport.

"Drummond. Just so we're clear. It doesn't amount to a hill of beans what Delaney thinks of you. If you give us trouble, you'll be on the next plane outta here. Understood?"

"Understood."

Hammond nodded towards the baggage claim. "When you leave the terminal, get in line for a cab. Wait a little ways back from the end of the line. Solomon will pick you up."

Drum didn't know who Solomon was, but he nodded and headed

for the exit.

He walked out into a chilly, New York evening. It was six o'clock, and the line for the Yellow Cabs was long. He did as he was told and crossed the lane of traffic leaving the terminal and stood at the end of the line, a few metres back.

He didn't have to wait long. An old battered cab broke out from the rank and pulled up next to him. The other drivers honked their horns in protest and expletives echoed down the rank. The driver, a West Indian with long dreadlocks and a brightly coloured hat, jumped smartly out of the cab, ignoring the abuse, and walked around to meet him.

"Mr Drummond? Solomon."

Before Drum could answer, he snatched his bag and threw it in the trunk.

"Let's go, man. We have company."

Drum looked around and noticed a black sedan parked across from them. Two suits were hurriedly getting inside, while a third was starting the engine. Drum opened the back door and slid onto the battered back seat. It smelt of old leather and sweat. Delaney could have at least sent a limo.

"Who are they?"

"Ya reception committee. Ya a popular guy."

Solomon pulled out quickly, cutting up a fellow cab driver who was forced to brake hard.

Drum looked back and saw the sedan attempting to pull out into the traffic, but a stationary cab had blocked their exit.

"Don't worry, man. We'll lose them at the toll."

Drum had to admire his driver's skill. "You work for ROD?"

Solomon let out a loud laugh. "Shit, man. I'm FBI."

Drum smiled and sank back into his seat. Not much point getting excited about the situation, it looked like Solomon had it all under control.

Solomon drove fast out of the airport and onto the Van Wyck Expressway. Traffic at this time of night was always going to be heavy, but Solomon made up time by occasionally turning off the I-495 and doubling back onto side roads, returning a few miles later ahead of the queues. After an hour, Drum could see no sign of the black sedan. Up ahead the Manhattan skyline came into view with the Empire State, and Chrysler buildings lit up like beacons in the night. He never got tired of that view.

Drum noticed Solomon looking at him in his mirror.

"So what's your story, Solomon?"

"Me? I'm here to keep ya safe."

"I meant, are you part of this task force?"

"Yeah, you could say that. I'm part of a unit that keeps track of organised crime. Our friends back there are probably Russian. Why would they be tailing you?"

That was a good question. He didn't think Abramov's reach would stretch this far. Perhaps he had underestimated him, something he wouldn't do again.

"I guess I have friends in low places."

Solomon frowned. "You don't need friends like those, man." He glanced at his side mirror. "Shit, they caught up."

Drum turned and looked back through the rear window. The black sedan was racing to catch up, weaving in and out of the traffic. Not very subtle.

Traffic began to slow. They had reached the toll. Solomon pulled into a cash lane and wound down his window. The black sedan manoeuvred into the same lane and was just a few cars behind.

The officer in the kiosk of the toll was a small, round man with a balding pate. He smiled when he saw Solomon.

"My man. How goes the struggle."

"Ya know. Shit happens. Black sedan a few cars down. Three goons. If ya could do ya thing, it would be appreciated."

"It shall be done. You have a good day, now."

Drum noticed that Solomon didn't pay any toll, but the barrier opened nevertheless. Solomon floored the engine, and the cab took off towards the Midtown tunnel. Drum turned to see the sedan reach the toll, the driver frantically waving cash at the officer. The officer shrugged and left his booth. They were boxed in with nowhere to go. A neat manoeuvre.

"Where ya heading, man?"

"Sixth Avenue. Drop me off at the Carlton on 45th."

Solomon exited the tunnel onto 35th Street and made his way slowly up through the avenues until he hit Herald Square before turning right onto Sixth Avenue. The Empire State building towered brightly above them, lit in red, white and blue. Once they had passed Bryant Park, Drum knew they had arrived.

Solomon turned onto 45th Street and parked outside the hotel.

"How much do I owe you?"

"Man, it's on the FBI."

"Thanks, Solomon. It's been a blast. Buy you a drink?"

"Another time. Ya keep ya head down."

Drum grabbed his bag from the trunk and watched Solomon drive off. He looked across the street where a black monolithic tower rose up and disappeared into the dark New York sky. Somewhere up there sat Phyllis Delaney and the offices of Roderick, Olivier and Delaney.

The 45th entrance took him through the hotel lounge and bar area. The place was buzzing for a Tuesday night. Office workers were getting their last drink in before the commute home. He walked on through to the marbled lobby to check in at reception. A smartly dressed young man wearing a purple tie welcomed him to the hotel.

"Checking in," said Drum. "Name of Drummond."

The clerk tapped a few keys on his terminal, and they both waited a few seconds.

"Yes, Mr Drummond. You have a suite: 1705."

A suite? Phyllis was certainly pushing the boat out. He must be in trouble.

The clerk looked down and retrieved a card key and entered it into the terminal. "Here you are – and you have a message."

The clerk handed him an envelope addressed to 'Drum' in a neat, sloping script.

"Who left it," asked Drum, turning the envelope over. It was hotel stationery.

"A lady, sir." The clerk lent in closer. "A very tall lady."

14

It was close to 8:45 pm by the time the cab dropped Drum off Downtown. The note had read: Surprise! Meet me in the whisky Bar, 8:30 pm, Fern. It was an address on the corner of Broadway and Canal Street. He'd just had time to shower and sling on a clean T-shirt; he kept to his jeans and jacket. He felt comfortable. If this place had a formal dress code, they'd have to relent. He was looking forward to seeing Fern.

The whisky Bar turned out to be a converted warehouse, a popular venue in the Tribeca area of Manhattan. A suited doorman nodded as he approached, and opened a large iron door for him to enter. Drum found himself in a small lobby with a cloakroom off to one side. A staircase spiralled up to another level. He declined to check his jacket and took the stairs up to the bar above.

What was once a large industrial space had been converted into a spacious lounge. Rough wooden boards covered the floor; the ceiling was kept exposed, displaying the air ducts and pipework above, paying homage to the building's past. Drum was reminded of Abramov's pad in Wapping, except in this case a large oval bar took centre stage, lit red from beneath and surrounded two large wooden pillars that supported the roof above.

The lighting was subdued and matched the slow, smooth melody of the music playing against a background of hushed conversations. Once his eyes had adjusted to the dim light, Drum scanned the interior and saw the usual mix of suits and the occasional lost soul wishing they had chosen an alternate rendezvous.

A waitress in a skin-tight jumpsuit placed a hand on his shoulder as she slid by carrying a tray of cocktails.

She smiled. "Can I get you a drink?"

"A Hendricks and tonic would go down nicely." He looked down the long bar where a small group of men had congregated. "I'll be at the bar."

"Sure thing."

As he walked towards the bar, a tall figure rose up from the throng of men, towering above most of them. Alex Fern turned and waved. She looked stunning in a short gold cocktail dress that hugged her trim and toned body. She made her excuses to her friends and strode over to meet him.

"Surprise!"

She bent down and kissed him on the cheek, a familiarity he wasn't expecting. She smelt of citrus and honeysuckle.

"You look amazing," said Drum.

She beamed at him. "Yeah, well – a girl has got to make an effort once in a while. And it's not every day I'm in New York."

They both took a stool at the bar, away from the crowd. The waitress returned with Drum's drink in a tall glass, complete with a slice of cucumber. Perfect.

"What are you drinking?" Fern asked him.

"Gin and tonic."

"Great! I'll have the same." The waitress nodded and disappeared.

"Of all the whisky Bars in New York …" he parodied.

She laughed. "I was made an offer I couldn't refuse."

"Let me guess. Phyllis Delaney."

"That woman has some serious influence. Next thing I know, I'm transferred over to this DOJ task force. Rubbed a lot of people up the wrong way in London, I can tell you."

The waitress returned with Fern's drink. Drum tipped her a few dollars.

"At least that's one thing Delaney has got right." He picked up his glass. "Cheers."

They clinked glasses, and he watched as she sipped her drink, her eyes lifting to meet his over the rim of her glass.

An impish smile spread across her face. "What?"

He returned her smile. He just wanted to sit there and breathe her in and pretend they had nothing better to do. He was content just to let the world roll by and let the alcohol smooth away the tension he had been feeling since leaving the airport.

"I'm sorry about Sunday," she said. "I was pissed about the case. I felt I'd let you down."

He shrugged. He didn't want to get into it right now. The Delaney hatchet would be heading his way soon enough.

"Not your fault." He gazed into her eyes. "You know, you look seriously hot without your tactical gear."

She laughed. "This is not the first time you've seen me out of uniform."

He shrugged. Puzzled.

"I saw you ogling me in the van."

He laughed. "Oh, yes. Guilty as charged."

She suddenly looked serious. "I'm a little worried about Raj and Alice. Abramov probably knows by now you have the laptops. I wouldn't put it past him to try to take them. I should have taken back the evidence. At least then you'd be in the clear."

"I wouldn't worry about Alice. She now has a Sig Sauer with a full clip and knows how to use it."

They both burst out laughing.

The mention of the laptops reminded him of McKay. He stared down into his glass, trying not to get angry.

"What's the matter," she asked.

He must have a terrible poker face. "I think we may have a bigger problem."

He recounted McKay's visit, leaving out his name and rank. The less Fern knew, the better.

"Why would the security services want you off the case?" she asked. "It doesn't make any sense."

He finished off his drink and caught the barman's eye: same again. "It gets better. They red-flagged me at the airport."

"What! How did you get in?"

"Delaney pulled some strings." Drum didn't mention his association with the M.O.D.

"What does it all mean?"

"I have a theory – but I'm guessing at this stage."

"Let's hear it."

Two more gin and tonics appeared on the bar. He could feel the jet lag kicking in.

"Someone is running some serious interference to stop the investigation – at least the London operation. Your case was closed down, and the security services are threatening to close me down. That can only mean one thing: someone in government or with government contacts is working against us. The answer lies inside the vault of RBI."

"So what you're telling me is we're likely to pick up some serious heat down the road."

He nodded.

"Oh, well. And here's me thinking all I had to worry about was the Russian Mafia. Cheers."

They clinked glasses. Drum could tell she was beginning to flag.

She noticed him staring and smiled. She reached out and placed a hand at the back of his head. Her fingers moved through his hair, caressing the nape of his neck. She drew him in, her eyes half closing. They kissed, her lips were full and sensuous.

"I have a suite," she whispered.

"Your suite it is."

She froze, her hand clenching the back of his hair. "Oh, fuck!"

He pulled back, surprised. "What is it?"

"I don't believe it. Molotok!"

It took a while for Drum's brain to register the name. He turned towards the stairs. Misha spotted him and nodded in recognition. He was smartly dressed in dark-grey suit, white shirt and tie. His thick blond hair, trimmed and neat.

"I don't suppose you have a gun secreted in that dress?" said Drum with a sigh.

"If we had left a few minutes earlier, you'd have found out," said Fern.

Misha strode up as if meeting old friends. "Good evening, Benjamin."

"Misha."

"Alex, you look ..." He struggled for the English word.

"Ravishing, is the word you're looking for," replied Drum, with a hint of irritation in his voice.

"Yes, very beautiful." He bent down, took her hand and drew it towards his lips. "Ravishing."

Drum rolled his eyes. If anyone other than the Russian had just kissed a woman's hand, he would have said it was corny, but Misha did it so gracefully that he could tell that even Fern was impressed.

The bastard.

"What are you drinking?" inquired Misha.

"Gin and tonics," replied Fern.

Misha caught the bartender's eye and indicated a new round of drinks.

Drum turned to Misha. "Can I make a suggestion?" He gestured to the bartender and lent over and whispered in his ear. The bartender nodded and went to complete the order. Misha looked at him. "Don't worry. You'll love it."

Fern turned so her back was to the bar, facing both men. "Why are you here, Misha, if that's your name."

The Russian lent against the bar so he was face to face with Fern. He looked as if he was going to eat her. "Vlad sent me. He is very unhappy you left London, Benjamin."

Drum stood up. "Tell Vlad –" Fern placed a restraining hand on Drum's shoulder.

"Why is Vlad unhappy?" asked Fern. "Drum – Benjamin told him no."

Misha stood up. "He knows you have Pinkman's laptop. He thinks you and Victor are working together. He wanted me to have – words with you, Benjamin."

"And what do you think," asked Fern.

The Russian turned to face her. "I think Vlad is a fool."

The barman returned with their drinks. Two gin and tonics, and what looked like a highball glass of orange juice.

The Russian picked up his glass and looked at it. "What is this?"

Drum smiled. "Orange juice and vodka over ice."

The Russian sipped his drink. "It is good. What do they call it."

Drum's face broke into a broad grin. "A Screwdriver."

Fern started to giggle uncontrollably. "I'm sorry …"

The Russian looked puzzled at first, then understanding spread across his face. "I think you are a smart ass, Benjamin."

"Ok, that was below the belt."

Fern took a tissue from her purse and wiped the tears from the corner of her eyes. "Ok, sorry - no really. I'm better now. I think I'm pissed …"

The Russian grinned and took a slug of his drink. "These are not the words I was supposed to have with you, Benjamin."

Drum said, "Listen, Misha. I don't know what Abramov is thinking or why you're here, but it's likely you're wasting your time."

"How so?"

"The investigation," said Fern, now a little calmer, "it's closed."

Misha paused and drained the rest of his drink. He raised his glass to the barman. "So, what about Pinkman's laptop? You still have it,

...

...

yes?"

Drum downed his drink. He was dead beat. He tried to think clearly. "Yes – and no."

Misha sighed. "Don't be smart ass."

"It's encrypted. We can't break it – at least not before the authorities confiscate it." Drum neglected to tell him that MI5 may well have their hands on Pinkman's laptop by now and that GCHQ would eventually break it.

Misha ran his hand through his hair. "Vlad will not be happy."

"Oh, fuck Vlad," said Fern, her face screwing up into a comical sneer.

"Tell me, Misha. Were those your guys following me from the airport tonight?"

Fern looked at him and frowned. "What guys?"

"Yes. Complete amateurs. They tell me they lost you. I tell them, don't be stupid. He'll be staying at the Carlton. I bribe the doorman. He tell me where you go. No big deal. They want to send two others with me. I laugh …"

Fern looked at Misha with a serious look on her face. "But I may be armed."

The Russian looked at her, his gaze raking the full length of her body as she slouched against the bar. "I don't think so – not in that dress."

It was Drum's turn to laugh, but he quickly stopped when he saw the scowl on Fern's face. Misha was smiling.

Drum saw them first. Solomon was standing by the stairs with two suits. They didn't look as if they'd come for drinks.

"Misha, are you carrying?"

"Of course. Why?"

Fern looked at him, her eyes half closed. "What's up?"

"Just keep your hands on the bar where they can be seen."

Misha turned towards the stairs and saw the three agents. He picked up his drink and placed his free hand on the bar.

Solomon strode over. The other two agents kept back, their hands resting on their guns.

"Drummond. Making friends, man?"

"Solomon."

Misha drained his drink and slammed the empty glass down. He then placed both hands back on the bar and bowed his head.

Solomon frisked him and retrieved a heavy looking handgun. He handed the gun to one of the agents then pulled the Russian's hands behind his back and cuffed him. Misha glanced back one last time before he was led down the stairs.

15

Drum woke early and alone. Misha's arrest the previous evening had killed the moment between him and Fern. It was probably for the best. They had to work together.

He still didn't know why Misha was here. He seemed very relaxed for an enforcer. He sensed the big Russian had another agenda but he didn't know what. *Vlad is a fool.*

He dragged himself to the shower and let the hot water pound his body. He closed his eyes and waited for the fog of alcohol and bad dreams to fade. The meeting wasn't until 9:00 am, but he needed time alone with Phyllis to mend some of the bridges he had burned the last time he was here.

He put on a clean white shirt and his best charcoal-grey suit; he polished his oxford brogues to a shine that his Sergeant Major would have been proud of, and left for the office across from the hotel by 8:00 am. Phyllis was always at her desk by 7:00 am, but he didn't want to face her until she'd had at least two cups of coffee. It was always hard getting to see Phyllis and he might just end up kicking his heels until the start of the scheduled meeting.

He entered the marble lobby of the black monolith on 46th Street and made his way over to reception. A familiar face was manning the desk.

"Maurice, how are you doing?"

Maurice - which is what everyone called him, but which Drum guessed wasn't his real name - had been with the company from the very start. He was built like a tank and looked formidable in his black suit, crisply starched white shirt and small black tie. He was responsible for ROD internal security and took responsibility for driving Delaney, acting as her personal bodyguard. He was a man of few words.

"Fine, Benjamin. She's expecting you."

"I'm a little early."

"Yes, she said you would be. Floor forty-four. You know the way." Maurice handed Drum a security pass.

He made his way over to an area marked private and entered an elevator designated for ROD employees. He held his pass over the security panel and hit the button. The elevator accelerated upwards only stopping at his floor. Penny Martin, Delaney's PA, was waiting for him.

"Ben! It's good to see you again." She stood on tip-toe and kissed him on both cheeks. Penny liked to watch European films, but it was nice to be greeted so warmly.

"Hi, Penny. I'm a little early. I thought I might grab some time with Phyllis before the meeting."

Penny looked at him in mock seriousness. "She told me to bring you straight in as soon as you arrived. I hope you haven't been a bad boy?"

Let's see. Since arriving at JFK, he'd been red-flagged by his own security service, warned to stay out of trouble by the head of the DOJ task force and caught by the FBI drinking with a known member of the Russian Mafia.

"Oh, you know. Quiet night."

She raised an eyebrow and smiled. She led Drum through the reception area and into the main office space. Several ROD investigators were already at their desks, hard at work on their various assignments. A few hands went up in recognition of his arrival; he waved back. They passed Harriet Seymour-Jones' empty desk before arriving at Phyllis Delaney's corner office.

Penny stopped at the door.

"She's with Sir Henry Minton, the RBI chairman. She wanted you to meet him."

Drum couldn't think of a reason not too and shrugged. Penny knocked lightly on the door before striding in.

Phyllis Delaney, the managing partner of Roderick, Olivier and Delaney, had chosen her place of power well. Her office was in a spacious corner of the building with views of the Chrysler Building to the West and the Empire State Building to the North; an expensive Persian carpet covered the floor in front of her large desk, and two black couches lined the walls on either side of the door.

"Ah, Benjamin," said Phyllis Delaney, rising from behind her desk. "Come in. I'd like you to meet Sir Henry Minton. Sir Henry, this is Benjamin Drummond, our lead investigator."

For someone with so much power and influence, Phyllis Delaney cut a diminutive figure. Drum always thought of her as being in her early sixties, but it was difficult to tell. She had a youthful, animated face. Her platinum blond hair was cut stylishly short. She was dressed for the New York weather with a cream cashmere sweater and a mid-length, grey wool skirt.

Sir Henry Minton rose from the couch and shook his hand.

"Glad to meet you, Drummond. I've heard lots about you."

"Take a seat," said Phyllis, indicating the other couch.

Drum sank down and thought he might never get up. He wondered what Phyllis had been saying about him. He really wasn't up to speed on the investigation and thought the less he said, the better.

"Ms Delaney tells me you're based in London," said Sir Henry, all smiles. "Glad to have a local man on the job."

Phyllis turned to Drum, "Sir Henry has been meeting with the DOJ, and he knows they have certain questions that need answering."

"Quite right," nodded Sir Henry, emphatically. "The board and I will give you our utmost co-operation."

Drum had met a dozen Sir Henry's in his corporate career. They were well-meaning but generally clueless on the day-to-day operation of the business. He knew that Sir Henry would be no help once he confronted the real power brokers and gatekeepers back in London.

"Thank you, Sir Henry," said Drum. "That's a great help. I'd just like to reiterate what you've probably been told: that this is an investigation and I'll expect full access to material back in London. That's full access."

Sir Henry looked a little shocked by Drum's direct approach. He looked at Phyllis who smiled.

"Why yes ... yes, of course. I'll make sure all senior managers are made aware." He paused and looked pained at having to mention the next topic. "And of course, there's the question of the vault."

Drum looked at Phyllis. "The vault?" He was intrigued and a little surprised that Sir Henry had brought it up.

"Apparently," said Phyllis, leaning back in her chair, "there is an issue with the bullion inventory."

"You mean gold from the vault has gone missing?" said Drum, thinking of his Russian problem.

"Good Lord, no. Nothing like that," retorted Sir Henry, sitting forward on the couch. He looked like he was about to bolt out of the starting gate. "Simply a discrepancy with our inventory system not being updated – at least that is what our MD assures me."

"That would be Damian Rhodes," added Phyllis. "He runs the Precious Metals division of the bank."

"Quite so, excellent chap. Full confidence in him."

"But you would like us to perform an audit of the physical inventory."

"Bang on", replied Sir Henry, looking Drum straight in the eye. "Every bar - every ounce." He gave Drum a conspiratorial smile.

Drum reappraised his opinion of Sir Henry. Not as clueless as he makes out to be.

"Rest assured, Sir Henry. Benjamin will leave no stone unturned," said Phyllis standing.

Both Drum and Sir Henry rose from their respective couches. Phyllis had decided the meeting was over.

"Well, I think that's everything," said Sir Henry, buttoning his jacket. He walked over to Drum and held out his hand. "Good to meet you, Drummond." He shook Drum's hand with some enthusiasm. "Just one last thing."

Drum hesitated. "What would that be."

"Do you have any experience of gold bullion?"

Drum looked at Phyllis. She offered no clue to what Sir Henry might be getting at.

"I'm familiar with aspects of its security. Bank vaults – that sort of thing. Why do you ask?"

"In that case, can I suggest you talk to this chap." He handed Drum a card.

"Sir Rupert Mayhew?" More knights than the roundtable, thought Drum.

"Who," echoed Phyllis.

"He's an old school chum. Now works at the Treasury. Specialises in the buying and selling of gold and other precious metals for the Bank of England. He'll be able to brief you." He opened the door. "Well, I look forward to your report." He leaned closer to Drum. "Every ounce."

Drum slumped back into the couch still holding the business card Sir Henry had thrust upon him. He felt dog tired. He rolled his neck to ease the tension.

"You look like shit," Phyllis told him, moving out from the safety of her desk.

"People keep telling me that."

"And what's with the hair? You look like some sixties hippy."

"Thanks, mum."

"Anyway," she sighed. "It's good to have you back."

"Look, Phyllis. I said some harsh things –"

Phyllis raised her hand before Drum could continue. "Listen. We all said things we shouldn't have said. And goodness knows I made mistakes with that last assignment. It sticks in my craw, really it does. Let's leave it at that."

Penny came carrying a tray of cups and a large pot of coffee. "Alex Fern is waiting outside." She glanced over at Drum. "You alright?"

"Skipped breakfast."

"Penny, be a dear and get some of those awful cookies the Brits like to eat – you know the ones," said Phyllis.

"Ginger nuts?"

"Whatever. Send in Commander Fern."

Drum smiled. "Thanks, Penny."

Phyllis poured the coffee and handed him a cup. "Might wake you up."

"Sir Henry. What was that all about?" said Drum, gratefully accepting the coffee.

Phyllis smiled. "Pompous prick, don't you think?"

Someone once described Phyllis Delaney as a shark, endlessly swimming in a sea of corporate corruption, seeking out her prey. That, someone, was probably up to no good. Roderick, Olivier and Delaney – or ROD, as it had become to be known – was formed in the wake of a number of high profile, corporate scandals. It specialised in investigating corporate malfeasance of the major kind. And Delaney had made it her mission to route it out.

Fern strode in dressed in her corporate best. She looked very New York, very ROD. She glanced at Drum and pointedly took a seat on the opposite couch.

"Ah, Commander –" said Phyllis.

"Call me Fern."

"Coffee?"

"Thanks. That would be great."

Phyllis poured coffee for Fern and perched on the corner of her desk.

"Sorry you missed Sir Henry," said Phyllis.

Fern gave Drum a hard look. He shrugged. "It was a surprise to me too."

"Sir Henry is the chairman of RBI," continued Phyllis. He's been in meetings with the DOJ these past few days. They're building a case against the bank and he knows it."

"We heard it was for money laundering," said Fern.

"Among other things. But that's the nub of it. He knows the bank is probably facing a heavy fine, and he's preparing the board. It's this missing gold that worries him."

Fern turned to Drum with a look of surprise.

"Apparently, Sir Henry has asked us to perform an audit of physical inventory at the bank," added Drum.

"Blimey."

Phyllis looked from him to Fern. "Ok, what are you two not telling me?"

Drum recounted the events of the raid and his subsequent encounters with the Russians.

"You have been busy," said Phyllis, returning to her seat behind her desk. "That partly explains why the FBI caught you hanging out with a Mafia hitman. Tom Hammond was – how can I put it –"

"Pissed," volunteered Drum.

"In our defence," added Fern, hastily, "we had no idea he was following us."

"And why was he following you?" asked Phyllis.

Drum and Fern both looked to each for inspiration.

"I have no idea," said Drum. "He has an agenda that is not part of Abramov's –"

"That would be Vladimir Abramov," interrupted Phyllis. "And the NCA has intelligence on this criminal?"

"Runs to several volumes," added Fern.

"Will you be able to take care of him if he causes trouble?" asked Phyllis.

"That's what the NCA is there for," said Fern, with a hint of annoyance in her voice.

Phyllis ignored Fern's change of tone and turned her attention to Drum.

"And you think the Auditor at RBI could be Harry?"

"I'm certain of it. That was last Monday. According to Victor, she was taken on as a contractor then terminated after the incident at the vault."

"And the Custody Officer has been conveniently reassigned back to Hong Kong," continued Phyllis. "And no sign of the Vault Manager – Harvey Pinkman?"

"Nope," replied Drum.

"I can understand why Sir Henry is worried," said Phyllis.

"Surely, he'll be more worried about the DOJ?" asked Fern.

"Not really," explained Phyllis. "They'll get a fine – millions of dollars, for sure – but that's par for the course. RBI will have made contingencies, and they'll continue on their merry way. No, if even an ounce of gold is missing, then confidence in the bank will evaporate. Investors will pull their accounts, and the board will be finished. Worse, Sir Henry's reputation and family name will be forever tarnished."

Phyllis sat in silence for a while. Drum knew she was weighing up all her options, making a tally of resources she could bring to bear. The grand chess master, moving her pieces.

"So what's the plan," said Drum. He was anxious to make a start.

Phyllis said, "The DOJ has a fairly long shopping list, but basically it boils down to proving the case against RBI for money laundering. I suspect the answer has something to do with the missing gold – if it is indeed missing."

"But?"

"I want Harry back, of course," replied Phyllis. "The Russian connection worries me. I don't want a repeat of the Mexico debacle." She gave Fern a sideways glance. "You still have … resources at your disposal?"

Drum nodded.

"What was your investigator doing at the bank," asked Fern. "Jones. Is that her name?"

"Seymour-Jones, Harry," corrected Drum. He looked at Phyllis.

Phyllis said nothing. Instead, she studied her manicured nails, flexing and straightening her fingers before resting her hands in her lap.

"Harry was supposed to be on assignment in Zurich – a routine background check on a new CEO for one of our clients. A company called Hoschstrasser & Buhrer. A law firm. Standard stuff, really. She'd requested the job. Not been herself since Mexico City – goodness knows, no one has – I thought it would keep her busy. Anyway, after a week, Harry requested more resources. She wanted a cybersecurity specialist assigned to the case – a hacker if we're honest about it. We thought she must have unearthed something, so we assigned her a young German called Mueller. That was three weeks ago. Not heard from her since."

"What was she looking for," asked Fern.

"I don't know. But I'm sure it had something to do with Mexico City – Harry couldn't let it go. I think she was moonlighting the case – following up on leads. I believe she'd traced the Mexican gold to Zurich and was using Mueller to obtain information."

"And this Mueller found something?"

"Oh, yes," said Phyllis, matter-of-factly. "I'm pretty sure he found something. He was discovered dead in his hotel room."

16

The meeting continued for another hour. Phyllis had prepared a detailed assignment brief and walked them both through it. Drum was starving: he didn't get his ginger nuts.

Penny handed him a note as they were leaving the office. "From Tom Hammond. Said it was urgent."

"And?"

"Someone ate your ginger nuts."

"What does Hammond want," asked Fern, closing the door behind her.

"Misha. He'll only talk to us. Tom wants us down at Federal Plaza."

"Great. That's all we need."

It was a bright crisp morning when they exited the building. It was good to get out into the open air, and Drum suggested they walk a block to 5th Avenue where they jumped a cab downtown. Fern was lost in thought, and neither of them spoke until they had passed the Flat Iron Building.

"What happened in Mexico City? Phyllis mentioned it in the meeting."

He didn't answer immediately but looked out of the window as 5th Avenue rolled by. They turned down 8th Street and then onto Broadway.

His thoughts took him to a deserted airstrip outside of Mexico City. Brock hammering an M16 while he drove; Harry and Jimmy Miller cowering in the back of the SUV as shattered glass cascaded down around them.

"I'd left the army and set up the consultancy. I kept in touch with Brock and some of the SAS troop I served with. You have to remember that these guys have some very specialist skills – they don't really take to stacking shelves. So I started a close protection unit."

"Bodyguards," said Fern.

"That sort of thing. We also specialised in K&R."

"Sorry …"

"Kidnap and Ransom," said Drum. "We would make exchanges or in special cases, extractions."

"And that's what you were doing in Mexico City?"

"Yes. But Phyllis got it very wrong. A case of bad intelligence," said Drum.

McKay sprung to mind. It seemed that lousy intelligence followed him around; or was it just him?

"What happened?" asked Fern.

"Phyllis sent in a relatively young team to what she thought was a routine investigation of a small company. A local bank had flagged up some irregular transactions, and the DOJ was cracking down on possible money laundering. Harry was the lead with a guy called Jimmy Miller and a computer tech called Rachel Mansfield. They should have been in and out in a few weeks …"

"But?"

"Miller stumbles upon a massive gold smuggling operation run by one of the drug cartels. Harry should have known better – should have let it go and returned to New York and reported in. Instead, she gets Rachel to hack their main server to obtain further evidence. Unfortunately, she ended up dead."

"What! How?"

"It was unclear. A tragic accident they said. Next thing I know, my team is scrambled to extract Harry and Miller. We barely made it out."

"And you blamed Phyllis?"

He thought about what McKay had said back in London. In war, shit happens. Afghanistan and Mexico City; the war had never stopped. He'd always been fighting someone whether they be insurgents or the drug cartels. He hadn't really spoken about either incident. He'd bolted down his feelings. He'd blamed others. But he must share some of the blame.

"I guess I did. She made a call. It didn't go as planned."

"Shit happens."

He looked at her. "I guess so."

His phone rang. It was Alice.

"Hi Alice, everything alright?"

"Ben. Listen, I have bad news. It's Raj."

"What about Raj?"

"The security services," she said. "They've arrested him."

Drum briefed Fern on the latest developments back home. McKay had been true to his word and returned with a warrant. All the evidence from the raid had been seized, but he never suspected they would arrest Raj. Someone had just made it very personal.

"What are you going to do?" asked Fern, as the cab slowed and came to a stop.

"I don't know. Try to sort things out when I get back. Alice is phoning some of her contacts in the Foreign Office. I can't stand the thought of Raj being holed up in a detention centre somewhere."

They got out on the corner of Broadway and Worth Street and walked the short way over to the tall building that was home to the FBI on 27 Federal Plaza. Solomon was waiting for them. He had lost the hat and was dressed more formally than the last time they had met.

"Drummond."

"Solomon. This is Commander Alex Fern."

Solomon nodded and handed them both a security pass. "Keep this visible at all times."

They dropped their phones and wallets into a grey plastic tray and walked through a security scanner. Once they had been deemed clear of any firearms, they moved on through to the elevator bank.

"Where are you keeping our man," asked Drum, as they waited for the elevator.

"Our man?" said Solomon, raising an eyebrow.

Fern shot Drum a sideways glance.

"Our drinking buddy."

Solomon cracked a smile. "Yeah well, Hammond wasn't too happy about that."

"Look on the bright side. At least he wasn't shooting at us."

"Ain't that the truth. We're holding him in interrogation, though he ain't saying much."

The elevator announced its arrival with a loud chime and Solomon escorted them inside. They rode up in silence to the twentieth floor where they were greeted with the general din of a busy FBI office.

Solomon said, "We're holding him in a secure interview room up here. Hammond would like to talk to you first."

They walked down a busy corridor, passing agents hurrying about their investigations. They eventually came to a door marked Interview Room One. Two suited FBI agents stood guard outside. They nodded to Solomon and glanced at Drum and Fern's security passes.

The room was sparsely furnished with two metal chairs on either side of a small metal desk. A yellow legal pad and pencil sat neatly on the desk beside a modern IP telephone and an old desk lamp that had probably belonged to J.Edgar. Tom Hammond was waiting patiently. He faced a window and stared fixedly at the unmoving mountain of a man they knew as Misha.

"Drummond. Commander."

Drum realised that the window was a two-way mirror; another door led to the room beyond where Misha was shackled to another metal table.

"He looks comfortable," said Drum. "What has he told you?"

"Diddly-squat. Wants to talk to you." He turned to face Drum. "Why is that?"

Drum shrugged. "I've no idea."

"Commander?"

"Same here. The NCA has him on a watch list. He's known under several aliases, but there's nothing concrete to link him to a crime in the UK we could deport him for. How did he enter the US?"

"Using a passport under the name Mikhail Fedorov. Unlike you, Drummond, he walked straight through immigration without being flagged. If Solomon hadn't been following you, we would've missed him."

"What will happen to him?" asked Drum, ignoring the slight at his immigration status.

"His passport looks bona fide. The only thing we have on him is the concealed weapon. We'll revoke his visa and deport him back to Russia."

"Let me talk to him," said Drum. He looked at Fern.

"Go right ahead," she said. "It's you he wants to talk to."

"We can listen in," said Hammond.

Hammond retrieved a card key from his pocket and swiped it through a reader attached to the door connecting the two rooms. The door buzzed open, and Drum walked in.

The big Russian looked up. "Benjamin. It is good that you are here."

The room was brightly lit, white and sterile; the two metal chairs and desk were the only furniture. Drum sat on the metal chair facing Misha. His once crisp, white shirt was now tieless and looking a little crumpled. Other than that, he looked in good shape. A half-empty plastic bottle of water stood beside another yellow legal pad and pencil.

"Writing your memoirs?"

Misha gave him a slight smile. "Still a smart ass."

Drum glanced around the room. The security consultant in him liked to spot the hidden cameras. He only found two. They were also being recorded as a matter of course.

"What can I do for you, Misha?"

The Russian sat up and flexed his shoulders in a slow circular motion and rolled his thick neck, trying to ease the stiffness of his confinement. Drum understood why the FBI would want to restrain him.

Misha asked, "Is Alex with you?"

"She's outside and sends her love."

Misha broke into a broad grin and tilted his head to one side to glimpse the mirror where he knew Alex would be watching. He pouted and blew her a kiss. Hammond was probably having to restrain her from coming in and beating the crap out of the Russian. He'd blown any future nights of gin and tonics with Commander Fern.

"I cannot be sent back to Russia," said Misha, his face taking on a look of seriousness that Drum had not seen before. "Bad things will happen."

Drum was a little taken aback. "That kinda goes with being a gangster, don't you think."

"Not gangster, soldier. We are both soldiers, Benjamin."

Drum remembered the time in the market; this was about the only thing they had in common. But it seemed important to the Russian.

"We were both soldiers once, Misha. Our war is over."

Misha looked amused. "We will always be soldiers. It's what we do. And the war … it is never over."

Drum thought back to the cold of an Afghan desert. The smell of cardamon brewing in thick black tea. The raw firepower that had rained down upon them. Misha was right: he'd never really stopped fighting. But who was he fighting now?

"Why is going home a problem?" asked Drum.

"I have a son."

Drum frowned. He hadn't imagined Misha as a father.

"And?"

"There are certain … people that would see me dead. If I return home, I would be arrested. They would use the boy – make an example of him."

"How old is this boy?" asked Drum

"He is eighteen. Studying in St. Petersburg to become an engineer – not soldier."

"Who is protecting him now?"

"Vlad. I make deal with him. He sees that the boy is supported –"

"Provided you work for him."

Misha nodded.

"I don't see how I can help."

"I need to get back to London. Show Vlad – business as usual."

Drum shrugged. "And?"

The Russian picked up the pencil. Drum was suddenly alert. In the hands of a normal individual it was just a pencil; in the hands of a Special Forces soldier it was a deadly weapon. Drum watched him closely as he wrote on the yellow legal pad, tore off the page, folded it and handed it to him. He placed the pencil back on the table.

"Get me back to London, Benjamin. You need me."

There was nothing more to say. Drum stood up and started towards the door.

"Benjamin." Drum stopped and turned to face the Russian. "Victor is not your friend."

Drum banged on the door. A buzzer sounded, and the door clicked open.

Fern was waiting for him. She looked 'madder than a wet hen' as Hammond would say.

"You don't believe that sob story about a son, do you?" she asked.

Drum looked at Hammond for support. He shrugged. "I've heard similar stories. These guys get sucked into working for criminal elements."

"Oh, give me a break," protested Fern. "This guy's a stone-cold killer. We should ship his arse back to Moscow."

Drum looked down at the folded note. There was something Misha wasn't telling him – or wouldn't say to him in the company of the authorities. *We will always be soldiers.*

"I need him back in London," said Drum eventually. He looked at Hammond. "Is that a problem."

Fern stared at him. "You're joking, right. Why would you want this guy back in London?"

"Not for us," said Hammond, ignoring Fern's protest. "But I'm with the Commander. Why have him back in London?"

When put like that, it did seem like a crazy idea. But there was something about what Misha had said. *Vlad is a fool.* "I think he still has a part to play in all this. Ultimately, it's your call what you do with him ..."

Hammond said, "I'll do the paperwork." He paused. "What'd he write on the paper?"

Drum hadn't looked. He unfolded the note. There was only one word, printed in neat block capitals: OMEGA.

17

Sir Henry Minton was not accustomed to being summoned, but summoned he was by one of the few men he couldn't refuse. Sir Rupert Mayhew had been an old school chum back in the day but, in truth, he'd been a real shit. Regardless, he was now one of the most prominent civil servants in Her Majesty's Treasury and a key advisor to the Cabinet Office on matters of banking regulation. As in most things in life, the biggest shits always floated to the top.

The club on Mayfair was not his first choice for a meeting, but Mayhew was always one for the dramatic. By day the club was a respectable meeting place for well-heeled bankers and those cabinet ministers who wanted to escape the Commons for a few hours or entertain in private; by night, the club transformed itself and played host to members with more carnal pursuits in mind. Becoming a member was coveted by many well-connected individuals. Money, power and influence were all keys to being accepted. Needless to say, the Minton family had been members since 1869.

It was midday when Minton arrived at the club. He was tired. The red-eye from New York had deposited him back in London at 6:15 am. Fortunately, he'd had a change of clothes at his Chelsea apartment and freshened up before his meeting. He entered the main foyer, which was decorated with ornately carved walnut panelling, polished to a warm rich brown and smelling pleasantly of beeswax. He was greeted by Giles, the concierge, an old duffer who had probably welcomed his father back in the day.

"Good day to you, Sir Henry. Nice to have you back."

"Morning Giles. Looking for Sir Rupert."

Minton waited patiently while Giles laboriously extricated himself from behind his desk, his aged joints cracking as he straightened himself. He moved with the purpose of one determined to do their duty. Minton knew that Mayhew was probably ensconced in the library and could have walked there in less than a minute, but that would have deprived Giles of the very purpose of his life, which was to escort members to other members within the club and announce their arrival. Custom can be a real pain in the arse sometimes.

Minton followed Giles as he shuffled across the checkerboard marble flooring of the main foyer.

"Terrible weather for this time of year," said Giles.

Minton didn't know what the poor fellow was on about. It was a perfectly sunny day outside.

"Brighten up later," added Minton.

They had made it to the library entrance.

"Roll on summer is what I say."

Minton felt his life slipping away.

"Sir Henry Minton," announced Giles to anyone who was listening.

"Thank you, Giles. Have the kitchen send up a pot of tea, there's a good chap."

"Yes, Sir Henry."

Sir Rupert Mayhew OBE sat alone in the exquisite library of the club in his favourite Chesterfield armchair, reading the Financial Times. The garish pink of the paper seemed somehow at odds with the somnolent browns of the leather seating and the languid greens of the window drapes. He was dressed in the regulation, three-piece navy pinstripe of a senior civil servant and exuded the smugness of a man who had shinned up the greasy career pole of Whitehall to become one of Britain's top Treasury mandarins.

"Ah, Minton. How are you," said Mayhew, folding his paper, but not rising from his chair.

Ignorant bastard, thought Minton.

"As well as can be expected, under the circumstances."

Mayhew glanced past his guest at the slowly diminishing figure of Giles.

"That old bugger should have been pensioned off years ago."

Minton ignored the comment and sank into an adjoining armchair, feeling the aged leather envelop him. He regarded the man before him with a mix of loathing and trepidation. They had never really been friends at school. Mayhew had just been another junior boy who was required to perform the ritual act of fagging: in effect, performing menial tasks for seniors back in the halcyon days of public schools. As far as he could recall, Mayhew was only ever called upon to warm his toilet seat.

Mayhew Peered at him over the rims of his tortoiseshell half-moon glasses, which were perched on the extremity of his hawk-like nose. "How was New York?"

"As we expected. They're going to settle on a fine," said Minton.

"That's good then. Operation OMEGA can proceed as planned. So why do you look like you've swallowed a turd?"

"The whistleblower –"

"That's been taken care of. The investigation has been closed." Mayhew hesitated. "Why, what did they say?"

There was a clinking of china announcing that the tea had arrived. A young butler – young by the club's standard – placed a tray of bone china cups and a pot of tea on the small reading table between them. They waited until he had left.

Minton lifted the lid of the teapot and gave the tea a quick stir. It needed to brew for a few more minutes.

"The DOJ has set up a new task force, run by a chap called Tom Hammond. Looking to become the next DA. Got the bit between his teeth. Not happy that the NCA investigation was halted on this side of the pond."

Mayhew shrugged. "Not much he can do. Not his jurisdiction."

Minton poured two cups of tea, adding the milk first as all public school boys were taught to do. It was the attention to such detail that had made the British Empire great.

"I agree," continued Minton. "But we have another problem. There's an irregularity with inventory."

"Inventory? You mean gold is missing from the vault?"

"Let's not jump to conclusions," Minton replied.

Mayhew stopped drinking his tea and placed his cup back on the tray with a loud clunk.

"You have a problem with your bullion inventory, and this is the first I'm hearing about it? Good Lord, man. How many fires do I have to put out for you?"

Minton sipped his tea calmly. "There was nothing I could do to contain the situation. The cat was already out of the bag. The Custody Officer went straight to the Audit and Risk Committee, who took it to the board. They want a full investigation and the DOJ are insisting on ROD."

Mayhew stood up and thrust his hands into his pockets and began to pace. He stopped and turned to face Minton.

"You've been talking to that witch, Delaney!"

"Had no choice, old chap. She's now running the show. She's assigned their top man in London. A man called Drummond."

"Drummond, you say. Good grief. I thought we had closed him down."

"It would seem that your friends in the security services weren't very successful. What's so special about this chap, anyway."

Mayhew placed both hands on the back of his armchair and was silent for a moment. Minton knew he was weighing up his next move. But the mention of ROD had rattled him. He drained the rest of his tea, smiling into the bottom of his cup as he did so.

"Captain Benjamin Drummond, Signal's Intelligence, two tours of Afghanistan and a tour of Iraq. Assigned to a special unit of GCHQ – at least, that is all my man knew about him."

"Army," interrupted Minton. "Thought the man had mettle. But I don't understand where the GCHQ part comes in?"

"It is a little-known fact that personnel of GCHQ were heavily involved in both wars. Signals Intelligence – or SIGINT - evolved into Cyber Warfare."

"And you know this how?"

"Because, my dear Minton, I pay all the bloody bills. Much of this is covertly funded. Some of it comes across my desk."

"At the Treasury."

"A special subcommittee. The rest I can't talk about."

A thought occurred to Minton. "What I don't understand is why your friends at Thames House couldn't close him down?"

"Good question. He's a bit of a dark horse. His file is locked down tight. Top Secret."

"How could that stop you," argued Minton. "Surely you have that kind of access."

Mayhew smiled, grimly. "Officially, yes. Unofficially, I was told to fuck off. Eyes only."

"By whom, dear chap."

"Vauxhall Bridge – MI6."

"So, you have a problem," said Minton.

"No, Minton. We have a problem. If any gold is missing from that vault then OMEGA is dead in the water and so are we."

"Rhodes assures me there's no gold missing. It's an administrative

110

error."

"It's time I talked to Rhodes."

"Is that wise? At the moment he knows very little about your involvement in the operation. Why take the risk?"

"Let me worry about that."

"What about the Captain? He starts next week, and he still holds evidence from the previous raid."

"Not any more," said Mayhew, smiling. "I arranged for my man to pay him another visit. It should, at the very least, slow him down."

"Very good," said Minton standing up. "I'll be glad when this is all over. Getting too old for all this cloak and dagger nonsense."

Mayhew didn't reply. He had walked over to the window and was lost in thought.

"Oh," said Minton, pausing on his way out. "Nearly forgot. I suggested to Drummond that he pay you a visit."

Mayhew turned from his reverie at the window.

"Why on earth would you do that?"

"Ostensibly, so you could brief him about the bullion market in your capacity at the Bank of England. Get to meet the man. Know what you're up against. Throw him a few curve balls, as our American cousins would say."

Mayhew frowned. Then his lips twisted into a pale imitation of a smile. "That might not be a bad idea. Let me think about it." He walked over to Minton and took him by the arm. "Come, let me walk you out. Got to take a leak."

"Jolly good," said Minton smiling. *Don't forget to warm the toilet seat for me.*

18

Fabio DeLuca felt pain. His whole body was on fire. He tried to open his eyes, but they felt glued shut. He attempted to move his head but stopped when a sharp pain lanced his scalp. He had a metallic taste in his mouth and realised his lip was bleeding. If this was a dream, it was a very painful one. He managed to open his right eye, just a crack, and a room swam into view, blurred at first but gradually getting clearer. A mans face appeared before him.

"Fabio, Fabio. You are awake at last."

Fabio didn't recognise the face but knew that he spoke with an Eastern European accent. There were many such people working at the bank.

"I am sorry, Fabio. The idiots I sent to fetch you were clumsy oafs."

The face turned and spoke harshly to someone behind him who Fabio could not see. He recognised a few words. The man was speaking Russian. He tried to talk but his throat was dry, and only a croak came out.

"Get this man some water, you idiots. He's no good to me if he cannot speak."

Someone approached with a small towel and a bottle of water. He went to reach for the water but discovered he could not move his hands. Water was poured onto the towel, and his face was roughly wiped. He managed to open his other eye and realised that he was shackled to a pulley suspended from an iron beam above his head, his arms stretched tight. He looked down. His feet just touched the floor which had been covered with thick sheets of polythene. He realised he was inside a warehouse.

The water bottle was pushed between his lips and upended. Water poured into his mouth and down his throat. He drank what he could until he choked and coughed. A searing pain stabbed at the back of his head and down his neck. He felt nauseous and wanted to sleep.

"Fabio, wake up, Fabio."

A hand slapped him around his face, causing the pain to lance through his neck and scalp again.

"Stop, stop. Please God, stop," cried Fabio.

The man came into view again. He had a sharp angular face with small black eyes. He gazed at Fabio, his thin hard lips curling into a mirthless smile.

"Good, good. Let us talk. My name is Vladimir Abramov. " He paused. "Have you heard this name before? Someone in the bank, perhaps?"

"No, no. No one has mentioned that name, I swear."

Abramov started to pace.

"Very well. Tell me about Harvey Pinkman."

"Harvey …"

Abramov stopped pacing and slapped him around the face. Sparkles of light danced before his eyes followed by the searing pain in his head and neck.

"Harvey Pinkman, yes, yes. What about him?" asked Fabio.

"Where is he?"

"I don't know. I swear. He didn't come into work on Monday. There was a big fuss with the vault –"

"What do you know about the vault?" asked Abramov.

"One of the Auditors told me about it. She was there – Jones, she called herself. Harriet Seymour-Jones," said Fabio.

"And?"

"There was a big fuss. Something about missing gold. Everyone running around trying to find out what was going on," continued Fabio.

"Jones, you say."

"Yes, yes. Seymour-Jones."

Abramov paused. He spoke to someone in Russian who scribbled down a note. "When was the last time you saw Pinkman?"

Fabio thought for a while. His head was spinning. "I think it was the Friday before."

"You talked to him, no?" queried Abramov.

"Just a chat," said Fabio. "He was anxious about something. Had a big shipment to move. Thought it would take him the whole weekend.

That's all I know."

Abramov started to pace again. "I'm told by people at the bank that you are whistleblower, no?"

"I ... not exactly," said Fabio.

"What does that mean? You are, or you are not. What is it to be?"

"It was Jones. She took all my trades and saw what was going on," said Fabio.

Abramov stopped and put his face close to Fabio's. "Choose your next words carefully. What was going on?"

Fabio tried to swallow, but he had no more spit. He mouth was dry. "Rhodes was dumping large amounts of gold on the Hong Kong market. Pushing down the price," he croaked.

"What does this mean. Why would he sell gold to push down the price?" Abramov questioned.

"He was making large bets on the price of gold falling – on the Futures market," explained Fabio. "It's a type of trade. He was insider trading – for himself or someone else. I'm not sure. It's all recorded on the system. Jones made me copy all of my trades to my local laptop. She didn't trust Rhodes screwing with the computers."

"And you have these records?"

"No, no. My laptop was seized during the raid by the NCA," said Fabio.

Abramov pulled back from his face and resumed his pacing. "And so you went to the authorities. Told them about these trades. I think you did, yes?"

"She made me –" whimpered Fabio.

"Seymour-Jones, the Auditor."

"Except she really wasn't an Auditor. She was working for ROD," said Fabio.

Abramov's face contorted into a sneer. "She was a ROD agent. This is what you are telling me?"

"Yes, yes. I had no choice," sobbed Fabio. "It wasn't my fault."

Abramov lent in and gripped Fabio's chin. "Tell me. From which account did this gold come – the gold that was dumped?"

Fabio coughed. He tried to answer, but his throat was dry and tight. "Could I have some more water, please."

"Yes, yes, but tell me the account. Was it from one particular account?"

"Yes," croaked Fabio. "It was always from the same two accounts: Borite Metals Holdings and Renkov Investments."

Abramov froze. He let go of Fabio's chin.

"Thank you, Fabio. You have been most helpful. Cut him down."

"Thank God," croaked Fabio, his voice reduced to a hoarse whisper. "Where are you taking me?"

"On a little boat ride. Not far from here. Then you can have as much water as you can drink."

19

It was Friday morning when Drum and Fern landed at Heathrow. They had caught the last flight out of New York after wrapping up with Hammond and Delaney. Fern had hardly spoken to him during the flight. Once they cleared customs, she made her excuses and caught a separate car service back into town. She was still pissed at him for wanting Misha back in London.

The driver took him back via central London and the Embankment. He was dog-tired and dozed most of the way. He woke as they passed Old Billingsgate Market and headed up Lower Thames Street towards Tower Bridge. The driver deposited him outside his favourite coffee shop beside Butler's Wharf.

He was surprised to see William manning reception.

"Morning, son."

"Morning. Didn't think I'd see you here. Where's Alice?"

"Gone to get the coffees. Thought you might be tired after your flight. I've come to give you a hand."

Drum took a step past the reception area and looked into what had been his office. It looked like a bomb had hit it.

"Good grief …" He dropped his bag behind the reception desk and, examining the carnage.

"Yeah, the bastards. Alice said they took great delight in wrecking the place."

"William, I'm sorry. If I'd known they were going to do this … Alice not too upset, is she?"

"One thing I've learnt about Alice is that she's as 'ard as nails."

Drum sat down on one of the seats in the small reception area and stared up at the ceiling. He was tired.

116

"Sorry about Raj," said William. "He was a nice bloke."

"He was – a nice bloke," echoed Drum.

"And he still is," said Alice as she bustled her way through the door, balancing a cardboard tray of three coffees. "Don't you two go all maudlin on me. We have work to do."

Drum smiled. "You're right." How did he manage before Alice?

They spent the rest of the morning clearing up the mess. As promised, McKay had removed all material related to the RBI case. Whatever evidence was on the two laptops was now in the hands of MI5 – or at least in the large hams of McKay.

Alice poked her head around the door.

"Got a minute?"

"Sure, Alice."

She looked behind her then slipped in, gently closing the door.

"I've got William tidying up the kitchen." She looked behind her again. "I cleared out the safe before the raid, just as a precaution."

"You did? Well done," said Drum.

Alice unbuttoned her jacket and proudly displayed the Sig Sauer secured in a leather holster.

"I thought we might be needing this. Things are going to get worse before they get better."

"Crumbs, Alice …"

"Just don't tell William. He'd faint if he knew I was carrying a gun."

"Is there something we need to talk about?"

She tilted her head to one side and pursed her lips.

"You mean about William and me?"

"No, Alice. I mean about your past career in the Foreign Office." He frowned. "Wait, what about you and William?"

"Good Lord," exclaimed Alice, buttoning her jacket. "That man is impossible –"

"Alice," said Drum. "Victor Renkov and Anna Koblihova have just walked in. Better show them in."

"Do you want me to stick around," said Alice looking over her shoulder.

"Just keep William busy out back. Not sure how this is going to play." *Victor is not your friend.*

"Right you are," said Alice, patting the side of her jacket as she left the office.

Victor came in wearing his best corporate smile and his coat over his shoulders. Anna remained outside talking to Alice.

"Benjamin, how are you!"

"Hi, Victor," said Drum, offering Victor the couch. "You're looking better."

Victor looked around and raised an eyebrow. He winced, automatically touching the tender side of his brow. Battered and bloodied, but not out.

"Having a tidy up?"

"Something like that," said Drum, noticing Anna and Alice having another animated conversation. "I see you still have your minder."

Victor scowled. "That woman will be the death of me." He calmed himself. "But I guess I'm stuck with her – at least for a while." He looked outside into the reception area. "What do those two have to talk about?"

"What do you want, Victor?"

"We were wondering if you had any information on Harvey Pinkman?"

"We? Are you working for Vlad now?"

"We're all working for Vlad, one way or another. Even you, Benjamin. Only you haven't realised it yet." He glanced behind him. "I thought you might want to know that Misha is back."

Drum shrugged.

"I only mention it because the New York side of the operation told us he was arrested. Vlad is wondering why he was allowed to return to London."

Before Drum could reply Anna walked into the office. She was in wearing a smart suit and matching heels. She looked all business.

Alice came in behind her. "Can I get you some tea, Mr Renkov?"

Victor replied smoothly in his native Russian. Alice smiled politely and left the office.

"Such a charming woman," said Victor, stealing a sideways glance at Anna.

"Are we still playing at Victor's PA, Anna?"

Anna sank back into the couch and placed her small leather purse beside her. She smiled.

"I think the time for pretence is over, don't you Benjamin? Vladimir wants the two laptops you have in your possession."

"If we're talking about the two laptops from the raid at RBI, I can't help you."

Anna scrutinised him. "It is best not to lie to me. Vlad wants those laptops."

"I wish I could help, but the security services have them now. That particular case has been closed down."

Anna frowned. "What security services?"

"I'm assuming MI5. An old army friend stopped by and picked them up. I really don't have them."

Victor grinned. "Oh, well. A wasted trip then, Anna."

Anna stared at Drum, her eyes narrowing. "I don't think Vlad will believe that."

"Vlad can believe what he wants. I gather Mr Pinkman hasn't turned up."

Anna didn't answer. She suddenly stood up.

"If you have any information on Harvey Pinkman, it would be best if you let us know." She walked out of the door and out of the office.

"Well, thanks for everything Benjamin. Be seeing you."

"Victor," said Drum standing. "How deep are you in?"

"One metric ton of gold bullion. You do the math. If that gold doesn't turn up, I'm a dead man walking."

He followed Anna out of the office.

Drum sat back down in his chair and sighed. He had a feeling he'd not seen the last of Victor and Anna. He wondered if Misha was looking at the wrong end of a pulley.

Alice walked in. "Anna looked like she left in a huff," she said.

"Wanted the laptops from the raid," said Drum.

"What did you tell her?"

"The truth. The security services have them."

"Did she believe you?"

"Not in the slightest."

"What are you going to do?"

Before Drum could answer, William poked his head around the door.

"Alice, gotta go. Problem with one of my rentals. See you later – at bowls."

"William –", said Alice, but William had made a swift exit giving Drum a wave as he left the office.

Drum laughed. "Ok, what am I missing here?"

"That man," said Alice, letting out a large sigh. "He's bloody impossible."

"It seems you have the measure of my father."

"He was supposed to tell you."

"Tell me what, Alice?"

"Oh, sod it. William has moved in with me. There, I've said it!"

Drum looked on in stunned silence. Then a smile spread across his face. He got up from behind his desk and walked over to Alice. He bent down and enveloped her tiny frame in a giant hug.

"Oh, Alice. That's wonderful news."

She pulled back from his embrace. "It is?"

"Of course it is. I've never seen William so happy."

Her eyes began to well with tears. She reached inside her jacket pocket for a tissue.

"He is, isn't he. Happy I mean."

Drum sat Alice down on the couch.

"I've been so worried," she said, her voice wavering. "We didn't know what you would think. We haven't known each other long."

"I've been a complete idiot for not realising the obvious," said Drum. "I haven't been the best of sons."

"Oh, nonsense. So much has been happening ..."

"About that," said Drum. "I think things could start becoming a little too hot around here. It might be best if you and William stayed away from the office – until things blow over."

Alice gave him a hard look. "Oh, tsk, tsk, that won't be necessary. I can take care of myself – and you have that nice Commander Fern to help you."

Drum thought about Fern. She hadn't checked in since leaving him at the airport. He really should give her a call.

"We should get cracking," said Alice.

"Oh, no you don't. We're going for a drink. It's Friday."

Alice beamed. "Great idea. I'll get my bag."

"And Alice."

"Yes, Ben."

"Lose the gun."

20

Drum said goodbye to Alice after spending an enjoyable afternoon over gin and tonics at a local bar on the wharf. He'd brought her up to speed on events in New York. She agreed with Fern: it was a mistake letting Misha back in the country.

She told him she wouldn't be in on Saturday. She was helping William pack his things. He was pleased that she and William had hit it off and the thought of them living together made him smile. He wondered what William really knew about Alice. Whatever she did at the Foreign Office, it wasn't merely typing. She was comfortable around firearms, spoke fluent Russian and seemed unfazed by the fact that the Russian Mafia might want to kill him. Whatever Alice was hiding, he trusted her to tell him in her own good time. *I know how to keep a secret.*

There wasn't anything more he could do that night so he sauntered back towards the office. The weather was mild for the time of year and the sun was sitting low over the rooftops of the converted warehouses, casting long shadows across the narrow cobbled street of the wharf. He should really call Fern. Perhaps she would consider dinner?

He had just entered the gloom of a small arched alley that led back to the office when a large man stepped out from the shadows, blocking his path. He heard footsteps behind him and quickly turned. Too late. He felt a crushing blow to the back of his head before blackness took him.

He woke briefly, his head spinning. He felt sick. Two men were holding him up, one on each arm. They were dragging him down the steps of a small landing where a dinghy was moored. The last thing he remembered was being man-handled into the boat before nausea and blackness consumed him once more.

He came to staring up at a darkening sky. A sharp pain lanced through the back of his head and the world seemed to be slowly rolling from side to side. He heard a Russian voice.

"Benjamin, are you awake?"

He heard the voice again, this time speaking angrily in Russian. Someone grabbed him and tried to sit him up. He slumped forward, unconsciousness threatening to take him. He was roughly thrust into a sitting position once more. He smelt a woman's perfume: lemon and a hint of jasmine. He felt something cold on the back of his head.

"Were you trying to kill him?" said the woman. It sounded like Anna.

He looked around and saw the City skyline moving up and down. He immediately felt nauseous. He was on a large motor launch, swaying and rolling in the middle of the Thames. He lifted his head and fought back the bile in his throat that threatened to overwhelm him. He reached for the back of his head and felt a small hand holding a cold compress to his scalp.

"Take your time", said Anna. "They were supposed to bring you to the boat, not kill you."

"Don't make fuss of him, Anna." Drum looked up and saw the dark-suited shape of Vlad looming over him. He was grinning. "He is one tough soldier. I think so."

He appeared to be on a soft leather couch with his back to the stern of the boat. More seating surrounded a large central table on the deck where drinks had been placed. He cautiously moved his head. Misha was standing off to one side, looking bored. Three of Vlad's henchmen were situated about the deck, hands folded, looking on. They were grinning like hyenas at their bosses' interrogation.

"You only had to pick up the phone," said Drum, trying not to throw up.

"You see, Anna," said Vlad. "He's fine. Englishmen have thick heads, dull brains." He repeated his joke in Russian to the amusement of his men.

"Take it easy," said Anna. She left him and walked over and sat on a couch near the table.

"Listen, Benjamin. I play nice with you. I offer you work. I send the lovely Anna to reason with you …" He leaned on the corner of the table and took a battered gold case of his jacket pocket. He opened it, one-handed, and extracted a long, black cigarette. One of his minions walked over and lit it for him. He snapped the case shut with practised ease and returned it to his pocket. He sucked deeply, drawing the thick grey smoke into his lungs.

"And you shit on me," he continued, exhaling the spent smoke down through his nose.

"I can't give you what I don't have," said Drum, wincing as he pressed on the cold compress.

"Don't fuck with me, Benjamin. That would be a bad idea."

"Look, Anna must have told you about the visit I had from the security services. They have the laptops."

"Yes, she told me. So I check. I think someone is fucking with you, yes?"

Drum wondered what contacts Vlad had that could confirm an MI5 operation. If this was true, he had serious influence with someone. A thought occurred to him.

"Listen, I suspect that we're both being fucked over. Someone doesn't want the information stored on those laptops coming to light. It must be someone at the bank."

Vlad stood up and moved to the side of the boat next to him. He casually flicked ash over the side of the railings and looked out at City skyline.

"I think you are right. I have come by information that Damian Rhodes might not be treating his customers fairly."

Drum didn't ask about the source of his information, but he guessed it involved pain and blood loss.

"I think whoever wanted Pinkman's laptop, also wanted Pinkman out of the way. Probably Rhodes …"

Vlad stared down at the end of his cigarette, thinking. "I don't think Rhodes had anything to do with Pinkman's disappearance."

"What makes you say that."

"Because Pinkman was working for me and Rhodes needed him."

Now Drum was confused. "So who would want Pinkman out of the way?"

"Beats me," said Vlad, dropping the end of his cigarette into the river below. "He was a little shit. Big drug and girl problems." A grin split his face. "Of course, we help him with these habits. I would have liked to have killed him myself, but he was useful." He moved back to the table and poured himself a drink. "Tell me, what were you doing in New York."

Drum glanced over at Misha who was standing stock still with his hands folded in front of him. He was looking as stoic as ever. There was no telling what Vlad would do if he knew he was working for ROD, not to mention the DOJ. He decided to steer a course between two half-truths and hoped that Misha wouldn't contradict him.

"I was on a date."

"A date?" said Vlad. "You expect me to believe that?"

"You know her. Alex Fern."

"You took Alex Fern to New York for –"

"Romance."

Vlad's face contorted with a lascivious grin. "You're fucking the policewoman?" He turned to Misha who nodded. He repeated this piece of news in Russian to his henchmen. On cue, they started to laugh.

Vlad regarded Drum with cold dark eyes. He was thinking, considering his next move. "What am I going to do with you, Benjamin? You don't have laptops and you don't have Pinkman. Why don't I just throw you over the side?"

Drum thought this was a good question. He needed to buy himself some time and get Vlad off his back. He needed to find Harry and not have to keep looking over his shoulder for a Russian hitman.

"You need me, Vlad. I know from my contacts that RBI are looking to audit the vault. Apparently, the board doesn't trust Rhodes either. I'm certain I can get a contract at the bank as part of the audit team. It'll give me the perfect opportunity to find out what's going on." Vlad was still looking sceptical. "I'll make a deal with you. I'll find Pinkman, dead or alive, and find your gold – if it is indeed missing."

Vlad grinned. "Good choice, Benjamin." He issued an order in Russian to one of his henchmen. The man went below decks.

Anna was looking at him. She pursed her lips, then stood and poured herself a drink and sat back down. He wondered who she really was.

There was a scuffling noise and then what sounded like cursing. Drum's Russian only amounted to a few dozen words – all of them bad. Whoever was being shoved up from below decks had exhausted his entire vocabulary.

A young woman was literally thrown onto the deck with the henchman following, cursing loudly. She was dressed in ripped jeans and a t-shirt with a deaths-head skull emblazoned on the front. Her hair was blond and short. The side of her nose and left eyebrow were pierced by small metal rings.

The henchman was now shouting at her angrily. Drum noticed Misha walking over towards them. The man went to strike the woman, only to have his arm held in an iron grip by the big Russian. The henchman looked up at the big man and backed off, muttering under his breath.

Vlad grinned. "This is Svetlana. She calls herself Stevie. Why? Who knows? She is to work with you."

The young woman knelt on the deck. She had fire in her eyes. She reminded Drum of Harry.

"What am I supposed to do with her?" said Drum, puzzled by this turn of events.

"She is my best computer hacker. Very skilled. You need her help. Your man Raj is being deported, no?"

Stevie looked at him. She obviously trusted no one. He shrugged. He figured she was better off coming with him that staying on the boat.

"Good," said Vlad. "I expect reports on your progress."

Drum removed the compress from the back of his head and realised he was holding a bag of semi-frozen peas. He dumped them on the seat.

"One last thing," said Vlad. "There is someone else at the bank who we are interested in tracing. An Auditor. Her name is Harriet Seymour-Jones. You know her, perhaps?"

Drum was having trouble thinking. He didn't understand why Vlad wanted Harry. Perhaps Victor had said something. "I've never heard of her," he lied. "But I'll find out …"

"Good. Now fuck off computer boy and find me my gold."

He tried to stand. The world swam around him. He wanted to sleep. He heard Vlad speaking. Then strong arms hoisted him up and the world spiralled into darkness.

21

Drum woke with a drill in his head. He was lying in his bed. At least he thought it was his bed. It was hard to tell. The room was in semi-darkness. He tried to sit up and groaned as pain shot through his skull and down his neck.

"Lay back," said a woman's voice.

The voice sounded familiar but he couldn't place it. He smelt the aroma of coffee and he forced himself to try to sit up again.

"Stay down," said the voice, more harshly. Then he remembered. The young woman on the boat.

"Svetlana?"

"Stevie. My name is Stevie." He felt a small hand press against his chest – his bare chest.

There was a movement on the end of the bed and then the blinds to his apartment opened a crack. Light from the Autumn sun flooded into the room and pierced his eyes. The drill inside his head spun-up to a high pitched whine like a dentist's drill scouring his brain. He laid back and covered his eyes with the back of his hand.

"You need to rest," said Stevie. "You probably have a concussion."

Her voice was low and husky with just a hint of an accent. She sounded much older than she looked when she was screaming in Russian on the boat.

"What time is it?" he said.

"It's nearly 11:00 am. It's Saturday morning."

"Christ, I need to call Fern." He struggled to sit back up.

He felt her sit on the edge of the bed. "Here, take two of these."

He gingerly opened his eyes, squinting into the bright room. Stevie sat on the edge of the bed wearing what looked like one of his white shirts and very little else. The shirt extended down to the top of her bare pale thighs.

"You can't be that badly injured if you have time to ogle my legs," she said, pressing two pills into his hand.

"What are they?"

"They're painkillers – for the crack on the skull those idiots gave you. What else?" She pushed a glass of water into his other hand. "Drink and don't be such a baby."

"Thanks." He carefully touched the back of his head, felt a large painful lump and winced.

"They almost killed you," she said. You must have pissed someone off. Guess they wanted you more alive than dead?"

He handed back the glass. Now that he had time to focus, he realised that she was a beautiful young woman.

"I had to borrow one of your shirts. Thanks to you, I left in a hurry." She looked at him and smiled. "Don't get any ideas. You're in no fit state for that type of exertion."

"That coffee smells good," he said.

She jumped off the bed, the sudden jerking movement awakening the drill inside his head. She was right about the exertion. She padded over to the kitchen and poured him a coffee.

"Hope you don't mind, I had a shower. Those pigs kept me locked in that boat for a whole day."

He watched her carry the coffee back to him. He carefully sat up and gratefully took the mug as she resumed her vigil on the edge of the bed.

"How did I get here?" he said.

"Misha brought you." She stared at his chest. "How did you get that?" She traced a finger gently down the scar that ran from his collarbone across his right breast to his sternum.

"Jealous Afghan tribesman," he replied.

"Really. Why was he jealous?"

"I was sleeping with his wife."

She looked at him, wide-eyed. "No!"

He raised an eyebrow and sipped his coffee.

She laughed. "You're such a joker."

She got up and went back into the kitchen. He watched her open his refrigerator and look in. The light from the door illuminated her lean body in silhouette against the luminescence of his starched, white shirt.

"You don't have any food in your fridge." She closed the door and the apparition vanished.

"I normally eat out," he replied.

She cast an eye around the kitchen. "Do you live here?"

He thought it an odd question. "Where else would I live?"

"Somewhere comfortable."

He looked around his apartment. "I guess I find it comfortable."

She shrugged and padded back to the end of the bed. "Why were you on the boat?" she asked.

"I could ask you the same question."

She looked at him as if trying to figure him out. "You work for Vlad, but I've not seen you around before."

"I don't work for Vlad," he protested.

She gave him a knowing smile. "We all say that, but here we are doing his bidding. He says jump and we say how high."

She had a point. He remembered what Victor had said. *We're all working for Vlad...*

"So, why are you working for Vlad?" he asked.

She looked down at her hands and twisted the duvet into a small knot.

"I was studying for my Masters – computer sciences. A friend asked for my help with a small banking problem she was having ..."

"Only she wasn't much of a friend," he said.

"No, right. The ex-pat Russian community is very small, and my so-called friend blabbed to another friend and the next thing I know I'm talking to Vlad. He has powerful contacts. Wanted me to do more and more. Hacking really. When I said no, he threatened to have my visa revoked."

"And the more work you did for him, the deeper the hole got."

She looked up. "I'm starving. Let's go eat."

"Wait, how did you and Misha get into the office?"

"Right. About that ... I bypassed your security system. Hope you don't mind. We were kinda in a bind." She gave him a lopsided smile.

There was the sound of a door closing in the lobby downstairs.

"Who's that?" said Stevie, crawling across the bed to Drum.

Fern's voice echoed up the stairs. "Drum, are you there? Your door was open."

"Who's Drum?" whispered Stevie.

"That would be me." He put his coffee mug down. "Up here, Fern," he shouted and then winced as his head throbbed.

There was the dull metal sound of heavy footsteps on the spiral staircase that led up to his apartment. Fern appeared at the top of the landing. She was wearing a pair of faded denims and a red plaid shirt. She stopped when she saw Drum and Stevie in bed together.

"Good grief, I am sorry. I didn't know you had company." She started to back down the stairs.

Stevie moved closer to Drum. "Is that your girlfriend," she whispered. "She's very big."

"Wait, Fern. Don't go." He was trying to get out of the bed, but Stevie had wrapped herself around his arm.

"You can't get up," said Stevie."

"No, really. I should have called," said Fern, starting downstairs.

Drum managed to get an unsteady foot on the floor. The rest of him seemed to be tangled in the duvet and Stevie.

"Will you let me go …"

"You really shouldn't get up," said Stevie, releasing her grip.

Drum managed to get both feet on the floor and staggered over to the landing. "Fern, wait. We need to talk."

Fern stopped halfway down the stairs and looked up. She was about to say something then stopped, open-mouthed.

"I tried to tell you," said Stevie smiling. "We couldn't find your PJs."

22

Drum woke with just a mild hangover. The lump on his head had subsided. He looked at his watch on the bedside table. It was Sunday morning. After Fern had stormed out of the apartment, he'd crashed and spent the rest of Saturday in bed. Stevie had pottered about the place making him tea and buying takeaways. She had been put out when he insisted she sleep downstairs on the couch. He needed to sort out a place for her to stay. He called his father.

"Hi, William. It's Ben. Can you I buy you breakfast?"

"Sure, son. What's up?"

"I need your help."

William suggested a rendezvous he hadn't been to in a while. He showered and put on a pair of jeans and a pale-blue shirt. He grabbed his leather jacket and went down stairs. Stevie was still fast asleep on his couch. He left the office, closing the door quietly behind him.

William had suggested they meet in Borough Market which was a brisk fifteen minute walk from his current location. He made his way under Tower Bridge and onto the Southbank. Riverboats filled with tourists cruised along the Thames, sounding their horns as they motored by. He walked briskly towards London Bridge.

He was soon looking down upon the sprawling commerce of Borough Market from the bridge above, a hotchpotch of stalls and restaurants that surrounded the splendour of Southwark Cathedral. It was still early, and the market had yet to fill with tourists. At lunchtime, during the week, they would be forming lines at the food stalls that offered everything from falafel to paella. William sat alone on a bench in the sanctuary of the cathedral grounds reading a newspaper.

An iron gate, just off the bridge, gave him access to the cathedral below. He sauntered down the granite steps, scanning the grounds for signs of trouble. All he saw was a tramp sleeping on one of the benches. He took a seat next to his father.

William was dressed in his now-familiar green waxed jacket and flat cap. He casually folded his newspaper.

"Hello, son. Were you followed?"

"I don't think we've got to that stage yet."

"What stage is that?"

"Me on the lam."

"Oh, right. It's just that Alice said that the security services would probably want to keep an eye on you." William looked at his son, a frown creasing his forehead. "You're not in any trouble are you son?"

"No more than usual. What did Alice say exactly?"

"Said to tell you that …" William paused as he tried to recall the message. "The bloke from Thames House – you haven't seen the last of him."

"McKay."

"Yes, that was the one. Do you know him?"

"You could say that. It's … complicated. We served together."

William waited for him to continue but when he didn't, he sucked his lip and pressed on.

"Your last tour of Afghanistan," said William, softly. "You never did tell me what happened over there. Want to talk about it?"

Dark memories came flooding back. The smell of cardamon in the rich, black tea brewed on their small campfire. That had been their undoing. They had rested. Got sloppy. It was the keen eyes of the Poacher that had saved them. He'd spotted them while on watch, advancing on their position. A troop of well-armed men had tracked them all the way from the LZ. It was if they had known their final objective. Not your regular insurgents was Poacher's expert opinion. They were carrying the Russian made AN94. Spetsnaz for sure. Get the man in, avoid capture at all costs. McPherson and Cairns had paid the price of getting him out.

Drum said nothing. They sat in silence for a while.

"Why don't we grab some breakfast," said William, breaking the silence. "I could do with something to eat."

Drum looked at his watch. It was time for brunch. He thought this ironic. It was usually months between visits to his father, and now here he was meeting with the old man twice in as many weeks.

Drum surveyed the market. "What takes your fancy?"

"No, not inside the market. It's closed on a Sunday. There's the place near the Clink. D'you remember? I used to take you there as a boy."

He remembered the Clink, one of the oldest prisons in London, now a museum. William would take great delight in showing him the ghoulish exhibits and would threaten him with the Clink for various misdemeanours at home.

They walked out of the cathedral grounds, away from the bustle of the market, and towards the river. They entered a narrow street with converted warehouses on either side; his life was suddenly full of them. After a short walk, they came to Clink Street and a small cafe squeezed in an unlikely space between two office conversions. He recognised the place and was surprised it was still there.

They took a table within the confined space and sat beside each other on a rough bench against a wall. A burly man with a ruddy face, wearing a white apron, came out from behind the counter.

"Morning, William. Haven't seen you in a while."

"Morning, Lionel. Two teas and two full English, please."

"Right you are." Lionel was about to leave when he hesitated. "Blimey, is that young Benjamin?"

Drum smiled but for the life of him couldn't remember the man.

"Yes, Lionel," said William, beaming from ear to ear. "Little Benjy."

"Blimey, well I never. The little skinny kid in shorts with grazed knees? Used to come in 'er and eat all of my pickled onions. Well, I never."

Drum carried on smiling awkwardly. He had a vague recollection of those onions.

"The very same. Time flies, don't it."

"Ain't that the truth. Well, let me get your order."

"That was Lionel," said William.

"So I gather."

"It was a long time ago."

"Time flies."

"Don't it just. Tell me what happened in New York."

"Picked up a new assignment – working for Delaney."

"You patched things up with her then?"

"I think so. It's difficult to tell with her. But everyone was pleased to see me."

"Why wouldn't they be?"

He thought about it. He didn't know. After the debacle of the last assignment, he had mixed feelings. *Shit happens.*

"Don't know, really." He shrugged. "Got me a new partner. We're working this new case together. The policewoman who helped with my Russian problem."

William sat up, suddenly interested. "Alice told me about her. The big girl."

"Her name's Fern. Not the 'big girl'."

"Right, right, Fern. Lovely woman, Alice says. Liked her a lot."

He thought about calling Fern. Then he remembered Stevie.

"Look, can I ask a favour? I have someone new starting. A young woman who needs a place to stay for a few weeks. I was wondering if she could rent your place ..." He gave his father a wry smile. "Considering you and Alice are moving in together."

"Yeah, right. I meant to tell you about that," said William looking down at his hands. "There was never the right time."

"I think it's a great idea."

William gave his son a broad smile. "Yeah, Alice said you were pleased. Sorry I didn't tell you sooner."

"She's a lovely woman. Just don't upset her. I need her. Practically runs the office now."

"Is that right. Said she was good at typing."

"Yeah, right. A good typist."

Lionel walked over carrying a large tray with two mugs of tea and two large plates with enough food to feed a SAS troop.

"Lionel, you're a star," said William.

Lionel beamed and left them to their meal.

Drum tucked into his breakfast. He made a note to come back and visit Lionel again.

After eating, William and Drum sat back, drinking their tea. Both men had demolished the food on their plates.

William put his mug down and turned to his son.

"What I don't understand is why the security services are giving you so much trouble. After all, don't you work for them?"

"I don't know. I guess that someone wants me off this new case. Probably someone with government contacts."

"This bloke, McKay. Sounds like a wrong'n. Do you think he's on the take."

Drum wondered about that. Whatever he thought about the competence of the man, he'd always considered him a loyal soldier.

"More likely he's just obeying orders. A blunt instrument, trying to slow me down."

Drum remembered why he was there.

"About the flat ..."

"Of course, son. I'll give Alice the key. She can drop it off tomorrow." He looked wistfully over his cup. "Hopefully, I'll have less of a problem renting my old place ..."

"Problems?" said Drum.

"Just some of my tenants complaining about noise – you know the sort of thing. They live in the middle of Wapping and expect it to be like the country. One of the warehouses down there has been causing problems. Workers coming and going all hours of the day and night. I dare say I'll sort it out."

Drum thought of Vlad's pad in Wapping. "What's this place called?"

"Tenants Wharf. Leased it to a company. They're not supposed to work at night."

Drum's phone rang. It was Stevie.

"Where are you? I'm starving."

"I'll be back soon. Make yourself a sandwich."

The phone went dead.

"Gotta go, William. Thanks for the flat."

He walked over and paid Lionel, complimenting him on his breakfast. Lionel beamed. "Don't be a stranger, Benjy."

He waved goodbye to William and walked back towards the cathedral. The tramp he'd seen on the bench shuffled by. He looked down when Drum passed him.

He walked through the cathedral grounds and followed the same route back along the Southbank towards Tower Bridge. The weather was mild and sunny, and it felt good to be out of the apartment and in the fresh air. He gingerly touched the back of his head. It was tender but no longer painful.

His phone rang. If it were Stevie again, he'd give her a piece of his mind. Vlad had turned him into a babysitter.

"Drummond," he said into his phone, not looking at the number.

"It's Fern."

Drum stopped walking. His heart leapt a little. "Fern! I was about to call you –"

"Yeah, course." Her voice sounded harsh. All business.

"Listen, Fern. About Saturday –"

"We're all grown-ups. You don't have to explain yourself to me," she said. "Listen. Just got a call from one of my contacts in the Thames

Police. About Fabio DeLuca."

Drum remembered the name. "One of the dealers at the bank."

"Right," replied Fern. "They just fished his body out of the river."

23

Damian Rhodes got the call early Monday morning. Victor Renkov wanted an urgent meeting. He was one of RBI's biggest customers – at least on the precious metals front. When he looked up the account he knew he had no choice but to meet the Russian. Victor Renkov was the name behind Renkov Investments Ltd. Gold had been flooding into that account from Zurich for the past year. He knew who was really funding the operation. Victor was just the front man for a much bigger enterprise. And now a good portion of that gold was missing. If Victor kicked up a stink about his account, it was game over.

He cleared his diary for the afternoon and asked Sam to book a table at the club for lunch. They should at least get some privacy and he knew Victor was also a member. He remembered meeting him there briefly on another occasion. Vladimir Abramov had introduced him. He thought him a prissy little prick with a limp handshake. The woman hanging off his arm was a completely different story. A pretty thing with a nice arse. Another Russian called Anna … something or other. He couldn't remember all the Russian names. The City was awash with them. More importantly, it was awash with their money.

He arrived at the club in Mayfair shortly after 1 pm The decrepit old man behind the desk immediately accosted him.

"Morning, sir. Can I have your name, please."

"Damian, Rhodes. I'm a member."

"Of course, sir."

"Giles isn't it?"

"Yes, sir. Are you meeting someone, sir?"

"Yes, a Mr Victor Renkov for lunch."

"Very good, sir. I'll announce you." Giles started to rise with a monumental effort.

"Good grief," exclaimed Rhodes. "I haven't got all day. Stay put man. I know the way," and with that, marched off.

"Very good, sir …"

Rhodes walked swiftly to the dining room which was situated next to the library on the ground floor. The elegant room was laid out for lunch with tables covered in stiff white linen and set with silver cutlery. He spotted Victor at a table, discreetly tucked away in the corner next to a large window. The general hubbub of the room quietened down as he walked over to Victor's table – unannounced.

"Afternoon," said Rhodes taking a chair and pulling it back from the table.

Victor looked surprised and stood up, extending his hand. "Damian, glad you could come." He looked around. "No Giles?"

"Silly old bugger," said Rhodes. "It would have been Christmas if I'd waited for him to walk me here." He shook Victor's hand in a perfunctory manner and sat down.

Victor waved the waiter over. "Get you a drink?"

"Whisky Soda," said Rhodes, not looking up.

"I recommend the steak," said Victor, unfolding his napkin and draping it across his lap. "The turbot is also very good."

The waiter returned with Rhodes' Whisky and Soda. "Same again, sir?" the waiter asked Victor.

"That would be nice."

Rhodes looked around the dining room. He didn't recognise anyone from the bank, although he thought he recognised a few MPs. Was that the Foreign Secretary?

"Anyone famous," asked Victor, smiling.

"What can I do for you, Mr Renkov?"

"Please, call me Victor."

"Victor, how can I help you?"

The waiter returned with Victor's refill.

Victor cupped his hands around the crystal tumbler and looked down into its amber contents as if divining inspiration. "Tell me, Damian – I can call you Damian?" Rhodes nodded. "Do you participate in some of the … evening activities that the club provides?"

Rhodes had heard about some of the more outlandish parties the club hosted. Only the most celebrated members and their guests were invited – usually those members with political clout or money. He knew Abramov had hosted a few. Rumour had it they could become quite raucous.

"I haven't had the pleasure," said Rhodes, fiddling with his knife and fork.

"I've heard your chairman is quite the partygoer."

Rhodes stopped rearranging his cutlery and looked up. "Really! Sir Henry Minton?"

"I've heard he likes a good spanking," said Victor, with a salacious grin on his face.

Rhodes stared at Victor. "Why are you telling me this?"

"Oh, just something that you might like to bank for a rainy day – to show good faith."

Rhodes looked at the Russian, wondering what he was driving at. He took a swig of his drink. He relaxed a little as the fine malt scotch slipped down his throat.

"Sorry, Victor. You've lost me."

"Harvey Pinkman was also a bit of a partygoer."

Rhodes sat up. "What about Pinkman?"

"I should say more of a party animal," continued Victor. "He didn't just burn the candle at both ends, more like from every orifice." He laughed. "Not even I could keep up, and that's saying something."

Rhodes had heard that Pinkman had issues, but he always seemed to have them under control. Sex, drugs and rock n'roll were all part of City life. People were always under pressure to perform, to deliver, especially in a dealing environment. But Harvey was back-office. He was primarily responsible for shipping gold and other precious metals between bank vaults. What was he doing partying with Victor Renkov?

"Will you get to the point," said Rhodes, downing his whisky. He looked for the waiter.

"And of course, there was the gambling. Not just a flutter on the gee-gees that would have been too mundane for Harvey. No, Harvey was full on. Didn't do things by half, did our Harvey."

"What are you trying to tell me," said Rhodes.

"Damian," said Victor, tracing a finger down the side of his glass, "you look like a reasonable man."

Rhodes didn't trust the Russian but had no choice but to listen to his crap. "I'm all ears."

"There was an audit of the vault – of my gold account. You have probably been told about this?"

Here it comes, thought Rhodes. "I think I was."

"Then you know," continued Victor, "that the vault was empty."

"That was a computer mistake with our inventory system," said Rhodes, hastily. "I can assure you, Victor –"

"Not according to Ms Seymour-Jones, one of your Auditors," interrupted Victor. "She was most insistent that something was not right with my account."

"Utter rubbish," protested Rhodes. "We've had to let the woman go –"

"You realise, of course, she is a ROD investigator?" said Victor, smiling.

"What! That can't be …"

"Why yes," continued Victor. Probably singing like a lark as we speak. She'll cause problems for both of us."

Rhodes stared at Victor. "There's nothing to sing about."

"Come, come, Damian. Don't bullshit me. I'm an expert." Victor took a sip of whisky. "I'll get to the point. I have your gold – or I should say Pinkman has your gold."

"Pinkman has the gold?"

"Yes, yes – incredulous, I know. 'Victor,' he says, 'I can make us rich!' I tell him he is crazy – full of shit. I think he must be drunk. He tells me no. He has barged six tons of gold to my Warehouse. We can all be rich – live happily ever after. At first I think he's mad, out of his brain. Of course, I know now that Pinkman owed a lot of money to some very bad people. He was desperate."

"Are you telling me," said Rhodes, his voice rising, "that Pinkman transported all the gold from the vault to your warehouse?"

Victor nodded. "That is precisely what I'm telling you." He looked over Rhodes' shoulder. "And please keep your voice down unless you want the Foreign Secretary to hear you."

Rhodes thought that Victor Renkov was full of it. But, if so, why was he telling him this ridiculous story. It didn't make sense. "Where is Pinkman now? More important where is the gold?"

Victor once more returned to his whisky. "Ah, I'll come to that." He took a large gulp of the amber liquid. "I say to Pinkman, 'Harvey, do you know who this gold belongs to?' But he does not care. He is only thinking about how rich he will be. I tell him we are all dead men walking. Do you not know what these people will do to you when they hunt you down? Not just to you, Harvey, but anyone close to you. There can be no 'happy ever after', I tell Harvey."

Rhodes stayed silent and fixed Victor with a glare.

"Of course, Damian, we both know who that gold belongs to. It is Abramov's gold. If that gold is not returned to your vault, we are all dead men walking."

24

Drum woke early and mentally prepared himself for a busy Monday morning. He stood beneath the shower and let the hot water hammer his body. He felt clear-headed for the first time in days. Perhaps Vlad was right: Englishmen do have thick skulls.

He padded into the main living area of the apartment and stood in front of a full-length mirror. He examined his body, still lean and battered. He touched the scar across his chest that Stevie had found so fascinating. If she'd taken a little more time, she'd have seen plenty more. He pulled at his damp hair. Phyllis was right. It was far too long. He needed to get it cut.

He put on a suit and and shirt. He polished his brogues and went downstairs. Stevie was snoring quietly on his couch. He left the office and made his way to Tower Bridge. He took the steps up to street level and joined the morning commuters walking into the City.

He spotted him at the base of the steps. The tramp from the cathedral. Experience told him that running into this character twice might be a coincidence, but three times probably meant he was an observer. He looked behind him, and sure enough, he saw two marks, tailing him at a discreet distance.

Once across the bridge, he took a shortcut past the Tower of London, along the river, until he came to a large art deco building belonging to an Insurance Brokers. From there he made his way to Leadenhall Market. It was still only 7.00 am. He pulled out his phone and hit redial and waited.

"Alex Fern."

"If you're in the neighbourhood of Leadenhall Market, I thought we could have breakfast at Ives. He's cooking your favourite."

There was silence on the end of the phone. "Can you give me forty-five minutes. I'll meet you there." The phone went dead.

Drum smiled and phoned Brock to let him know they were coming. Brock sounded pleased. He casually looked around and spotted one of his tails: a young woman in a salmon-pink sweater pretending to window shop. Drum placed another: a man in a dark suit reading the newspaper, leaning against one of the columns in the market. He couldn't see the third, which bothered him.

He walked past Ives and to a small barber shop tucked away in the corner of the market. He'd been going to the place for years. A bell jangled as he pushed open the heavy glass door and walked back in time into Henry's Shaving Emporium. The air was thick with steam from dozens of hot white towels and redolent with the scent of sandalwood that Henry always used as an aftershave.

"Morning, Henry. Can you squeeze me in?"

Henry Morgan was the epitome of a well-groomed Victorian gentleman, transported into the twenty-first century. He sported an immaculate waxed moustache that Hercule Poirot would have been proud of and had shiny black hair, parted with military precision and slicked down with a liberal application of macassar oil.

"Good Lord. Is that you Drum?"

"The very same." He smiled. Henry always made him laugh.

"Clear the decks, lads. We have an emergency. Someone has kidnapped Captain Drummond and transported him back to the seventies."

Drum looked at himself in the mirror. "That bad, eh."

"Take a seat, sir. We'll soon have you back on parade and looking dapper."

Drum sat in the ancient barber's chair as Henry covered him with a crisp, white sheet with the flourish of a matador. They chatted, as barbers do, about this and that as Henry clipped, trimmed and shaved his way through his thick, brown hair. Drum occasionally glanced out of the window to see if his tails were still in place. The young woman in the pink sweater was again shopping.

Once Henry was satisfied that his hair had been cut to a decent length befitting a military man, he started on his thick, black stubble. First the hot, steamed towel wrapped around his face. This was followed by an application of luxuriant thick shaving cream. Then, with a flourish, Henry produced a cut-throat razor from his pocket which he proceeded to swipe up and down against a thick leather belt attached to the wall. This, William had told him, was a strop. It honed the razor's edge. Drum held his breath as Henry moved the honed, bare steel closer to the base of his throat.

"You always do that," said Henry, pulling the razor back. "You can relax, you know. I won't cut your throat."

"I had a similar conversation with an Afghan."

"The one whose wife you were sleeping with? Lucky he was going for your throat."

Drum made himself relax. He and Henry carried on with the banter as Henry skilfully played the razor up and across his face until he was whisker-free.

"There you go. Much better."

Drum wiped the remaining shaving cream from his face and inspected his new self. He hardly recognised the person staring back at him. He looked about ten years younger.

"You worked your magic this time, Henry."

Henry reached behind him and splashed a small amount of lotion onto his hands and gently slapped Drum's cheeks with both palms. "The finishing touch."

Drum smiled and paid Henry. It was time to meet Fern.

He left the barbers and immediately spotted his two observers. He looked around for the third but didn't see anyone else. He walked around the corner and made his way towards Ives. A black van pulled up with a squeal of brakes. A door in the side of the van slid open, and three men and a woman jumped out. The three men were dressed in jeans and casual jackets, but their combat boots and close-cropped hair marked them as military. They looked fit and hard and moved with a purpose. He recognised the woman from the wharf. He'd noticed her in his local coffee shop on several occasions. She was tail number three, and this looked like a snatch squad.

He was about to turn and make his escape through the market when he heard the roar of an engine and the shrieking of tyres. A bright red Ferrari with black tinted windows slid around the corner at the bottom of Lime Street and roared towards him. He had no idea where the car could be going as the entrance to the market was barred by three silver bollards. The Ferrari accelerated towards the snatch squad who cursed and scattered. He heard a hiss and the three bollards suddenly descended below the road surface.

He jumped back as the Ferrari skidded to a halt beside him, the four big exhausts chortling playfully as the big V12 engine slowed to an idle. He looked around. The three men were now running hard towards him. He turned in time to see the woman walking briskly across the market. She reached inside her bag and pulled out a gun.

The passenger door of the Ferrari slid out and up revealing the diminutive figure of Anna Koblihova in the driving seat.

"Get in!"

He ducked around the open door and slid into the passenger seat. The woman dropped her bag and crouched into a firing position. The passenger door quickly floated down and locked itself shut as three shots rang out. Drum instinctively ducked as the bullets ricocheted off the door and windscreen. Anna didn't flinch. She stamped on the accelerator causing the big V12 engine to roar into life. The big, fat Pirelli tyres screeched and smoked and the Ferrari lurched forward just as the snatch squad came up behind it.

The woman in pink barely had time to dive out of the way as the car accelerated towards her and into the market. Anna sounded the horn causing tardy office workers glued to their phones to scatter before the speeding vehicle.

Drum looked behind him to see the snatch squad racing back to the van. Anna slowed and manoeuvred the Ferrari past dining tables of a restaurant before heading for the market exit.

Just as before, three silver bollards guarding the entrance to the market slipped silently below the surface of the road. Anna floored the accelerator and the Ferrari fish-tailed onto Gracechurch Street and roared towards the Monument.

"Where are we going?" asked Drum, pulling his seat harness tight as Anna dodged parked vans and jaywalking pedestrians.

"Someone wants to meet you," she said, concentrating on the road ahead.

"Could have just picked up the phone," said Drum.

"Good point," replied Anna. "Stash your phone in the bag in the glove compartment. They're probably tracking you."

He slipped his phone into a thick, foil bag. At least she wasn't insisting he throw it out of the window. He loved that phone. He suddenly realised he'd left Fern waiting at the restaurant.

Anna turned smartly at the Monument and roared up Cannon Street, accelerating quickly past the station, heading towards Blackfriars Bridge.

He looked at Anna, she was driving in bare feet. Heels probably weren't an option when driving a high-powered sports car. "Why are the security services shooting at me?" he asked.

"They're not. They're shooting at me. They think I'm working for the Russians."

"I thought you were working for the Russians?"

She smiled before turning sharply down White Lion Hill and onto the Embankment. She red-lined the engine, accelerating rapidly through the underpass of Blackfriars Bridge, heading towards Temple, along the Victoria Embankment. Drum looked behind him. The black van was nowhere in sight.

"There's a table booked in your name at Rothmanns on the Strand. You know the place?"

He knew Rothmanns well. Brock and the rest of the troop used to meet there between postings. They had all assembled there for one last night when he had resigned his commission. He remembered the great slabs of beef served on silver platters and carved at the table by waiters in regimental red. The meal was followed by jugs of port and cigars in the oak-panelled drawing room reserved for special guests. They had been serving military men the same meal at Rothmanns for over one hundred and eighty years.

"Who am I meeting?" asked Drum.

Anna didn't reply. She slowed and indicated right, turning into a side street and parked just before the Strand. "I've got to drop you here."

"This is Victor's car. Where is Victor?" asked Drum.

"That's part of the problem. Victor has disappeared."

"I thought you were his minder?" said Drum.

"That's what Vlad wanted. Victor had other ideas," said Anna.

His door clicked and slid open. He removed the bag containing his phone from the glove compartment. "I'll keep this secure until after the meeting."

Anna nodded. "And Drummond …" He turned to face her. "You can trust Alice."

He got out of the car. The door slid shut, and with a roar, the Ferrari took off down the Strand.

He started walking. He really should call Fern. He removed his phone from inside its tin-foil bag and thought better of it. He continued up the Strand at a brisk pace until he came to the gated entrance to restaurant. Rothmanns only served lunch and dinner and never opened for breakfast. He rattled the ornate iron gates, but they were locked. He found a brass doorbell and pushed hard for several seconds. An oak door opened and a man dressed in a livery coat and tails walked out and stood by the gate.

"Drummond. I have a reservation."

"Yes, sir. You're expected." He unlocked the gate and allowed Drum to enter.

"This way, sir."

They walked through a lobby of ochre-coloured colonnades and ancient chequer-board tiled flooring and into a private dining area lit by the sombre orange glow of Victorian wall lights. A single table was laid out for service, it's starched white tablecloth in bright contrast to the dark oak-panelled walls and luxuriant black leather seats. Major Timothy Weekes sat alone, cradling a cup of black coffee.

The waiter indicated he should take a seat. Weekes stood and extended his hand.

Tim Weekes' lean frame hadn't changed much in over ten years. The blond hair was now touched with grey, and his once gaunt features had filled out a little with age. But there was still an intensity about the man.

"Drummond, thanks for coming."

The two men shook hands warmly. "Major. It's been a while."

"It's Colonel now, I'm afraid."

"Well-deserved, I'm sure," said Drum, slipping in between the table and the bench.

"Let's order shall we?" Weekes got the attention of the doorman who was standing nearby. "Simmonds, tell the kitchen we're ready, thank you."

The doorman nodded and left the room, closing the door behind him.

"Coffee for breakfast, if I remember," said Weekes, "although in Afghanistan you always drank that awful tea."

"And you probably ordered your favourite: devilled kidneys on toast with two poached eggs."

Weeks smiled. "I guess we're both stuck in our ways."

"Why am I here, Colonel?"

Weekes poured a coffee into a bone china cup from a silver coffee pot . The luxuries of rank, thought Drum.

"It's all a bloody mess," said Weekes. "Sorry I had to involve you. I had no choice. There was no one else I could trust."

"It was you who requested me on the night of the raid," said Drum.

"Yes," continued Weekes. "I was out of options. All last minute.

Heard you had a spot of bother with a Russian."

Drum relaxed into the soft leather of the bench. "Just lent him my screwdriver."

Weekes smiled and stared down into his cup, ruminating on a problem.

Drum pressed on, "Why are the security services attempting to close me down? I thought we were supposed to be on the same side?"

"Bloody mess," repeated Weekes. Finally, he said, "There's a war going on."

"A war? Between who?"

"We believe there's a rogue element operating within MI5 – more likely within government instructing MI5. They've been interfering with our operation – specifically, this operation."

Drum thought it was a bloody mess. "I gather you represent Vauxhall Bridge in this matter?"

Weekes looked up. "Yes, that's right. I head up the Russian desk now. We've been working to track an operation that's connected to some of the top brass in the Kremlin. It involves the movement of large amounts of dirty money from across Europe, all heading for London. We think it's being used to fund intelligence operations against this country."

Drum thought he knew what this operation was called. "OMEGA."

Weekes looked up from his coffee, surprised. "Yes – how did you come by that name?"

"I've been hanging out with too many Russians. I may have a source close to the problem."

Weekes said, "I'm afraid I've put you in a difficult position – a dangerous position. If our Russian friends find out you have this information …"

"It wouldn't be the first time," said Drum. "But I need to see this through. I need to find someone. There's a ROD investigator that's caught up in all of this. I need to bring her in."

"The Auditor at the vault," said Weekes. "Yes, Anna mentioned her. She thought there was something about the woman. And she's missing?"

"It's been a while since she went dark."

Weekes cradled his cup in both hands and looked down. "It doesn't look too good for her, does it."

"I know Harry. She's holed up somewhere …" But even Drum wasn't entirely convinced. Time was running out.

"Look, Drummond. I need you on this one. You're in a prime position to find out what's going on inside that bank." Weekes stopped fiddling with his cup and looked Drum squarely in the eye. "I've been authorised at the highest level to use whatever means necessary to stop this Russian operation. I'm sanctioning you, and whoever you need, to find the primary actors of OMEGA and eliminate them.

25

Drum was officially reactivated. The government made a habit of keeping people with his sort of skills. Weekes had agreed to use Ives and Davis. He'd served with the men, and knew you couldn't pick up experienced SAS soldiers from the local Job Centre. He'd mentioned a third person which surprised Drum.

Weekes had made several calls before he left the restaurant and reined in the attack dogs at MI5. He didn't know how long the truce would last, but he mentioned talking with McKay. Drum wished him good luck with that one.

Drum made his way down the Strand and slid his phone from its protective bag. He called Fern. She answered on the first ring.

"Where the fuck were you?"

"And a good morning to you too," said Drum, flagging down a cab.

"There were reports of gunfire in the market. Was that you?" asked Fern.

"Probably a Ferrari back-firing. Where are you now?"

"I'm heading back to the office – hungry."

"Sorry about that. I was taken for a ride. Look, can we try again. We need to meet before starting work at the bank. How about coffee at the office?" he asked.

There was silence on the line. "Fine. Just be there this time." The phone went dead.

Drum arrived back in time for a minor skirmish of office personnel. Stevie was standing in the reception area in just his shirt. He thought she looked adorable. Alice had other ideas and was letting her know in no uncertain terms that her attire was not appropriate for 9.30 am in the office. Stevie was surprised when Alice returned her expletives with equal venom in her native Russian.

"Sorry, am I interrupting?" said Drum, making his way between the warring factions.

"Ben, thank God. Found this one asleep on your couch when I came in this morning," said Alice.

Drum sat at his desk and retrieved a laptop from one of the drawers. He had a lot to do before the start of the RBI investigation.

Stevie stomped in, firing off a tirade in Russian, with Alice following promptly behind her.

Drum slammed the palm of his hand down on the desk and stood up.

"Enough!"

Stevie's mouth dropped open and Alice looked down at her feet and shuffled on the spot.

"Stevie, go and get dressed, I'm going to need you later."

"But I haven't had breakfast yet," she pouted.

"I'm not your keeper. Alice is in charge of the office. What she says goes. Sort yourself out or fuck off back to Vlad."

Stevie's lower lip stuck out in abject defiance, then quivered. She turned to Alice and said something to her in Russian. Alice nodded in agreement. Stevie padded out of the door and made her way up the stairs to Drum's apartment.

"Can I get you a coffee, Ben?" said Alice, regaining some of her composure.

"Grab a seat, we have work to do."

Alice sat on the couch, carefully smoothing her skirt. Drum noticed she never took notes but could easily repeat any instruction or recall any detail of every meeting.

"Sorry about that," she said. "Didn't mean to cause a ruckus."

"What did Stevie say before she left?" asked Drum.

"Thought you looked very handsome now that you've cleaned up your act. I agreed," said Alice, smiling.

"Right … well, ok then."

Drum went over the events of the morning. Alice listened attentively.

"You were wise to make a run for it. MI5 have a habit of making people disappear. This is a serious escalation," she said.

If Alice was surprised that Anna Koblihova was an MI6 agent, she never showed it. But then Drum guessed that she already knew.

Tell me, Alice," said Drum, leaning back in his chair. "You never really worked at the Treasury, did you?"

Alice gave him a sly smile. "Oh, yes. That part of the story is perfectly true. For the last two years of my career, I was posted at the Department of Special Procurement."

"Special Procurement? Not heard of that one. What was its purpose?"

"It's a special subcommittee of the Treasury." Alice paused and thought for a moment. "Tell me, Ben. What is your current security clearance?"

"Top Secret," said Drum. "But I think you already knew that when you accepted the job."

"Yes, well my last employer insisted on a background check when they knew I was applying for another job."

"You mean the Treasury wanted a background check on me?"

"Oh no," said Alice. "I did work at the Treasury, but I was employed by Her Majesty's Secret Service."

"You worked for MI5?"

"Good Lord, no," said Alice. "Not Thames House – Vauxhall Bridge. I served on the Russian Desk of MI6 for over thirty years. The Treasury posting was my exit ramp out of the service. I was supposed to retire with a full pension, but I ended up butting heads with a real pig over there and I left under a cloud – and without my full pension."

Drum could see that the revelation had hurt Alice. "I'm sorry, Alice. You should have said something."

"Well, it wouldn't be much of a Secret Service if every retired agent blabbed about it, would it?"

Drum nodded. *You can trust Alice.*

"When did you know that Anna was an MI6 agent?"

"On the first visit, really." She glanced up at him. "You have to remember that, during my time in the service, I trained many a young recruit. I recognised Anna – not her real name, you understand."

Drum nodded.

"Of course, I said nothing. I'm retired. And anyway, years of training kicked in. I kept schtum."

"You kept schtum," said Drum.

"Well, what could I do? She knew who I was. I'd marked her down on her language skills. Must have been quite a shock to see me behind the desk." She smiled." I did say to you there was something strange about her accent, but you didn't pick up on it."

"Right," said Drum, "I should have picked up on that one. Anyway,

I met with Colonel Weekes and he suggested I recruit you to the cause. Said I needed you."

"I met him just the once, at a briefing. Didn't know he was your old CO. Small world." She hesitated. "But I'm retired."

Drum stood up. He looked out at the City skyline. It looked dull and grey this morning. The Autumn sunshine had all but disappeared.

"MI6 agents are like old soldiers, Alice. They never retire. They go out fighting. Someone has declared war on us and I need you in my corner. You in or out?"

"I'm in, of course." She cocked her head to one side. "But let's not tell William."

Fern arrived as promised, and Alice discreetly left the room to make the coffee. Fern sat down on the couch. "Well?"

"Sorry about this morning," said Drum. Got called away to an urgent meeting."

She gave him a look, expecting more of an explanation. For some reason he felt reluctant to go into any more detail. Something stopped him mentioning his meetings with Weekes and Anna. For now, he would stick to the assignment brief provided by ROD.

"You're looking nice," she said, grudgingly. "Got a date?"

"Just had a haircut," said Drum, surprised by her comment. He looked at her and smiled. "Anyway, I was hoping for a date with you, once this is all over."

"Maybe," said Fern, trying to hide a smile. Her face softened, and she relaxed into the couch. "What's the plan?"

"We head over to RBI tomorrow and pay Rhodes a visit," said Drum. "The sooner, the better. If Sir Henry is true to his word, he'll be expecting us which means he'll have been covering his tracks."

Fern shifted uneasily. "But what are we going to do there? I'm not up with procedure on these types of operations."

"That's ok. The thing to remember is that this is an investigation. Ostensibly, we're there to audit the bullion inventory."

"But ..."

"That's our way in. From there we try to prove the case of money laundering or corporate malfeasance - they're doing something really bad."

Yeah, right. I do understand what that means."

Alice backed her way into the room carrying a tray of coffee.

"Morning Commander. Nice to see you again," said Alice.

"Morning Alice. You're a life-saver."

Alice put the tray on Drum's desk. "Can I get you anything else, Ben?"

Drum thought he'd have to bite the bullet sooner or later. "Can you send Stevie in."

"Stevie?"

"The Russian woman with a ring through her nose," said Drum. "Make sure she's dressed."

"If you say so." She left and closed the door.

"Good grief," said Fern. "Do you mean to tell me she's another Russian?"

Drum explained the comprise he'd reached with Vlad.

She said, "Are you out of your mind?"

"Well, after the smack on the back of the head – almost."

"Seriously, Drum. She'll compromise the whole operation. She's only here to blab our plans back to Vlad."

"If she's as good as Vlad says she is, I'll need her for the data analysis and cybersecurity side of things. I don't have time to do it all myself."

"You mean she's a common hacker?"

"I'm hoping so. Listen, Fern. It's not ideal. We'll keep her here – strictly back-office. Alice will sit on her."

This seemed to make Fern a little happier. "What a mess. Pour me some coffee," she said.

"Harvey Pinkman," said Drum. "We need to find him. Can the NCA track him down?"

"Technically, the case is closed. But Pinkman is still a person of interest. I'll make some discrete inquiries – I'll start with drug enforcement. He might have a record for possession."

Drum poured coffee as Alice escorted Stevie into his office. Stevie was a little taken aback to see Fern.

"Stevie, this is Commander Fern of the NCA. She'll be working with me on the bank job," said Drum.

The two women eyed each other with suspicion. "Never told me your girlfriend was the fuzz," said Stevie.

Alice let rip with a flurry of Russian that instantly subdued the petulant Stevie. Fern rolled her eyes. Drum asked Alice to stay. He then proceeded to outline the game plan.

"Rhodes and his team will be expecting us. They'll throw all sorts of bullshit and obstacles in our way to hinder the investigation, but our first priorities is to get access to their trading and inventory systems and to check out that vault."

Drum looked over at Stevie who was only half listening.

"Stevie, your job will be data analytics. There'll be a ton of data to sort through – thousands of transactions. Are you familiar with that type of work?"

Stevie looked up. "Sure, but it's a waste of my talents. I'm a much better hacker."

"We call it penetration testing in this business," said Drum.

Stevie gave a little smirk. "Is that what you were showing me the other night?"

"Oh, good grief," exclaimed Fern. "Do I have to listen to this –"

Drum smiled. "Let's just call it hacking. You can use Raj's office and his computer suite."

Stevie shrugged. "Fine."

He turned to Alice. "Any news on Raj?"

"I'm afraid not. My friends at Immigration can't find him. He may well be in an MI5 safe house, somewhere."

Drum wondered if Weekes could do some digging. Failing that, he would have to have a word with McKay. A real close and personal word.

"Don't worry, Ben. We'll find him and bring him home."

They spent the rest of the morning going over their strategy for the investigation. Drum needed to put an actual plan on paper to fire off to Rhodes and the bank's Audit team. They would want to be involved. Drum knew from experience that Internal Audit teams would be ineffective when it came to an investigation, but they'd have a great deal of local knowledge if they were prepared to share. Rhodes would be the problem.

As they were finishing, Alice mentioned another meeting which he had entirely forgotten.

"I've scheduled a meeting at the Bank of England for tomorrow morning," said Alice, as she was about to leave.

"I don't think we have time for this meeting, Alice. Fern and I need to be at the bank at eleven for our opening meeting."

"Trust me on this one, Ben. There is something odd about the chairman suggesting this meeting. I know these Treasury types. Arrogant bastards. Wouldn't give you the time of day, so it's odd that he's agreed to see you. It's only a morning. His secretary has arranged it for 9:30 am. Plenty of time to get back for your meeting with

Rhodes."

They finished up, leaving Drum in the solitude of his office making notes. He had dozens of memos and information requests to type up. Specifically, he wanted access to the RBI computer systems. He knew that the bank would resist this or only give him limited access.

Alice popped her head around the door. "I'm taking Stevie to William's flat. Won't be long."

A thought occurred to Drum. "This meeting tomorrow at the Treasury. Why was it odd that they would want to talk to us?"

Alice closed the door to his office leaving Stevie waiting outside. She hesitated. "I told you I left under a cloud. The person who caused me so much trouble and the reason I left …"

Drum could tell she was fighting something inside – a secret she wasn't supposed to disclose. "Oh, fuck it," she said, finally, and let out her breath with a huff. "The person you're meeting tomorrow … it was Sir Rupert Mayhew."

26

Drum and Fern arrived at the entrance to the Bank of England on Threadneedle Street in time for their meeting with Sir Rupert Mayhew. They walked through the heavy doors and were met by a security guard in a pink livery coat and top hat. He escorted them across the ornate lobby with its mosaic floor and high ceiling supported by pairs of black marble colonnades. The thick granite stone of the masonry and high arched porticos exuded the power of money and the people who controlled it.

They were shown into a room with a large dining table. The table was covered in thick green felt and was surrounded by a set of ornate Edwardian chairs. The ceiling was high and finished with lavish plaster cornices.

"Sir Rupert will be with you shortly," said the Top Hat.

They sat silently beside each other, like two naughty schoolchildren waiting for the Headmaster. They didn't have to wait long. A side door opened and a tallish, thin man bustled in, his steel-grey hair in sharp contrast to his dark, pinstripe suit.

"Rupert Mayhew, sorry to keep you waiting," he said, walking briskly over to Drum with his hand extended.

Drum stood and shook his hand. "Ben Drummond, thank you for seeing us, Sir Rupert."

Sir Rupert shifted his attention to Fern and extended his hand. Fern started to rise and kept rising until she was a good head taller than Sir Rupert. Fern gripped his hand firmly and smiled. "Alex Fern. Pleased to meet you."

Sir Rupert looked up and raised an eyebrow. "Pleasure, I'm sure."

They sat down, Sir Rupert leaning back in his chair.

"Sir Henry thinks you can help us with our investigation at RBI," said Drum.

"Strictly speaking I can't interfere with any investigation of a bank," replied Sir Rupert, "but RBI is an important player in the market, and as someone who has a role to play in the governance of banks, Sir Henry thought we should meet."

"What is your role, exactly?" asked Fern.

Sir Rupert looked over the rim of his glasses and regarded her with a frown. It was clear to Drum that he wasn't used to people asking him for his job description.

"Well … I have a number of roles in the Treasury and advise the Cabinet on banking regulation, among other things." He turned his attention back to Drum. "I'm largely responsible for the buying and selling of gold bullion for the Treasury, which is why Minton thought I could advise you. You're there to audit the bank's inventory I understand?"

Drum noticed that Sir Rupert had dropped Sir Henry's title.

"Yes," said Drum. "The Custody Officer at the bank raised an issue with their Audit and Risk Committee who raised it with the board."

Sir Rupert frowned. "And what issue was that?"

"Someone has made off with all the gold," replied Fern, with all the finesse of a police officer during an interrogation.

Sir Rupert turned to her and smiled. "I don't think that would be possible, my dear girl. There was obviously a computer error. No one makes off with a bank vault of gold bullion."

Fern's brow creased into a deep frown and she sat up a little straighter. "And why not may I ask?"

Drum thought that calling Fern a 'dear girl' may have been an unintended slight by Sir Rupert, but something made him think otherwise. The man had an arrogance about him. Alice was right to despise him.

"Well for one thing," explained Sir Rupert, "you would need a train to transport it – providing, of course, you could bypass all of the security." He paused as if considering something. "This is probably the reason why Minton wanted us to talk. Let me show you." He rose and walked over to a telephone. He punched in a number. "Jarvis? Mayhew. Can you bring up the sample I requested? Yes, all reasonable precautions. Yes, yes, I'll take full responsibility."

Sir Rupert returned to the table with a satisfied smugness. "Won't be long."

"I'm sure you're right," said Drum as they waited. "Sir Henry's been told it's an error with the inventory system not being updated. We'll probably find it's been logged to a different vault."

"Precisely," said Sir Rupert, smiling warmly. "So what will your investigation entail, exactly?"

Drum kept a mask of conviviality in place and smiled. "Oh, you know, the usual things. Check vault security. Audit the inventory. Standard stuff really."

"Right, right," agreed Sir Rupert. "Standard Audit Program I would imagine?"

Before Drum could answer, there was a knock on the door.

"Come," bellowed Sir Rupert.

The door opened and in walked two security guards. One was carrying a small, rough wooden crate, held by rope handles at each end. He placed the crate on one end of the table. The second security guard then removed a pair of white gloves from his pocket and opened the lid of the crate. He reached inside with both hands, withdrew a large bar of gold bullion and placed it in the centre of the table. The guard then took off his gloves and set them beside the bar.

"Thank you, gentlemen. Please wait outside," ordered Sir Rupert.

Drum and Fern both stared at the bar of gold on the table. Drum was in awe of it's lustre. He'd seen small pieces of gold before, but never so large an amount. It seemed to radiate a warm glow. It was hypnotic. Fern also seemed captivated by its presence.

Sir Rupert chuckled, "It's a thing of beauty, isn't it. I'm always amused by people's reaction to the stuff. I see these bars every day and still …"

"It's incredible," said Fern. She went to touch the bar.

"Put the gloves on, please. We mustn't damage it."

Fern put both gloves on and waited for Sir Rupert's instruction.

"What you're both ogling at is what we in the trade call a 'good delivery bar'. You can't buy this over the counter. It's what banks trade between themselves. It's what is stored at RBI – or should be."

Drum examined the bar. It didn't look that big, about the size of a house brick but longer. "What are those markings on the top?" asked Drum pointing to an elaborate crest stamped into the gold.

"The big mark is the assayer's stamp," explained Sir Rupert. "This bar was smelted in Zurich. There are only a few assayers that can smelt good delivery bars. The long string of numbers is the serial number. Every bar should have a unique number. Finally, there's a series of digits denoting the fineness, usually 99.999. This tells you the purity of the metal to three significant digits."

"There's no weight?" asked Drum.

"No, that's right. Every bar varies slightly to within a few troy ounces. When the Vault Manager accepts a bar, he or she must weigh it and confirm the weight against the delivery note which records the serial number of the bar and the weight when it left the smelters."

"I see," said Drum, half to himself. He was thinking of the task ahead with the audit of the RBI vault. This could be quite a job.

"Now, you look like a strong girl, Ms Fern," said Sir Rupert. "Try and pick it up – but with only one hand."

Fern looked at Drum. He shrugged. Looked easy. She reached across the table and gripped the bar firmly – and heaved. The bar hardly budged.

"Go on, put your back into it," roared Sir Rupert, egging her on.

Fern gritted her teeth and heaved again. This time she managed to lift the bar a few centimetres off the table.

"It's incredibly heavy," admitted Fern. "It doesn't look it, but I could barely move it."

"Gold is one of the heaviest materials on the planet - well, barring uranium," explained Sir Rupert. "But you wouldn't want to pick that up." He chuckled. "The only metal that comes close to its density is tungsten."

"The stuff they make the lightbulbs from?" asked Drum.

"Yes, that's the stuff, but it's a dull grey colour and not as pretty. The bar you see here is close to four hundred troy ounces or thirteen kilos. Dealers tend to work in ounces, but our European friends prefer kilos. The same size bar of tungsten would be slightly lighter and far less expensive."

"What is this bar worth," asked Fern.

Sir Rupert considered the question. "Let me see. The spot price of gold per troy ounce on the market today is around $1,200." He laughed. "Even though we are the Bank of England, we still price gold in US dollars. So you do the maths."

"So this four hundred ounce bar would be worth ..." Drum paused for just a second. "Four hundred and eighty thousand dollars."

"Bloody hell," exclaimed Fern.

"Quite so," agreed Sir Rupert. "And I would imagine there would be hundreds of such bars in the vault of RBI."

Drum remembered Sir Henry Minton's words back in New York.

Every ounce ...

27

The meeting with Sir Rupert finished amicably. It wasn't a long meeting, just enough time for Sir Rupert to persuade them that nothing untoward was happening at RBI. Drum was surprised by how much he had learnt about the gold bullion business. He and Fern both agreed that the meeting had been useful. It was clear that to audit the vault they would need the original delivery notes of all gold shipments to and from RBI. Drum made a mental note to add that to his list of materials he'd requested.

They now had just enough time to get to their meeting with Rhodes. Outside the bank, Drum flagged down a taxi.

"What did you make of our friend, Sir Rupert?" asked Fern, as she clambered into the back of the cab.

Drum gave the driver the address of The Undershaft. He thought about the question. There was something odd about the meeting. Alice was surprised Sir Rupert had agreed to it.

"He clearly has an interest in the investigation," said Drum. "But then he does advise the Cabinet on banking. He doesn't like Sir Henry very much, that is clear."

"Yeah, I kinda picked up on that as well," agreed Fern. She turned to face him. "Are we really going to have to weigh hundreds of bars of gold?"

"Looks like it," said Drum. "But if Victor is right, the vault should be empty."

The cab made good time through the busy City traffic and turned into a small road beside the building most Londoners referred to as The Gherkin. Drum and Fern walked the short distance to the Victorian, red-brick building that now housed RBI's secondary dealing centre. Drum realised they were at the back of the Leadenhall building.

Drum paused just before the entrance. "Before we meet with Rhodes, just a word of advice."

"What word would that be?" said Fern raising an eyebrow.

"I've dealt with these types before. They think they are the real power-brokers behind the business. Rhodes is likely to throw all sorts of obstacles at us and try to deny us access to sensitive areas of the bank. All we have to remember is that this is an investigation, not an audit. We're here at the request of the RBI board."

"Right," said Fern. "Got it."

They entered the reception area and were greeted by Rhode's PA. She introduced herself as Samantha Jenkins. But they could call her Sam.

"Mr Rhodes is expecting you," she said, with a smile. "He's with the Audit Director, Mr Simmonds."

She led them through a large room where rows of dealers were standing and shouting out there trades over the tops of computer screens, mobile phones pressed to their ears. They came to a set of large oak doors. Sam knocked and then heaved open one of the doors and walked in.

"Mr Drummond and Ms Fern, Mr Rhodes." She turned to them. "Can I get you anything?"

"No thanks, Sam. We're good."

Fern rolled her eyes and shook her head. "At least she's not Russian."

Rhodes was seated behind a large ornate desk in front of a tall arched window. The place reminded Drum of an Edwardian drawing room with dark oak bookcases lining one wall and two dark brown couches. The floor was covered with a large Persian rug. Rhodes appeared to be engrossed in a document. A short, balding man in a poorly fitting suit was standing next to the desk, looking anxiously in their direction. Drum assumed he was the Audit Director.

If Rhodes was aware that they had entered the room, he did not acknowledge the fact. He carried on scribbling on the sheets of paper in front of him. Drum realised the sheets were his Request for Material – all the documents and data that he would need to complete the investigation.

It was Fern who first broke the silence. She was not accustomed to being kept waiting.

"Good morning," she said, in a tone that was more suited to felons being read their rights.

Rhodes looked up but made no attempt to introduce himself or to offer them a seat. It was typical of the reception that he was subjected to during the opening meeting of an investigation.

Rhodes eventually put down his pen with a sigh. "I understand you're here to audit the operation, Mr ... Drummond. Make sure you submit your audit plan to Simmons here for his approval before you start." He nodded in the general direction of his Audit Director. "That way it will give us time to provide you with the information you need and allow us to get our ducks in tow."

"That won't be necessary," said Drum, calmly.

Rhodes pushed the papers away and sat back. "And why not?"

Fern jumped in before Drum could continue. "Because Mr Rhodes, this is not an audit. It's an investigation." She smiled with satisfaction.

Drum waited for the inevitable riposte. Rhodes would want to protect his client's confidentiality.

"Nevertheless," pressed Rhodes, "we must protect our client's confidentiality so it's important we are clear that you have the authority to see our client list and any transactions."

Drum smiled grimly. Rhodes was not used to having his authority questioned. He was the gatekeeper to this part of the RBI enterprise.

"You misunderstand the nature of this ... investigation," countered Drum. We have the full authority of the board to see all and any information we deem necessary. I'd also like to remind you that we're here at the behest of the FCA and the DOJ and they'll be expecting that we leave no stone unturned – to paraphrase Sir Henry."

At the mention of Sir Henry Minton, Rhodes' face went bright pink. Sir Henry appeared to be a popular chap, mused Drum.

"Of course," replied Rhodes, standing up from his desk. He looked at Simmonds for support.

"It's just that this request you've sent," responded Simmonds, looking with some anxiety to his superior. "It's just ... well, you've asked for a lot of information."

"It's bloody ridiculous if you ask me," retorted Rhodes. The information you've asked for ... must be thousands of transactions?"

Fern stared down at Rhodes. "Don't worry we have big computers."

Drum smiled. He wondered if Fern had meant to be sarcastic. Apparently, Rhodes was beginning to piss her off.

"We'd like to start by inspecting the vault," said Drum.

At the mention of the vault, Rhodes' face turned a deeper shade of pink. "I can assure you, Drummond," he retorted," there is nothing to worry about regarding the security of our operation. It's first-rate. And anyway, I think it's out of scope."

Drum had come across people like Rhodes all too often in his career, and he was beginning to tire of the game. "I understand that your vault manager is missing –"

"Not missing, Drummond," replied Rhodes, an air of smugness returning to his voice. "Harvey Pinkman was let go."

Drum and Fern looked at each other. This was a new but not unexpected development. Pinkman was key to this whole fiasco. Drum wasn't surprised that he was no longer around to answer an awkward question like 'where is all the gold'?

"Regardless", said Drum, "we'll want to start with the physical security of the vault. Standard stuff. Have your people meet us down there this afternoon. And I'll want full access to your vault and any anterooms. It would also be helpful to have your head of security meet with me today so I can explain the access we want to your systems." With that he did a sharp about-turn and headed for the door. Fern followed hard on his heels.

"A little prickly, wasn't he," said Fern, under her breath, as they were walking out the door.

"Yeah, a right little prick," replied Drum. "C'mon let's get to the vault before evidence starts to disappear".

There was something he'd forgotten. Something he needed for the audit of the bullion. He suddenly remembered what Sir Rupert had said in their meeting at the Bank of England. He stopped and walked back into the office.

"There's one more information request that I'd like make before we visit the vault," said Drum.

"What might that be?" ventured Simmonds.

"I'd like all documentation on all shipments of bullion to and from the bank's vault for the last month," replied Drum.

Simmonds' frowned. He looked anxiously at his master. Rhodes simply smiled.

"You have that information already," said Rhodes with a smirk.

Drum was confused. "I do?"

"Yes," answered Simmonds. "All delivery notes and Bills of Ladin are digitally scanned and stored on computer by the Vault Manager. We don't keep paper records any more."

"Then I'll need access to those files," said Drum, getting a little frustrated by the runaround.

"What Simmonds is trying to tell you, Drummond," said Rhodes, "is that Pinkman always scanned them directly onto his laptop." He smiled once more. "And I believe you already have that."

"You're angry," said Fern as they left The Undershaft. The sky was overcast and threatening rain.

Drum stopped and looked across the street to the Cheesegrater. They were at the rear of the building, a vertical wall of polished glass and steel that reflected back the threatening sky. "How can you tell?"

"You ignored the smiles of the skinny Samantha."

"Skinny Samantha?" said Drum, raising an eyebrow.

Fern gave him a sideways glance. "Well, she could do with a bit more meat on her bones."

Drum relaxed. "I'm just pissed that Rhodes thinks he got one over on us."

"Yeah, you said that might happen. I could easily have beaten the crap out of the little creep."

"Right," said Drum. "Let's put that on our to do list."

"What now? We're screwed without Pinkman's laptop."

"Maybe. But first things first." Drum started to cross the street.

"Where are we going?" asked Fern as she strode across the road to catch up.

"We need to pay a visit to Human Resources. We'll need a list of all personnel that have recently joined or left the company. We need to confirm if Pinkman and Harry have actually left RBI as everyone keeps telling us."

They reached the back entrance to the building. Fern flashed her credentials, and they were escorted to the elevator bank.

Fern looked up at the vertical glass shaft disappearing above them. "I hate these things," she said.

Drum looked at her. "You've never struck me as the nervous type?"

Fern gave him a withering look. "I just hate these exposed elevator cars … "

They exited on the tenth floor and stepped out into a familiar reception area.

"The floors must all be built to the same layout," said Drum as he approached the desk. A young man was busy at a computer terminal.

"Deja vu," said Fern.

"Hello," said the receptionist, looking up from his screen. "Can I help you?"

"We're looking for Beth Flack, HR," said Drum.

"Who shall I say is here?" said the young man.

Fern was just about to flash her warrant card when Drum stayed her hand. "Just say that it's Roderick Olivier and Delaney."

"Oh, right. We were told you might be coming. Hold on." He picked up the phone. "Hi, Ms Flack. The two investigators are here … right." He put the phone down and smiled. "She's expecting you. Go straight through."

They walked down a short corridor and were met by a stout lady in her mid-forties with cropped brown hair. "Hi, I'm Beth Flack, Head of HR," she said, extending her hand.

"New York," said Drum, as he took her hand. She spoke in a husky breathlessness, possibly the result of too many cigarettes. "Long Island, I'm guessing."

"Well … yes! That is very observant of you, Mr …"

Drum gave her his warmest smile. "Ben Drummond. But call me Ben."

Beth Flack returned his smile. She wore a dark-pink lipstick, accentuated by a slightly darker lip pencil, so it looked like she had a permanent pout.

"Alex Fern. Pleased to meet you," interjected Fern, thrusting out her hand.

"Goodness. Yes … Sorry. Pleased to meet you. This way."

They followed her into a well-furnished office. She sat down behind a large desk and waved in the general direction of a couch. "Please take a seat. I've been preparing for you."

"You have?" said Fern, as she seated herself beside Drum.

"Oh yes," Flack replied. "All senior staff received a memo from Sir Henry. We're to help you in any way we can." She gave them both her very best Human Resources smile.

Drum wondered how many people she had fired over the years, all receiving the very same smile with a pout of her pink-lined lips.

"What can you tell us about Harvey Pinkman?" said Fern, cutting to the chase.

"Ah, yes." Flack turned to her desktop computer. She typed a few keystrokes and stared at the screen. "He has been terminated."

Fern looked at Drum in surprise.

"Beth means he's been let go. Moved on to pastures new –"

"Right, I get the idea," said Fern with a scowl.

"That's right," said Flack. "I forget I'm not in New York. You use different expressions over here."

"When was he let go," asked Drum, but thinking that termination was probably a more likely explanation of Pinkman's disappearance.

Flack made a big show of studying the information displayed on her screen. "About two weeks ago," she said, smiling.

"How convenient," said Fern under her breath.

"How about Harriet Seymour-Jones," continued Drum, although he knew what the answer would be."

Again, Flack stabbed a few keys and stared at her screen. "Term … she was also let go."

"At the same time," said Fern.

"Well … yes! Now how did you know that?"

"Just a lucky guess," said Fern, with a look of exasperation on her face.

"But Seymour-Jones was a contractor," continued Flack. "It says here her contract was up."

Drum thought he would try for an address, but knew the answer he would get. "Could you provide us with a contact address for Seymour-Jones?"

Flack looked at her screen and then back at Drum, her lips pursed into a perfect bow. "Well … I would like to help, but you guys have such strict Data Protection laws, over here. I just couldn't give out that information." She tilted her head to one side and smiled.

Fern was starting to get up when Drum grabbed her hand. "You feeling alright, Alex?"

Fern sat on the edge of the couch and looked at him. "I'm fine," she said, frowning.

"No, really," pressed Drum, squeezing her hand. "You're looking a little queasy."

"Oh, dear …" exclaimed Flack. "Can I get you some water?"

"You look like you're going to throw up. Something you ate, perhaps?" continued Drum.

"Oh, no," said Flack, fearing a mess in her lovely office. "Let me take you to the bathroom."

Fern rose from the couch as Flack ran from behind her desk and tried to help her up. "It's alright," said Fern as she towered over the shorter woman. "Just lead me to the loo." She scowled at Drum as she and Flack left the office.

Drum quickly closed the door and moved over to Flack's desk. He had less than a minute before her screen saver kicked in and locked him out. He punched a few keys and brought up Harry's address. He heard footsteps outside in the corridor. He quickly memorised the information on the screen then hit the Esc key. The RBI corporate screen-saver appeared. He quickly made his way back to the couch just as Flack opened the door.

"False alarm," said Flack, with a cheery smile. Fern filed in behind her and stood in the doorway.

"Well," said Drum jumping up, "we mustn't take up any more of your time." He extended his hand to Flack who took it gently in hers.

"You're welcome," she said, huskily, giving him her very best pout. "If you need anything else, Ben ..."

"I know where to find you ..."

"C'mon ... *Ben*. I'm starving," shouted Fern as she strode down the corridor.

Drum caught up with her at the elevator. "Feeling better?" he asked, with a grin.

"Good grief, Drum. If you laid on the charm any thicker, I might really want to puke."

28

The next day Drum visited Fern at the NCA offices just off Vauxhall Bridge. By the time they had reviewed the paperwork needed for the investigation, it was late afternoon when they left for the vault. Drum hailed a taxi and gave the driver the address of the RBI vault in Blackfriars. Fern sat moodily beside him. He wondered why she was so irritated.

"You got Harry's address, right?" asked Fern

"Right."

"So why are we going to the vault? Shouldn't we head for Harry's apartment? The gold won't be going anywhere."

"Probably not – if it's there at all. And I doubt we'll find much at Harry's apartment either. She's not going to be there."

"It's your call," said Fern, and went back to staring moodily out of the window.

The taxi dropped them outside the RBI building on the banks of the Thames. A light rain was falling, and the horns of the pleasure boats passing beneath Blackfriars Bridge sounded mournfully in the darkening gloom of the day.

Fern looked up at the building. "This is a bank vault? Looks more like a French chateau."

They were met in the lobby by a thick-set security guard. He escorted them to a large room, ornately furnished in a Regency style. They were greeted by a tall, slim woman dressed in the corporate dark-grey of RBI who looked like she hadn't slept in a while.

"Rosalind Baxter," she said. "I'm the Security Administrator."

"Ben Drummond, Senior ROD Investigator," said Drum, taking her hand. "And this is my partner, Alex Fern."

Baxter smiled weakly at Fern. "We've been expecting you," she said and moved to her ornate Regency desk where she retrieved two cards.

"Your security passes. They'll get you into most areas. Keep them on you at all times. But ..."

"But what?" asked Fern, opening her jacket and attaching her card to a zip holder on the front of her belt. Fern looked up and saw Baxter staring at her gun."

"We don't allow firearms in the building, I'm afraid," said Baxter, looking anxiously between Drum and Fern.

Fern reached into her jacket pocket and retrieved her warrant card and waived it in front of Baxter's nose. "I'm authorised to carry a firearm by her Majesty's government." She snapped the card shut. "So let's get to the vault, shall we?"

Drum's mind seemed elsewhere. He appeared to be scanning the room and looking up at the high ceiling with its ornate, plaster cornices.

"You coming?" asked Fern.

"Right behind you," he replied.

They followed Baxter out into the lobby and walked further into the building before reaching an elevator beside a large wooden staircase. Baxter waved her card over a side panel, and the doors to the elevator slid open.

"The vault is below us," she said, pressing a button marked one. There was a whine of a motor and they started to slowly descend.

Drum continued scanning around him. So far he had counted six security cameras, not including the one in the elevator.

"Mr Rhodes phoned through this morning," continued Baxter. "Said you might be stopping by, so I've arranged for the Vault Manager and someone from the Custody department to meet us there."

"Who is representing Audit?" asked Drum.

"That would be Mr Simmonds. Head of Internal Audit," replied Baxter.

The elevator bumped to a stop. They walked out into a marbled corridor, illuminated warmly by up-lights running along the length of each wall. At the far end of the corridor was the huge, steel door of the vault, brightly picked out by two spotlights in the ceiling.

"Bloody hell," exclaimed Fern. "It's huge."

Drum counted three more security cameras in this area.

Three people were waiting for them. "This is Walter Baker, our Vault Manager," said Baxter, indicating a young, nervous-looking man. "Mr

Simmonds, our Head of Internal Audit, who I believe you've already met, and Sarah French from our Custody department." She waited until introductions were over and said "Right. I'll leave you in the good hands of Mr Simmonds. I'll be upstairs if you need me." She turned back to the elevator.

"There is just one more thing," said Drum. "I'll need security access to the RBI network and some of its systems."

Baxter looked at Simmonds who nodded. "See me upstairs when you've finished down here," she said and walked briskly back up the corridor.

Fern turned to Drum. "Can we get this show on the road? It's getting late."

Drum glanced at his watch. It was nearly three o'clock. He turned to Simmonds. "Mr Simmonds. Nice to see you again. Can you give us a tally of the contents of the vault?"

Simmonds turned to the Custody Officer. "Sarah?"

"According to our records we have approximately six metric tons of gold bullion stored in the vault, as of today," she said, clutching her tablet with both hands.

Drum recalled that this was the number of tons of gold Victor was expecting to see in the vault. If Victor's account was correct, the vault should either be empty or have gold missing. He turned to the Vault Manager. "Do you have a list of inventory – a breakdown by bar, weight and serial number?"

Walter Baker glanced at Simmonds and then back to Drum. "Yes … of course. I can print one for you now." He looked over at Sarah. "Sarah, be a love and print Mr Drummond the bar list."

She blinked. "Oh, sure. No problem." She looked at her tablet and stabbed at the screen. The sound of a printer could be heard in a small anteroom just off from the vault. "Won't be a minute," she said and disappeared into the room.

"Right," said Drum. "Let's open her up."

Walter walked over to a side panel, fixed to the wall beside the vault door. He activated the panel with his card key then placed his hand on its surface. A bright, green bar of light appeared at the top of the panel and moved slowly down to the bottom, scanning his hand in the process. The panel turned blue, and he stepped back. "Can you all please move back from the door," he said.

A klaxon sounded. A small vibration was felt beneath the floor and then the whine of electric motors spinning up. The huge steel door began to open – centimetre by centimetre.

Lights inside the room began to flicker on as the vault door completed its arc and slowly came to a stop. Drum was the first to move inside, followed swiftly by Fern.

Drum was standing in the middle of a well-lit room with a high ceiling and a smooth concrete floor. On the far wall were rows of numbered safety deposit boxes. The two side walls were recessed to form large alcoves within which were placed wooden pallets, piled high with stacks of bright yellow bars of gold bullion.

"Good grief," said Fern. "There must be hundreds of them."

Sarah French walked into the vault, followed by Simmonds and Walter Baker. "Sarah," said Simmonds, looking around in awe. "How many bars are stored in here?"

Sarah checked her tablet. "Six metric tons stored as four hundred and eighty-two bars." She held up a several page of printout. "Here's a list of bars and their individual serial numbers and weights."

Fern turned to Drum who was busy looking around the vault. He had his hand pressed to the floor. "What now?" she asked.

Drum stood and looked up at the ceiling and noted two more cameras. "We count, weigh and record the serial numbers of each bar," he said matter of factly.

"I was afraid you'd say that," said Fern with a sigh. Drum started to walk out of the vault. "Hey, where are you going?"

"I need to talk to Ms Baxter – before she goes home," said Drum.

"How am I supposed to record all of this?" shouted Fern. "I haven't brought a laptop."

Drum turned to Sarah French. "Sarah, please create a new spreadsheet for Fern. Record the details of each bar as they are weighed and email it to me." He handed Sarah his business card and started back up the corridor

"What am I supposed to do?" asked Fern dejectedly.

"Shoot anyone who tries to run off with any of the bars," Drum said, disappearing into the elevator.

Drum found Rosalind Baxter at her desk, poring over a computer screen. Two new security guards, heavily-built, had also materialised and were standing at the back of the room, keeping silent watch on a nervous Baxter. They looked more like muscle than security, thought Drum. This was confirmed when one of them shifted slightly revealing the bulge of a weapon beneath his jacket.

"Hello, Rosalind," said Drum, cheerily as he took a seat in front of her desk. "Sorry to keep you so late."

Baxter looked up. The computer's glow washed over her face adding to the pallor of her skin and the tiredness of her eyes. "Hello, Mr Drummond. That's ok."

"Call me Ben," he said. "I wanted to ask you about the level below the vault. The red button in the elevator … "

Baxter's eyes flickered sideways and then back to him. "A storage level … it's closed."

He glanced to the back of the room. "Never mind … not important." He gave her a reassuring smile. "About that security clearance."

Baxter nodded and smiled weakly. "I've given you this level of access. Hope it's what you wanted?" She quickly turned the screen around to face him.

One of the guards behind Baxter suddenly took an interest, peering to try to get a better look at what she was revealing. Drum glanced at the screen. A standard security profile was displayed, except that in one of the boxes marked 'Comments' Baxter had written a telephone number and the words 'Call me'. Drum nodded, and she flipped the screen back again.

"That looks fine," he said, rising from his chair. "I won't keep you any longer." He made his way back to the vault, saving her number into his phone.

29

It was gone eight o'clock when Drum and Fern finished their audit of the vault. It was dark, and a cold wind blew off the Thames. It had started to rain.

"Great!" said Fern. "Now I'm going to get soaked."

Drum braved the rain, leaving the shelter of the lobby to flag down a taxi. They were soon bundled into the back and driving along the Victoria Embankment towards the City.

"You look beat," said Drum.

"I've just shifted six tons of gold from one room to another and back again."

"What did you learn?" asked Drum.

"That gold is very heavy," replied Fern, exasperated.

"Yes," said Drum, thoughtfully. "They knew we were coming. They must have covered their tracks."

"Or Victor Renkov is a lying shit," said Fern.

"There is always that." He looked at his phone. There was the email from Sarah French with a spreadsheet attached. "The only way to check if the gold in the vault is complete is to compare our tally with the inventory on the Rhodes computer system. But even that could have been altered by now. And we really need the original delivery notes from Pinkman's computer to be doubly sure."

"So we're screwed," said Fern. She looked out of the window. "What a waste of time."

"Not necessarily," replied Drum. He hit the speed dial on his phone.

"Hi, Rosalind. Ben Drummond. Sorry to call you so late." He listened for a short while. "Ok, I understand. I'm texting you the information I need. Send it to the secure location in the text ... right. I'll be in touch."

Fern turned to him. "Baxter?"

"She had company when I went to see her. She couldn't talk. I think she's being coerced. She's sending me some information I think will be useful."

"What now?" asked Fern.

"I think I owe you dinner," said Drum, trying to read her expression in the dim interior of the cab.

"You owe me more than dinner," replied Fern, turning to look at him.

Drum smiled. "I think that can be arranged." There was silence. She moved a little closer to him, bent her head towards him and kissed him on the lips. The street lights of the City invaded the darkness of the cab, and he caught her smiling.

"But first …" He reached for his phone and scrolled down until he found the note he was looking for. He read out a new address to the cabby.

"What! You have got to be joking," said Fern, slumping back into her seat.

"We're not far from Harry's apartment. It's close to the Barbican … and Smithfield market is nearby. A quick in and out and then a great steak."

"Yeah, right," sighed Fern. "I've heard that one before."

Harry's apartment was on the first floor of a relatively new building. It was accessed via a gated lobby. They waited until a couple came out and then breezed in before the door could close and lock. They took the stairwell to the first-floor landing and walked along it until they came to the door number that Drum had memorised from the HR directory. There were no lights from inside the apartment.

"I hope you realise that this counts as breaking and entering," said Fern as she bent down and inserted her credit card between the lock and the door jam.

"That's probably the reason you're so good at it," retorted Drum.

Fern gave the door a sharp push, and the lock clicked open. She reached inside her jacket pocket for a pen light, drew her gun and pushed the door open with her foot.

Drum followed her inside. Fern played her light down the length of a narrow hallway. She moved through a doorway on her right, her gun raised, her light illuminating the space beyond. She relaxed and lowered her weapon.

"Looks like it's empty," she said, straightening and holstering her gun.

Drum found a light switch and flicked it on. They were inside a spacious lounge with a small kitchen-diner towards the rear. It had been minimally furnished; now it looked like a bomb had gone off inside the place.

Fern took a few steps, her feet crunching glass underfoot as she surveyed the scene. "Looks like someone's trashed the place."

Drum carefully manoeuvered his way through the debris, careful not to disturb the scene. "Someone was looking for something, but don't ask me what." His foot crunched down onto a glass photo frame. "Blast …" He bent down and picked up the shattered remains. Harry and a young Jimmy Miller smiled back at him. He recognised the place. It was taken while on their last assignment together in Mexico City. He peeled out the photo and turned it over. 'Zurich', a date then a long string of numbers were written on the back. He frowned and put the photo in his pocket.

Fern moved through an adjoining doorway and switched on the light. "Bedroom."

Drum followed her in, and they started to search the place, rifling through drawers.

"Hello," said Fern, peering into a large closet. "What's this?" She held up a slim, red leather corset and a long pair of black leather boots. "Looks like Harry was into some kinky stuff."

Drum came over and examined the corset. He looked at Fern.

"Don't get any ideas, sunshine. I'd never squeeze into something like this."

Drum smiled, raising an eyebrow. "I didn't think Harry was into this sort of thing."

Fern frowned and gave him a hard look. "Were you two … y'know?"

Drum laughed. "No … nothing like that."

Fern sighed. "That's alright then." She was in the process of putting the clothes back when Drum noticed a card on the floor. He picked it up.

"Looks like an invitation to a club in Mayfair. Some special gala."

Fern looked at the invitation. "It's for tomorrow night."

Drum reached for his phone and walked back outside into the lounge. He dialled William.

"Allo, son. Everything alright?"

"Sorry to call you so late. Is Alice there?"

There was a pause.

"Hi, Ben."

"Sorry to disturb your evening Alice –"

"Oh, tsk, tsk. What do you need?"

"Ever heard of the Lantern Club?"

"Why yes," whispered Alice, after a brief pause. "It's an upmarket S&M club. We kept a close eye on the place, back in the day. Frequented by members of the Cabinet who should know better. Why'd you ask?"

"Right," said Drum, amazed at the secrets Alice kept. "Got a lead on Harry. How do I get in?"

"Well … it's pretty exclusive. A private members club by day and a knocking shop by night." There was a pause on the line. "For a start, you'll need a female companion with suitable attire."

"Sorry, Alice. I think this goes way beyond your job description."

A high-pitched cackle erupted from the phone. "Oh my. You're so like your dad. No, I was thinking of Commander Fern."

Drum's thoughts were dragged to the sight of Fern in a slim, red leather corset. "I don't think I could ask Fern –"

"Oh poppycock," said Alice. "She'll be glad to go. Anyway, she likes you. You men can be so dense sometimes."

Fern came out of the bedroom. She tilted her head to one side querying who he was calling. He smiled warmly back at her.

"If you say so, Alice. Now how do I get an invite?"

"Well … I still have a contact at the club. He can get you in."

"Great," said Drum. "What's his name?"

She went silent for several seconds. Alice was not used to disclosing information over an open line. Eventually, she said, "His codename is Giles."

30

"There was no blood at the scene?" asked Alice. She and Stevie perched on Drum's office couch.

It was nine in the morning, and he was dog tired. Yesterday had been a long day – and the night even longer. "No. None that I could see."

"That's a good sign," added Alice.

"How do you figure that?" asked Stevie.

Drum thought she was looking more presentable in a new pair of jeans and a clean, white t-shirt.

"It shows she's probably still alive – maybe in hiding," said Alice. "Whoever trashed the place was looking for something. If they had Harry they would have found it by now."

Drum picked up the photo from Harry's apartment. "What do you make of this?" He leant over his desk and handed the photo to Alice.

"Is that Harry? Beautiful hair."

"Is she your girlfriend?" asked Stevie, her eyebrows raised.

Drum sighed. "No Stevie. Not every woman I work with is my girlfriend."

Stevie pouted her lips. "Pity."

Drum smiled. He liked Stevie's impish sense of humour. Well, most of the time. "What do you make of the note on the back?"

Alice flipped the photo over. Stevie peered over her shoulder. "A location and date – not sure what the number is," said Alice, passing the photo to Stevie. "What about it?"

"I remember the location," said Drum. "It's not Zurich. It was taken in Mexico City – and not on that date."

"What was special about Zurich?" asked Stevie, running her finger over the long number.

"Harry was working on an assignment with a guy called Mueller," said Drum.

"Hans Mueller?" said Stevie. "The hacker?"

Drum sat forward. "Yes, do you know him?"

"Heard of him. He was outed and arrested a few years back for hacking a government database. He claimed to have reformed and turned 'White Hat' … that's a good guy, Alice."

"I'm not that old, dear, or technically inept."

"Where is he now?" asked Stevie.

Drum sat back and sighed. "He's dead."

"Oh …"

"Keep hold of it," said Drum. "You might figure out what it means."

"You have data for me?" asked Stevie, smiling. "Or did you and Commander Fern not get around to that?"

Alice tittered.

"I've sent you a link to a secure cloud location that Raj and I both use," said Drum, ignoring Stevie's jibe. "You'll find a list of all the inventory we found in the vault. Approximately six metric tons of gold made up of 482 bars."

"Vlad's gold?" said Stevie, a little surprised. "Shouldn't we tell him?"

Drum paused. "We don't know who that gold belongs to. Victor reports the gold missing and a week later it magically reappears."

"Perhaps it was just a massive cock-up," said Alice.

"I'm not buying that," replied Drum. "Something's not right at the vault. Someone is hiding something." He told them about Rosalind Baxter.

"Who were the heavies?" asked Alice. "Vlad's men?"

"I don't think so," said Drum. He shrugged. "Either way, she was very nervous. But she did send me digital copies of the vault security tapes for the past week and the bullion inventory as listed on the RBI computer system." He turned to Stevie. "They're stored on our secure cloud service. I've installed the encryption key on Raj's desktop. Compare the list of bars we audited last night to what's recorded on the RBI database."

"What am I looking for?" asked Stevie.

"Any anomaly. If everything is kosher, both lists should be the same."

"I'll run a few statistical analyses on the data and see what pops up," said Stevie. "What about the security tapes? There must be hours of them."

"I can help with that," said Alice. "Not the first time I've had to pore over hours of security footage."

"Really?" said Stevie, giving Alice a puzzled look.

"A woman of many talents is our Alice," said Drum with a chuckle. "What about tonight?"

"I've spoken to my contact at the club." She gave Stevie a sideways glance. "The one we spoke about last night. It's a gala evening so just black tie for you and a cocktail dress for Fern." She paused. "You asked her, right?"

"She's out buying a dress as we speak," sighed Drum.

"You have a tux?"

"I'll hire one."

"Tsk, tsk," replied Alice. "Go to this place." She scribbled an address in the City on a pad on his desk. "Tell them Alice sent you. They'll provide you with a jacket with a little more room."

"A little more room for what?"

"The Sig Sauer of course," replied Alice.

Drum stood under an awning erected at the entrance of an Edwardian terrace that was home to the Mayfair club. It was eight in the evening and Commander Fern was fashionably late. The night was chill, and the earlier rain had subsided to a light drizzle leaving the London streets smelling fresh.

Limousines pulled up, together with the occasional black cab, depositing elegantly dressed couples onto the wet pavement.

The tailor recommended by Alice had fitted him with a more than decent Tux. She had insisted he take the Sig with him. The tailor, unfazed by the sight of the weapon, had nipped and tucked the jacket to hide the bulge of the firearm.

A quarter hour of an hour later, a black cab rolled to a stop next to the awning. The door swung open, and the tall and elegant figure of Alex Fern stepped out into the cool evening air. She shivered then smiled when she saw Drum.

He moved from under the awning to meet her. She was wearing a wine-coloured, sleeveless cocktail dress with a choker-like halter neck that exposed her broad back and shoulders. The hem of the dress had an asymmetric cut that rode high upon her bare thigh. It fitted her like a silk glove. Her only accessory was a silver purse. Alex Fern was indeed a beautiful woman.

"Good evening," he said, extending an arm for her to take. "You look gorgeous."

She beamed at his compliment. "And you're looking very handsome." She drew him closer and kissed him on the cheek. "Love the Tux."

They walked up a short flight of steps to the club's entrance where a doormen in a bright-red lively coat awaited them. Drum handed over his invitation. The doormen inspected the card, nodded and the front door of the club clicked open.

Giles was waiting for them when they walked through into the ornate, wood-panelled lobby with its checkerboard of marble flooring. He stood almost to attention in his bright-red livery coat over a white, wool waistcoat and sported a white bow tie around the collar of a starched white shirt. His black, regimental-style trousers were ironed to a knife-edge crease, and his black patent shoes had a shine that any Sergeant Major would have been proud of. Drum could tell from his bearing that he was an army man. Only age had stooped his once strong shoulders. He smiled warmly when he saw them, the corners of his eyes wrinkling with satisfaction and betraying a sharp mind that was rarely on display.

"Good evening," he said. "My, such a handsome couple. This way please." He turned and walked quickly to a door just off the lobby which he unlocked with a small key attached to a silver chain on his belt and walked through.

They found themselves in a small drawing room. Giles closed the door behind them. "This room has no security cameras, so we can speak freely." He turned to Drum. "Are you armed, sir?"

Drum opened his jacket to reveal the Sig Sauer nestled under his arm.

"Really?" said Fern, a little surprised.

"It was Alice's idea," replied Drum.

"Quite right, sir. Alice always did favour the bigger weapon," said Giles.

"Alice?"

"A story for another time," said Drum, looking at his watch. "Alice sends her regards, by the way, Giles."

"A wonderful woman," sighed Giles. "We had such times …"

"Giles," said Fern. "We're a little pressed …"

"Quite so, quite so," said Giles, straightening a little. "And you madam … are you carrying?"

Fern smiled. "If you can find a place to hide a gun in this dress, you're most welcome to try."

Giles raised an eyebrow. "No, madam. I was thinking of your purse."

Drum grinned.

"Right," said Fern, "of course. No, I'm not armed."

Giles moved over to a bureau and opened a drawer. He came back with a small, compact gun. "May I suggest this nine millimetre Beretta. It should fit nicely in your purse." He handed her the pistol.

"We expecting trouble?" said Fern.

"I always expect that every function, here at the club, will go off smoothly," replied Giles. "But as Alice used to say: 'it's best to prepare for the worst.'"

Fern studied the compact weapon. It seemed small in her hand compared to her trusted Glock. The Beretta was a woman's gun. She ejected the small magazine. "Six rounds." She re-inserted the clip and slipped the gun into her purse.

"One more thing," said Giles. "Should things go pear-shaped, there's a back exit. Go out of the patio doors next to the stairs and follow the path all the way back to a wall. There you'll find an iron gate." He handed Drum a small brass key. "This will get you out onto the street."

Drum took the key and slipped it into his jacket pocket. "Anything else?"

"If you need me, I'll be manning my desk. Good luck," said Giles.

He led them back out into the lobby. "Take the stairs up to the next floor. That is where the action is."

Just then another couple entered the lobby. Drum glanced in their direction. He was a tall, grey-haired man, perhaps in his sixties; she was a bright young thing, old enough to be his daughter and had on a small, blue dress the size of a postage stamp. The man nodded to Drum then turned his attention to the woman hanging off his arm. She giggled and squealed as she looked around wide-eyed at the grand lobby of the club. Giles excused himself and made his way over to greet the new guests, his movements now much slower and the stoop of his shoulders more pronounced.

Drum took Fern by the arm, and they made their way up the dark-oak stairway to the floor above. As they neared the top, they could hear soft music coming from behind two large closed doors. Two more liveried men attended the doorway. They nodded to Drum and Fern as they approached and pulled open each door.

Drum and Fern walked through and entered a large, white high ceilinged ballroom, and lit by three huge Murano crystal chandeliers. The cacophony of people talking and the clink of champagne glasses were mixed with the subdued background sound of a string quartet, stationed in one corner of the room. The noise in the room subsided, and heads turned in their general direction. Drum guessed their stares were not for him but for the statuesque Alex Fern.

Drum commandeered two glasses of champagne from a passing waiter and handed one to Fern.

"Cheers," he said, clinking his glass to hers.

"Now what?" asked Fern, looking around.

Drum led her further into the ballroom. "We mingle."

"What are we looking for?"

Drum reconnoitred the room. Large round dining tables with starched white tablecloths and ornate floral centrepieces dotted the dance floor. He moved over to a vacant table.

"I suggest we split up and just engage people in polite conversation. We need to understand what Harry was looking for."

"Probably didn't need to be armed," said Fern. "Seems a pretty tame event."

"Over there," said Drum. He nodded to a side room located off the central space and closed off by glass-panelled doors. Two heavy-set men stood guard outside. "Something's going on in that room," said Drum. "And it looks like the goons on the door didn't have the benefit of my tailor."

Fern glanced behind her. "I see what you mean. I don't think the bulge in their jackets is due to the size of their wallets."

"Let's keep an eye on it," said Drum. He walked off.

"Hey, where are you going."

"I'm mingling."

He left his champagne. It wasn't his drink. He spotted a bar in another side room and made a beeline for the door.

Heads turned his way as he entered the room. He ignored their stares and ordered a gin and tonic. The hubbub of conversation soon resumed. He stood at the bar sipping his drink and surveyed the room. People congregated in small groups and talked in hushed conversation. They appeared to be bankers or City types – grey-haired captains of industry thrashing out the next big deal. But it was hard to tell who was who or what they were discussing. He didn't recognise anyone in the room.

He was on his second drink when he noticed a woman looking in his direction. She was in her forties and the centre of two older men's attention. She appeared to be listening attentively to their conversation, but Drum could tell from her body language that she was bored. She interrupted one of her party who then looked in Drum's direction. She walked over.

"Hello, I don't think we've met? Amelia Makin."

Amelia Makin was a dark-haired, attractive woman and wore a full-length modestly cut white gown which accentuated her shapely figure. She offered Drum her hand which dripped with diamond rings and a gold bracelet around her slim, elegant wrist.

"Ben Drummond."

"I've not seen you here before," she said, giving him a bright smile.

"I heard the drinks were free so I gate-crashed the place," he said, returning her smile.

She laughed. "So what do you do, Mr Drummond?"

"Call me Ben. I'm in the gold bullion business."

"Oh, really. Then you must know Damian Rhodes?"

"Our paths have crossed," admitted Drum.

"I hear the bank is in trouble. They're here tonight looking for a cash injection. I've already turned them down."

"What is it that you do, Amelia?"

"Oh, I run a hedge fund." She looked over at the two gentlemen she had abandoned. "Those two are bankers. They're looking to invest in my fund. Tedious, really." She studied him carefully. "You don't look like a banker – too well-built."

"It comes from shifting tons of gold every day. It's very heavy."

She laughed, her hand moving to a gold chain around her long, slender neck. Her fingers traced down the chain until they came to a large, teardrop pearl nestled deep within the canyon of her breasts. "Are you looking for anything particular tonight, Ben?"

He was about to answer her question when in walked the diminutive figure of Anna Koblihova. She was wearing a small red dress which appeared to Drum to be made of the sheerest of fabric. She sashayed over to them, a smile on her face.

"There you are, darling," she said in a husky tone. "I look for you everywhere."

"Oh," said Amelia, "I didn't know you were with the Russians."

"Sorry Amelia, darling," purred Anna. "Big demand for Benjamin tonight." She took Drum by the arm and started to lead him out of the room.

"Excuse me, Amelia," said Drum.

Anna led Drum out into the ballroom and towards the patio doors. Heads turned when she walked by. Drum looked for Fern, but she was nowhere to be seen. Two attendants opened the patio doors as they approached and they stepped out into the chill night air.

"You'll catch your death in that outfit," said Drum, watching as Anna folded her arms around herself.

"You shouldn't be here," whispered Anna. "Vlad arrived some time ago. If he sees you… "

"We're following up on Harry –"

"We?"

"I'm with Alex Fern."

"What! You should leave – right now." She looked around anxiously.

"What was Harry doing here," he pressed.

"Jones poked her nose into things she shouldn't have," admitted Anna. "And now she is missing."

"But you don't know where she is?"

"All I know is that Vlad is now looking for her."

"Vlad?"

"Leave now, Benjamin," said Anna, her voice rising. "I cannot protect you here." She walked back to the patio doors and tapped on the window. The doors opened, and she disappeared back inside. It was time to find Fern.

Drum followed Anna back into the warmth of the ballroom. He found Fern sitting alone at one of the tables. She rose and smiled when she saw him.

"Hello, stranger. Thought I'd lost you," she said.

"We need to go."

She moved closer to him, one hand extended, holding a glass of champagne. "But I need to give you my intel."

"Perhaps later," he replied.

She placed a hand on his shoulder and looked serious. "Well, Sergei over there," she nodded towards a tall man in the corner, "is only interested in threesomes. But I had to pass on tonight. And Sir Reginald's into whipping –"

"Fern, we really need to go."

She smiled and leaned towards him. "You can be such a party-pooper ..." She draped her arms around his neck and pulled him closer, her lips brushing his ear. "And Victor owes a lot of money on a warehouse lease in Wapping – at least that's what Sergei tells me." She lightly bit his ear lobe. "God, you taste nice," and started to giggle.

"I think you're pissed."

"God, I hope so after all the Champers I've drunk." She gave him a lopsided smile. "Just doing m'job, guv'nor."

"I'm not going to have to carry you home, am I?" said Drum.

"Bigger men than you have tried, believe me," she said and started to giggle again.

He unwrapped her arms from around his neck and liberated her glass. He took her arm and headed for the main door.

"Why are we leaving?" she said.

"Vlad's here."

Fern suddenly became alert. "Oh, fuck."

They had made it halfway across the ballroom floor when the door to the guarded room opened and out walked Vladimir Abramov. He was closely followed by Sir Rupert Mayhew. The two men shook hands. Sir Rupert looked up and locked eyes with Drum. He turned to Vlad and nodded in Drum's direction.

"Shit, we've been spotted," said Drum. Let's pick up the pace."

They reached the main set of doors and Drum rapped on the wooden panel. The doors swung open. Drum glanced back to see two of Vlad's heavies following close behind. They started quickly down the long staircase.

"The escape route," said Drum, pointing to the garden exit.

A large hand appeared on Fern's shoulder. One of the guards had caught up.

Fern grabbed the guys wrist and turned to face him. She twisted and locked his wrist. The guard screamed. In one fluid movement, she flipped him forwards sending him crashing down the stairs.

Giles moved swiftly from behind his desk and advanced towards the patio doors. He swung them open just as Drum and Fern reached the bottom of the stairs.

"Out you go," he said. "Quickly now. I'll delay them."

They ran out into the cold darkness of the garden. A light rain was falling.

Drum looked back. Giles was busy trying to close the patio doors as the second of Vlad's guards descended the stairs.

There came the loud retort of a gunshot.

Fern and Drum stopped in their tracks and turned to the patio doors. Giles was on his knees, clutching his stomach, a dark red stain spreading out across his starched, white shirt.

The second guard was now advancing towards them, his gun outstretched.

"Bastard," shouted Fern. She drew the Beretta, discarding her purse in the process. She racked the small gun and extended her arm.

"No, Fern." Drum drew his weapon.

Fern strode back towards the advancing guard. He was surprised by the sudden confrontation and fired a round that went wide of its mark. Fern fired back, hitting him in the shoulder. He grunted and with an effort raised his gun. Drum came up beside her and fired twice in quick succession – a double-tap to the guard's chest as he had been trained to do. It was an automatic response. The guard fell face down into the cold, wet earth of the garden.

31

Alice sat in her dressing gown sobbing.

"Who's Giles?" asked William. He placed an arm around her, but she was inconsolable.

It was a little past midnight and Drum sat slumped in an armchair, still in his tux in Alice's apartment in Chelsea. Fern sat across from him, a look of anguish on her face, her hands clasped tightly together.

Alice pulled a tissue from her pocket and dabbed her eyes. "He was someone I used to work with."

"But I thought you worked at the Foreign Office?" said William.

"Why don't you make us some tea, dear," said Alice, forcing a smile.

William sighed. "You can't keep asking me to make tea whenever you want to get rid of me. What's going on?"

"Why don't you pour us a drink, William. We could all use something stronger," said Drum.

"Right," said William, knowing that it was useless to argue. He heaved himself up from the couch and pulled his dressing gown tightly around him. "Bushmills it is then." He ambled into the kitchen.

Fern got up and sat next to Alice. She enveloped the small woman with her arms. "I'm so sorry Alice. It happened so quickly ..."

"He went out fighting," said Drum, angrily. "Like a true soldier."

"Ben!" exclaimed Fern.

"No, dear. Ben's right. And you shot the bastard," said Alice.

"I only winged him – too pissed. It was Ben ..."

Alice gave Fern a hard look. "You've never shot anyone, have you dear?"

Drum looked surprised. Until now, it hadn't occurred to him that Fern had never used her gun in anger. He remembered their first encounter with the Russian. She had been reluctant to draw her weapon.

William came in carrying a tray of tumblers and a bottle of Bushmills whisky. He placed the tray on a small table. "What will happen to Benjy?"

"Have you been listening?" asked Alice.

"I'm not deaf or stupid," replied William. He splashed whisky into all the glasses and handed them around. "Will he be arrested?"

Fern took a glass and sat forward nursing her drink. "I honestly don't know. Technically, I should report the whole thing."

"Technically, you'd be stupid to do anything of the sort," said Alice. She knocked back her drink in one gulp and held out her glass for a refill.

"I don't understand," said Fern.

"There'll be a cover-up," said Drum. "They won't risk exposing what's going on at the club."

"You've lost me ..." said William.

"The club – it's a black market for laundered money. The place was filled with City types looking for investment and the Russians only too happy to help," said Drum.

"But we should report what we saw," said Fern. "I'm supposed to be a police officer."

Alice took a swig of her second whisky. "I think you're naive. The first thing they'll do is arrest Ben and probably suspend you. And that will be the only arrests they'll make."

Fern stared down into her drink.

"You're an NCA Commander," added Drum. "You're supposed to fight organised crime. No, the only way to clear this mess up is to find out what's going on in that vault."

"This is the place at Blackfriars?" asked William. "Close to the river?"

"You know it?"

"My father did. I remember him telling me stories. Used to be a school before it was a bank. They stored paintings in the cellars during the War. My dad told me how he and a mate barged valuables into the place from the river. Stopped them being damaged during the Blitz."

"In the vault?" asked Drum.

"No. There wasn't a vault in those days, just large cellars that led straight to the river. You can still see the entrance."

Drum turned to Fern. "You still have a mate in the Thames River

Police?"

"Yes, why?"

"We should take a look at the location from the river. Just a hunch."

Drum downed his whisky then made their excuses to leave. William lent Fern a raincoat which she draped over his shoulders as she stepped out into the chill, night air.

Alice took Drum to one side as they were leaving. "They'll come for you now, Ben. You know that, don't you?"

"I know, Alice." He hesitated. "Perhaps it's time you came clean with William."

She looked down at her feet. "I know I should ... I just don't want to screw things up between us."

"He adores you, Alice. He'll understand."

Alice started to cry again. Drum drew her to him and held her tight. "It'll work out, Alice. Don't you worry."

She pulled away. "Abramov is going to pay, Ben. He's going to pay ..."

32

Rhodes was summoned once more to the Mayfair club, this time by the Treasury Mandarin Sir Rupert Mayhew. He was beginning to dislike the place. Rhodes was only a member because social etiquette demanded he take part in the charade. He entered the lobby expecting another run-in with the old duffer behind the desk but was greeted instead by someone much younger.

"Hi. Can I help you?"

"Damian Rhodes. I'm meeting Sir Rupert Mayhew for lunch. Who are you?"

"Er, George. Just started. Hang on …" he fumbled for the visitor's book and started to flip the pages.

"Where's Giles?" demanded Rhodes, put out that he had been denied the courtesy usually afforded him by the old man.

"Don't really know. Just started, like I said … Ah yes, here you are. Go straight through."

Rhodes stomped off towards the dining room. A group of cleaners were furiously scrubbing at the marble flooring as he passed the patio doors that led to the garden. He found Sir Rupert sitting alone, the dining room deserted.

"Sir Rupert? Damian Rhodes."

Sir Rupert Mayhew didn't rise, simply indicated to Rhodes to be seated. "Drink, Rhodes?" he waved over a waiter.

"Thank you. whisky Soda." The waiter hurried off.

Rhodes waited as his host studied the menu. He looked around and wondered why the dining room was empty. It was one o'clock and by the now the place was usually buzzing.

"Where is everyone?"

Sir Rupert looked up. "Some trouble at the club last night. Too much free champagne – things got a little out of hand ..."

"Right," said Rhodes. He picked up the menu and browsed the mains. It hadn't changed since the last time he was here.

"I can recommend the turbot," said Sir Rupert.

"I see, yes. Good idea. The turbot then."

The waiter returned with his drink and waited to take their lunch order. Rhodes took a good swig. Sir Rupert was making him nervous. The man had the power to make or break a bank, and the fact that he wanted to see him wasn't a good omen.

Sir Rupert snapped his menu shut. "Two turbot." He dismissed the waiter with a wave of his hand. He removed his glasses and placed them on the table. "You have a problem at the vault, I hear."

Rhodes wondered how Sir Rupert had come by that information. Then he remembered that Victor Renkov had mentioned that Sir Henry Minton was also a club member.

"I can assure you, Sir Rupert, that things are tidy our end ..."

"Complete bollocks and you know it. You're missing a Vault Manager – this Pinkman – and one of your key traders turns up dead. And to top it all, you now have two ROD agents sifting through your underwear."

"Well, we do have a regulatory audit in progress, but it's routine and I've taken steps –"

"What do you take me for? You have two ROD agents investigating your operation, for Christ's sake. Have you any idea what that means?"

Rhodes shifted uncomfortably in his chair. "Well ..."

"No, you bloody well don't, that's for sure. You don't think the FCA called in ROD, do you?"

"Well, I assumed it was another regulatory audit. We have so many. And anyway, I can assure you I've tidied up the loose ends."

Sir Rupert laughed. "Another regulatory audit. Dear God, man. When the shit hits the fan, they call in Roderick Olivier and Delaney. And when I say 'they', it usually means the Fed."

"Why is the Fed interested in our operation?" asked Rhodes.

Sir Rupert raised his empty glass and beckoned over a nearby waiter. He waved his hand around the table. *Same again.*

"RBI - their money laundering controls haven't been as effective as they could have been – especially when comes to our Russian friends," said Sir Rupert. "Then, of course, there's the whistle blower ..."

Rhodes thought of Fabio DeLuca, his body found floating face down in the Thames. "But DeLuca –"

"I'm talking about the Auditor, Rhodes. The one present when the vault was opened. It's likely she was also a ROD investigator, working undercover."

"Harriet Seymour-Jones," confirmed Rhodes.

"Yes, that's the one."

Rhodes smiled.

"What's so funny?"

"Let's just say I have that under control," replied Rhodes.

"Really!"

"She's my insurance. A hedge, if you like."

"A hedge against what?" inquired Sir Rupert.

"When you, Sir Henry or whoever decide I'm no longer of any use," replied Rhodes.

Sir Rupert smiled grimly. "I see …" He paused as their drinks arrived. He picked up his heavy, crystal tumbler and swirled the clinking ice around. "There are people looking for her – Ben Drummond for one."

Rhodes frowned. "The ROD auditor?"

Sir Rupert shook his head in dismay. "You still don't get it, do you?"

"I'm afraid not," said Rhodes, getting irritated.

"Captain Benjamin Drummond is a highly decorated officer. Fought in two wars and served with some of this country's most effective killers. He was part of a unit so classified that his file is sealed, even to me."

"So what's his connection to Jones?"

"Not much of a team player, are you, Rhodes?"

Rhodes shrugged.

"She's a fellow ROD investigator. Someone like Drummond is not in the habit of leaving his people in the shit."

Waiters appeared with plates of food which they served to each man.

"Ah, lunch," said Sir Rupert. "I'm starving."

Rhodes looked down at the steaming pile of white fish. He suddenly wasn't hungry. He sat back and studied the Mandarin. "So what's the worst that could happen? He writes me up in his audit report."

Sir Rupert paused, his fork midway to his mouth. "Good Lord, no," replied Sir Rupert. "He's going to kill you."

33

Harry was cold and tired. She sat atop an old packing crate in the gloom and shivered. A single wall lamp cast a pitiful orange light over the crumbling Victorian brickwork of the damp cellar. The River Thames was rising, bringing dirty water trickling down the old brick tunnels that led to her make-shift prison beneath the main floor of the vault.

And with the rising of the river came the rats. They scurried past the rusty iron bars that enclosed the alcove where she sat, stopping, sniffing and staring at her presence in their domain.

An old porcelain toilet sat in one corner, thick with grime. It was now beginning to smell. She had been using it on and off for a few days now, but with every rising tide, water gurgled up and spilt over the bowl followed silently by the rats.

Her once pristine white blouse was covered in grime and her pencil skirt was torn and tattered. She longed for a wash and something to eat. Her stomach growled. Those bastards hadn't fed her in over twenty-four hours.

She wanted to pee. Harry cautiously peered into the toilet bowl. There was a splash and a large, grey rat raised its whiskered snout and then swam back down the u-bend. She would hold on just a little longer.

She left the sanctuary of the packing case and splashed through the cold, black water to the iron gate of her prison. She'd lost her shoes in the struggle when they took her. That was four days ago. One shoe was lost between the legs of the Russian who tried to grab her by her hair. He'd returned the favour by smacking her across the face and busting her lip. She'd lost the other when they dragged her down here.

Her mistake had been returning to the apartment. They were waiting for her. After the fiasco of the empty vault, the trail of smuggled gold that led to London had gone cold. She'd quit and left for Zurich. She needed to speak to Mueller who was still working on hacking Hoschstrasser & Bührer. She needed another lead. But Mueller was dead. She still had the original cache of documents from the first hack. There might be something in there that she had missed. She reasoned they hadn't found it. It was the reason she was still alive.

She gripped the rusty bars and rattled the locked gate. "Hey, I'm hungry you bastards."

She pressed the side of her head against the bars and peered to her left. A wide brick tunnel disappeared into the blackness. She knew that way led to the river. Days earlier, the tunnel had been brightly lit and busy with men pulling small carts loaded with gold bricks. They were returning gold to the vault. Why? She had no idea. They had ignored her shouts and curses.

She heard the splash of water, and a guard appeared down the tunnel off to her right. He was one of the Russians that had dragged her down here. He was a large man, unshaven and in the grey of the bank's security personnel. One of Victor's men. He put his finger to his lips. *Quiet.*

"I'm hungry you bastard. Get me some food." She rattled the gate in her frustration.

The guard simply laughed. He looked down and noticed the water flowing into the tunnel. It was getting deeper. He looked up and mimed the water rising above his head.

"Go fuck yourself. Bloody idiot."

"Now, now Ms Jones." There was more splashing and Rhodes appeared, dapper in a navy suit and expensive shoes that were at risk of filling with water. "Oh, dear. I see what you mean."

"Get me out of here, Rhodes," demanded Harry.

"Patience. Not long now."

"How long are you going to keep me here?"

"Just one more transaction for our Russian friends then … well, they appear keen to meet you. Apparently, you have something they want – badly."

"You realise they're going to kill you after their last shipment of gold is sold," said Harry.

"That's why you're still here," he replied. "You're my insurance policy. They can have you after I'm long gone."

"ROD will find me. They don't leave their people in the shit."

"And yet here you are," sneered Rhodes, looking around him. "In the shit."

"They'll figure it out. ROD always does."

"There's nothing to figure out," said Rhodes. "Pinkman lost his mind and emptied the vault. Renkov had the good sense to return the gold. Abramov and ROD are none the wiser. Everything is as it should be."

It was her turn to sneer. "Think about it, Rhodes. Why would Victor return the gold? It stinks, like the water I'm standing in."

He laughed. "That's as may be. I don't trust Renkov either. All the bullion has been accounted for – every ounce." He paused. "In fact, one of your ROD colleagues has been carrying out an audit of the vault above you. He's found nothing. Benjamin Drummond. You may know him?"

She felt a flutter of hope at the mention of the name. "Ben is here?"

"He's been counting and weighing bars. He'll finish his audit and tell us the usual crap: our money laundering controls need improving. Then we'll wave him goodbye."

Harry watched Rhodes' smirk slip from his face. He apparently didn't believe that either. She wondered what he knew about Ben Drummond. She had touched a nerve. Ben would find her. Then Rhodes would be toast. Her stomach growled.

"You forget the whistle blower," she said. "He'll have alerted the FCA. It's only a matter of time before the Bank of England steps in …"

There was a gurgle of water. "I don't think so," said Rhodes, stepping back from the encroaching Thames. "The Bank of England is buying the gold."

34

Stevie worked the keyboard of Drum's computer. She looked up from the screen at her assembled audience, her fingers continuing their staccato dance.

"There," she said, stabbing one last key in triumph. She turned the computer screen around to face them.

Drum stood brooding by the window, watching the heavy rain falling. The inky, black river raged around the piers of Tower Bridge. There was talk of raising the Thames Barrier to protect against a surging tide.

Alice peered at the screen from the end of the couch. "I must get new glasses," she confessed. "Can't see a thing."

Fern slouched in her corner of the couch. She glanced at the screen, bored. "What are we looking at?"

"Geez," sighed Stevie, "don't all rush at once."

Drum dragged himself into the present and turned to examine the screen of data Stevie had brought up. "You've been analysing the data from the vault audit?"

"Yes," confirmed Stevie. "There isn't much to go on – just 482 data points, each representing a bar of gold."

"Six tons of gold," groaned Fern.

"Right," said Stevie. "The weights and serial numbers of each bar match exactly those recorded in the RBI computer."

"So, a complete waste of time," sighed Fern.

"And you recorded the data," said Stevie, stating the obvious.

"Right," said Fern. "I watched them weigh every bar and record the serial numbers. I stood and watched the Custody Officer email Drum the spreadsheet at the end of the session so that nothing could be altered."

"That's precisely my point," said Stevie. "It's a perfect match with the RBI computer."

"I see what you're saying," said Drum. "It shouldn't be perfect."

"I don't understand," said Fern. "We weighed every bar very accurately."

"But there should be some slight variation in the weights," explained Drum.

"Correct," replied Stevie, feeling pleased with herself. "They simply uploaded the audit data into the RBI computer."

Fern looked puzzled. "I still don't get it."

"Their original data didn't match the gold in the vault," said Drum. "Sure, the gross weight is the same – six tons – but this inventory doesn't match the original."

"You're saying they moved six tons of gold into the vault from another location?" said Fern.

"It looks that way," replied Drum. "Although without the original bar list tied to the delivery notes, we have no way of knowing where this gold came from."

"You mean we're back to square one?" asked Alice. She looked mournful.

"There's something else," continued Stevie. "I also performed some basic analytics – simple stuff really – just to be sure." She tapped a few keys and another screen appeared.

Drum examined her report. "There are duplicate serial numbers."

Fern stood up and moved to the screen. "But they should all be unique – at least that's what Sir Rupert told us."

"That's right," said Drum. He turned to Stevie. "Have you run a Benford's Law analysis on the data."

"Sorry, I don't know what that is."

Drum moved the screen back around. He leant close to Stevie and tapped a few keys. "Bedford's Law tells us that certain digits appear more frequently than others in numeric sets." He tapped a few more keys. "In simple terms, this analysis will tell us if the serial numbers on the bars are forgeries." Drum stared at the report on his screen.

"Well?" inquired Alice. "Don't keep us in suspense."

Drum looked up. "There's a high probability that someone simply made up the serial numbers - at least on many of the bars."

"What does that mean?" asked Fern.

"It means that these bars couldn't have come from a certified bullion refiner. Certainly not from Zurich," said Drum.

"But we checked," said Fern "The bars were all marked with the Zurich refinery stamp."

Drum stood and moved back to the window. The wharf outside was awash with water. He was at a loss. If the bars didn't come from Zurich, where else did they come from?

"Well I have something which might cheer us up," said Alice, moving over to the computer. "Roll em, Stevie."

Stevie tapped few keys and brought up video footage from the bank. She swivelled the screen to face the couch and moved from behind the desk with the keyboard.

"What are we looking at?" asked Drum.

"That's the vault reception area," said Fern.

"This is one minute past eleven, Monday evening," said Alice. "Please play it, Stevie."

The video footage began to roll. Two big men, dressed in the dark-grey of RBI guards could be seen dragging a struggling Harry. One of the guards stopped, turned and struck Harry hard across the face.

"Bastard," said Fern.

"I recognise one of the guards," said Drum, bitterly. "He and his mate were at the vault the night of the audit. They were keeping Baxter company."

"Stevie has patched together more footage," continued Alice.

The video feed jumped to inside the elevator. Harry was limp between the large arms of the guards. One them reached forward and punched a button.

"Hold it there," said Drum. The footage froze. "There – he pressed a red button."

"There must be a level below the vault," said Fern.

"Yes," said Drum. "Baxter told me it was disused."

The video footage continued, but all they saw was Harry being dragged out of the elevator.

"Well, at least we know she's alive," said Alice. "At least she was four days ago."

"And we know where she is," said Fern. She stood back up and smoothed down her skirt. "We'll need a warrant."

Alice looked at Drum and raised an eyebrow.

Drum returned his gaze to the window. Large, black clouds scudded over the City, turning day into night. There was a rumble of thunder.

"Forget the warrant," he said. "We're going to need a boat."

35

Sir Rupert Mayhew hated coming into the City on a Saturday, but the Russians had insisted on a meeting. After the fiasco at the gala, he thought it wise not to meet at the club. Instead, he chose a private room in the Sky Garden restaurant at the top of Twenty Fenchurch Street. City folk called it the Walkie Talkie building.

Vladimir Abramov arrived punctually with just the one bodyguard, a large man with blonde hair who assumed a stoic position by the door.

"We have a problem," said Sir Rupert.

Vlad downed his vodka. "No, Sir Rupert, you have problem."

"However you want to slice it, the bank has two ROD investigators putting Rhodes through the wringer." Sir Rupert poured himself some wine. "And after the debacle at the club ... they need to be taken care of."

"We are aware of the investigators Benjamin Drummond and Alex Fern. Unfortunate they saw you," said Vlad.

Sir Rupert was surprised. "You know them?"

"Our paths have crossed," said Vlad. "What about the bank's Auditor - Seymour-Jones?"

"I'm told that Rhodes may be able to help you there. Why is she important?" asked Sir Rupert.

"She holds sensitive information. We have been trying to trace her – no success."

"Well, our immediate concern is the two ROD agents," said Sir Rupert. "This chap Drummond appears to be some type of security specialist. He's tearing through all of the bank's transactions. Tried to have him closed down, but no luck. My contacts say he's ex-military with connections to GCHQ. Has a security clearance that's off the chart. My contact also believes someone in Vauxhall is protecting him."

"Vauxhall?" enquired Vlad.

"Vauxhall Bridge. A British euphemism for MI6," explained Sir Rupert.

"Ah, big problem," said Vlad. "We need to accelerate OMEGA. One large deal. Your bank needs to accept the next shipment of gold."

"I can probably swing it, but it's going to look odd," said Sir Rupert.

"Good, good. Then that's settled. Have your people prepare to receive one million ounces –"

" One million ounces!" exclaimed Sir Rupert. "Are you mad? That's close to $1.5 billion. The price of gold will plummet and –"

"Then, Sir Rupert, you will make a lot of money, I think," said Vlad.

"I don't understand …"

"Your options trading. You bet on the price of gold falling, no? I think so. Mr DeLuca was most talkative before his end. So, Sir Rupert, you'll make even more money on this last shipment - providing, of course, you can find someone to trade the gold."

"But, but …"

"No buts," said Vlad. "Prepare your vault to accept the gold. One last trade. In meantime, I deal with Benjamin Drummond.

36

"Please don't eat those dreadful things," pleaded Alice.

She watched as William speared a gelatinous piece of eel.

"If you just tried one, you might find you like them," said William. "Full of vitamins and the like."

Alice gave him a withering look. Love William, love his jellied eels. It was something she would have to stomach. "Wait til I'm gone."

"I don't know why you need to go into the office today," said William. "After all, it's a Sunday. I'm sure Benjy can do without you for one day. I've hardly seen you all week."

Outside it was threatening rain and the old covered market was growing dark and gloomy. Why William loved this place she would never know. She pulled up the collar of her old trench coat against the chill September morning and thrust her hands into its deep pockets. Her right hand rested upon the cold metal of the Sig that she had secreted there the night before. She casually took in her surroundings, scanning for signs of a threat with a practised eye. A big man in a black mac, sitting on his own, reading a newspaper. A young woman with a pram, looking at her phone. Years in the field had given her the uncanny ability to spot another agent. She saw nothing. But she had not been in the field for many years and this worried her. She knew the Russians wouldn't let sleeping dogs lie. Whatever Ben had witnessed at the gala, the Russians would want to clean up loose ends.

"I need to talk to you about something," she said. "It's about my past."

William smiled weakly. "We don't have to do this, Alice. The past is the past. We're together now, that's what's important."

Alice heaved a sigh, suddenly weary. "I've done things, William –

bad things. Things I can't talk about – for the country …"

William reached forward and held both her hands. "I don't need to know this, Alice. I don't."

She looked at him and held his gaze. "It's important you know – who I am."

William smiled and said "Look, Alice. We've all done things that we regret. In our youth. I only know the Alice I'm with now."

She smiled. This was why she loved William. What good comes of digging up the past? But in her heart she knew the past had a habit of catching up with you.

"Things happened – a long time ago. I'm not proud of what I did …"

William squeezed her hands. "Don't tell me, Alice. Please don't tell me. I understand."

"Do you, William?" She looked into his eyes, pleading, hoping that he did understand.

"I'm not a complete dope, Alice. I guessed you were trying to keep something buried. I've seen it before – in Benjy. After he came back from the war – well, he wasn't the same. Troubled he was. He'd get upset about things – silly things. Things most of us wouldn't give a fig about. He'd lose his temper or get depressed."

Alice squeezed his hands. "War does that, William."

"I'm sorry if I've been a bit insensitive to you at times. I know I can be a silly old bugger …"

Alice smiled. "No, you've been marvellous – you have." She pulled her hands from his and reached inside her pocket for a tissue. She picked one from beneath the Sig and remembered why she had started this conversation.

"Listen to me. I have something to tell you – about the Russians." She looked around the market one last time. The big man was still reading his paper. That's what people do on a Sunday – read the papers. But Alice noticed he was reading the Times – a weekday copy and had yet to turn a page. Her hand tightened around the grip of the gun.

"What about the Russians?" asked William. "Is Benjy in trouble …"

"I think we're all in trouble, William. It's what I'm trying to tell you …"

The woman with the pram was walking towards them. The big man was now folding his paper and heading their way.

"I'm all ears, Alice." He paused when he saw Alice wasn't listening.

"What is it?" he asked, looking around.

"Time we left." She kept her hand inside her pocket, gripping the Sig and stood up from the bench.

"But we only just got 'ere."

Alice watched as the big man approached; the woman with the pram was now close by. The man or the woman? She couldn't decide which was the greater threat. Logic told her the man was the obvious choice, but her gut told her the woman would make the first move.

"William, quickly. Come stand by me ..."

The woman let go of the pram and moved towards William. She pulled what looked like a fat pen from her pocket and grabbed his arm.

"Er, what do you think you're doing," said William, trying to pull his arm away.

Alice drew the gun from her pocket – too late. The big man was upon her. He grabbed her wrist in a crushing grip and wrenched the weapon from her hand. Alice cried out in pain.

William had started to stand when the woman rammed the pen into the side of his neck. The pen let out a soft hiss and William sat back down. He swayed, his eyes rolling back up into his head. Then with a crunch, he slumped forward onto the bench.

"William!" cried Alice.

The big man laughed.

A red mist of rage swept over Alice. She started to shake. With her free hand, she reached back until she found the butterfly pin keeping her hair in place. She gripped the enamelled wings and withdrew the pin – a disguised blade of hardened surgical steel. Her hair tumbled down across her shoulders as she swung the weapon in a graceful arc, ramming it into the ear of her assailant, penetrating his skull, lodging it deep within his brain.

The big man fell silent, a look of astonishment on his face, before releasing his grip and dropping to the floor like a stone.

The last thing Alice remembered was a feeling of satisfaction followed by a sting on the side of her neck. She instinctively raised her hand before the world spun into blackness.

Rage Against the Machine

37

Drum pressed himself against the side of the police motor launch as it pitched and rolled in the swell of a raging Thames. He steadied himself with one hand on the slippery handrail while trying to operate his mobile phone with the other. The police skipper throttled power to the small engines just to keep them from drifting back against the surge of the tide. He was cold and wet.

"Any news?" asked Fern.

Drum glanced up at his partner standing tall with her legs akimbo against the roll of the small craft. She looked imposing in her black waterproof jacket branded with the white logo of the NCA and her now familiar peak cap. It was the first time Drum had seen her back in uniform since starting the assignment. He thumbed the screen of his phone one last time.

"No joy," he said. "I can't reach either Alice or William."

Brock rested effortlessly on the opposite side of the boat, absorbing the movement of the swell with the ease of a seasoned professional. He ran a hand through his shaggy hair causing the white stripe down the side to flash in the gathering gloom of a cloudy Monday morning. He pulled up the collar of his old combat jacket against the light drizzle that was now falling. "Probably having a lie in," he ventured. "Better than sitting out here."

Drum pocketed his phone and zipped up his jacket. He could understand William missing a call, but Alice was not the type to be late or lose a day in the office. Alice was a trooper, a real pro. He'd never met anyone more dedicated – well, perhaps Brock.

He shouted to the skipper. "Let's get under the bridge and closer to the Embankment."

The helmsman applied power to the engines, and the small boat crept forward under the shadow of Blackfriars Bridge. The structure shook and suddenly shuddered as a commuter train moved out from the station overhead, rumbling on its way out of London.

Brock swung himself across the deck to join Drum on his side of the boat and handed him his binoculars. "Over there." He pointed to a row of lighter barges tied to a makeshift mooring.

"What am I looking at?" asked Drum.

"To the right of the mooring."

Drum moved his line of sight to his left and refocussed the binoculars. Then he saw it. A large opening in the stone wall of the Embankment with an iron grill across the entrance.

Fern staggered over and Drum handed her the binoculars. "Looks like it's in use," she said.

"How so?" asked Drum.

"There are two brand new padlocks attached to the gate."

She gave the binoculars back to Drum. He took another look. Fern was right. The gate was in use. They had found another entrance into the vault – if indeed it did lead to the vault. He also spotted another problem: two security cameras on either side of the gate.

Drum turned to Brock. "What do you think?"

Brock leaned over the side of the small boat. "It's doable, providing the tide don't sweep us downstream and we can cut our way in."

"You can't be serious," said Fern. It must be thirty metres to the gate – and with this current ..."

"We go tonight," said Drum. He nodded to Brock. "How's Poacher doing?"

"On his way with his gear. Be here this afternoon."

"Wait," said Fern. "We need to get this authorised – get a warrant. We can't just bust in, guns blazing."

"Harry will be dead by the time you obtain a warrant," replied Drum. "You can bow out now if you need to."

Fern frowned but said nothing.

"What about gear?" asked Brock. "Well need wetsuits, scuba and cutters."

"We can supply that," said Fern.

"Really?" said Brock, looking doubtful.

"You're going to do it anyway. This way, you'll have more of a chance."

Drum turned to Fern and gave her a slight smile. "Let's get back to the office."

Fern cupped her hands over her mouth, turned to the wheelhouse and shouted. "Skipper. Let's get back."

The helmsman nodded and throttled up the engines, steering a course back down the river towards Butler's Wharf.

38

Harry stood up to her waist in water and gripped the rusty iron gate of her prison. She let out one last scream. "I'm down here ..."

She felt, more than heard, the engine reverberating down the brick passageway that led to the river. It was the first time in days that a boat had come close to the tunnel entrance. She strained to hear above the rushing of water and the low growl of the wind that had been increasing all morning. She thought she heard a woman shout. Something about a kipper? That can't be right. Sounded more like 'slipper'. Her brain was turning to mush from the lack of food and sleep. She rested her head against the bars of the gate and closed her eyes. God, she was tired. The rhythmic thumping of the engine slowly faded until all she could hear was the splashing of the rats.

Something brushed against her skin. She yelped and jumped back. A giant rat surfaced from between her legs and escaped through the rusty iron gate. She squeezed her head into the bars and shouted one last time. "Get me out of here!" There was no reply. Her captors had deserted her. The last Russian she'd seen was after Rhodes had left. Friday – or was it Saturday? He'd thrown her a bottle of water and waved goodbye. She occasionally heard a snatch of muffled conversation drifting down one of the tunnels. They seemed content to leave her to the rising tide.

She waded back to her wooden crate and heaved herself up and out of the water. It provided a temporary respite against the frigid Thames. The water was rising by the hour and would soon claim her island sanctuary. After that ...

She drew her legs up to her chest and hugged her knees, resting her forehead on her arms. She could have comfortably slept if not for the continued probing of the rats. Several had now taken up refuge on the crate. She had long ago given up trying to kick them off.

She heard a soft buzz and the wall light flickered. Water was seeping into the electrical system. She wondered how long the light would last? Perhaps an hour?

She brushed aside dark thoughts. It ain't over til the fat lady sings, she mused. Or in her case, the skinny lady cries. Her stomach growled. What was it that Rhodes had said? One last deal for the Russians. She had not seen that coming. Too fixated on finding the smuggled gold from Mexico City. She hadn't figured on another player. And Vlad Abramov wasn't just any player. His connections led straight back to Moscow. The Kremlin's own money man. That had been evident from the cache of documents from Hoschstrasser & Bührer - lawyers to the wealthy and to the mob. They handled all the transactions, creating the network of shell companies and registering the nominee directors. Bills of Laden and delivery notes for all of the gold shipments were all stored on their servers. And Mueller – poor Mueller. Brutally murdered. She had pushed him to hack the server, just like she had bullied and cajoled Rachel in Mexico City. Both dead. Was there no limit to her obsession?

Her only consolation was that she had the original H&B cache. Somehow Mueller had hidden them on the net – a private location hackers called Altair IV. He'd scribbled the key on the back of her photograph.

And what of Ben Drummond? Her heart had leapt when Rhodes had mentioned his name. He would figure it out. Why hadn't she contacted him when she arrived in London? It was her pride – and her shame. He had resigned over the Mexico City affair. She couldn't involve him again. Yet he had been here – above her, inspecting the vault. Figure it out, Ben.

She heard the rats in the passageway and the sound of splashing. She strained to listen. The rats on the crate raised their heads and began to sniff the air. As one, they plunged into the water and headed up the tunnel. She craned her neck trying to see what the commotion was all about, not wanting to leave the relative safety of the crate. The orange light flickered and fizzed. She sniffed the air and then smelt it. Something bad. Something rotten. The smell of decay. The smell of death.

Then she saw it. The body of a man in a suit floating face up, slowly drifting past the gate. His head swollen. His eye sockets empty and black. He'd been dead for some time. Maybe dumped in a cell further in the tunnel. Now the rising tide had claimed him – as it would claim her. Despite the blackened head, she recognised the decaying form of Harvey Pinkman.

39

Rhodes was holding court in the dealing room of the Undershaft. The anointed king of bullion trading addressed his devoted courtiers. They hung on his every word, on his every instruction, all eager to learn from the master and grab a slice of the action. This is where he loved to be. In the thick of it. Making money. The cut and thrust of trading precious metals.

And today would be exceptional.

There was a rumble of thunder and black clouds scudded across the large windows of the Victorian building, momentarily darkening the room. Rhodes ignored the threatening storm and stood, raising both hands like a messiah. "Ok, listen up. You have your dealing instructions for today?" He waited until they had all finished nodding and muttering their acknowledgements. "We have a million ounces of gold sitting in the vault, waiting to be sold. Make a note of the client: Borite Metals Holding. John, as the senior trader, will lead and the rest of you will pile in after. I want the order sold by the end of today's trading." He paused for effect, waiting for the first Judas to show himself. He didn't have to wait long.

A young trader broke first. "A million ounces … That's a lot of gold to place in one day. What happens if we can't place it all?"

"You can fuck off back to New York, Henry," retorted Rhodes. The room filled with laughter.

Henry squirmed in his seat.

"Look," continued Rhodes, "I know it's a lot of gold. That's why we're the best." The traders cheered and fist-pumped the air. "Don't worry. London is the biggest precious metals market in the world. There's a whale out there, waiting to gobble up our trades."

Of course, he didn't tell his traders that he already knew of a whale in the guise of the Bank of England ready and waiting to buy the gold. That would have been tantamount to admitting that the game was rigged. Neither did he tell his band of merry men and women that Borite Metals Holding was nothing more than a shell company for the Russians, a way to funnel billions of dollars illegally out of the Kremlin and into the financial system of London. But if their gold was good enough for the Bank of England, it was good enough for him. He scanned the room, but there were no more dissenters. Still, he would need to sweeten the deal.

"One last thing. The first trader that succeeds in placing a hundred thousand ounces will receive a ten grand bonus this month." The room went wild. He could feel the greed, feel the ambition as each trader digested the announcement. Money. It's what drove them. It's what they lived for. "Right, get to it!"

The room suddenly became a hive of activity. Traders flung themselves into their seats and fired up their dealing systems. Computer screens flickered into life and calls to clients were made. Rhodes smiled. It was all going according to plan. He knew that a little after the London market opened the Bank of England traders would begin placing their orders. Small at first, so as not to spook the market, then increasing their orders in both size and frequency until the bank's order books were full. Of course, the price of gold would plummet. But one could always hedge against that eventuality and make a killing in the process.

Yes, everything was going to plan. The only fly in the ointment was ROD. Drummond, had completed his audit of the vault. Of course, he found nothing – but the man made him nervous. There was an intensity about him. He seemed driven. *He's going to kill you.*

His hand reflexively reached for his passport in his jacket pocket. He had his exit from London planned. A private plane would take him back to South Africa and from there, Venezuela. Free from the Russians – free from Vladimir Abramov.

His mobile pinged. He glanced at the screen. It was that idiot of a chairman. Sir Henry was badgering him to place another futures contract. He may be chairman of the bank, but he wasn't averse to turning a blind eye to an illegal trade. Hypocrite.

He turned to his computer screen, about to enter Sir Henry's trade, when a secure message popped up demanding his attention. One of Victor's men had sent him the briefest of notes on the condition of the vault tunnels: Tunnels flood. Girl?

Renkov had insisted on using his men to transport the gold through the tunnels and into the vault. He had no choice. He needed the gold back in the vault. But they were thugs, common criminals. They'll provide security, insisted Renkov, until the deal is complete and the gold is sold. He didn't trust Renkov. Why would Victor return the gold?

There was a lightning flash, and thunder reverberated around the dealing room. Rhodes' thoughts turned to Seymour-Jones alone in the tunnels with the water rising. A pretty little thing with beautiful red hair. He admired her grit. What did the American's say? She had moxie. He liked that in a woman. Sticking her nose into his business had been a bad idea. He hadn't time to deal with her now. He needed every man at the vault. The tunnels had flooded before. The little story he had told Sir Henry had only been half true. The vault had a damp problem – but nothing that would make him move six tons of gold. Seymour-Jones would have to tough it out with the rats. Nasty buggers, as big as cats.

He quickly typed a reply to the secure message: Leave the girl.

40

The small police launch slowed, bobbed and rolled in the Thames as it manoeuvred close to the Butler's Wharf slipway. The skipper expertly throttled the engine back and forth until it lightly bumped against a mooring buoy. Brock jumped out and secured a temporary line through a mooring ring and heaved back, holding the stern of the small craft until Drum and Fern had disembarked. He slipped the line and threw it back onboard the launch and waved the skipper off. The boat's engine powered up and thrust it's bow back into the raging swell of the Thames. They watched as the launch rose up and slammed down, wave after wave, until it disappeared.

Fern turned to the two men. "You think you have a chance in that?"

Drum knew she had a point. He pulled up his collar against the wind and rain. They had no choice. He wasn't prepared to lose Harry. He turned to Brock looking for words of advice from his old friend. Brock shrugged.

"We go as planned," he said.

"You're crazy," said Fern. "You'll both drown."

"Maybe."

They walked up the steps and onto the main path that led back to the office. Rain blew in off the river. The sky darkened and was pierced by an electric-blue flash of lightning, shortly followed by a rolling peal of thunder. They reached the office and piled into the small reception area as a torrent of rain flooded the walkway. They stood dripping water as they removed their coats and hung them up. Stevie peered around the corner of the kitchen.

"Oh good. You're back. You have a visitor. I parked him on the couch." She nodded in the general direction of Drum's office. "You look like you've had a great time. Tea?"

"Any news from Alice?" asked Drum.

"Nothing. Tried calling her several times, but all I get is her voicemail." Stevie disappeared back into the kitchen.

Drum looked through the glass wall of his office but could only see the back of someones head. He opened the door and walked through, followed by Brock and Fern. A lanky man with receding hair was stretched out on the couch, arms folded across his chest, his long legs crossed in front of him. He appeared to be asleep. He was wearing a large brown waxed coat and black army boots. A black canvas bag had been dumped unceremoniously on the floor in front of the desk.

Brock laughed. "Poacher."

At the mention of his name Poacher opened one eye and closed it again. "Hello, my lovelies."

Corporal Dick (Poacher) Davis spoke in a slow West Country accent. Every syllable was laboured as if the effort of speaking was too taxing for him. Drum was relieved to see the man. They had served together for many years in two theatres of war. Other than Brock, there was no one he trusted more; they had often placed their lives in his hands. In the coming hours they would need all the skills of this tall, softly spoken and unassuming man.

Stevie came in and placed a tray of steaming mugs on Drum's desk. She regarded the sprawling shape on the couch. "Is he asleep?"

Poacher opened his eyes, yawned and sat up. "God I'm tired. Been driving all day" He spied the tea. "Ah, you're a lovely girl. That you are." He pushed himself up out of the couch and kept on rising until he was standing above nearly everyone else; Fern looked him straight in the eye and smiled.

"Dick Davis, a.k.a Poacher, meet Commander Alex Fern of the NCA. You've already met Stevie," said Drum. Introductions over, he grabbed a mug of tea and sat by the window.

Poacher smiled back at Fern and held out a large hand. "Commander." He took her hand. "I must say, Commander, you're the best-looking copper I've seen in a while."

Fern gave him a wry grin. "Charmed, I'm sure."

Brock rolled his eyes. "You haven't changed."

"Come 'er," said Poacher and enveloped the short stocky man in a huge embrace.

Brock laughed, "Git off me, ya big lanky lump of mutton."

Poacher turned his attention to Stevie. "And another gorgeous young lady. Thanks for the tea. You're a real life-saver."

Stevie's face broke into a broad grin. Drum could have sworn she was blushing. The sharp-tongued, wise-cracking young Russian was as warm as a toasted marshmallow in Poacher's hands.

"What's in the bag?" asked Stevie.

The Poacher looked between Fern and Drum. Drum nodded.

"Tools of the trade, my lovely." He cleared some papers on Drum's desk then unzipped the large canvas bag. There was a clatter of metal as the bag's contents spilt out onto the floor.

"Bloody hell," said Stevie. "You planning to start a war?"

"We're at war already," said Drum. He put down his mug. "What did you bring?"

Poacher bent down and started to unload the bag. "I cleared out the arms cache up North." He placed two square-looking handguns on the desk. "Two Glock 17s." He retrieved two more slightly bigger handguns. "Two Sig p320s." He dipped back down. "Managed to wangle two H&K G36s with scopes. And Brock's favourite, a Remington shotgun." He smiled.

Fern moved closer to the desk and picked up one of the rifles. "A Heckler & Koch assault rifle. Even my team doesn't have access to these." She checked the safety then sighted through the scope. "You realise that it's illegal for civilians to own these weapons?"

"Good job we're not civilians then," said Brock taking one of the Glocks. He slipped the magazine and inspected the rounds. He replaced the clip, checked the safety and placed the gun back on the desk.

"What about your weapon, Poacher?" said Drum.

Poacher moved back to the couch and picked out a long case from the floor. Brock moved some of the guns to one side as Poacher placed it on the desk. He released two catches and flipped open the lid. "My pride and joy."

Fern cast an experienced eye over the weapon. It was broken into several pieces so it could be stored and transported in its case. It consisted of a very long barrel, fitted with a bulbous flash guard, a short black body, complete with a small magazine and pistol grip, and a thick stubby stock. A large precision scope was stored at the side. "What is it?"

"It's an Accuracy International AS50," said Poacher. British made."

"Which is what?" asked Stevie.

"A very accurate rifle. Gas operated for low recoil with a semi-automated action." He paused. "I'm a sniper."

Stevie looked up at him, wide-eyed. "You shoot people?"

"Usually only the once," said Poacher with a lopsided smile.

Stevie's mouth dropped. It was beginning to dawn on her what was about to happen. *We're at war already.* She looked at Drum. "And this is what you do …"

"He's the Package," said Brock. "We get him inside the vault …" He paused, picked up a Glock from the desk and racked the slider. "And hopefully, we get him and Harry out."

41

It was late afternoon when Fern made her excuses, leaving the three ex-soldiers planning the night's mission. She needed to organise the boat and prep the scuba gear, she had told them. Drum reminded her that insertion would take place at midnight and extraction no later than one thirty in the morning.

Stevie helped with logistics. She'd scoured the net and sourced several architectural documents that they hoped would provide them with a route into the vault.

Brock was looking at the documents. "Assuming we get you in," he said, stabbing a pencil at Drum, "how do we get Harry out?"

Stevie was perched on the end of the couch sipping tea. "Why can't you just swim out the way you came in?" asked Stevie.

Drum looked out at the black clouds scudding past. "Too dangerous in this weather and the tide too strong. We don't know the shape Harry's in. I don't even know if she can scuba."

"That leaves the elevator," said Brock.

"Which takes us either to the vault area or to the ground floor reception area and a room full of Russians," said Drum.

"We create a diversion at the front of the building," said Poacher. "Plenty of noise and smoke and I'll pick off anyone who pokes his nose out. Keep 'em busy." He pointed to a Google Map of the building and surrounding streets. "The two buildings either side are no good for a sniper – angles are all wrong and the field of fire is too narrow." He pointed to a structure on the mooring in the river, just across from the bank's entrance. "That should have sufficient elevation and allow a field of fire above the pedestrians and traffic. Perfect. I'll set up there."

Drum remembered something. "Stevie, can you get us a schematic of the other floors? I remember a staircase leading to another level."

"Right. I'm on it." She headed for the other office and her computer.

"You're thinking you can exfil from the roof?" said Brock.

"I was thinking of these windows on the second floor," said Drum. He pointed to the map. "They appear to look out onto the glass extension of the adjoining building. From there ..." He shrugged. He was worried about Harry. Could she walk? Could she climb? Was she injured? There were too many unknowns. Too many possibilities for failure. He couldn't lose Harry.

There was a buzzing from the reception area.

The three men stopped talking. Brock grabbed the holdall and stowed the rifles. Poacher slid his gun case behind the couch and grabbed a Glock giving the second one to Brock. Drum grabbed a Sig, ejected the mag and checked the clip was full. Satisfied, he snapped the clip back and racked the slider. Poacher and Brock repeated the procedure with their weapons: slip the mag, check the load, lock the clip, chamber a round. It was a choreography of action that they had performed many times. The sounds of the preparations resonated with Drum. They were the sounds before a battle that all soldiers remembered.

Drum saw Stevie reaching for the exterior door. "Stevie ... wait!"

Too late. She'd disappeared and buzzed the door open. There were the sounds of a scuffle, of Stevie crying out. A tirade of angry Russian expletives gave way to the harsh, deeper voice of a man with a Scottish accent: "Fuck off you silly bitch and get out of my way."

A bear of a man came barreling into view. He barged through the office door, rattling the glass of the walled partition as he did so and came to a complete halt with the realisation that three handguns were pointed squarely at his chest.

He stood there, water pooling on the floor from his rain-soaked coat and dripping trilby. No one moved.

Lightning lit up the room, throwing black shadows against the white walls and illuminating the features of the intruder. A clap of thunder finally broke the silence.

It was Drum who recognised him first, lowering his gun. "McKay!"

Brock and Poacher were less inclined to lower their weapons. Brock said, "Major fucking McKay of Her Majesty's Secret Service. Never thought you would have the nerve to show up here."

"McKay?" echoed Poacher.

Drum caught sight of Stevie slipping into the kitchen. "What are you doing here, McKay?"

McKay's eyes darted between Brock and Poacher who eventually took the hint and lowered their weapons.

"Spit it out, McKay," said Brock "I'm not going to kill you … at least, not yet."

"The Russian girl," said McKay, "you know she works for Vladimir Abramov."

"Yes," replied Drum. "Is this about Stevie?"

"It's about you working for the Russians."

Brock looked at Drum. "What's he talking about?"

"It's complicated," said Drum. "I thought I was helping Victor."

"And our American friends tell me you've done a deal with one of Vlad's henchmen," said McKay.

"I admit, it doesn't look good," said Drum.

"I warned you to drop the case, but you were never very good at taking orders."

Drum took a step forward, his fists clenched.

Brock placed a hand on his shoulder. "Just hold on a minute. Why are you here, McKay?"

McKay removed his trilby and ran a hand through his hair. He stood there, a frown creasing his brow, an internal debate raging within him. He sighed, having made a decision, and said, "We received an alert a few days ago – two Russians were flagged entering the country. We track a lot of Russians, but these two were different. GRU operatives, sent over for a specific purpose we believe. So we put surveillance on them."

"Is this going anywhere?" asked Drum.

"They give us the slip. We lose them for eight hours. Then one turns up dead."

"Killed by one of our people?" asked Brock.

"No," said McKay. "Killed by one of Drummond's people."

All eyes turned to Drum. "One of my people?"

McKay pointed to his pocket, indicating he wanted to take something out. Brock nodded. Poacher raised his gun a fraction. McKay slowly put his hand into his coat and removed a long thin blade with an enamelled butterfly on one end. "Recognise it?"

Drum knew immediately who had killed the GRU agent. "Alice."

Brock held out his hand and McKay gave him the blade. Brock gripped the enamel wings and made a thrusting motion with the blade. "A disguised stiletto. Where did you find it?"

"Inserted through the eardrum of the GRU agent, and with enough force to penetrate his cranium," said McKay.

"Bloody hell," said Poacher, "I hope the poor bugger's dead."

"He would have died instantly," said McKay.

"And who's Alice?" asked Poacher.

"She's my office manager," said Drum.

Poacher raised an eyebrow.

"Not the woman who's seeing your dad?" said Brock.

Drum considered all the possibilities that would have led Alice to kill a man in this fashion. None of them were good. "Where was the GRU agent found?"

"Spitalfields Market," said McKay. "Sunday afternoon."

"Then they must have William as well," said Drum. "I've got to find them ..."

This time it was McKay who stepped forward and placed a restraining hand on Drum's shoulder. "Which is what they want you to do."

"I'm lost," said Poacher. "Who're we talking about?"

"The Russians," said McKay.

"Which ones? There's so many," said Brock.

"Vladimir Abramov," said Drum. "He's trying to close me down – or has been told to. Fern and I stumbled on his money laundering operation run from a club in Mayfair. Somehow its connected to this bank vault and the gold bullion market. Harry must have figured it out. She has information on the operation. Harry is the key."

"It's important we find this Harry then," said McKay.

The three soldiers looked at each other in confusion.

"I don't understand. Why did Thames House close down the initial RBI investigation?" said Brock.

McKay turned to Brock, his eyes narrowing. "Because we *do* obey orders."

Drum shook his head. "You're being played, McKay. Someone in government is colluding with the Russians – someone with connections to the security services." McKay was silent. Drum pressed on. "It was probably a back channel request. On a need-to-know basis. You were singled out because of our history. Warn Drummond off, you were told. Low-key stuff. Do a soldier a favour. For old times sake. Don't kick up too much of a fuss. No paperwork." McKay looked down and gave the slightest of nods.

"He probably asked you deal with him directly, which means you know him. Someone connected to the service but not in an operational sense. Someone with enough weight in the government that no one questioned his demands." Drum paused. He looked down at the gun in his hand and realised that he still had his finger on the trigger. He relaxed, removed his finger and flipped on the safety. "But something didn't feel right, did it, McKay? Things didn't add up. Which is why you're here."

McKay stared at Drum, his eyes narrowed into two thin slits. He wanted a name. A name that would either confirm his suspicions about the whole operation or prove that Drum was full of shit and was working for the Russians after all. "Just give me the fucking name."

"Sir Rupert Mayhew," said Drum.

McKay's face dropped and softened. Then something happened that none of the men had seen before: he smiled. "I knew you were full of it, Drummond."

"If Mayhew didn't contact you, who did?" said Drum, surprised.

McKay looked behind him and sat down. He was working something out. That's what McKay always did. Thought through the moves. Drum reflected on the operations they had worked together. It was always McKay who saw the fly in the ointment, McKay who would question, probe, explore all the angles.

"You're half right," said McKay, eventually, "I'll give you that. And it was a back-channel request. Doing you a favour, as you said. Then things started to get a bit weird. Not exactly kosher. I was told to close you down. In the national interest. I was asked to hand over all data retrieved from the bank. Again, it didn't add up. So I put you under surveillance. And that's when things got interesting."

"I'm lost," said Brock, also sitting down. "If this Mayhew wasn't pulling strings, who was?"

McKay said, "Mayhew is almost certainly the puppet-master. From what Drummond tells me, it now makes sense. But it wasn't Mayhew who approached me. It was Tim Weekes."

42

Alice heard talking. A conversation in Russian. A man and a woman. They were speaking softly, making it hard to understand what they were saying. She slowly opened her eyes. Her head was fuzzy and she felt spaced out. There was a sour taste in her mouth and her throat felt dry.

She was in a large space, brightly lit, sitting in a chair beside a wrought-iron column. The walls of the space were bare brick and the floor was rough wooden boards. Industrial chic, she mused. A converted warehouse. Her eyes travelled up and found wrought-iron roof beams and a rusty pulley wheel. Not a good sign. A large oak desk sat in the centre of the space and was where the conversation was taking place. A man with a short-cropped beard in a dark suit gave the appearance of being in charge; the woman he was talking to was slowly raising her voice. Alice recognised her as the agent pushing the pram in the market, only now she was dressed in dark jeans and a short black leather jacket.

Her heart suddenly leapt at the memory of Sunday morning. Where was William? She slowly turned her head to her left and he came into view, slumped in a chair beside her, his breathing shallow. What time was it? What day was it? She had no idea. How long had they been here? A little further to her left was a glass window stretching almost the entire length of the wall. It was dark outside, but exterior lights shone on a small balcony – a wooden deck and, below that, a small mooring. They were beside the river. She strained her eyes and many more lights came into view, moving along a stretch of inky blackness. It must be the Thames. They couldn't be far from the office. Where had Ben been taken? Wapping. They must be in Wapping. A low rumble of thunder filled the room.

The man stopped talking and walked over to her. He spoke to her in Russian. "Ah, Alice – if that is your name – you are awake at last."

Alice shifted in her seat and was surprised to find she was not bound. She moved a hand to her hair which was loose around her shoulders. "Where are we?" she asked.

The woman moved closer to the man. "You should tie this one up. She is dangerous."

Alice smiled, remembering how she had lost her pin.

The woman scowled, stepped forward and slapped Alice hard across the face almost knocking her off the chair.

"Enough," said the man. "Alice. Do you know who I am?"

"Vladimir Abramov," said Alice.

"So, you know my name. That is good." He stepped back and sat on the edge of the desk. "She is angry with you, Alice. I don't blame her. You killed her partner. They had been together a long time." He reached inside his jacket and pulled out a battered gold cigarette case. He flipped it open and withdrew a long black cigarette and placed it between his lips, unlit. "My God, Alice. That trick with the pin ..." He took the cigarette out of his mouth and mimed stabbing it in his ear. "Amazing."

He reached over and grabbed an old battered table lighter and lit the end of his cigarette. He sucked in the smoke with a look of lazy satisfaction. "I remember speaking to an old KGB man, back in Moscow, many years ago. He tells how he also lost a partner to a hairpin such as yours. He claimed the assassin was a petite woman – attractive. A British agent. But no one believed him." He inhaled the smoke, deep into his lungs. "Was that you, Alice? Are you British Intelligence? MI6, perhaps?"

"Don't be ridiculous," said Alice. She turned to look at William. He was still unconscious. His breathing was becoming irregular. She was worried. Why wasn't he awake?

"He is a problem," said Abramov. "He did not react well to the drug. I hope we can wake him up. Otherwise ..."

Alice looked at Abramov, her eyes narrowed. "Why are we here?" she spat.

Abramov ground the end of his cigarette into an ashtray and stood up. "I need you to call Benjamin. We need to persuade him to cease his investigation. He is digging too deep and upsetting people. He also has something we need."

Yes, thought Alice, he saw you with Sir Rupert Mayhew. And Giles –
poor, poor Giles – he paid the price. She never imagined that Mayhew
would stoop so low. But why? Was it some play – a means to an end?
What did he gain by dealing with these gangsters? And if he was in
bed with the Russians, then it meant that the security services were
compromised. Who could be trusted?

"What is it you think he has?" said Alice.

"He's been looking for a ROD agent – Seymour-Jones. So have we –
or more precisely, so have the GRU. I think he knows where she is
hiding. I propose an exchange. You and the old man for this Seymour-
Jones."

"What makes you think Ben knows where she is?"

"Come, come, Alice. He's been asking questions at the bank and
been spotted at her apartment. He knows her. She's a fellow ROD
agent. He pretended to look for Pinkman, but he was looking for
Seymour-Jones."

Alice couldn't think straight. Her head was spinning. "I don't
understand. Why are the GRU interested in a ROD investigator?"

The woman stepped forward and struck her again.

"Alice, Alice," said Vlad. "Does it matter?" He shrugged. "She has
something – stole something. Information that could harm our
operation here in London. Then we need Benjamin to finish his work at
the bank. Write a nice report and piss off. Simple."

"Ben won't give up Harry," said Alice. "Not for me."

"You're right, Alice. Not for you. For his father. William. That is his
name? Come, come Alice. Don't play games with me. William doesn't
have time. He needs a hospital. Make the call, Alice."

43

It was 11 pm and preparations were being made for the raid on the vault. Drum was still angry at the revelation concerning Weekes. He and McKay had both been played. If Mayhew was the puppet-master, did that make Weekes the puppet? Where did that leave Anna? Was she a player or a stooge? And who was Weekes ultimately working for? The thought of his ex-CO being a double agent didn't sit well with him. The other men were struggling with the same realisation.

Drum had gone over the plan with the Major. He had agreed to sanction the operation. At least they now had MI5 on their side. After their conversation McKay had been on the phone for most of the evening.

He pushed the thoughts aside and concentrated on prepping the gear they would need for the op. It was going to be a lot of equipment to carry. Sidearm, the H&K, which at least had a folding stock, knife, flashlight, webbing, ammo and assorted tools. And that didn't include the scuba gear. It wasn't going to be an easy swim.

Brock was prepping the weapons for a water borne assault. He wanted to make sure they fired after a soaking. Poacher was stripping down the AS50, checking and re-checking every piece of the mechanism, and going through the ammo he'd brought. McKay had camped out in the small conference room and had set up a makeshift command and control centre. He was currently arranging for the Blackfriars Underpass to be temporarily closed for maintenance around midnight clearing the area of traffic and civilians in case a full-blown firefight ensued. Stevie had been in contact with Baxter who had provided remote access to the vault's security cameras. Stevie would be their eyes and ears once inside.

227

At 11:30 pm the buzzer sounded in the reception area. Drum moved to the main office door and cautiously opened it, the Sig in his hand.

"Expecting trouble?" said Fern. She was now in civilian clothes: black jeans, a black waterproof jacket. She was hauling a large nylon bag. The rain outside was lashing down, flooding the decking of the wharf walkway. "The police launch is moored up and waiting. The rest of the scuba gear is onboard."

Drum smiled and lowered the gun. "Sorry, we had a visitor. We're all a little edgy."

Fern frowned. "Everything OK?"

"We'll see."

They walked into Drum's crowded office. Fern held up the bag. "Your wetsuits. I had to guess sizes: lean and not so lean."

"Very funny," said Brock grabbing the bag. "Let's go change upstairs."

Drum and Brock made their way to the apartment above. Fern followed. Both began to strip down to their briefs.

"You gonna just stand there?" asked Brock.

"I'm not shy," said Fern. "Anyway, Drum owes me an ogle."

Brock rolled his eyes. They proceeded to pull on the wetsuits.

Fern walked over to Drum. The top half of his wetsuit hung around his waist. "You're really going to do his?" she said, her finger tracing the scar across his chest.

"I have to."

"Sorry to interrupt, but did you bring the van, Fern?" said Brock, padding over to the stairs in his wetsuit.

It's outside," said Fern not taking her eyes off Drum. "Don't worry. I know what to do."

"Right," said Brock. "I'll see you downstairs in five," and he headed down the stairs.

Fern smiled, wrapped her arms around Drum's neck and kissed him lightly on the lips. "Make sure you come back in one piece."

Drum was about to say something when his phone started to ring.

"Can't a girl catch a break?" sighed Fern.

Drum picked it up. He didn't recognise the number.

"Drummond," he said, pressing the phone to his ear.

Silence, then in a hoarse whisper. "Ben, it's Alice."

Drum braced himself in one corner of the rolling police launch as Fern heaved a scuba tank onto his back. Stevie was hanging over the side being sick. She had insisted on coming against Fern's better advice.

Fern shouted in Drum's ear, trying to make herself heard over the storm. "I've given you a small ten-litre steel tank. It's heavier and less buoyant than the aluminium ones you may have used. I figured the less buoyancy the better in this current."

Drum nodded.

"Listen carefully," continued Fern. "Swimming in this current is going to be hard and the tank is relatively small. If you get lost in the flooded tunnels …"

Drum squeezed her hand to acknowledge he understood. He checked his dive watch. Midnight. Brock gave him the thumbs up and he moved to the side of the boat. He took one last look around then pulled down his face mask. Fern had positioned the launch upriver, above the entrance to the tunnels. It meant they would be swimming with the current and not against it. They just had to make sure they weren't swept past the entrance, or they would never make it back. He took a bearing and fell backwards into the cold turgid water.

Drum felt the force of the impact on his back, followed by a muffled explosion of air and water in his ears. Then the world turned black, the only sound coming from his shallow breathing through the tank's regulator. There was another muffled thump as Brock followed him into the river. Already the tide was carrying them away from the boat. Drum turned on his torch and struck out for the Embankment and the entrance to the tunnel, swimming just below the surface. They would be invisible in this weather.

Drum kicked hard – strong sweeping strokes of his legs, no arms. He needed to conserve his energy if he was to reach the entrance in decent shape. He checked his wrist compass and kept to a bearing that he estimated would allow them to intercept the entrance. He tried to control his breathing but the sheer physical effort of swimming in the current was causing him to take long ragged breaths. He looked back. The light from Brock's torch shone dimly in the gloom behind him. He carried on, his legs burning with the exertion, his breathing laboured. He felt a tug on his leg and looked back. Brock was pointing for him to come up. He kicked upwards and raised his face mask just above the surface and looked around. They were about five metres from the iron gate, but drifting fast. Drum gave Brock the OK sign. Brock turned and, with several short flashes of his torch, signalled the boat that they were in position. It was up to Stevie now to disable the security cameras over the gate.

Both men slid under the water. Drum kicked hard, one final effort, to make it to the gate. He was within half a metre when he felt the sharp tug of the tide. He increased his efforts. Despite this, he wasn't going anywhere. He was within minutes of being swept away.

Stevie looked green in the harsh light of the cabin. The skipper of the launch applied power to the engines to keep the boat from drifting back, causing another bout of pitching and rolling. Stevie groaned and put her head between her legs.

"There's the signal," said Fern. "Get your shit together and do your hacker stuff – and don't puke in the cabin."

Stevie stood up and ran outside..

"Good grief," said Fern. "Now you tell me you're not good in boats."

Stevie staggered back inside and grabbed her bag. She unzipped it and withdrew her laptop and started tapping at the keyboard. "Shit, the signal's too weak." She turned to the skipper. "Can you get us any closer to the building?"

The skipper nodded and powered up the engines. The boat manoeuvred closer to the Embankment wall. "That's about as close as I dare get," he said.

Stevie stabbed her keyboard several times, a frown creasing her forehead. Then her face lit up. "Got you!" A green and yellow schematic slowly appeared on the screen. "I'm in the bank's security system. It's slow, but it will have to do." She clicked on two camera icons which turned from green to flashing amber. "There. I've not turned them off, just put them in standby. Anyone monitoring the feed should see a frozen picture."

Fern grabbed a torch and moved out of the cabin into the wind and rain. She flashed the light in the direction of the gate. Four short bursts. I hope they can see this, she thought. She waited.

"Anything?" asked Stevie.

Fern peered anxiously through the veil of rain. Come on, come on.

"Well?" said Stevie.

"Will you shut the fuck up." Fern wondered if she should signal again. Then she saw it. Four short bursts. They were safely at the gate. "They made it," shouted Fern. She poked her head into the cabin. "Right, let's get to the next mooring and meet with Poacher."

Poacher drove the van at a leisurely pace, down Upper Thames Street and towards the Blackfriars Underpass. The high-sided van proudly displayed the name 'Ives in the City'. Traffic was light at this time of night but he checked his watch anyway. It would be bad form to turn up late for a gig, and people were counting on his diversion. His hand moved instinctively to the long case on the passenger seat. All he needed was the right elevation and a fair wind. He hummed a little ditty.

There was the sound of static in his earpiece. "Poacher, sitrep." It was the dulcet tones of McKay from his makeshift C&C in Drum's conference room. Fucking McKay. He'd never thought he'd hear from that bastard again.

Poacher keyed his radio. "Approaching Blackfriars Underpass."

"Roger, receiving. The plod should be expecting you. Out."

Fucking well hope so, thought Poacher. Otherwise he would have some explaining to do. He imagined the conversation. *And what's in the case, sir?* One of Britains best-kept secrets: an AS50 semi-automatic sniper rifle. An effective range of eighteen hundred metres. *And do you have a licence for that weapon, sir.* Fuck off, sonny.

He approached the Underpass and, as promised, it was cordoned off. Two police cars blocked the road. He slowed to a stop and wound down his window. He waited for someone to approach.

"Evening sir."

Poacher leaned out of the window. "Poacher".

The policeman looked at the side of the van then back to his colleague who was examining his onboard computer. The policeman nodded.

"Thank you, sir ..." He hesitated. "What's in the case?"

"You don't want to know. Now open up. I'm in a hurry."

The policeman ran back to his car. Engines started and the two police cars pulled back allowing Poacher to drive through.

He drove for a short way before re-emerging onto the Embankment. He passed the vault on his right. He slowed and glanced to his left. An elevated wooden hut rose up from a mooring on the river. Bingo. It was perfect. He cruised on by until he spotted another mooring a few hundred metres further on. He slowed the van and stopped. It was quiet. No traffic and no pedestrians. McKay's planning had come good.

Poacher spotted them. Two women coming up from the mooring. Little and Large. Best keep that thought to himself. Fern tapped on the window. He opened the door and jumped out, looking around as he did so.

"Good timing," said Fern. "Any problems?"

"Sweet as a nut. Keys are in the ignition." He leant inside the cab of the van and grabbed his rifle case and kit bag. "Communications?" Stevie was staring up at the Poacher with a big grin on her face. "That's you, my lovely."

"Oh, right," said Stevie. "All good." She gave him a smile.

Poacher took a small round item, the size of a hockey puck, from his bag. "When you drive by, stop and slap that on the door. It's sticky on the back. Make sure the cameras are off."

Fern gingerly took the puck.

"Catch you later." And with that, he jogged back to the mooring opposite the vault. All he had to do now was break in and set up. He hummed a little ditty.

Drum was making one last monumental effort to reach the iron gate when a hand came out of the blackness and grabbed his arm. Brock held on to the gate with one hand and pulled Drum in with the other. Eventually, Drum grabbed hold of an iron crossbar and relaxed. He tried to calm his breathing. He checked his air gauge. He'd used more than half his supply. He turned to Brock and pointed up.

They broke the surface, pulled up their masks and spat out their mouthpieces. Rain lashed down around them as they bobbed up and down beside the gate. The tunnel was completely submerged.

"Thanks," shouted Drum. "I'm knackered."

"Let's get moving. We're behind schedule."

Brock unhooked a pair of bolt cutters from his belt. He shouted in Drum's ear, "I'll go back down and cut the locks. Careful the gate doesn't swing out and knock you off." He replaced his mask, bit down on his mouthpiece and slid beneath the water.

Drum heard a clanking and then a dull snap. The gate moved suddenly but stayed shut. Drum clung on. Eventually, Brock resurfaced and replaced the cutters back on his belt. He pointed down. Drum pulled down his mask, inserted the mouthpiece of his air supply and sank below the surface. Brock was pointing to one side of the gate. Drum grabbed hold and both men pulled. There was a dull clunk and one side of the gate swung open.

Even with both flashlights, visibility was down to just a few metres. The only good point was the current had diminished. Drum checked his watch. They were fifteen minutes behind schedule. They needed to make up time. They carried on swimming, keeping as close to the tunnel roof as their tanks would allow. After five minutes they came to a junction – which was a problem because it wasn't on the map.

Brock turned to Drum. Left or right, he mimed. Drum had no idea. It was fifty fifty. He checked his air gauge. Just a quarter of a tank. He didn't have the luxury of making a wrong turn. *Don't get lost in the tunnels.*

Drum was still trying to decide on a direction when a large rat swam past his mask. He pulled back instinctively. Another rat followed. Then a partially decomposed corpse drifted into view. Both men recoiled and let it drift past along the roof of the tunnel. It had come from the right-hand fork. Drum made his choice.

They swam up the right-hand fork for several more minutes. The water level had still not dropped. Then they saw it. A gated alcove. Drum shone his flashlight through the bars. All he saw were old packing crates, bobbing against the roof. He checked his air gauge. He had only a few more minutes of air. He decided to press on. He indicated to Brock to keep swimming.

Soon, Drum noticed a change in the water. An air gap of about half a metre appeared above them and he could make out stone steps coming up from the bottom of the tunnel. They paused and moved forward slowly, keeping just below the surface.

The stone floor came up to meet them allowing Drum and Brock to push up their masks and spit out their mouthpieces. They gulped in the air. It tasted rank and smelt bad – as if something had just died. Then Drum heard it. A whimpering sound and a slight cough, a little further up the tunnel. They pushed forward and found a second gated alcove. Drum again shone his flashlight through the bars. It was Harry, standing on a packing crate, up to her knees in water.

44

Drum played his torch around the alcove. Harry stood there, shaking from the cold and sheer exhaustion. She slowly turned towards the light.

Drum put his finger to his mouth. She acknowledged with a barely perceptible nod. A tear rolled down her cheek.

Brock tapped Drum on the shoulder and indicated with his hand to look further up the tunnel. Drum could make out a faint glow. He nodded. He would clear the tunnel; Brock would free Harry. He undid his weight belt and let it sink slowly around his feet, then he carefully removed his air tank and lowered it gently to the tunnel floor. He discarded his mask and removed his fins. He unstrapped his H&K and unfolded the stock, checking the mag and screwed the suppressor onto the short stubby barrel. Drum knew the suppressor would not completely silence the weapon, but he hoped it would be enough to prevent the sound of gunfire from reaching the upper levels of the vault. He racked the slider on top and chambered a round. He flipped off the safety and selected single fire. He would need to conserve his ammo. He turned off his torch and waded up the tunnel.

Drum headed towards the glow, moving slowly and as silently as possible through the dirty water. The lights in this section of the tunnel had blown. He could barely make out the sides of the walls. The water receded with every stride. He came upon another alcove on his left, the iron gate open against the wall. He pressed himself against the gate and listened. Nothing. He peered inside the dark recesses of the alcove but it was empty. He pressed on.

The water was now up to his ankles allowing him to move a little faster. The light grew brighter. He could make out markings on the tunnel walls. He took another stride, stubbing his toe on the bottom of a stone step. He swore quietly under his breath. He could hear the sounds of a conversation. He raised his weapon and mounted the steps.

He rounded a shallow bend, crouching low. The floor was wet but had yet to flood. Bulkhead wall lights illuminated a widening corridor that ended in a large space and the elevator shaft. The sound of conversation intensified as Drum crept closer. A room came into view to his left. Two men were drinking and playing cards, the door ajar. Drum pressed himself against the opposite wall to lessen the chance of being seen and crabbed closer. He reached the elevator and slid silently against the wall, coming to the side of the door. The men were talking in Russian, relaxed, enjoying their game. Drum stepped into the middle of the door frame and kicked the door fully open.

The conversation stopped. Both men frozen at the shock of his entry. Drum put a single bullet in the chest of the furthest man who was reaching for a gun. The impact spun him backwards over his chair. In his peripheral vision, Drum saw the second man coming for him. Too slow. Drum put two bullets into his chest at close range, the impact felling him like a tree, pushing him back against the wall. Drum entered the room and put a second bullet through the head of the first man, just to be sure. He quickly surveyed the scene, then left the room and headed back down the tunnel.

He rounded the bend, splashed down the stone steps and switched on his torch, flashing the light four times. Brock returned the signal. There was a dull clang followed by the screeching of rusty metal hinges. It took him only a few more minutes to reach Harry's makeshift prison.

"Give us a hand," said Brock, struggling to get Harry down from the crate. "I think she's suffering from hypothermia." His hand struck the water. "Fucking rats ... get off me you bastards."

Drum handed Brock his H&K and waded into the alcove. He reached up and grabbed Harry around the waist. "I've got you. Let's get you out of here."

Harry looked down. "Ben ..."

"Later," said Drum. "We gotta move."

Harry stepped off the crate, clinging to Drum's neck, her body shaking. Brock took her arm and they waded out.

"I've got her," said Drum.

Drum half carried and cajoled her up the tunnel. Brock followed close behind. They had reached the stone steps when Harry sank to her knees.

"Sorry ... legs are cramping. Been standing for hours."

"Not far now, Harry. A few more steps." Drum heaved her up and they staggered on until they were back at the room near the elevator.

Drum lowered Harry to the floor and propped her up against a wall. Her head drooped forward. She didn't look good. He went into the room and spotted a flask, a half bottle of vodka and a couple of mugs. He stepped over the two dead men and retrieved the flask. He opened it and sniffed. It was coffee and still warm.

He knelt beside Harry. She looked asleep. Brock was trying to wake her.

"Let me try." Drum poured out some of the flask's muddy contents into a mug. "Wake up Harry. Drink this."

Harry's eyes flickered open. She smelt the coffee, grabbed the cup with both hands and downed the contents in one gulp. He refilled the cup, adding a slug of vodka.

"Slowly this time."

Harry sipped from the cup. She half-closed her eyes and rested her head against the wall. "Thank God you found me ..."

"Better late than never," said Brock. He broke out the comms, donned his headset and turned on his radio. "Comms check, comms check. Stevie are you there?" All he heard back was static.

Drum donned his headset and secured his radio on his belt. "We're still too deep. The tunnels are shielding the signal." He tightened the straps of his webbing and checked his gear.

He looked down at Harry who was now shivering. He went back into the room and looked behind the door. Sure enough one of the guards had a parka hanging there. He brought it out and wrapped it around Harry's shoulders. "Let's go, Harry."

They helped Harry to stand and then moved over to the elevator. "The only way is up," said Brock. "You find an access card?"

Drum thought for a moment then searched each pocket of the parka and pulled out a plastic access card.

"How did you know it would be in the coat?" asked Brock.

Drum smiled. "Because that's where I keep mine." He placed the card against a panel on the wall. A light illuminated green and they heard the soft whine of the elevator motor as it descended to their level.

Brock stepped back and trained his rifle on the door. He waited. The doors slid open. The car was empty. "All clear. Let's go."

They piled in, Drum supporting Harry. Brock tried the radio one more time. "Comms check. Stevie, are you there." Again, just static. "No joy."

"Punch it," said Drum.

Brock leant forward intending to punch the button for the lobby when the doors suddenly closed. "What happened?" The elevator motor spun up and the car lurched upward. "Shit, someone's called the elevator."

Fern sat in the cab of the Ives van. All the traffic on this stretch of the Embankment had ceased, leaving things eerily quiet. Only the occasional riverboat broke the silence of the night with a mournful sounding of its horn. She had parked the van in a dimly lit side street, as close to the wall of the vault as possible. The rough brick wall blocked out the driver's side window, adding to the gloom of the cab's interior the only light came from Stevie's laptop screen. She wondered what she was doing here, sitting and waiting on someone else's command. Usually, she was the one in control and it irked her that all she could do was count down the minutes. She checked her watch.

"That's the fifth time you've checked your watch," observed Stevie.

"What are you, the clock police?"

"Just saying … there's no need to be nervous."

Fern turned around. "I'm not nervous, just frustrated at being stuck inside this van listening to you fucking poke at that laptop." She gripped the steering wheel and turned to face the street once more. "Try them on comms. That's your job right?"

Stevie touched a small bone mic attached to her ear. "Comms check. Comms check. Come in please." She paused. "Nothing but static."

"Are you sure your gear is working?"

"We always knew they would be in a radio black spot in the tunnels … or perhaps their radio wasn't as water-resistant as we thought."

Fern slumped forward and rested her head on her hands. "That's just great!" She looked up. "Try Poacher."

Stevie sighed. She switched channels on her radio. "Comms check, Poacher. Still awake?"

The dulcet tones of Poacher floated over the airwaves. "Hello, my lovely. I was thinking of you."

"Good grief," sighed Fern. She touched her bone mic. "Any activity at the front of the building?"

There was a pause then a crackle of static. "As quiet as a graveyard, Commander."

"You all set?" asked Fern.

There was another pause, longer than before. "As ready as I was the last time you asked me, Commander."

Stevie quickly interrupted, "Thanks, Poacher. Comms check out."

Fern groaned. "I can't believe I just asked a SAS veteran if he was ready."

"Ben will be alright."

"Ben?" said Fern.

"Yeah. Why do you two call each other by your last names? What is that?"

"You wouldn't understand. Drum's ex-military ..."

Stevie smiled sweetly. "Well, he certainly stood to attention when he was in bed with me."

Fern turned to face the young Russian. "Listen, you little Russian tart. I have a Glock 17 strapped to my thigh. So I'd quit with the aggravation."

"Right, just kidding ..."

A crackle of static filled the cab. "Which channel was that?" asked Fern.

Stevie checked her radio. "It's Ben's channel." She made a few adjustments. "Ben, Ben are you receiving." She waited. There was another crackle, then what sounded like 'Evie'.

"It's Drum," said Fern.

Stevie kept trying to tune the radio. "They must be up from the tunnels. But where?" She fiddled with the radio again. "No good I can't get them back."

"Fuck," said Fern. "If we go too early they won't make it to the second floor."

"What do we do?" asked Stevie, her voice rising.

Fern pounded the steering wheel with her palms. "Wait, wait. If they've made it out of the tunnels then they must be in visual range of the security cameras. Can you punch them up?"

"Right!" exclaimed Stevie. She turned to her laptop. The video feeds from several cameras appeared in neat squares across her screen. "They're not on the first floor." She punched up more feeds. "Not on the second floor. Nor the lobby ..."

"What about the vault?"

Stevie frowned. "Why would they be in the vault?"

"Just do it ..."

Stevie brought up the vault feed. The square of video blinked onto the screen and the vision of Drum and Brock, walking down from the elevator towards the vault, guns blazing.

Drum sat Harry down in the corner of the elevator. "Stay down."

"Let me help," said Harry.

"You can help by not getting shot."

"Ready?" asked Brock.

Drum moved beside Brock and readied his rifle. "The only way is down the corridor, to the left, towards the vault door. Watch for a room on the right."

"Roger that."

The elevator car bumped to a halt and the doors opened. Two big men in the grey uniform of the bank's security guards froze in front of them. Drum recognised them as the ones who had dragged Harry to the vault. Drum fired first, taking out the guard directly in front of him with a head shot. The second guard only had time to move his hand to his jacket before Brock took him out with a similar shot. The force at point blank range threw each man back onto the opposite wall, adding their blood and brains to the decorative marble. Despite the use of suppressors, the noise from the weapons echoed off the walls.

Drum and Brock trained their weapons down the corridor. The vault's monstrous door was open as was the balance room beside it. Drum saw no movement. He waved Brock towards the wall while he moved over to the opposite side. He crouched down and keyed his mic. "Stevie, are you receiving?" Static filled his earpiece. He adjusted his radio, trying to fine-tune the frequency. "Stevie, are you receiving?" He shook his head and indicated they should move forward. They needed to clear the area. Both men crouched and moved towards the vault, weapons raised.

A movement in the vault caught Drum's eye. He flipped the H&K selector to semi-automatic. A hand holding a gun appeared around the side of the balance room door and blindly fired off several rounds down the corridor, the concussion of sound bouncing off the solid Carrera marble of the walls. The shots went wide of their mark.

Brock sighted down his H&K at the gun protruding from inside the balance room. He fired once. The round found its target and smashed into the gun, removing several fingers from the hand. An easy shot for the veteran SAS Sergeant at such close range. They heard a scream and the gun clattered to the floor. A guard stumbled from the balance room into the corridor, one hand clutching the mangled and bleeding wreck of the other. Brock fired twice more, a double-tap to the chest and the the guard collapsed to the floor.

They continued their advance towards the vault. Drum could see inside: the racks of safety deposit boxes at the back, the stacks of solid gold bars around the sides. They were no more than ten metres from the entrance when a shape appeared from behind a wall of gold bricks. "Gun. left-hand side," shouted Drum.

They both opened fire, short bursts. A cacophony of sound filled the enclosed space, the metallic hammering of bullets ricocheting around the steel walls of the vault and off the gold bars, the clattering of spent and smoking cartridge cases falling onto the marble floor. Drum held up his fist. The metallic echoes faded. Nothing moved.

Drum waved his hand forward and to the right. Brock moved cautiously into the balance room; Drum moved into the vault. The smell of cordite hung in the air. The vault had only one occupant, a guard lying dead in the centre. Probably the result of several ricochets.

Brock walked into the vault. "Clear." He looked around him, eyes wide. "Bloody hell. We're in the wrong business."

The room was packed with gold bars. A small trolley stood in the middle of the space near the dead guard. They were about to move the shipment to another location, obviously not via the tunnels this time. On the trolley was a stack of small 100g gold ingots. Drum picked one up and examined the serial number. He replaced it and examined another. There were ten ingots in all. He chose one at random and slipped it into his webbing.

Brock gave him a look. "We helping ourselves, now?"

"I'll explain later. Let's go. They must have heard that racket upstairs."

They headed back up the corridor and were approaching the elevator when the doors suddenly closed. Drum ran to the wall and slammed the access card onto the side panel. The panel light lit up amber with a small arrow pointing up. He heard the soft whine of the elevator motors as the car ascended with Harry inside it.

Fern switched channels on her radio and keyed her mic. "Poacher, it's Fern. I'm coming round."

Stevie looked wide-eyed at Fern who was now clambering into the back of the van. "Fern! Where are you going?"

"I'm not sitting here while they're in trouble. Keep trying Drum."

Fern pushed open the back doors of the van and jumped down. She ran out of the side street and onto the main road. "Poacher?"

"I see you, Commander."

"Blow the doors. They're in trouble."

"Roger that. Blowing the doors."

A thunderous explosion ripped through the air followed by a cloud of smoke and a shower of debris. Fern ran towards the newly created opening.

A crackle came over the radio. It was Poacher. "Commander wait. Keep down. I need eyes on the lobby."

Fern crouched down below the low wall of the building's entrance. She looked up, her breathing ragged. The smoke was clearing. A man in a grey jacket with a gun in his hand came out onto the steps . Fern drew her Glock and racked the slider. She stood up and aimed, her arm outstretched. The man saw her and turned to fire.

Fern heard a faint high-pitched whine and then the guard's head explode in front of her.

Poacher's calm voice came over the radio, "If you're going in, Commander, keep to your left. I wouldn't want you as collateral."

A chill ran down Fern as she watched the disfigured corpse collapse and roll down the steps.

"Commander?"

Fern broke free of her reverie. "I'm going in."

She took the steps two at a time. She needed to get to the elevator at the back of the lobby as quickly as possible. She stumbled over the broken remains of the oak doors, almost dropping her gun. She cursed, looked up and saw a guard rising from behind the front desk, gun raised. I'm too slow she thought. She heard another high-pitched whine and ducked instinctively. The guard's chest exploded.

Fern pushed on, crouching, weapon raised. She hugged the wall and crabbed her way around to her left. She chastised herself for her sloppy technique. Focus, Fern focus. The first reception room came into view on the opposite side of the lobby. She remembered the layout from her previous visit. The ornate, Regency desk. She thought that she was exposed when the glass door of the reception room suddenly shattered and a bullet zinged past her ear. A guard had emerged from the side of the room and had fired through the door. She shuffled sideways and returned fire. Two shots. The first missed but the second hit the man's shoulder and spun him around. She fired once more, hitting him squarely in the back and sending him crashing to the floor.

Fern keyed her mic. "Room on your right. One down. Looks clear. I'm moving to the back of the lobby."

"Roger that, Commander."

She heard a woman's voice. She moved over to the central desk and peered around one corner. The smoke and dust had now dissipated and she could make out the entrance to the elevator. Two guards were dragging a tall woman out.

She keyed her mic. "Two guards, wrestling with a woman ... could be Harry."

There was a brief pause. "I see them. Yep, that's her." There was another pause. "I can only take one out. The other guy's too close."

"Take the shot." She heard another whine and the guard furthest from Harry was thrown back against the wall.

The second guard froze in shock for just a few seconds before grabbing Harry around the neck and yanking her in front of him.

Poacher cursed. "Damn, I've haven't got a shot."

Fern left the safety of the desk and moved to the left side of the lobby. The guard holding Harry managed to fire twice, both shots going wide of their mark.

"Still no shot," Poacher announced calmly.

Fern crept towards the elevator, crouching low, trying to reduce the firing angle between her and the guard. There was no cover and she still had two more reception rooms to pass. She'd made a stupid mistake. Where was Drum? Why hadn't he left the vault? Then it occurred to her. How stupid not to think of it. They were stuck waiting for the elevator.

Fern switched channels. "Stevie. Are you there?"

"What's going on? I'm wetting myself sitting here all alone. You're supposed to protect me."

"Stevie, focus. Do you have eyes on Drum?" Another shot rang out, this time much closer. Fern crouched lower.

"Wait ... yes. They're in the vault area, by the elevator doors. Still can't reach them."

Fern switched to the Poacher's channel. "Poacher, can you put a shot close to the guard?"

"Commander?"

"We need to force him back into the elevator."

"I think so ..."

There was a brief pause. Then she heard it and the flooring to the

242

right of the guard exploded upwards in a cloud of dust and fragments.

"He's moving back inside the elevator," announced Poacher.

Fern stood up. The guard raised his gun. Too late. The doors to the elevator shut and the motor spun up as the car descended.

Drum slapped the access card against the elevator panel for the tenth time.

"It's no good," said Brock. "Someone must be holding it at the lobby."

Drum continued to hold the access card against the access panel. An orange down-arrow blinked slowly. Of all the stupid things to happen, he mused. They couldn't go up and they couldn't go down. And Harry was stuck upstairs. The question was, who else was upstairs?

He felt a vibration run through the marble floor of the corridor.

"Did you feel that?" said Brock.

Drum pressed his ear to the elevator doors. "Sounds like gunfire."

"They must have blown the doors," said Brock. "Try your radio again."

Drum tweaked his radio. "Stevie, Stevie, come in, Stevie." He paused. "Still nothing."

Drum pressed his ear to the door again. He heard a few more shots. Someone was having fun.

The arrow on the panel turned green and pointed down. Drum looked at Brock. "Against the wall." They pressed themselves on either side of elevator doors and readied their H&Ks.

The elevator stopped with a thump and the doors opened. Harry was flung out roughly into the corridor. Drum and Brock half turned and opened fire killing the guard before he had time to realise he was not alone. Brock stuck his foot in the door.

"See to Harry. I'll hold the doors."

Drum moved to Harry's side. She looked all in. "Sorry. We lost you for a moment."

Harry placed an arm around Drum's neck and heaved herself up. "It's a war zone up there. A tall woman … seems to be storming the place."

Drum smiled. "That'll be Fern. I guess she grew impatient."

"Let's go, guys," said Brock.

Drum helped Harry back into the elevator, stepping over the dead body of the guard. He pressed the button for the lobby, keeping it depressed with his finger. "Please go up," he murmured. It sounded like more like a prayer.

Harry let out a short laugh, followed by a fit of coughing. "If it goes back down, you're both fired," she croaked.

The elevator gave a small lurch and started to ascend.

"Thank God," sighed Brock.

"Can you stand, Harry?" said Drum.

"I'll be alright. Just don't leave me in this elevator again."

"Roger that," echoed Brock.

The elevator slowed. They could hear more gunfire. The car lurched to a halt and the doors opened. Brock stuck his foot in the door but made no attempt to leave the car. He selected a channel on his radio. "Poacher, Brock. Receiving?"

"Nice of you guys to show."

"Can we exfil out the front?" asked Brock.

"Negative," Poacher replied. "Four hostiles heading through the front entrance ..." There was a brief pause, followed by the sound of a high-velocity round that blew a hole in the wood panelling at the back of the lobby, close to the elevator doors. "Correction, three hostiles heading in your direction with automatic weapons." There was another pause then the sound of automatic weapons fire from the front of the lobby. "I think I've been spotted. I'll have to bug-out soon. Be advised: you have the Commander coming your way ..."

Drum broke into the channel. "Hold fire, Poacher. We're making for the stairs."

"Roger that."

Drum peered around the elevator doors. Three men with automatic weapons were pinned behind the lobby desk. They hadn't noticed the elevator and thought they were safe.

Drum noticed the body of a guard sprawled on the lobby floor, half-in, half-out of the reception room closest to the elevator. Poacher's handiwork. Then he saw Fern. She had taken cover behind a large stone urn. If she kept her cool, she might be able to make it up the stairs without being detected. If she was spotted, they would have to contend with three men bearing down on them with automatic weapons. She looked up and gave him a grim smile.

Drum turned to Brock. "Watch out for Fern. She'll be moving to the stairs with you."

Brock frowned "And what about you?"

"If they clock you, I'll lay down covering fire from the elevator." He smiled. It wasn't much of a plan but they needed to get out. "I'll lay down smoke then leg it. Whatever you do, don't wait. Get to the van."

Brock nodded. "C'mon, Harry. Hope you can walk."

Drum peered out of the elevator. The three guards were changing mags. They turned to face the door, trying to pinpoint the Poacher's location. "Go, now." He looked over at Fern and pointed to the stairs. She nodded and started to creep around the urn. Brock helped Harry out of the elevator, her arm around his neck. She limped and staggered out into the lobby. Drum changed mags and crouched just inside the doors of the elevator, sighting down at the three men.

Brock and Harry made it halfway across the lobby and hooked up with Fern. She took hold of Harry, freeing up Brock, and headed for the stairs. They had made it to the bottom of the stair when Harry cried out. Drum looked over and saw blood pooling beneath her foot. She must have trodden on some broken glass. One of the men looked back and shouted and then all three turned towards them, weapons raised.

"Go, go," shouted Drum. He opened fire, a sustained burst from the cover of the elevator and took out the man who called out, raking a line of bullets up his body. The other two men immediately scattered left and right. Fern continued to drag a limping Harry up the stairs. Brock had stubbornly stayed and was laying down short bursts of weapons fire from the base of the stairs. Drum pulled a smoke canister from his webbing, snapped the pin and rolled it down the lobby. Thick smoke billowed out obscuring visibility.

Automated fire immediately raked the side of the elevator forcing Drum back inside the car. Brock returned a sustained burst of fire. It's now or never, thought Drum and ran out of the elevator for the stairs. He reached the first few steps and caught sight of Brock now kneeling halfway up, waiting for him. He barely made it off the lower level of the stairs before a burst of fire raked up the lobby obliterating one of the handrails.

"Shift your arse," said Brock, "I'm almost out of ammo."

"I thought I told you not to wait"

"Yeah, right."

The radio crackled and Poacher came over the airwaves. "Two cars just past my position. McKay reckons they broke through the cordon. They look to be heading for the entrance. Wait … one has stopped. Ok I have a group of hostiles heading my way. Bugging out."

"Time to leave," said Drum.

Drum and Brock ran up the stairs, each taking a turn to lay down short bursts into the thickening smoke to discourage anyone from following. Fern and Harry were waiting at the top. A narrow landing led back into the building with two further rooms leading off to the right. Both rooms had solid wooden doors. Both doors were closed. They hadn't time to check and clear the rooms. More hostiles could be heard entering the lobby. They would be coming up the stairs very soon.

Two window openings, complete with ornate marble colonnades, were on their left, five metres apart. Drum ran over to the first window. He looked down. He could make out the glass roof of an annexe of an adjoining building. It was only a short drop.

Drum called over to Fern. "Out the window. I'll lower Harry down."

"Really?"

"You're the tallest. It's only a short drop for you." Drum took Harry from Fern and they moved over to the window.

Fern looked at the glass roof. "I'm also the heaviest."

"It'll hold your weight," said Drum.

The window looked old, a single pane affair with an elaborate pattern of lead-lights. Fern tried the handle. It moved up. She pushed and the window opened. There was a loud click and an alarm sounded.

A burst of gunfire came up from the lobby, chewing up the stairwell.

"I think we've been rumbled," said Brock.

Fern holstered her gun and clambered up onto the windowsill and climbed out of the window. She turned, hanging from the window ledge, her feet dangling over the glass roof of the annexe. Drum looked back as Fern let go and dropped. There was a loud crack.

He looked down. Fern was crouching on top of the glass roof, a large fracture radiating out from beneath her. She gingerly stood up and slowly moved beneath the window, her arms stretched up.

"Your turn," said Drum, lifting Harry and sitting her on the windowsill. He gripped her wrists and hands as she backed out over the edge, lowering her gradually until Fern had grabbed hold of her. The pair shuffled off over the glass roof towards the alley where Brock's van was parked.

He switched channels on his radio. "Stevie, come in Stevie." There was the crackle of static but no reply. Shouts came from the lobby. The smoke was clearing and another burst of gunfire raked the stairwell. Brock broke out another smoke grenade and tossed it down the stairs. This evoked more shouts and a sustained burst of gunfire.

"Out you go," said Brock calmly. "They're getting ready to rush the stairs."

Drum looked over the window ledge. The two women were almost to the alley side of the building. Harry was limping badly. He applied the safety to his H&K, folded the stock and strapped it to his back. He climbed up and squatted on the sill. His wetsuit which had served him well in the chill waters of the Thames was now causing him to burn up in the heat of battle and he was sweating profusely. He turned and jumped backwards, grabbing hold of the sill in one smooth motion. He hung there, swinging for just a second, before dropping onto the roof. There was an ominous crack from the glass beneath him. He froze and looked down. The fracture of glass had widened but was still holding. He moved carefully off the broken panel and stood beneath the window and waited.

It wasn't long before Brock appeared. He handed down his weapon then jumped back and grabbed the ledge. He hung there before dropping like a stone. He landed hard, falling backwards. Drum heard the roof crack. Brock froze. Drum leaned forward and grabbed Brock's arm. There was another loud crack. Drum pulled Brock towards him just as part of the roof crashed to the floor of the annexe beneath them.

They crouched low and crept along the roof, hugging the back wall of the vault. They reached a small ledge that led down onto a flat roof and jumped down. From here it was a ten-metre drop to the alley below where Stevie was waiting in the van. Fern had stopped at the edge of the flat roof and was supporting Harry around the waist.

"We have a problem," said Fern.

Drum looked down. The van was gone.

45

Alice awoke with a start to the sound of Abramov barking orders to his men. She must have dozed off. She straightened her back and rolled her head from side to side to ease the stiffness in her joints. Fuck old age.

Abramov had returned to the warehouse with his enforcer, Misha. The big Russian took up position by the door. His presence seemed to fill the room. Alice remembered Ben's description of the man and their meeting in New York. He acknowledged her with the slightest of nods. She stared back at him but did not return the nod. She wondered what part he was playing in this game.

She looked at her watch. It was just after two am and there was still no word from Ben – but then, she didn't think Ben would show anytime soon. And certainly not with Harry. Which begged the question: what was Ben's play?

William's breathing was still ragged but had not deteriorated. He needed a hospital, but she knew Abramov had no intention of letting any of them live beyond the end of the night. If Ben was going to make a move, it had to be soon.

She eased herself up from the chair and stretched. One of the guards moved towards her. "Sit down."

She smiled at him. It was a smile she'd practised over the years. "Be a dear and make me some tea."

He hesitated, taken aback by her demeanour. It was as if his mother had given him the order. Abramov laughed. "Go and make tea, Dmitri. Russian tea." He walked over and perched himself on the edge of his desk and lit a cigarette. "You're good, Alice. I can understand why the GRU are wary of you."

Alice walked over to the window and stared out into the night. Apartment lights from across the river twinkled like distant stars. She regarded Abramov's reflection. "Why not let William go? He knows nothing, he's seen nothing."

"I can't do that, Alice. You know how this game works. You shouldn't have involved the old man." He looked at his watch. "And where is Benjamin? You said he would be here tonight."

Alice turned to face him and shrugged.

A buzzer sounded. Abramov turned to Misha and nodded in the direction of the door. Misha drew his gun and moved over to the entrance. He looked at the video feed from the security cameras and buzzed the door open. The diminutive figure of Anna entered the room, wrapped in a Burberry mac, water dripping from a small umbrella. She stopped when she saw Alice.

"Ah, Anna. Nice of you to join us," said Abramov. "I think you and Alice know each other."

Anna ignored him and walked over to a coat rack, hung up her mac and dropped her umbrella onto the floor. Her tight black woollen dress hugged her toned figure. She moved casually over to a couch, some distance from Alice, and sat down. "Why is she here? More to the point, why am I here?"

Abramov smiled. "I wanted you to be here. Our GRU friends insisted on it. I am expecting them shortly. Dmitri is making some tea. Would you like some tea?"

Anna turned to look at Alice then back to Abramov. "No, I want to get back to my bed. What is this all about, Vlad?"

"Patience, Anna."

Alice didn't like this new development. From Anna's expression it was clear she wasn't too happy either. Abramov knew something. What, Alice had no idea. If Anna was working for MI6 then it was looking like her cover had been blown. If that was the case, she would be handed over to the GRU and would probably never be seen again. As far as Alice was concerned, death was a better option. The question was, how many friends did she have in the room?

The front door buzzed. Misha again drew his gun and walked over and inspected the video feed. Was this Ben? The door opened and the other GRU agent entered, rain dripping from her leather jacket. She walked quickly over to Abramov and whispered something. Abramov smiled.

Dmitri returned with a tray of cups and a small samovar and placed it on a table close to Anna. Abramov nodded in Anna's direction and Dmitri moved over and stood by her side at the end of the couch.

Alice noticed that Misha was still waiting by the door. She heard footsteps over the timpani of falling rain. Someone could be heard stamping their feet and removing a wet raincoat. A tall lean man dressed smartly in a light-grey pinstriped suit, his City brogues polished to a military shine, stood in the lobby. Alice thought she recognised him. She had trained her memory over many years to observe and recall the smallest of details of a person. She remembered his lean features, the intelligence in his eyes, his lank blond hair now greying at the temple. She remembered Tim Weekes of MI6.

46

"That little bitch has left us." Fern heaved Harry up.

"You don't know that," said Drum, peering into the gloom of the alley. All seemed quiet after the recent sounds of gunfire. He looked down. They had estimated the height of this side of the roof at just over two storeys. Could he drop down? Even if he could, what about Harry? That was the point of having Brock's high-sided van.

"Then where is she?" pressed Fern. "I knew it was a mistake to trust her."

"Then you shouldn't have left her," replied Drum. "Your job was to stay with the van." He knew he was risking Fern's pent-up anger, but her entry into the firefight had complicated matters. Now their escape route had disappeared.

Fern turned to face Drum. "What! I can't believe you just said that …"

Brock sighted down his H&K. The open window was just visible from their location. "We can't stay here. They'll work out where we are pretty quickly. So I suggest you both zip it until we find a way down."

Harry looked as if she was about to drop. Fern helped her to the back of the flat roof and sat her down with her back against the raised edge of the adjoining roof. "Let me take a look at that foot."

Drum moved back from the edge of the roof and knelt, trying to keep his profile as low as possible. He pulled his radio from his belt and examined the channel frequencies to make sure they were set correctly. He selected Stevie's channel. "Stevie, this is Drum. Come in Stevie." He waited.

"Poacher here. Receiving you. Sorry to keep you. Stevie ran into a spot of bother. We hooked up further down the Embankment. You should see us reversing back anytime now. Be advised: hostiles heading for the alley."

They heard the van before they saw it, the whine of its gearbox screaming in protest as it rounded the bend in the road. Two red tail lights blazed like angry fireflies as the van weaved a drunken path into the alley. There was gunfire from the main street. The van wobbled before scraping the driver's side against the bare brick wall, the soft aluminium siding screeching like nails down a blackboard. The passenger side door was flung open and Poacher jumped down, a Glock 17 in his hand.

"Get a move on people," said Poacher over the radio. "McKay advises that SCO19 are responding. We need to be gone before they arrive."

Drum knew that SCO19, the police armed response unit, would not be able to distinguish between the Russians and themselves. To the police every person carrying a firearm would be a potential target. They couldn't get caught in a full-blown firefight with law enforcement.

"Hostiles coming out of the window," announced Brock. The suppressor of his H&K whispered twice. They heard a cry followed by the crashing of falling glass and then the loud wail of an alarm. "He didn't land well."

Drum turned to Fern. "I'll jump first. Then you hand Harry down. Watch for hostiles firing into the alley."

Fern nodded and hefted Harry up. "Keep your head down."

Drum shouldered his H&K then clambered down the side of the brick wall until he was hanging over the van. He dropped and landed on the roof with a loud clang.

Gunfire echoed in the alley, breaking the silence of the night. They had been detected. Poacher returned fire.

A pair of legs dangled over Drum's head. He reached up just as Fern dropped Harry down. He barely caught her in time and the two of them collapsed onto the roof. "Ok, down into the van."

Harry clambered over the roof and stumbled headfirst through a skylight. Drum heard a crash as she landed heavily in the cargo area at the back.

Automatic weapon fire raked the wall close to Drum. He knelt and un-shouldered his H&K, extending the stock. He sighted down the scope. Two men with automatic weapons had appeared around the side of the building and were laying down fire.

Drum spoke calmly into his mic. "Time to go, people." He switched the selector of his H&K to semi-automatic and fired, the attached suppressor reducing each burst to a barely audible whisper. The two men quickly retreated around the corner of the building as Drum's bullets ricocheted of the Victorian brickwork.

Fern dropped onto the van. She drew her Glock. "No time," said Drum. "Get inside." She reluctantly re-holstered her sidearm and lowered herself down through the skylight. "Time to go Brock."

Brock appeared over the edge of the roof and slowly slid down. He dangled over the van for a few seconds before dropping as Drum grabbed him. "They're coming over the roof," he said and jumped down into the back of the van.

Drum banged on the roof of the cab. "Let's go." He lowered himself onto the edge of the skylight facing the rear of the van, his feet dangling inside. Poacher jumped back into the cab and slammed the door. Drum held on as the van lurched into gear and moved out of the alley, turning a sharp left onto the main road that led off the Embankment towards Queen Victoria Street and back into the City. He caught sight of several guards exiting the front of the vault. He was preparing to return fire when the van swerved around a bend in the road and they were gone.

Drum clicked his H&K to safety and lowered himself down inside the swerving van. He heard the wails of police sirens in the distance. SCO19 were en route which meant the Russians were probably bugging out. He surveyed the back of the van. Fern sat with her back against the rattling side panels, her long legs outstretched, an arm around Harry, cradling her head against her shoulder. Brock, his wetsuit undone to his waist, his webbing and gear discarded, squatted with his knees held against his chest. Drum had seen this many times before. Soldiers caught up in the heat of battle, surviving one firefight after another, their screaming muscles fuelled by adrenalin, their aches and pains ignored. And then the fight is over; the silence deafening. The realisation that they have survived. The body reacts to the silence and closes down.

He suddenly felt weary. He stowed his weapon and removed his webbing. The van swerved then came back on track. Drum turned to face the cab and realised Stevie was driving, her small frame hunched over, her knuckles white from gripping the wheel.

"Slow down, Stevie," he said.

Poacher looked back from the passenger seat and raised an eyebrow.

He turned to Stevie and placed a large hand on her arm. "Pull over, my lovely. Let me drive."

Stevie slowed and pulled into a bus lane, crunching the gears until the van came to a stop. She slumped forward.

Poacher pulled her towards him. She buried her head in his chest sobbing. "It's alright, my lovely. We all cry the first time. You're safe now. We all are."

47

The black Range Rover with tinted windows sat dormant on the Wapping street not far from the narrow entrance to the Regency Wharf warehouse complex. The heavy rain had subsided to a light drizzle leaving the shadowy cobbled street glistening in the subdued orange glow of the street lamps. The three men sat in silence, each harbouring their thoughts of the night's events.

A radio crackled causing McKay to sit forward and listen intently to the tinny voice coming from his earpiece, his face creasing into a deep scowl. "Fuck it. Victor's gone."

Drum sank deeper into the plush leather of the big SUV. He'd thought as much. Victor's men at the vault would have warned him ahead of time that their operation had been compromised. He'd had an escape plan set up well in advance. Victor was ever the wily dog. He'd played him and Abramov and still managed to elude capture.

Brock shifted in the back of the vehicle. He was dressed in the tactical gear of the NCA, courtesy of Fern. His H&K rested on his lap. "What about the gold?"

McKay half turned. "It's where Drum said it would be. SCO19 reports there's tons of the stuff."

"Blimey," said Brock. "Any opposition?"

"Just a few guards – the rest appear to be immigrant labourers. SCO19 have rounded them all up and secured the warehouse."

"And this is your dad's place?" asked Brock.

"Right," said Drum. "I remembered William telling me he was having trouble with a lease – people working at one of his warehouses, day and night. Fern and I came by information that Victor had borrowed money to pay for a lease. I put two and two together." Drum looked at his watch. It was 4.15 am.

"You don't have to do this," said McKay. "We can send in SCO19."

"I can't risk Alice and William by going in mob-handed. I trust the old team. I trust us."

McKay nodded. "Our man was reported entering the building about an hour ago. He was with the remaining GRU agent. A woman. It looks like we were right." He paused, staring out into the gloomy night. "Vauxhall Bridge wants him alive – and the GRU agent if possible."

"What do you want?" asked Drum.

McKay sat back and gripped the wheel of the SUV with both hands. He stared into the night, a look of anguish on his face. He was never a man to show much emotion, but Drum could tell he was struggling to keep himself under control. "He betrayed his country – fuck it, he betrayed us. I've lived for years with the failure of that last mission. I believed I screwed up …"

Drum nodded and opened the door. "I can't guarantee what will happen in there. Shit happens."

"Focus on getting Alice and William out," said Brock. "Fuck Weekes. Fuck em all."

"Everyone in place?" asked Drum

McKay nodded. "All set."

Drum turned to Brock. "If I'm not out before daybreak, send in the cavalry."

Brock grabbed his arm. "I hope your friend comes through for you or you really are fucked."

Drum mounted the steps to the warehouse and buzzed the door. He waited, looking up at the security cameras. He pulled up the collar of his coat against the light drizzle of rain and the occasional plop of water dripping from the roof above. The door opened and he walked through into the small lobby.

Misha was waiting for him – gun drawn and pointing straight at his chest. "Turn around, Benjamin."

Drum turned to face the wall and placed his hands on top of his head. Misha searched him thoroughly, his big hands running down his arms, his waist and legs. He patted each of the coat pockets and stood back. "Coat pocket. Remove it."

Drum delved into his pocket and retrieved the small 100g ingot he'd taken from the vault. He handed it to Misha. Misha took the bar and waved Drum into the main lounge.

Abramov had assumed his usual position in the centre of the room, perched on the edge of the oak desk. He drew lazily on one of his Russian cigarettes, watching with interest as Misha approached and handed him the ingot. Alice was seated next to William by the patio doors. Drum wondered why William was still asleep. He could tell that William's breathing was erratic and his skin looked pale. Standing close to Alice was Tim Weekes. He stood like a man apart from the others in the room, one hand casually slipped inside his coat pocket and the other resting on the back of Alice's chair. Beside him stood the female GRU agent, slightly built, black leather jacket and jeans. She stared at Drum with a mixture of disdain and self-satisfaction. She thought she had won. Drum finally turned his attention to Anna, sitting impassively on a couch. A guard stood next to her holding a gun. At least Drum knew where Anna stood in all of this. She too had been betrayed by Weekes. Misha returned to his usual position by one of the supporting pillars, his handgun trained on Drum.

Abramov hefted the ingot in his hand, feeling its weight. How could something so small be so heavy? Gold had a habit of defying the senses. "Benjamin. You came." He drew on his cigarette and sucked down the thick smoke. "But you came alone. That was not the deal, I think."

Drum stared at Weekes. He wanted the man to say something, to atone for his guilt. How many had died under his command as a result his betrayal? Weekes said nothing.

Abramov looked from Drum to Weekes and smiled. "You know each other? I think so. I'm told by the GRU that he is a Colonel in your MI6. I am surprised, Benjamin. How easily you were played."

It was Drum's turn to smile. "I think we've both been played, Vlad. And don't worry about Seymour-Jones – Harry. She's safely out of harm's way, helping MI5 retrieve the cache of information from Hoschstrasser & Bührer, your law firm in Zurich." Drum directed his next question to Weekes. "You remember Major McKay? He sends his regards."

Drum noticed Alice smiling.

Weekes turned pale. "You're bluffing. The woman is dead."

Abramov frowned. "And you know this how?"

Weekes hesitated. "She must be. It's the reason she's not here."

"I did find Pinkman, however," said Drum. And he *was* dead. At least we think it was Pinkman. Harry told us it was."

"And where was Pinkman?" asked Abramov. He stood and examined the ingot under one of the lights. "And why have you brought me this?"

Drum took a few steps to his right so he was facing Weekes at a slight angle. "We found Pinkman floating in the flooded tunnels beneath the vault. He'd been there for some time, his face was half eaten away by the rats that live down there. It's where we found Harry."

"Beneath the vault, you say?" Vlad glanced at Weekes. "Who killed him?"

"Probably one of Victor's men – or Weekes."

"You're full of shit, Drummond ..."

Abramov raised a hand. "What has Victor got to do with this? And why would the Colonel kill Pinkman?"

Drum noticed that Weekes had slipped his hand inside his jacket. He looked over at Anna. She was now sitting upright, her hands on her knees. Misha pushed himself away from the column, gun in hand. The GRU woman had stepped away from Weekes.

"You thought Pinkman was your man," continued Drum, "when in fact, he was really working for Victor. And Victor ... well, Victor was working for Victor, but he had help from Weekes."

"He's talking nonsense," said Weekes. "He's playing for time."

Abramov turned to Weekes. "Speak again and I will shoot you myself."

Weekes shifted uncomfortably.

"You were right to be suspicious of Victor, Vlad. He played us both. And all the time he was stealing your gold – with some help from the Colonel here."

Abramov looked surprised. "But you audited the vault. Rhodes told me you found nothing. All the gold was accounted for. You talk shit."

"And you would be right," said Drum. "When we eventually returned to the vault, all the gold was there – but it wasn't your gold."

"You're talking in riddles," said Abramov. "Get to the point or I start shooting people. I'm fucking tired of this shit."

"The gold you have in your hand is one of ten 100g bars. I took it from the vault a few hours ago. It is part of your inventory. The rest made up of standard good delivery bars."

"You took it from the vault ..."

"All ten bars have the same serial number," said Drum.

Abramov's eyes narrowed. He examined the ingot once more under the light. He rattled off a command to Misha who pulled a knife from his belt and handed it to him. Abramov grabbed the knife and placed the ingot on top of the desk. He slammed the knife into it, gouging a deep rent in its surface. He moved back over to the light to examine his handiwork. He cursed loudly, his face contorted in anger.

Drum noticed that the GRU agent had moved closer to his side of the room. He wondered how this was going to play out. It all depended where the loyalties lay.

Abramov made an effort to calm himself. He glanced at the GRU agent and then at Weekes. He was obviously having the same thoughts as Drum. He tossed the bar to Drum. Drum moved under one of the spot lights. He had been right. Beneath a thin veneer of gold lay a dull grey metal.

Drum said, "On the surface this looks like a 100g ingot. It has the Zurich refiner's mark and a serial number. When we audited the vault we accounted for all the gold: one metric ton of your original consignment and five tons of gold that Harry was tracking; but there were duplicate serial numbers on many of the bars. In fact, it was clear that someone had just made up the numbers. Then I remembered my lesson from the Bank of England. Gold is one of the heaviest metals. But it's not the only heavy metal. This bar is comprised mainly of tungsten. It's a fake – along with the remaining six tons sitting in the vault."

There was silence. Weekes moved closer to Alice and placed his hand on her shoulder. He quickly reached inside his jacket and pulled out a small handgun. Drum heard the click of a hammer being cocked. The GRU agent had closed her distance to Abramov and was now pointing a gun at his chest. She spoke in Russian to Misha who still had his weapon trained on Drum. Misha had no choice but to lower his gun. He knelt slowly and placed his gun on the floor in front of him. She issued another order and Misha moved back and stood by Drum. Weekes issued a command to Dmitri who was looking from him to Abramov. Dmitri nodded and trained his gun on Anna. So much for loyalty.

Abramov smiled and sat back on the edge of his desk. He spoke to the GRU agent who nodded. He slowly extracted his battered gold cigarette case from his pocket and removed a cigarette. He regarded the end of the cigarette as if seeing it for the first time. He had resigned himself to the fact that he wasn't going to live to see the sunrise.

"You were right, Benjamin. We have both been played." He reached for a lighter and lit the cigarette, inhaling deeply. He absentmindedly flicked at its end, although there was no ash to flick. He smiled. "How do you remove six tons of gold from a vault without anyone noticing?"

"It doesn't matter, Vladimir," said Weekes.

"Shut the fuck up. I served Moscow for years and this is their thanks."

Drum waited. "The original plan was for Pinkman to remove the gold over a weekend," he said. "There are tunnels under the vault – a wartime relic. As the vault manager he could authorise the movement of bullion from one location to another. In this instance the gold was scheduled to be moved to the alternate vault – a move designed to frustrate the audit that Harry had arranged. She was interested in tracing contraband gold from Mexico City. She had no knowledge of Victor's scheme, although she suspected something was wrong from the information she had gleaned from H&B in Zurich. Instead of moving the gold to the alternate location, Pinkman used the underground tunnels to barge the gold to Victor's warehouse here in Wapping. It's where the gold was smelted and re-cast."

Abramov looked incredulous. "Wapping, you say." He laughed and shook his head.

"You told me yourself that Pinkman was a very fucked-up individual. Drink, drugs and rock n'roll had taken their toll. The plan was always to fake the bars and return them to the vault via the tunnels. Pinkman would then amend the shipment details on the bank's computers and no one would be any the wiser. All the original documentation was stored on his laptop, which is why everyone involved in the scheme wanted to get hold of it. It held too much incriminating evidence." Drum paused. He glanced at Alice. She looked grim and determined. He hoped she wouldn't do anything foolish. Anna was waiting patiently, biding her time. She was under no illusion as to what Weekes had planned for her.

"What went wrong?" asked Abramov.

"Pinkman," interjected Weekes. "He had lost control."

"So you killed him," said Drum.

"I had no choice ..."

"Which kind of put Victor in a bit of a bind," continued Drum. "There was no Pinkman to return the fake bars. When Victor turned up on the Monday, the vault was empty. He had no idea what the Colonel had done."

Abramov roared with laughter and shook his head. "Incredible.

What a fuck-up. How did Victor return the gold?"

"From what Harry tells me, Victor did a deal with Rhodes. He was in a fix. Six tons of gold was missing from the vault. He was desperate to get the gold back before the ROD audit. The gold was shipped back to the vault via the tunnels before they flooded. I don't think Rhodes had any idea the gold was fake."

Weekes shifted beside Alice, looking uncomfortable. Drum could see the cogs working. He was never the most spontaneous of leaders – even in his younger days in Afghanistan. "The incident at the vault tonight. That was you, Drummond?"

"I'm afraid we interrupted the last part of your plan. MI5 and SCO19 are already at the vault and have taken control. Most of your men are dead and we have seized the real gold in Victor's warehouse. Her Mastery's Government thanks you for your contribution to its gold reserves."

Abramov inhaled one last time before grinding his cigarette into an overflowing ashtray. He smiled grimly. "I think it is you who is fucked, Colonel Weekes. You have nothing to take back to Moscow. You have lost the gold and the OMEGA operation is dead in the water. Careless of you."

Weekes glared at Drum, "You always were a good soldier, Drummond. Always ready to do the right thing. It's why I chose you." He looked at his watch and moved towards the large windows of the patio doors. "But you had one weakness. You could never make the hard choice. Too sentimental." He turned and looked down at the small jetty. Satisfied, he returned to take up his position behind Alice. "Tell, me. How did you manage to get past my men at the vault? You couldn't have been working alone?"

Drum took in the complete scene. The stage was set, all the players were in position. The angles looked good. Drum shrugged in response to the question. "Teamwork. You remember that? McKay ran intelligence, Brock delivered the package." He paused. "And Poacher …"

At the mention of Poacher, Weekes's demeanour changed. His face dropped at the realisation of his miscalculation.

Drum pointed two fingers at Weekes, his thumb miming the hammer of a gun. The patio windows exploded.

The width of the river Thames is not great. In many places it is less that 265 metres. The Poacher had set up in an abandoned car park on the south side of the river. The perfect location for a sniper. From his vantage point, it was an easy shot for a marksman of his calibre. At that distance, not even bullet-proof glass could stop a round from an AS50. A British made weapon. One of the best in the world.

The Poacher had resisted a headshot and aimed just left of centre of the main body mass. The bullet of the AS50 was travelling at supersonic speed when it passed through the glass of the patio door.

The force of the sniper round exploded into Weekes' back, destroying his chest cavity, throwing him forward onto Alice and continued before finally embedding itself in the far wall of the apartment. Alice grabbed the gun from the lifeless hand of Weekes as he fell forward. She shrugged him to one side, stood up and calmly took aim at the hapless Dmitri. She fired twice – a double tap to the chest, killing him instantly.

The GRU agent quickly moved behind Abramov grabbing him by the shoulder in an attempt to shield herself from another sniper round. She held her gun to his temple, attempting to shuffle him back towards the lobby.

Misha did not hesitate. He took two strides towards her and placed his large hands around the small woman's head. In one fluid movement, he whipped his hands apart, snapping her neck cleanly. Her lifeless body crumbled to the floor.

Abramov was about to say something when Alice interrupted, her arm outstretched. "Misha, move aside, please."

Misha turned to Drum, perhaps seeking some form of confirmation on what he should do.

Drum shrugged.

Misha stepped back.

Anna rose smoothly from the couch. "Alice, don't. We need him. He has value …"

Alice laughed bitterly. "Not to me he doesn't. He is scum. Murdered countless people over the years. He murdered Giles without a second thought."

Realisation spread across Abramov's face. "The old man at the club. That was Giles?"

Alice fired twice more. The second bullet pieced Abramov's heart.

Alice lowered her gun. "Yes, that was Giles."

48

Anna drove the Ferrari in her customary manner: heels off and very fast. Drum admired the skill it took to handle the power of the car without wrapping it around a tree. Dawn was breaking as they left the warehouse complex in Wapping. Anna confidently navigated her way through the empty streets before accelerating onto the A13, heading for London City Airport.

Drum pressed his phone against his ear, placing a finger in his other ear to drown out the noise of the big V12 engine as it roared along East India Dock Road. He nodded and ended the call.

Anna glanced in his direction, "Everything alright?"

Drum stared fixedly on the road ahead. A light goods van flashed by as they overtook it at an unnerving speed. "A police launch took William to St Thomas' Hospital. They think he'll be fine. Slight hangover. Nothing he hasn't experienced before."

"And Harry?"

"Dehydrated, hypothermic, battered but not broken. Also St Thomas'. MI5 have her on lock-down. Fern is with her. She's pissed I asked her to stay behind."

"Harry?"

"No, Fern."

Anna gave him a wry smile. "Why did you do that? She can take care of herself."

Drum didn't know – or perhaps he did and didn't want to admit it. Why was his relationship with the Police Commander complicated? They liked being together, but they kept dancing around each other.

"Did you suspect Weekes?" asked Drum, changing the subject.

Anna was silent for a moment. "The short answer, no." She slowed as they turned onto Victoria Dock Road. The Royal Albert Docks, now home to London City Airport, was just ahead. "The long answer, I wasn't sure. The mission seemed to be deviating from its original goal, which was to close down OMEGA. If the top brass had any inkling they didn't let on. The funny thing was, he did activate you and Alice. Like it or not, you're still working for the British government."

Drum thought about this. He remembered what Weekes had told him during their original meeting: find the primary actors of OMEGA and eliminate them. It was Weekes' way of cleaning house. Well, they had certainly done that despite the protestations of MI5. McKay would get some flak over that, but would take it on the chin.

"How did you know Weekes was working with Victor?" asked Anna.

"I didn't at first. Victor's a schemer, a dealer. He's not comfortable around guns. It was only after I'd spoken to McKay that I realised Weekes must have been organising that side of things. He probably muscled his way in when you reported back on what Victor was up to. I doubt if Victor had any choice in the matter. His appearance at the Warehouse was a cleanup operation. He wanted to remove all evidence of OMEGA."

"And Pinkman?"

"Again, not Victor's way of doing things. It had to be Weekes – or one of his men."

They turned onto a roundabout and accelerated past some hangers.

"What will happen to Misha?" asked Drum.

Anna drove slowly over a bridge that linked the North and South sides of the docks. "He'll be debriefed back at Vauxhall. He's a valuable asset with his knowledge of OMEGA and other Russian networks."

Drum wondered if the man would ever escape his life of serving one government or another. He wondered the same thing about himself.

They turned into the small car park of a private aviation company. Anna pulled up in front of the security barriers, the V12 engine chortling on idle. Drum could see a Learjet on the tarmac not far from a small terminal building on the other side of the security fencing. Two armed police officers approached the Ferrari. Anna lowered her window and flashed her ID.

A burly policeman took the card and examined it. He scanned the inside of the Ferrari. "Your man is already onboard. His flight's being held. What are your orders?"

"Radio the tower and ask the pilot and crew to disembark. No one is to board the plane until we leave. Understood?"

"Yes, ma'am."

The security barriers were raised. Anna parked the Ferrari just outside the terminal building. The jet sat no more than twenty metres away, the crew already disembarking.

Anna turned to Drum. "Nothing about OMEGA can be revealed. Should it become known that London dealt in fake gold bullion, the London market would collapse and the integrity of the Bank of England would be compromised. Your original orders stand."

Drum nodded and checked inside his jacket. He slid out of the car. It was 6.00 am and the first flights of the morning were landing on the airport's small runway. Drum walked slowly across the black tarmac, wet from the night's rain and glistening in the early morning sunshine. He made his way up the steep steps of the Learjet and entered the luxurious cabin.

Rhodes was in the middle of the aircraft, lounging in a plush leather seat. A tray of drinks was on a table in front of him. He was holding a tumbler of whisky, waiting patiently, staring out of the small round window.

Drum took a seat opposite. If Rhodes was surprised, he didn't show it.

"Can I offer you a drink, Captain Drummond?"

Drum smiled. It was the first time Rhodes had referred to him by his rank. "Not when I'm working."

Rhodes turned to face Drum, a look of resignation on his face. He sipped his drink, savouring the moment. "When we didn't take off I guessed it was too late – although I was expecting the lovely Commander. By the way, how is she?"

"Sorry she couldn't make it. Presently with Harry. She doesn't send her regards."

Rhodes half smiled over the rim of his glass. "It was nothing personal. Wrong place at the wrong time. Glad she made it out."

"Who's idea was OMEGA?" asked Drum.

"Does it matter?"

"Sir Rupert Mayhew we know about. But what about Sir Henry Minton?"

"Both cut from the same cloth that pair," confided Rhodes. "Old school chums. The backbone of the British establishment. You won't find any dirt on Minton, but you can be sure he knew what was going on. Mayhew pulled all the strings. Probably his idea."

"Who did he report to?"

Rhodes put his glass down with a look of disdain. "God, don't be naive. You sound just like a policeman. Think about it. The UK is about to exit the EU - the most disruptive economic event in the past forty years. Sterling will fall off a cliff when that happens. The Bank of England needs to shore up its gold reserves. The Russians were only too happy to help. But if you think you can point the finger at anyone in the Cabinet or the Prime Minister's Office, then you're deluding yourself. Whether they knew about the scheme or not, Mayhew will take the fall." He slumped back and held out his wrists. "Time to put the cuffs on?"

Drum reached inside his jacket and pulled the Sig Sauer out from its holster. From another pocket he retrieved the fat barrel of a suppressor and screwed it in place. He sat back, the gun pointed at Rhode's chest.

Rhodes froze in disbelieve. *He's going to kill you …*

"It would have been better if the Commander had come. She *would* have put the cuffs on. Unfortunately for you I'm not a policeman."

"Listen Drummond –"

"There's a saying in our part of the service …"

Drum fired. Two bullets into the chest. Both aimed at the heart.

Don't declare war on a soldier.

He stared at Rhodes' body, but found no peace.

49

Drum woke early. He pulled up the blinds and stared out at the London skyline. The light from the low autumn sun danced playfully on the Thames. The storms of the last few days had all but dissipated, leaving the streets cleaner and fresher. It was as if the rain had washed away all the blood – at least temporarily. Even now new players would be entering the markets to fill the voids left by the failures he had cleansed.

He headed for the shower and stopped. Is this what he called home? Stevie was right: who lived here? The room bore no trace of him. It could be a hotel suite, featureless and generic. This wasn't a home, it was a billet. Why was that?

It was 7:30 am when Drum made his way downstairs. He was surprised to see Alice behind the reception desk.

"Didn't think I'd see you today?"

Alice was dressed in her smart business attire. She wore the same dark-blue suit she had interviewed in. Her hair was perfectly coiffed once more and held in place with her butterfly hairpin. She noticed him staring and moved her hand absentmindedly to it.

"Sorry. Can't be without this. Giles gave it to me, years ago."

He smiled and changed the subject, "How's William?"

Alice beamed. "Much better. Doesn't remember much – thank God. I blamed it on a plate of bad jellied eels."

Drum laughed. "Good I'll pop up and see him this afternoon." He looked at the small woman. She had been through so much and yet here she was manning his reception desk. Business as usual. "And what about you?

Alice considered the question. Her pale-blue eyes regarded him – a teacher examining her student. He always felt she was testing him. "Oh, I'm alright. Best to keep busy. No good sitting at home moping."

He thought he'd better broach the next subject, although he was dreading her answer. "What about your plans?"

"Well, I'd hoped you would let me stay on for a bit – until I sort out my pension, if that's alright? I'm seeing someone this afternoon."

He felt relieved rather than pleased or perhaps a little of both. He couldn't imagine anyone else running the place now. "Alice, that's great. I was hoping you'd stay on. I don't know what I'd do without you."

She smiled. "You're very sweet. I must admit playing bowls with your father all day could get a little tedious – but let's try not to get mixed up with any more Russians."

They both laughed.

He went into his office and made a start on a backlog of paperwork that had accumulated over the past month. Invoicing, bills, meeting schedules – a business didn't run itself.

He was working on a very large and satisfying invoice for Roderick, Olivier and Delaney when his email pinged. It was from Raj. McKay had assured him that there would be no issues over his assistant's immigration status but, after his detention, Raj had decided to spend some time visiting relatives back in Delhi. Drum scanned the email and realised that Raj wasn't coming back. He'd accepted an offer from a large Indian outsourcing company to be their Chief Security Officer. He thanked Drum for his mentoring over the past year and hoped he would understand. After his treatment at the hands of the security services, Drum understood completely. But this left him without a security analyst.

"Knock, knock." Stevie poked her head around the door. "Alice said it was alright to pop in."

Drum couldn't help but smile. "Stevie, of course. Come on in." He moved from his desk and hugged her. "How are you doing?"

Stevie looked up at him. "I'm fine. A bit shaky still, but Poacher said that was normal." She sat on the end of the couch while Drum perched on the side of his desk.

"I gather McKay was pleased with the H&B material," said Drum.

"The guys a pig. I told him about the number on the back of the photograph. It was similar to the encryption key you and Raj use to store secure information. Mueller used a similar service. He just snatched it out of my hand and stomped off. How do you put up with him?"

"We can't always choose who we work with. He came through in the end. That's all that counts," said Drum.

There door rattled as Alice backed in carrying a tray of tea and biscuits.

"Thought it was time for morning tea," she said. "Give it a minute." She took a seat next to Stevie on the couch. "I saw Raj's email. Pity. I liked him."

Drum thought that Stevie being here was not a coincidence. "So, Stevie. What are your plans?"

"I don't know. I haven't given it much thought. Probably go back to Cambridge and see if I can resume my Masters." She fished a key from her jacket pocket. "I thought I'd better return this." It was the key to William's flat.

Drum turned the key over in his hand. William was never going to go back to that flat. He looked at Alice. She raised an eyebrow and cocked her head to one side as if to say 'get on with it'. "Apparently, we have a vacancy. Raj's old position – if you're interested? It comes with an apartment to rent." He tossed the key back to her. "What do you say?"

Stevie broke into a broad grin. "Yes!" Then she started to sob.

Alice poured the tea. They chatted and made plans for the coming weeks. Alice insisted that Stevie finish her Masters – at least on a part-time basis. Drum told her to take a few days and sort things out. As she was leaving Alice spoke to her in Russian. Stevie blushed and said her goodbyes.

"What was that all about?"

"I told her that now you were her new boss she had to keep her hands to herself."

"Very thoughtful of you," said Drum.

It was mid-day when Alice poked her head around the door. "Commander Fern to see you." She shooed Fern into the office as if she was reluctant to enter. "I'll leave you to it, Ben. I have an appointment. See you tomorrow."

"Thanks, Alice," said Drum.

Fern crashed onto the couch and regarded him. She was back in civilian dress. The jacket of her smart grey suit had been tailored to accommodate the bulge of her sidearm. Drum guessed from her demeanour that he was in trouble.

"So, why didn't you call?" she asked.

"You're looking especially gorgeous this afternoon."

"Don't change the subject."

He reached over and pointed the desk lamp at his face. "It weren't me guv'nor. I was at home, tucked up in bed."

She laughed, despite herself. "I was told you went off with that Russian tart in her fancy car."

Drum was surprised. "Anna?"

"Whatever alias she goes by. I spent the night with Harry."

Why hadn't he called her? He seemed to have a blind spot for the women he cared about most. They were back to dancing around each other. "Sorry, Fern. You're right. I should have called. Anna and I had some unfinished business ..."

"I bet you did. What is it with you and Russian tarts?"

He'd never told Fern who Anna really was. He'd spent a lifetime keeping secrets, compartmentalising people according to the information he shared. "C'mon Fern. Don't be like that." He stood. "Let's go and grab a coffee."

"Harry's fine by the way. Wants to talk to you."

Drum paused. She was here to tell him something and whatever he said wasn't going to change her mind. He waited.

She said, "I've resigned from the force."

He was stunned. "Why did you do that?"

Fern looked down, a frown creasing her brow. He realised it must have been a painful decision. Having spent years working her way up to the rank of Commander, she now intended to leave it all behind. "I realised after the raid on the vault how ineffective being a policeman is. You and ROD achieved more in a few weeks than I did in the years I spent chasing Abramov and his mob." She slumped back. "I didn't exactly shine when I blundered into the vault that night."

He wondered if he'd been too harsh with her on the roof. He'd been frustrated with the way the operation had panned out. But then many operations ended up going awry. It was hardly her fault that Stevie had driven off. "You stepped up and made a call. Blowing those doors was the right thing to do. I had no right to question your decision."

"Anyway, I've gone as far as I can in the service. Time for a change."

He didn't think his reprimand on the night was the real reason she was leaving. And then he realised. "You've been talking to Harry. Which means you've been talking to Phyllis."

Fern stood and walked over to the window. "She's offered me a job in New York. I've accepted."

His heart sank. "Fern ... really?"

She moved closer to him and absentmindedly ran her fingers over the lapels of his jacket. Her face was close to his. She smelt of jasmine and citrus. "It wouldn't have worked out between us."

He took her hands in his. "We never really had a chance to try ..."

She pulled him towards her and kissed him gently on the lips. "You have too many secrets, Ben Drummond." She planted one last kiss on his cheek, then moved to the door. "Phyllis said it wouldn't be too long before you were back in New York. Don't be a stranger." She turned and walked out of the door and out of his life.

He watched her as she disappeared through the passageway that led back to the street. He continued to stare at Thames not entirely convinced that she was gone. A riverboat sounded it's horn as it approached Tower Bridge. He looked to the City beyond. Despite the events of the last few days, the vast financial machine would continue to turn, regardless. It did not pause and it did not sleep. Like the mighty Thames, a river of money would continue to flow into the financial heart of London, keeping the economy beating. And with it the flotsam of the criminal underworld.

And Ben Drummond would be waiting.

50

The lights were off when Sir Rupert entered Treasury room 4a. This was his domain, his bolt hole when things turned bad. He walked over to the oak desk and switched on the table lamp - a relic from the war. It was rumoured that Churchill had used it to read by in his bunker. It was his now. The dim light barely illuminated the desk, but was enough for him to find the bottle of Bushmills he kept in one of the drawers. He poured two fingers of the amber whisky into a crystal glass and then gently lowered himself into his favourite red leather chair beside the desk.

He was about to raise his glass when he noticed a shadow by the door. It rose slowly in one smooth motion. No sound. He peered into the unlit corner of the room, trying to get his eyes to adjust to the gloom. The shadow advanced slowly, moving silently towards the light until he could make out the silhouette of a figure.

"Who's there!"

"Hello, Sir Rupert." The voice was quiet, calm, a seasoned professional who had done this many times before. He thought he recognised it.

Sir Rupert put his glass down slowly on the desk. "Who is it? Show yourself."

The shadow moved a little closer towards the light. "Don't you remember me, Sir Rupert?"

Sir Rupert stared at the figure before him, now lit by the ghostly half-light of the lamp. His hand reached once more for his glass and rested there as if the touch from the cold cut-crystal would bring him some solace. He knew this person - this shadow - because that is what she always was - a ghostly apparition, appearing from the dark, bringing death.

"Hello, Alice … glad to see you're still alive."

Alice smiled grimly. "No thanks to you." She tilted her head to one side, the half-light catching the silvery-white of her hair and the polished breach of a gun.

"Thought you had retired?" said Sir Rupert. "You should have bloody well retired!"

Alice slowly reached into her jacket pocket. She pulled out the fat barrel of a suppressor and screwed it onto the gun. A Sig Sauer, if he wasn't mistaken. Alice always did favour a Sig.

"Don't think I didn't try," said Alice. "Even though you fucked me over my pension, I still tried. Water under the bridge and all that. Joined my local bowls club. Met a nice man. Things were going well …"

"My God! It was you – you were the MI6 insider protecting Drummond!"

Alice smiled and gave the suppressor one last twist. "Good Lord, no – although I did try to warn him about bastards like you." She brought the gun level with his chest.

Sir Rupert gripped the glass tighter. "Look here, Alice, I was only doing my job. Queen and Country and all that. Didn't know you were involved. Had no intention of hurting the old boy –"

"His name is William. He and his son … well, why am I telling you this? I gave the best years of my life to the service. Threw it away for self-serving bastards like you. And what did you give in return?" she spat. "Serve your country – you sanctimonious bastard! You're nothing more than a common criminal." Alice tilted her head slightly to one side. She favoured her left eye.

Sir Rupert began to rise from his chair, still gripping his glass. "Alice, Alice we can work something out. Alice –"

The sound of suppressed shots in quick succession cut him short, throwing him back over the chair. Hardly any sound at all. 'Phut, phut.' A double tap, just as she had been trained to do, all those years ago. The smell of cordite in the air … behind her. Alice spun around, almost a reflex, but age had slowed her allowing time for a hand to grab the barrel of her gun and pull it to one side.

Anna was standing there, her recently fired gun by her side. She held onto the barrel of Alice's gun. "Sorry, Alice – couldn't let you do it. You're not sanctioned anymore."

"Fuck me – didn't they tell you never to creep up on someone with a gun. I could have shot you."

"Maybe …" said Anna. "It's best this way. Can I take it?"

Alice relaxed her hand, allowing Anna to slip the Sig from her fingers. She suddenly realised she was holding her breath and slowly exhaled. Her fingers were stiff. Fuck old age.

Alice sighed. "Maybe you're right …"

Anna gently took her by the arm. "Come on, let's get out of here."

Alice hesitated. "Benjamin … He doesn't need to know about this"

"Of course not, if that's what you want."

Anna turned to leave, but Alice still hesitated. "And tell your masters at Vauxhall Bridge that he's not an assassin. He's served his country. He's out of the game. Tell them …"

Anna turned to face Alice. "Why does he matter so much to you?"

Alice looked at the young woman in front of her. How much she had changed. Anna was not the same person she once knew. She kissed her gently on the cheek. "Because, like you, he's family."

Be the first to hear about discounts, bonus material and much more! Subscribe now and never miss an update.

My readers are important to me, which is why I like to keep them updated with the latest news and release dates for new novels and other bonus material that I'm working on. I do this by sending out the occasional newsletter which contain special offers and new bonus material.

If you are <u>not</u> already subscribed, simply use the link *tomasblack.com/ newsletter.*

P.S. You can unsubscribe at any time.

Tomas Black was born in the UK and grew up in London's East End. He spent his formative years working in and around the great markets of Billingsgate, Smithfield, Borough and Petti Coat Lane. These markets feature in his books. After graduating from the University of Sussex, he taught in a College of Further Education for several years before taking a post graduate Diploma in Computer Sciences and found himself in the City of London, writing code to track the inventory of gold bullion for a major bank. He spent the next twenty five years working in the City and other major financial centres around the world as a computer consultant, specialising in the Audit and Security of financial systems. He now travels the world and writes.

His latest project is The Omega Sanction, the first novel in a series of thrillers set in the financial centres of New York and London. It follows the exploits of a group of investigators that work for Roderick, Olivier and Delaney. On Wall St. and the City of London, they are simply called The ROD.

Printed in Great Britain
by Amazon

36925567R00166